A WORLD AWAY

DATE DUE

APR 2 0 2018		
AUG 3 1 2018		
JUN 2 5 2019		
AUG 2 0 2019		
		PRINTED IN U.S.A.

A WORLD AWAY
THE QUEST OF DAN CLAY: BOOK ONE

T.J. SMITH

TATE PUBLISHING & *Enterprises*

TATE PUBLISHING
& *Enterprises*

Tate Publishing is committed to excellence in the publishing industry. Our staff of highly trained professionals, including editors, graphic designers, and marketing personnel, work together to produce the very finest books available. The company reflects the philosophy established by the founders, based on Psalms 68:11,

"THE LORD GAVE THE WORD AND GREAT WAS THE COMPANY OF THOSE WHO PUBLISHED IT."

If you would like further information, please contact us:
1.888.361.9473 | www.tatepublishing.com
TATE PUBLISHING & *Enterprises*, LLC | 127 E. Trade Center Terrace
Mustang, Oklahoma 73064 USA

A World Away
Copyright © 2007 by T.J. Smith. All rights reserved.

This title is also available as a Tate Out Loud product.
Visit www.tatepublishing.com for more information

No part of this publication may be reproduced, stored in a retrieval system or transmitted in any way by any means, electronic, mechanical, photocopy, recording or otherwise without the prior permission of the author except as provided by USA copyright law.

This novel is a work of fiction. Names, descriptions, entities and incidents included in the story are products of the author's imagination. Any resemblance to actual persons, events and entities is entirely coincidental.

Book design copyright © 2007 by Tate Publishing, LLC. All rights reserved.
Cover design by Jennifer L. Redden
Interior design by Leah LeFlore

Published in the United States of America

ISBN: 978-1-6024732-5-6

08.07.03

THIS BOOK IS GRATEFULLY DEDICATED TO:

the Holy Spirit for enlightenment,
my parents—Jean and Robert—for their inspiration,
my siblings and their spouses for their encouragement,
and
Michael McKee for his suggestion
to embark upon this literary journey.

ACKNOWLEDGMENTS

My grateful appreciation is extended to family members and friends who were instrumental in the composition and completion of this novel. Specifically, I acknowledge Archbishop Charles J. Chaput, O.F.M. Cap., Cindy Gallaher, Francis X. Maier, Marlene Murillo, Betty Jane Nelson, Caroline Rose, Ysella Fulton-Slavin, Celeste Thomas, Nancy Walla, and Rebecca Welborn whose patience and support throughout this undertaking made this literary work possible.

—T. J. Smith

TABLE OF CONTENTS

1. THE CROSSOVER	8
2. LIBRARY CONFRONTATION	20
3. THE RECLAIMERS	30
4. THE DOUBLE LIFE	43
5. THE DISTURBING CONFESSION	62
6. THE INVITATION	79
7. MYSTERIOUS NOTE	86
8. UNWELCOME PURSUERS	101
9. THE SOUL OF THE BEAST	117
10. SUBTERRANEAN DANGER	131
11. NIGHTMARE REVISITED	148
12. PREDATOR OF DREAMS	153
13. THE DELUGE	169
14. THE PRIESTLY VISIT	190
15. LAKESHORE DISCOVERIES	196
16. THE FEMALE WARRIOR	214
17. DUAL HUNT	232
18. THE FORMIDABLE FOOTSTEP	251
19. CEREMONIA	260
20. CALAMITY IN THE CLEARING	277
21. THE THREE-FOOT PROGNOSTICATOR	291
22. TORTUROUS THOUGHTS	303
23. DARK WATERS	315

CHAPTER ONE

The Crossover

EVEN THOUGH HE SAW IT APPROACHING FROM THE CORNER OF his eye, Dan Clay knew that any sudden movement to swerve from its path would prove fruitless. Moreover, while he also knew that this latest act of injustice from the class bullies would likely leave a cut on his forehead, he couldn't understand why his high school senior classmates ridiculed him so often and to such great lengths. Was it his above-average intelligence or his slim build and non-athletic disposition which caused others to view him as the school geek? Whatever the reason, Dan was determined not to let this latest infraction, a rubber band-propelled paper clip to the temple, distract him from today's sole objective–winning the esteemed *Newton Science Award*, which included a full-year scholarship at a university of the student's choice. The paper clip made contact.

Before the teenager had time to react to his throbbing temple, the closing school bell rang. Dan was relieved, not only because this signaled the end of his classmates' torments for a day, but it also announced the beginning of the science project judging in the gym. Unfortunately, the trip to the gym would be like any other journey down the long, narrow cinder block hallway. While pressing a damp cloth to his forehead, and within only yards of the gym doors, the two notorious bullies, Kevin Sur and Tony Malice, were lurking around the corner like two panthers ready to ambush their prey. Dan reached for the gym door when suddenly, and quite abruptly, he was forcefully thrown against the corridor wall.

"Don't set your hopes on winning the scholarship, freak," taunted Sur and Malice, "we'll make sure of that."

Then it hit Dan. For as often as he dreamed of leaving the small town of Lawton and moving to a metropolitan area as a science professor with a prestigious university, Sur and Malice's warning sadly reinforced what he refused to admit, even to himself; they were right, he was a freak.

The town of Lawton was a small rural community of nearly 20,000 residents, most of whom were poorly educated and apprehensive of big dreams. After all, dreams come at a cost. In addition to being academically gifted, Dan was also unique in being virtually the only Lawtonian with high aspirations of making something of his life. At eighteen, Dan was the only known living child of Jeff and Nancy Clay. While many Lawton residents of Dan's age lacked discipline and common decency, Dan had been conditioned from an early age to respect his parents and all elders. Sadly, this rare, but genuine, quality further distinguished Dan from the majority of his classmates. The teenager's slender build, quiet nature, disproportionate nose, and thick black-framed glasses proved valuable ammunition for the school bullies.

Even though Dan was aware from an early age that he had an older brother, it wasn't until Dan's early teen years that his parents attempted to explain the events surrounding his sibling's mysterious disappearance. For years, his parents had searched tirelessly and even hired a private detective, but to no avail. In the end, Jeff and Nancy completely exhausted their resources and failed to uncover the slightest lead on the whereabouts of their older son, William. While his parents never lost hope of locating their firstborn, they also never lost sight of Dan's future. Though Lawton was an ideal small town to raise a family, the undeniable fact remained that a metropolitan area would present Dan with better career opportunities, but something always prevented the family's escape. Now, in their early forties and with little hope of relocating, Jeff and Nancy strongly suspected that Dan's ticket to a better life rested in grasping the prestigious science award.

Out of the gym emerged Mr. Mark Williams along with Mr. Charles Simon who had received their degrees in natural biology and astronomy, respectively, at Summerton University, two counties over.

"Clay, what's the holdup?" demanded Mr. Williams. "The judges are beginning their deliberations now. You know the rules; all qualifying students must be present to explain their projects or they're disqualified."

Noticing Sur and Malice standing nearby, Mr. Simon insisted that the young men enter the gym or leave the school and stop lurking in the hall.

Trying his best to dismiss the latest incident in the hall, Dan entered the gym with unusually inflated expectations, only to discover that his science project–the effects of planetary motions on the earth–was strewn all over the floor.

Sur and Malice immediately came to mind as the prime suspects, though it was equally conceivable that any number of Dan's fellow classmates could have performed the disgraceful act. *But why would someone go to such malicious lengths to disqualify me from an advanced education?* thought the teenager.

His science project was crushed, along with his dreams. Dan stormed out of the gym in a rage and stepped onto Main Street.

Though it was only 4:30 in the afternoon, the full moon was visible over the horizon. It was winter.

Where do I go to calm myself, and how can I ease my revengeful mind? preoccupied Dan's thoughts.

Lost in his preconceived schemes of retribution, Dan wandered aimlessly, unaware that he had entered Eldritch Forest.

All Lawtonians were warned from their early childhood never to enter the forest after dark, especially unaccompanied. Some townspeople claimed that the forest was named thus because of its dense canopy which prevented even the noonday sun from penetrating to the forest floor. Other Lawtonians maintained that the unearthly happenings in the not too distant past conjured its name. Regardless of the name's origin, Eldritch Forest was not to be entered. In Dan's state of mind, however, he was oblivious to the fact that he had trespassed into forbidden territory.

Dan was nearly fifteen minutes into his 'therapy' walk before he realized that he had entered the forest; he also realized that he was lost. Nothing, absolutely nothing, looked familiar. After all, he had never been in the forest before ... or had he?

Now any eighteen-year-old would never deliberately exhibit signs of fear in any situation, especially when among friends, but Dan was alone. He trembled while feelings of abandonment and isolation invaded his thoughts. He intently scanned beyond the swaying limbs, hoping to spot a town landmark. Regrettably, nothing was recognizable. The stories he had heard from his youth about mythical beasts and demons among the rocks and trees of the forest fashioned grotesque mental images. Foremost was the tale of a sixty-year-old man who entered the forest twenty years ago, only to escape the hellish place with unimaginable and horrific stories on how he ultimately rediscovered Lawton. The townspeople laugh at and ridicule the man to this day and consider him one of Lawton's few mentally deranged. Dan wasn't laughing now.

Overcome with fatigue and fright, Dan sat upon a fallen tree for a moment to collect his thoughts. While gazing about, he spotted an unusually large oak tree which was barely visible, due to the dense canopy which prevented the recently risen full moon's beams from penetrating the forest. The teenager peered closer. Something about the tree *was* familiar to him. He *had* seen it before, but where? Unfortunately, the unsettling noises of the forest and his recurring thoughts of the woodland creatures which he had envisioned since his early childhood clouded his normally rational judgment to the point that he couldn't recall where or when he had seen the tree before. Intrigued, Dan cautiously rose to his feet and neared the oak.

Nearly fifteen feet in girth with massive knotty limbs and an undetermined height, due to the poor visibility in the forest, the tree soared into the moonlit sky. Now within arm's reach, Dan felt overly compelled to touch the oak, simply because he knew he had seen it before—somewhere. Nearly the exact moment the teenager made contact with the tree's surface, he immediately withdrew his hand. To Dan's astonishment, his hand penetrated the oak's surface. His passion for science, however, fed his curiosity. The teenager extended his hand once again, but this time, he placed it deeper inside the tree and for a few seconds longer. The texture of the tree was similar to ...

"What the heck?" Dan said to himself.

A loud screech from behind caused Dan to spin around rapidly, releasing his hand from the interior of the tree. He could actually feel the hairs on his neck stand on end and his heart race. Now there was nothing; complete silence invaded the forest which was more terrifying to Dan than the shriek.

The poorly lit forest floor offered no clues; no movement could be seen or heard. With great reluctance, Dan slowly turned to face the tree and was bent over to grab his glasses, which had flown from his face in the recent scare, when he was shoved from behind and tumbled through the oak. Even though the pass through the tree was nearly instantaneous, the unnatural sensation shook Dan to the core.

Dan remained prostrate on the ground for a few minutes, gasping for air. A sudden rustling sound through the dense trees in the distance caused the teenager to spring to his feet and take cover on the opposite side of the oak. The crackling noise grew louder as the separation of the lower tree limbs and the crushing of the forest's underbrush grew ever closer. Dan peered around the tree. In the darkness, the teenager couldn't make out anything. Only the rustling of leaves was heard. With his adrenaline racing, the teenager debated whether to run and dash toward town. Unfortunately, the sprint would lead him in the direction of whatever or whoever pushed him through the tree.

Dan was now presented with a frightening dilemma, *Do I continue racing through the forest for the safety of town while risking another encounter with whatever or whoever struck me from behind, or do I hide somewhere in the forest until sunrise risking an encounter with whatever or whoever is pursuing me?*

Trying to convince himself that it was probably a low-hanging branch swaying in the turbulent wind which knocked him through the tree, Dan began his sprint.

The escape from the forest to the edge of town seemed an eternity to Dan. Every stride presented new and unusual sounds to the teenager. Upon emerging from the forest, Dan realized that he was actually happy to be back in Lawton. Suspecting that it was about 5:00 in the evening, Dan thought it best to head home. Oddly enough, while he knew he had reached safety on Main Street, he still sensed that something wasn't quite right in town. Dan scanned the area: there stood the liquor store next to the diner and nearby was Mrs. Gogat's Bed and Breakfast.

I guess I'm still a little shaken, he tried to convince himself as he continued his brisk pace for another fifteen minutes.

Turning the corner and nearing his house, Dan noticed that the porch light was on which was rare, especially since his dad recently lost his job at the lumberyard. Cutting corners was now the rule, not the exception. Maybe his parents, realizing that he wasn't home, were concerned and left the light on for him. For a relatively small town, gossip took to the wind and Dan realized and resigned himself to the fact that the dreadful science fair fiasco would be discussed at the dinner table; it was inevitable. However, he swore to himself that he'd not mention his brief visit to Eldritch Forest. After all, why needlessly worry his parents when he was back in Lawton safe and sound.

The Clay's house was modest, nothing fancy, but all the necessities. The two-story Dutch Cape Cod had seen better days, but had never experienced more warmth and love than from its present occupants. Peering around the corner of the structure, Dan noticed the metal swing set in the back yard, quite dilapidated and rusty since it hadn't been used since he was a child. Reaching the first porch step, Dan heard the sound of laughter and the conversation of what seemed to be several people. It was then that he noticed a second car parked in the driveway; Uncle Bob and Aunt Vicky were visiting.

What's the occasion? Dan thought. *They haven't paid my family a visit in years, even during the holidays.*

The sound of laughter grew louder, which was something Dan hadn't experienced at that volume since he was a child, perhaps since before the disappearance of William. Quite elated, he advanced to the second step. Upon hearing his parents' laughter, which was seldom heard, the science fair disaster and his recent forest visit seemed to belong to the pages of ancient history. His parents were enjoying themselves. After ascending the third step, he quietly crossed the porch, and while touching the screen door handle, he instinctively peered through the living room window. Dan froze.

What's happening? he thought.

Seated on the frayed couch were his parents, Aunt Vicky, and Uncle Bob. Opposite the couch and seated on a smaller sofa were two young men. One appeared to be in his early twenties, and–Dan!

"How can I be there?" he questioned himself in a voice loud

enough to be heard by anyone who would have been standing next to him.

Totally and utterly confused, he released his grip from the door handle and withdrew a step. Nothing could have prepared him for what came next.

"William," remarked his father, "your mother and I weren't sure what to get you for your twentieth birthday, so we thought you'd enjoy a new set of skis."

Dan lost his balance and grabbed the porch railing. As much as he wanted to enter the house, he knew he shouldn't; he couldn't. Something was terribly wrong! Descending the three porch steps, Dan reached the sidewalk and surmised that maybe all of these events–the science fair, the forest visit, and William's birthday party–were part of a dream. After all, this wouldn't be the first time he had a dream about his brother.

But if it's a dream, thought Dan, *why do I have a cut on my temple?*

After a moment, Dan reasoned, *Perhaps even what I'm thinking right now is part of my dream.*

To escape his dream, Dan knew that the logical move would be to retrace his steps. But that would mean revisiting Eldritch Forest! Taking a deep breath, while squeezing his fists, and after glancing a final time through the living room window, he darted toward the forest.

Gifted with a scientific mind, Dan had often indulged in advanced scientific periodicals dealing with the abnormal. As he neared the forest, the theory of time travel immediately replaced his original theory of a dream. Dan recalled reading an article in last month's *Our World and Beyond* on the possibilities and ramifications of time travel.

Perhaps, Dan thought, *I've traveled a week, a month, or even a year into the future to a time when William has returned home.*

Ever closer to the forest's entrance, Dan racked his brain trying to establish a way to prove or disprove his assumption of time travel, while avoiding direct contact with the local townsfolk who would rightly interpret his question as most unusual. Concentrating on his dilemma and not on where he was walking, Dan was nearly knocked over onto the narrow and severely cracked sidewalk by two young men who bolted from the neighborhood liquor store. Though Dan was not personally familiar with the establishment, he did know that it was adjacent to the local diner. The two men anxiously pulled a bottle of Peppermint Schnapps from the bag, discarded the wrapping to the ground, and walked briskly out of sight into a dark alley.

The receipt, Dan thought.

Chasing the bag, which had momentarily become airborne due to the approaching storm, he eventually captured it, only a few feet from the forest entrance. With great apprehension at what he may discover, Dan slowly unwrinkled the brown bag and removed the receipt. Printed at the top of the receipt was today's date.

"Yes!" Dan mumbled to himself and breathed a heavy sigh of relief.

Now, the teenager knew beyond the shadow of a doubt that time travel was not the cause of the eerie happenings.

Even though his close brush with the men leaving the liquor store had ultimately discounted his time travel theory, there was still something terribly wrong.

When did my brother return home, and how could I be standing on the porch and sitting in the living room at the same time? thought Dan.

Arriving at no logical explanation, the teenager returned to his original thought that he was experiencing an 'out-of-body' dream. Now well within the forest, he caught sight of what appeared to be the shadow of a man slinking behind the waist-high shrubs far beyond the large oak tree which he was pushed through.

This dream must come to an end now, he thought.

Now, totally convinced that he was merely living a dream–actually, a nightmare–Dan thought, *But if a dream, how do I wake up?*

While entertaining options on how to awake from his dream, his thoughts reluctantly returned to his unknown assailant, or branch, which pushed him through the tree.

"That's it," he said to himself, "the tree."

About ten feet directly ahead of him stood the majestic oak. His stride increased, his heart raced, and his thoughts wandered; but no sign of the thing or person that shoved him through the tree a short time earlier. Even the shadowy figure of a man that he thought he glimpsed among the forest shrubs only minutes earlier had vanished. Finally, within arm's reach of the oak tree, Dan touched it and discovered that it was still penetrable. Since no one or no thing was there to push him through this time, Dan collected his courage, covered his face with his hands, and lunged into the tree. Once again, a strange and eerie sensation enveloped his entire body as he entered the tree, and ultimately fell to the ground on the opposite side of the oak, where he remained motionless for a brief time catching his breath. Eventually rising to his feet, Dan quickly placed a comfortable distance between himself and the tree, as he ran through the forest, increasing his stride with every step as if running a race to secure a prize. And the prize was Main Street which he soon obtained.

Once in the safety of town, Dan realized that he had been clenching the liquor receipt with his sweaty hand. Unfolding the receipt, he read it one final time, just out of curiosity, to verify that no time travel had occurred. The date was still correct.

As he was folding the receipt to stuff it in his pocket, Dan exclaimed, "What's going on?"

Unfolding the receipt, he read, *"Thank you for shopping Liquor Land."* The store's name didn't sound familiar; he'd never heard of 'Liquor Land.' Since he was already on Main Street, he walked down the road a short ways to the liquor store next to the diner. Once a short distance from the establishment, he clearly read its neon lights: *"Heavenly Spirits."*

Great, thought Dan, *on top of the mystery of my brother reappearing, now I've got the unsolved liquor store dilemma to contend with.*

Realizing that time travel was an impossibility, Dan maintained his original theory that he was still in a dream state and needed to get to his bed—and fast.

Making a right onto Beacon Lane, Dan could dimly see the Dutch Cape Cod in the distance. But this time, the porch light was off and there was no second car in the driveway.

As he entered the house, he was greeted with, "Where on earth have you been?" demanded Nancy Clay. "School let out hours ago and your supper is cold."

"Sorry, mom," replied Dan. "I was in town with Jimmy and I guess I lost track of time."

As much as it pained him to be dishonest, the teenager realized that if she knew where he really spent the last hour or so, she'd be furious.

"Well, sit down and I'll re-heat your supper," said Nancy. While removing a platter of food from the refrigerator, Nancy continued, "I heard from Mrs. Hart that her daughter, Kristen, won the *Newton Science Award* today. I'm sorry, son; I know you worked hard on your project."

To Dan's astonishment, his mom was completely unaware of the disastrous events which unfolded moments before the judging, namely, his planetary project shattered and scattered upon the gym floor.

But the paranormal events of his evening visit to the forest were now uppermost in Dan's mind; the idea of losing the scholarship barely registered to him. Dan's speculation that his forest adventure was merely a dream was being seriously questioned as he sat down to dinner. *If this is a dream,* Dan thought, *I can live with it; I'll eventually wake up. But, if it's not a dream and I haven't traveled through time, then how do I explain seeing William and another Dan Clay in another house beyond the forest? And how do I explain the two distinct names on the same liquor store?*

In his quest for answers, Dan was compelled to ask his mother something he rarely asked in the past, "Mom, what was William like?"

Nancy closed her eyes, tightened her lips, and abruptly turned from her son to conceal her emotions, while pretending to check the oven temperature. "Of all nights," snapped Nancy, "why ask me tonight?"

"I'm sorry, mom," replied Dan, "but I was just curious and wanted to know what... ."

His mother quickly left the room and ascended the stairway.

Dan was just rising from the kitchen table and nearing the oven when Jeff Clay entered the room.

"Where's your mother, son?" asked Jeff.

"I think I upset her and ... she's upstairs," answered Dan.

"Upset ... upset about what?" asked his father.

"I'm not sure," replied Dan. "I was asking her about William ... ."

"Son," interrupted Jeff, "of all nights to bring up William, why tonight?"

"I don't know," answered Dan. "It's just that I've been thinking about him a lot today and was wondering what happened the day of his disappearance."

"Can't this wait for another time?" asked his dad. "It's hard on your mother, especially today, this being William's twentieth birthday."

"His birthday?" blurted Dan.

Things were really getting weird. Dan had just witnessed William celebrating his twentieth birthday only a short time ago through the forest.

"Son," remarked his father, "we'll discuss William another time." After seating himself at the kitchen table, Jeff continued, "Actually, while you're here, there's something I wanted to talk with you about."

Taking a few moments to abandon his thoughts of William's birthday party and the coincidence of it taking place that very night, Dan eventually asked, "What's that, dad?"

"Well," replied his father, "remember a couple years ago when your mother and I were discussing the possibility of your attending summer camp?"

"Yeah," said Dan.

"Well," replied his father, "you're obviously too old for summer camp now, but your mother and I have discussed it and we'd like to send you to survival camp this year."

Unlike summer camp, survival camp was geared toward men and women in their late teens and early twenties to learn valuable life skills as they enter their adult lives. In addition to experiencing the great outdoors with limited amenities, camp participants gained essential personal and business knowledge, while developing lifelong friendships. The fact that the camp was located within the Fort Knee National Park and that park rangers directed the month-long excursion eased the safety issues which Jeff and Nancy felt for their son. In recent years, survival camp had quickly become a tradition for Lawton's graduating seniors for spending time with fellow classmates before embarking upon their college lives.

"But, dad," replied Dan, "what about your job?"

"Don't worry, we'll manage," answered his father. "Actually, I've got a good lead on a job in the glass factory. Anyway, that's not important. What is important to your mother and me is that you experience survival camp at least once in your life. As a matter of fact, just this morning, I was speaking with Jimmy's parents, and they're sending him to camp also."

Detecting an expression of disappointment on his son's face, Jeff added, "Son, it'll be fun."

Jimmy Parker was the closest person Dan could call a friend, since he had so few. Actually, Dan had none. And, while Jimmy actively pursued extracurricular activities, Dan's studies occupied much of his free time, much more than the average teenager. Living next door to the Clays, Jimmy witnessed the family's personal loss firsthand and noticed how Dan's mom—over the years—had become overly protective of her son, probably due, in part, to William's disappearance. On countless occasions, Jimmy tried to get Dan involved in social activities, but Dan's constant apologies and flimsy excuses, forced Jimmy to stop asking years ago. Curiously enough, as much as Dan was viewed inferior by his classmates, there was something about him that Jimmy admired. Perhaps it was Dan's commitment to his studies, or his courage withstanding the taunting of bullies, or perhaps Jimmy just felt sorry for him.

CHAPTER TWO

Library Confrontation

THE NEXT MORNING PROVED TO BE A COLD AND DREARY DAY AS Dan and Jimmy braved the rain on their walk to school. Even though the teenagers were neighbors and occasionally walked to classes together, Dan's introverted nature often precluded discussions between the two. But that particular morning, something quite unusual happened: a conversation developed, though somewhat forced.

"So, I hear you're going to survival camp," Jimmy said.

"Yeah," replied Dan.

"Aren't you excited?" continued Jimmy.

"Not really," replied Dan. "I was hoping to find a job this summer to help out the folks."

"Work?" asked Jimmy. "Dan, we've got the rest of our lives to do that. And believe me, that's one thing I'll put off as long as possible."

For a change, Dan made an effort to prolong the conversation by asking, "So, what's survival camp like?"

"Well," answered Jimmy, "you basically learn to survive in the wilderness and life in general. Personally, I'm looking forward to hiking and rock climbing. But the park rangers also teach gun safety, archery, self-defense, and tips for successful hunts."

"How do you know so much about survival camp," questioned Dan, "if you've never been before?"

"My older cousin attended camp a couple years ago," answered Jimmy, "and told me all about his adventures in the great outdoors." With a look of disgust, Jimmy shook his head and added, "He also told me that the most boring activities of camp were memorizing native plant life and learning personal skills like job hunting and budgeting."

"Oh," remarked Dan, in a half-interested tone.

That was the longest conversation the neighbor boys had in a long time. For the remainder of the journey, silence won out.

The first class period proved relatively uneventful. But then again, how excited can one get in Ms. Thomas' algebra class? The only benefit to her class was the absence of Sur and Malice. But that didn't mean Dan was immune from the torments of the lesser-grade bullies.

By lunchtime, things had resumed their normal course: Dan was eating alone at a six-foot table, while quietly reading as he ate. Lifting his head from his chemistry book, he noticed Jimmy and Jimmy's three closest friends–Richard, Ken, and Cindy–eating at the table directly across from his. Dan had always admired Cindy, from a distance of course, as his awkward social graces and shyness prevented him from even saying hello to her. As for Richard and Ken, they were pretty harmless, but went along with the crowds, halfheartedly, in humiliating Dan. He was just turning the page in his chemistry book when Sur and Malice approached his table.

"Reading a romance novel?" asked Sur. "Hey, everybody, the geek's looking for love. Any takers?"

A very low, but unquestionable, laughter echoed throughout the cafeteria.

"You have no friends, Clay," said Malice. "You're pathetic and a disgrace to this town, just like the old mentally deranged guy who hangs out at the library."

Knocking the tray of food on Dan's lap while leaving, Sur warned, "Clean up your act!"

All eyes in the cafeteria were fixed on Dan as he removed the food from his lap and shamefacedly bolted from the cafeteria.

Jimmy started to rise from the table to follow Dan, until Richard remarked, "That was great!"

Jimmy desperately wanted to check on Dan, but he knew he couldn't without losing face in front of his friends and classmates. Cindy, who viewed the entire appalling incident and was visibly upset, refrained from confronting the two bullies and continued with her lunch. She reasoned that a young lady coming to Dan's defense would only further deteriorate his classmates' perception of him.

Jimmy finally caught up with Dan at 3:30 as they were leaving school. But oddly enough, Dan was heading into town, the opposite direction of home.

"Hey, Dan, wait up," yelled Jimmy. Once at Dan's side, Jimmy painfully acknowledged, "Listen, I'm sorry about ... you know ... the cafeteria incident. Someday, Sur and Malice will get their rewards."

Dan remained silent.

"So, where are you going?" asked Jimmy, in an effort to engage a conversation.

"To the public library," answered Dan.

"The library?" questioned Jimmy. "Dan, don't you study enough as it is?" Quite unexpectedly, Jimmy felt the growing urge to repair their neglected friendship. "Come on, let's go home and hang out."

Sensing his neighbor's obvious attempt to resurrect an earlier friendship, Dan reluctantly responded, "No thanks. I really need to visit the library; maybe another time." As Jimmy turned to walk away, Dan quickly added, "Hey, Jimmy, tell my mom I'm at the library."

"Sure, Dan," replied Jimmy.

The teenagers parted. But as Jimmy glanced back and saw Dan cross Main Street, he suddenly sensed something which he'd never perceived before: Dan was in serious trouble. Jimmy resolved then and there that he would exhaust his efforts at repairing their broken friendship. For if something happened to Dan, he couldn't live with himself. After all, years ago, they were the best of friends. "I'll work on it tomorrow," Jimmy whispered to himself.

Towering four stories high and stretching an entire street block, the Gothic-style public library–in addition to hosting six exquisite sets of man-sized gargoyles, ready to escape from their cement encasements at the sound of the great trumpet blast–boasted the largest volume of books within a hundred mile radius. Once on the second floor, Dan entered an immense side room which housed the history section. Within minutes of locating the local history division, the teenager immediately set to work. Dan was determined to learn all he could about Eldritch Forest: its folklore, its topography, its indigenous species, and most important, its trees. Regrettably, his time-consuming

LIBRARY CONFRONTATION

research rewarded him with only sketchy facts. Finally, he pulled his nose from a book, glanced at the wall clock, and realized he'd be late for dinner if he didn't leave straight away. If a cold meal was awaiting him again, his mom would surely question his after-school activities.

Amid a fast stride to the doorway, the teenager noticed an older man leaning against a reading table near the hallway entrance. Dan recognized him. He was the man that the townspeople referred to as 'mentally deranged.' Trying to remain unflustered, Dan acted as if he didn't see the male patron and tried to pass him without making eye contact. But the man stepped directly in his path.

"You've crossed over, haven't you?" asked the man.

"Excuse me?" said a baffled teenager.

"You've crossed over," the man said again. "I know you have."

"What do you mean, crossed over?" asked Dan. There was a momentary pause before Dan resumed, "I think you've got me confused with someone else."

"Do I?" asked the man. "I know you've crossed over to the other side."

"The other side of what?" asked Dan.

"The other side of this world, to a world virtually identical to ours, but on a different cosmic plane; a parallel world," answered the man.

"I have to go," remarked Dan. "I'm really sorry, but you've got the wrong person."

As Dan passed to the man's left and neared the doorway, the man uttered, "I saw you enter Eldritch Forest last night, so I followed you."

Dan stopped in his tracks, spun around, and asked, "You followed me, why?"

The man leaned against the reading table again and replied, "I wanted the reassurance from at least one person–if only from a boy–that I speak the truth." After glancing about the nearby area to confirm the absence of eavesdroppers, the man continued, "You see, I'm getting older and I don't want to die labeled as 'deranged.' I know you've been to the other side, because ... God forgive me ... I was the one who pushed you through the tree."

"You ... but why?" demanded Dan.

Ignoring Dan's question, the man asked, "Tell me, did you see a "Reclaimer?"

"Did I see a what?" asked Dan.

"A Reclaimer, boy, a Reclaimer!" shouted the man.

"I have to go!" exclaimed Dan. Terrified, the teenager bolted through the doorway, down the long spiral staircase, and out into the cold evening air. Though visibly shaken, he was determined–now more than ever–to revisit the forest for answers.

As expected, he was an hour late for dinner. Thankfully, Jimmy remembered to tell Nancy Clay about Dan's visit to the public library. After enjoying the reheated meal, but before the table was cleared, Dan took the opportunity to ask his dad if he could speak with him in private. This was a conversation Dan knew he could not chance his mom overhearing. The two men stepped into the den.

"Is something wrong?" asked his father.

Perplexed at how to open the conversation, Dan blurted, "Dad, what happened the night of William's disappearance?"

"Why so many questions all of a sudden about your brother?" asked Jeff. "We told you that he disappeared thirteen years ago. Can't you let it rest?"

Dan persisted, "Dad, as his brother, don't I have the right to know?"

Knowing that eventually he'd have to disclose all the known details of his son's disappearance, Jeff eventually replied, "You're right, son; you do have the right to know. To this day, it's hard to think about, much less talk about. But, I'll do my best."

The father reclined in a worn chair, while the son remained standing. Jeff began, "Thirteen years ago, you, William, your mother, and I were on our way to Doctor Dixon's office–you remember his old location on Madison Street–because William had difficulty breathing that particular afternoon. I remember that day so clearly, as if it was only yesterday."

Jeff closed his eyes for a moment; he was reliving that tragic afternoon. Upon opening his eyes and looking upon his younger son standing nearby, he resumed, "We arrived at the doctor's office at 4:30. Within an hour or so, William was diagnosed with acute asthma. Doctor Dixon doubted seriously that he'd outgrow it, but told us that with present medications, it was a condition William could live with and wouldn't affect his life too adversely."

Growing more uncomfortable in recounting the worst experience of his life, Jeff rose from the chair, neared a bookshelf, and—with his back toward his son—continued. "After Doctor Dixon wrote us a prescription, we left the office. But, before we reached the car, we ran into an old friend who was visiting Lawton whom your mother and I hadn't seen in years. I suppose we were caught up in reminiscing, when within only a few minutes, both you and William were gone. We looked in the usual places: the nearby playground, the toy store, even the outskirts of the forest. We searched everywhere, but you two were nowhere to be found. The police arrived within fifteen minutes and decided it would be wise to search Eldritch Forest. I personally felt that their search would prove fruitless, since your mother and I strictly forbade you, and especially William—at a very early age—never to enter the forest. Anyway, your mother and I were looking in the park when suddenly we heard the cry of a child coming from the direction of the forest. Your mother, our friend, and I raced across the street and caught up with the police who found you sitting on the ground crying. We searched in desperation for William; we searched everywhere. But, even the light from the full moon that evening revealed nothing. After several weeks, the authorities called off the search and your brother was listed as a 'missing person.' The only thing recovered that evening was William's stuffed animal which was discovered several feet from the base of a tree. You know the stuffed animal of the tiger which your mother keeps on William's bed in your room."

Jeff paused for a moment to wipe his eyes, turned from the bookshelf, and asked, "So, why so much interest all of a sudden?"

"Just curious," replied Dan.

"Alright then," suggested his father, "let's go help your mother in the kitchen."

Nancy, who was now washing the dishes, asked the men upon entering the room, "What were you talking about?"

So as not to upset her, Dan immediately responded, "Survival camp."

"Oh," replied his mother, "then you've decided to take your father and me up on our offer?"

"Yeah," responded Dan, "it might be good to spend some time with Jimmy again." Dan mistakenly thought that his concession would end the conversation; his mother persisted.

"I understand that Jimmy's friend Cindy is also going," said his mother. "She seems like such a nice young lady."

It happened that Cindy shared many classes with Jimmy and Dan at school and lived only a block behind the Clays. She was an attractive brunette, slender–but solidly built–and possessed the uncommon ability to delve below the surface in people to unearth the real person. She had Jimmy pegged, but Dan was another story. Perhaps it was because Dan seldom spoke with her or perhaps because Dan was a complex person, much like his father.

"As fast as time's flying," continued Nancy, "the day of your departure to survival camp will be here before you know it. It's only four months away you know."

Dan's attempt to conceal his conversation with his father about William had obviously backfired. In truth, the teenager had no desire to attend survival camp.

"But the month-long camping trip is pretty expensive, mom," remarked Dan, "and ... well, you keep saying that things are pretty tight right now."

"It's already paid for," replied his mother. "I sent the final payment just last week. You concentrate on finishing the school year honorably, and I'll worry about survival camp."

Actually, Jeff and Nancy Clay had been discussing for months whether or not Dan should attend survival camp. Jeff reasoned that it would be good for Dan to spend quality time with youth his own age and learn valuable outdoor skills, whereas Nancy thought it might be too long for her son to be away from home and familiar surroundings. What Nancy never verbalized was her nagging fear that, like William, something dreadful would befall Dan. In the end, Jeff and his reasoning prevailed; Nancy conceded, but with great reservation.

Since it was a late dinner, Dan went to bed after reluctantly agreeing to survival camp. Once alone in his room, his earlier encounter with the man in the library inundated his thoughts. *What was the man's infatuation with a 'Reclaimer,' and what is a 'Reclaimer?'* Dan wondered. *Why did he push me through the tree? What or who did the*

LIBRARY CONFRONTATION

man expect me to see? There were too many questions and no answers. As uncomfortable as Dan felt around the man, he resolved that night to push his fears down into his shoes and search for the man in the library tomorrow. *Maybe the man has answers to the questions which have haunted my parents for over a decade,* Dan's thoughts continued.

Sleeping that night was nearly impossible with all that had happened that day in the library. As a result, Dan overslept and was late for school. As he ran down the steps, he yelled that he'd be late that night since he'd be visiting the library again.

"Be home before dark," Nancy yelled back.

The hours at school dragged more slowly than usual and the pranks—at Dan's expense, of course—were no less humiliating. But they didn't seem to faze Dan nearly as much; he had only one thing in mind: the library. He kept telling himself that if his older brother were with him now, William would leave Sur and Malice in sorry shape. A seldom-seen grin appeared on Dan's face. At long last, the closing bell rang and Dan was the first student out the school doors, even too fast for Jimmy who, because of his sheer dislike of knowledge, was typically the first student out the doors.

That day, the library never looked more inviting. Dan scaled the grand staircase two steps at a time in an effort to spend as much time as possible talking with the man and finally getting some answers. When he arrived at the history section, he was somewhat surprised that the man was nowhere around. While waiting, the teenager indulged in researching the history of Eldritch Forest. At 5:30 p.m., and with no sign of the man, with great reluctance, Dan closed the book entitled, *"Eldritch Forest: The Land of Enchantment,"* and walked slowly and quietly down the stairs. Suddenly, the library felt like a tomb.

"Where else could the man be?" Dan whispered to himself.

Coming up clueless, Dan decided he would visit the library every afternoon hoping that someday they'd meet again.

Days turned into weeks and weeks into months with no sign of the man. By now, Dan had acquired a first-name basis with the library staff that interpreted his daily visits as an undying quest for knowledge. In reality, he was on a quest for knowledge, but not of this world. Nearing the point of despair, Dan focused on survival camp which was now only two weeks out.

It might be nice, after all, Dan reflected, *to get away from the eerie events of Lawton and get to know Jimmy again.*

However, before attending survival camp, there was one last hurdle for Dan to overcome: senior graduation. Whereas most of his classmates looked forward to their graduations as a symbolic intellectual jump from adolescence to adulthood, Dan merely looked upon it as another dreaded occasion to endure more time with his classmates and the bullies. That particular Thursday night in late May was unusually warm, which made the already uncomfortable cap and gown, even more unpleasant. While his parents were enormously proud of their son's scholastic achievement, they knew that his beaming face was a sham. They desperately wished that he was more outgoing and had more acquaintances besides Jimmy, but they also knew it wasn't entirely his fault. After all, his reclusive nature became more and more apparent shortly after his brother's disappearance. Following the ceremony, the Clays tried to persuade Dan to go out and have some fun with Jimmy, Cindy, and their friends, but Dan politely declined. After the ride home with his parents, Dan immediately climbed into bed.

The next day, since high school was now delegated to the pages of history, Dan slept in and spent his Friday afternoon throwing away old school supplies and cleaning his room. At 4:00, Nancy entered her son's room and after a compliment on a job well done, gave her son a fair amount of money with instructions to visit the local sportsman's store and purchase a few camping essentials.

"But, mom, I don't need anything," Dan responded.

"I'll not have my boy exploring the great outdoors with inadequate equipment," replied Nancy.

In reality, Nancy incorrectly assumed that purchasing reliable camping equipment would ensure her son's safe return from survival camp.

The sportsman's store was several blocks north of Beacon Lane, but only four, if one cut through an alley, which Dan decided to do. As he neared the end of the alley, the teenager noticed a homeless person rummaging through a restaurant's dumpster. Proceeding ever so cautiously, Dan did his best to remain undetected. But his curiosity eventually won out as he turned and took notice of the individual. And a good thing too, it was the man from the library.

"You!" exclaimed Dan.

There was no response from the man, who continued his search amid the trash.

"Don't you remember me?" continued Dan.

"Yeah, I remember you," replied the man, as he turned his head slightly in Dan's direction. "You're the kid from the library who thinks I'm a nut, just like the rest of the town." The man returned his gaze to the contents of the dumpster.

"No, I don't ... well ... not anymore," admitted Dan.

The man removed his face from the garbage heap, turned to face Dan, and asked, "Why the change of heart?" Without waiting for a response, the man noticed Dan's clenched fist and added, "What's that?"

"Money for camping equipment," replied Dan. Looking at the tall, slender man, who was obviously looking for food in the trash, Dan took a deep breath and nervously proposed, "Tell you what; if I buy you a meal, can we continue the conversation we had a few months ago in the library?"

Closing the lid of the dumpster, the man replied, "You've got yourself a deal, kid."

CHAPTER THREE
The Reclaimers

NOT SURPRISING, THE MAN CHOSE THE RUN-DOWN DINER NEAR the perimeter of the forest, next to the *"Heavenly Spirits"* liquor store. Twice Dan tried to start up a conversation, and twice he met a brick wall. Finally, the man lifted his eyes from his plate and gave Dan a nod indicating that a conversation was now in order.

"Sir," said Dan.

The man interrupted and said, "The name's Sam White."

"Okay, Mr. White," said Dan.

The man interrupted again, "You can call me Sam."

Dan tried again, "So, Sam... ."

A third time, Sam interrupted and asked, "What's your name?"

"Dan ... Dan Clay," answered the teenager, who continued, "what exactly is a 'Reclaimer' and what's so terrifying about the other world?"

"Tell you what, kid," said Sam, "let me tell you my story and you can ask questions later." After wiping his mouth with a napkin, Sam continued, "When I was about forty, I took up the sport of hunting. It wasn't long before rabbit hunting became my favorite pastime. The thrill of the hunt and the victory of the kill made my adrenaline rise. Anyway, early one morning, oh, I'd say around 2:00, I geared up for the hunt and drove to Eldritch Forest. I'd heard from a friend that rabbit hunting was exceptional in the forest. I remember it so vividly as though it was yesterday. What I particularly remember was the full moon that crisp, clear morning. Its beams of soft light seemed to glisten off the forest canopy, partially illuminating the hunting area near the edge of the woods. Almost immediately, I heard a scuffle in the brush thirty feet ahead. I slowly and quietly reached for my prized arrow in my quiver and prepared to lance the rabbit, assuming that's what it was, as soon as it scurried from the bush. It couldn't have been more than ten seconds later, when the rabbit did just that. I drew the bow, took aim, and released my deadly weapon. But just before release, a sudden, but loud, movement in the distance startled me, throwing off my aim, and I completely missed spearing my prey. Most peculiarly though, the arrow went straight through a tree. I said to myself, 'Wow, I've got great power behind the bow.' Anyway, I circled the tree to retrieve my arrow, but it wasn't there. I circled the tree again to check the ground all around–nothing. Finally, I inspected the tree itself, only to discover that the tree had the texture of a mud paddy and that I could actually penetrate the tree with my hand. It was probably a mistake, but you know what they say about hindsight. Anyway, I stepped back a few paces and then took a running leap into the tree, landing on the other side and lodging my prized arrow in my thigh."

Sam quickly ended his story, as he witnessed the waitress approach their table and ask, "Is everything okay, here?"

"We're fine, thanks," responded Sam.

Glancing at Dan across the cluttered table and sensing that he was intrigued with the story, he asked, "Dan, your encounter with the tree also occurred during a full moon, remember?"

Dan remained silent.

"I take it," added Sam, "you've probably figured out that the majestic oak is only penetrable under the watchful eye of the full moon. But that doesn't surprise me. All our lives we hear of strange occurrences during a full moon, like its effect on the tides, the brain, and the like. Well, why should Eldritch Forest be any different?"

Reaching for the saltshaker, Sam continued, "Before I go on any further, I need to make something perfectly clear. Our world, the one which you and I are in right now, and the other world beyond the oak tree are virtually identical, but you must remember that they're not *totally* identical. For instance, there are good people in our world and there are plenty of good people in the other world, too. The main difference between our two worlds is the forest, not the forest itself of course, but what lives within the forest. The woodland in our world, just across the street from this diner, is dark and ominous; but that's about it. I mean, the stories of unnatural and weird happenings in our forest in the distant past that you and I have both heard for years are just that, stories. The only thing unusual in our forest is the oak tree. And thankfully, I think you and I are the only ones living that know of its transporting power. But, the forest in the other world, the one through the tree, in addition to being dark and ominous, is also infested with bloodthirsty creatures, a diabolical castle, and the Reclaimers."

After removing several napkins from the dispenser and shoving them into his pocket, Sam continued with his story. "The bulk of my knowledge about Eldritch Forest in the other world comes from the family that took me in after my accident with the arrow. The O'Briens–Mark and Sharon–were kind, loving, and extremely protective of their children and neighbors since their back yard was adjacent to the forest. They had heard time and again of the eerie creatures which inhabited the forest in their world. Anyway, it happened that their eldest son, Ron, was coercing a stray cat from one of the tree limbs on the outskirts of the forest when he spotted me resting on the ground, gasping for air, only about a hundred yards into the forest with an arrow stuck in my thigh."

Sam put a potato chip in his mouth and after chewing remarked, "I later learned that Ron faithfully patrolled the forest during every full moon, which explains why he found me so early in the morning."

After sitting back and relaxing in the booth, Sam resumed, "Anyway, Ron quickly, but cautiously approached me. He only whispered and worked fast to get me clear of the forest. Once free from the woods, he slowed his pace and helped me into his parents' house. The house was rather small, especially for five children, but it was well maintained, tidy, and efficient. Not a single square foot of the house was unused. I was placed on a chair in the kitchen and given a bit of liquor to ease the pain. Ron left the kitchen to wake his father. I was just taking another sip of the whiskey, when Ron's father and mother made an abrupt entrance into the kitchen. Mr. O'Brien was toting a black leather case; Mrs. O'Brien told me not to worry. She informed me that her husband was a medical doctor and that he'd have me walking in no time."

Sam stopped to clear his throat and order a cup of coffee, when Dan interjected, "You still haven't explained the 'Reclaimers.'"

"I'm coming to that, boy," replied Sam, "but first you need to understand their purpose of existence and how they ended up in Elysian Castle."

"Elysian Castle? What's that?" inquired Dan.

"If you keep interrupting," admonished Sam, "I'll never finish the story."

"Sorry," said Dan.

"Now where was I?" asked Sam. "Ah yes, the O'Briens. After stitching and bandaging my thigh, Doctor O'Brien helped me to a little room off the kitchen to recuperate. During the rest of the early morning, thoughts tossed in my head, thoughts which didn't make any sense. 'How, for example, was I able to penetrate a tree and what was Ron's obvious fear of the forest?' Eventually, the whiskey wore off, the pain set in, and I fell unconscious. Awakening rather late in the morning, the five children were already off to school, which presented me with the perfect opportunity to have a few questions answered. When Doctor O'Brien entered the room to examine my flesh wound, I seized the opportunity. 'So what's the deal with the oak tree?' I asked Doctor O'Brien. 'What oak tree?' inquired the doctor. 'The one I walked through,' I continued. 'Sam, I'd rather not discuss it. Some things are better left unsaid,' replied the doctor. Obviously, the doctor knew more than he was willing to share; I persisted, but it didn't pay off. As I painfully labored to my feet, the doctor asked, 'What are you doing?' I gratefully answered, 'Thanks, doctor, for your services, but I think it's time I left. I came here to hunt and hunting is what I intend to do.' 'You're to stay off that leg for at least a week and no hunting for at least two,' reprimanded the doctor. 'Look, doctor,' I said, 'if you won't provide me with some answers to the oak tree, then I'll find them out myself.' 'You won't survive even a day in Eldritch Forest!' the doctor responded. 'Why not? What's the danger?' I asked. The doctor remained silent. So I said, 'Good day, doctor.' As I was closing the back kitchen door behind me, the doctor reluctantly spoke up, 'The oak tree is a passageway—a portal if you will—between our two worlds.

Over the years, I've read many articles on the phenomenon referred to as parallel universes. And I suspect that's what exists in the forest, or more precisely, within the tree. All of the townspeople are aware of the darkness and dangers of the forest and its legends of ghastly events of the past. Thank God–to the best of my knowledge–only my wife, my son, and I know of the tree's power.' The doctor sat down, as if it was going to be a long story. The physician continued, 'I was working in my home office late one evening a few years back when my neighbor, John Schultz, came in quite breathless and disoriented. Little did I know that I wasn't actually talking with my neighbor, but with his twin–if you will–from your world. Anyway, he told me his story and this is how I came to learn of the tree.'"

"I said to the doctor, 'I remember reading in the *Lawton Gazette*, the paper in my world, about the questionable circumstances surrounding John Shultz's disappearance about four years ago. After a lengthy and costly search, he was ultimately listed as a missing person. John always seemed to be intoxicated. Heck, the last time I remember seeing him sober was in the seventh grade. In an inebriated state, he probably aimlessly entered the forest during a full moon and fell through the tree.' While taking a closer look at my injury, the doctor said, 'I'm not surprised that he was ultimately listed as a missing person. You see, John contracted a rare abnormality which increased in severity with each passing day until he finally gave up the fight and died in my house no more than three weeks after his arrival. As a matter of fact, I had no choice but to bury him alone without any mourners just inside the grounds of the forest. My gosh, if any of the townsfolk, especially the John Shultz from my world, learned of the situation and the circumstances surrounding the visitor's death ... well, you can imagine.'"

"'Go on,' I prodded. The doctor continued, 'Now most of what I'm about to tell you, Sam, has not been proven, nor has it been disproved. I mean, some is fact and some, I believe, is folklore. Anyway, the story is told that some nine hundred years ago, a cataclysmic event occurred in the netherworld. A certain number of men–fifty, I believe was the number–had committed such heinous and horrific sins before their deaths that they received the punishment of eternal damnation. But apparently, even their banishment to hell wasn't sufficient suffering for their transgressions. It's been told that their hell mates were so jealous and envious of their fiendish accomplishments before their deaths that a great upheaval took place.' 'Exactly what were the sins?' I asked. 'There have been many speculations over the centuries,' answered the doctor, 'but no one really knows for sure. Personally, I've always suspected that their abominable sins were deliberately unnamed to prevent future occurrences of such offenses. Anyway, in response, an enchanted tree transported these fifty evildoers from hell to Eldritch Forest, more specifically, to the Elysian Castle in my world. Legends say that the men would remain in the castle and its surrounding forest for all eternity, tormented beyond belief whenever they viewed their image. For in seeing their reflection, they view their own souls. After all, the eyes are the windows to a man's soul. No one really knows why this causes the Reclaimers unbearable anguish, but I'd speculate that their souls are so sinister that the mere glimpse of their immortal souls torments them, or maybe they see their missed opportunities to inflict pain on humanity. Regardless of the cause of their agony, these evil men are quite cunning and retained their awesome powers even after their banishment–powers of such magnitude that the most wretched souls in hell marveled at their abilities. Over time, their powers to relieve humanity of physical and mental sufferings gained wide reputation. This, by the way, is the origin of their name, the Reclaimers. Once inside the castle walls–which the Reclaimers cursed–humans afflicted with maladies of all sorts would *reclaim* perfect health through the powers–or, should I say sorcery–of the Reclaimers. Down through the centuries, their fame for curing diseases spread throughout my Lawton and the neighboring villages. Over nearly a millennium, many men and women from nearby towns and villages have voluntarily sought out the Reclaimers, simply because their sufferings became unbearable. As a matter of fact, legend mentions a family in the 1600's from the town of Tamorville that offered their son, who was stricken with paralysis, to the Reclaimers. The legend continues that the family soon came to deplore their act of betrayal with such intensity that they set out to rescue the boy from the castle. The story adds that no one escaped from the castle, except the ailing boy's older brother. Again, no one knows if this actually happened, but even if it did, nothing is mentioned on how the older brother escaped the clutches of the Reclaimers.'"

"But why haven't.... ?" interjected Dan.

The teenager was interrupted by Sam, "Boy, do you want to hear the story or not?"

Dan apologetically replied, "Yes."

Sam continued, "Anyway, the doctor told me, 'It's said that during their instantaneous journey from hell to the castle, a gruesome bodily transformation took place. Unlike their former bodies that they once possessed while among the living, they were now distorted into half-man and half-serpent creatures. While maintaining the head, shoulders, arms, and torso of a human, their lower body was serpent-like. Countless muscles in their lower extremity enable them to slither in an upright position. Beyond this, they're also cursed with a serpent's elongated tongue and red penetrating eyes capable of luring would-be guests into permanent residents of the castle.'"

"'Entrancing,' continued the doctor, 'is probably the best word to describe their inner grasp on the human mind and will power. You see, when an ailing person, or should I say victim, enters the castle, they are promised complete recovery from whatever ails them, as long as they remain within the castle walls. The moment they step foot beyond the fortress, their sufferings eventually return and often times, in greater severity. As a result, many residents freely choose to remain in the castle. But legend adds that the Reclaimers, with their supernatural mind-altering powers, go one step further to ensure they always have guests. Should an individual decide to escape the castle and endure his or her suffering, the Reclaimers' penetrating eyes become inflamed as the fires of hell, entrancing the guest, making the individual susceptible to the Reclaimers' wish to return to the castle. In short, the Reclaimers obliterate a person's will power to leave the castle. Basically, when one enters the castle, there's no leaving it.' There was a slight pause before the doctor continued, 'I know what you're thinking, Sam, and I don't know if, or how, the boy in the 1600's escaped the Reclaimers' clutches. But even if he did escape, there's no record of him ever making it back to Tamorville alive.'"

The waitress arrived carrying a cup of coffee.

After thanking the waitress, Sam resumed his story. "Then the doctor looked straight into my eyes and said, 'There's one last thing you should know about the Reclaimers, Sam. Don't be fooled by a pain-free life. I'm not an overly religious man, but I do believe there's a purpose for everything in the world; even suffering has a purpose. When I was a child, I remember learning in Sunday school that a suffering individual should offer up his or her pain for the world's salvation. The older I get, the more wisdom I see hidden in these words. After all, doesn't the Bible say that he who does not suffer cannot expect to receive the unfading crown of glory? Anyway, what I'm leading up to is this. Whereas the Reclaimers' fame for alleviating the physical and mental sufferings of humanity continues to spread to this day in my world, what is rarely circulated is what happens when the guests depart from this life. Here's where it gets rather complicated, Sam. I'll do my best to explain.'"

"'You must understand,' continued the doctor, 'that the Reclaimers—just by the mere fact of where they've been imprisoned for all eternity—are wretched, vicious, and unforgiving creatures. The precise moment a guest dies, his or her assigned Reclaimer is close at hand to consume their non-corporal being—their knowledge, strength, memories, thoughts, and ultimately, their soul. Yes, the Reclaimers claim the soul of the departing guest for all eternity! Knowing only too well that as humans age they gain greater knowledge and inner strength, the Reclaimers will stop at nothing to prolong an individual's life. After all, these qualities are highly desirable to the Reclaimers, because once a guest dies and is incorporated into the Reclaimer's being, the Reclaimer himself becomes more knowledgeable, more powerful, and for a brief moment, experiences a respite from his torment.'"

Dan interrupted again, asking, "Do you think the shadowing figure I saw in the forest's distance the night you pushed me through the tree was a Reclaimer?"

"I can't say for sure," replied Sam, "but it's entirely possible."

"Getting back to my story," said Sam, "the doctor informed me that, 'Over the centuries, the Reclaimers have perfected their approach to ensnaring mankind. It's even said that there's a hierarchy in their structure. Spiritus Malus is the headmaster, who is constantly perfecting schemes to ensnare humanity into thinking that suffering has no purpose and luring them to the castle. It's reported that nearly 200 years ago, a hunter who became lost in the evening twilight of the forest was visited by Spiritus Malus, who promised him everlasting relief of his epilepsy if he took up residence in the castle. Legend adds that Spiritus Malus deliberately refrained from luring the man with his unmatched power of mental persuasion, holding out for an even greater prize. And the prize he won. You see, even though the hunter refused the offer to end permanently his agony, he spread the news of his encounter with the local townspeople. In a short period of time, a number of villagers ventured to the castle seeking relief from their ailments. Even though myths abound of ghastly creatures inhabiting the forest preying on travelers, stories recount that a number of individuals over the years have reached the castle willingly, just like the boy from the 1600's.' Staring into space, the doctor continued, 'I've often wondered what would possess a healthy person to enter the forest. I suppose we humans have an undying curiosity for knowledge of the unknown, while I suspect that others enter the forest purely for the thrill to hunt its indigenous creatures. Anyway, nowadays the constant talk of residents in my world about the castle and its pain-free lifestyle and the frequent hunters from the surrounding villages who enter the depths of the forest for its rare species preclude Spiritus Malus from visiting the forest regularly. I suppose that once a person's pain becomes unbearable, even the idea of ravenous creatures won't deter them from seeking relief at the castle. However, it's said that Spiritus Malus still occasionally patrols the gateway during full moons hoping to coerce crossover victims from your world. Actually, Sam, that's what puzzled me about your entrance. You arrived during last night's full moon and yet you never encountered Spiritus Malus.'"

Back in the diner, Sam could tell that Dan was mesmerized, so he continued. "'This is utter nonsense,' I said to the doctor. 'No one in their right mind would dream up such a story. But for argument's sake, let's say it's true. Then why don't the Reclaimers cross over to my world in search of grief-stricken people?' Doctor O'Brien explained, 'Keep in mind, Sam, that this is just hearsay. Very little has been substantiated about the Reclaimers. But, it's been said that they *do* have the ability to cross over to your world, but choose not to. Crossing over drains them of all the knowledge, strength, insight, and experiences which they've stolen from their former guests upon their deaths;

basically, what they've pilfered is too precious to relinquish. Once a human penetrates the tree, he or she experiences exhaustion and confusion. A similar occurrence happened to you when you entered my world. This is why Spiritus Malus guards the portal at crossover times, eager to manipulate easily the will power of even healthy victims while they are briefly disoriented and fatigued.'"

Sam abruptly ended his story as three teenage patrons walked past the booth. After offering a backwards glance to confirm that no one was within earshot, Sam resumed his conversation he had with Doctor O'Brien twenty years ago. "'Sam,' said the doctor, 'you're probably asking yourself what's to prevent the Reclaimers from leaving the forest and preying on the citizens in my world. Some townspeople believe that the Reclaimers rarely leave the castle itself because of the light... not that they're fearful of it, but that the light of day exposes them to the handiwork of God's creation, a reflection of Him, which they find repulsive and insufferable. Others, mostly hunters, claim to have occasionally seen the creatures wandering in the far distance of the forest during daylight hours. But you have to remember that the thick canopy blocks much of the sun's rays from reaching the forest ground. Since the light is somewhat tolerable to them for short periods of time, I suppose that under extreme circumstances, the Reclaimers are compelled to venture outside their fortress when the situation dictates it.'"

After a poor attempt at silencing a burp, Sam wiped his mouth with an already soiled napkin and continued, "Doctor O'Brien was quick to add, 'You're also probably wondering why Spiritus Malus risks a visit to the oak tree during the brightness of a full moon. Again, the possession of one priceless mortal makes his exposure to the moonbeams and God's creation worth it. My son, Ron–who always remains within the fringes of the forest, so as not to be lured by the creature–suspects that when Spiritus Malus ventures to the tree, he arrives at the moon's rising but leaves shortly after midnight, so he suffers the beauty of creation for a shorter period of time.' The doctor paused, as he drew his hand to his chin, and then remarked, 'Now that I think about it, Sam, it was probably your arrival after midnight which prevented Spiritus Malus from enticing you.'"

"Then I asked the doctor," informed Sam, "'And why haven't

more humans made the journey between my world on the other side of the tree and your world, and vice versa?' Doctor O'Brien informed me, 'The reason why more individuals don't cross over between our two worlds is because very few people in either world are aware of the oak tree. Unfortunately, when one does stumble upon it and crosses over into my world, the individual soon develops a debilitating nervous condition within weeks, like John Shultz. I'm sure that over the centuries, a few mortals from your world have accidentally entered my world, but probably died or were taken directly to the castle. It's hard to say. I'd presume a similar nervous condition befalls those who cross over from my world to yours. Though everyone in my world's Lawton is familiar with the castle, I'm not aware of anyone crossing from this side to your world through the tree, since, to the best of my knowledge, my wife, my son, and I are the only ones in this world who know of the tree's quality. Sam, you must remember that while our two worlds are virtually identical, they're not *totally* identical. I'm told that even the creatures and plant life deep within Eldritch Forest in my world, which I'm grateful you haven't encountered, are like nothing one's ever seen. Legend also has it that during their transport from hell, the fifty men were allowed to bring their pets ... pets of a ghastly nature. But just like their owners, the pets try to avoid the light of day if at all possible and thus never adventure beyond the shadowy forest and into town. Their inbreeding continues to spawn more appalling creatures than the previous generation. That's why I forbade you to hunt in the forest, not because of your injury, but to save your life. Since we live near the forest and know of the tree's secret, my wife and I do our best to help Ron patrol the portal during full moons to assist any unfortunate traveler who may stumble from your world into ours. If someone enters this world, we would seclude them in our house to protect them from Spiritus Malus and to provide minor alleviation of their nervous condition, while making certain that they avoid all contact with the residents in my world. That's exactly what we did with John Schultz and you.'"

"'Shortly after John Schultz's death,' informed the doctor, 'I began researching the nervous condition from the tests I performed on John, hoping to find a cure, should another transworld traveler arrive. My preliminary results suggested that there exists an undiscovered toxin in my world's atmosphere which precipitates a nervous condition in travelers from your world. I can only assume that the inhabitants of my world have developed immunity to the toxin. As a matter of fact, only recently, I developed an experimental drug which I hope will delay the onset of this nervous condition in future visitors ... if there are any. My only regret is that I didn't develop the serum years earlier which would have permitted John Schultz to return home.'"

"'So what you're saying is that within a few weeks, I'll be afflicted with this nervous condition?' I asked. 'Unfortunately, I'm afraid so, Sam,' said the doctor, who quickly added, 'but I was hoping you'd be willing to try my experimental drug. Bear in mind, though, that it won't totally cure you of your approaching condition, but it should minimize the effects until the next portal opening. Once in your world, I suspect that the toxin levels in your body will decrease in a relatively short period of time. I'd suggest you take it now while you're a visitor in my house so that I can keep you under observation.'"

For a moment, Sam had forgotten where he was, until Dan interrupted him again with another question. "Did you take the serum?"

"Yeah," replied Sam, "and the pill tasted like rotten seaweed. Enough for now, boy, you need to get home; your folks will be worrying."

Glancing at the diner's clock, Dan realized that, yet again, he was late for dinner and no camping equipment to show his folks. *I'll think of an excuse on the way home,* he thought.

As the two were leaving the diner, Dan asked Sam where and how he could reach him. "There's something you should know," said Dan, "about my older brother and his walk into Eldritch Forest thirteen years ago."

"Oh no," replied Sam. After a slight shake of his head, the older man directed, "Let's meet tomorrow in the library at noon."

As Dan walked along Main Street, a spine-chilling thought crept into his mind, *What if, at this very moment, William is a prisoner at the castle with no means of escape? I must enter Eldritch Forest the next full moon; but how can I slip away without my folks or Sam noticing?*

Once Dan glanced at the town hall clock, he promptly focused his attention on resolving a crisis of a more immediate nature: late for supper again and what excuse to fabricate this time. *I suppose,* he thought, *I could say I was testing camping equipment at the sportsman's store, everything from tents to fishing lures to lanterns, and lost track of the time.* Dan loathed the idea of lying again to his parents; it seemed to be becoming more and more frequent and even easier and easier to dismiss the moral consequences. *But maybe this could be practice,* he thought, *for the big lie I'll have to produce convincingly in three days. Besides, after Monday, I won't have to lie anymore,* Dan tried to convince himself.

CHAPTER FOUR
The Double Life

IN AN ATTEMPT TO GO UNNOTICED, DAN SLOWLY OPENED THE back door. The door always had an annoying creak, but that night, it was accentuated. It seemed, to Dan, the more slowly he opened it, the louder the noise. On the other hand, maybe it wasn't the noise which bothered him as much as his conscience, which was about to hatch a lie. He had just made a successful undetected entry into the kitchen when a boisterous laugh was heard from the living room area which commanded a complete view of the main level. Then he remembered it was Friday night, the night when several middle-aged women checked in their frustrations and unfulfilled dreams at the front door in exchange for a few hours of bridge. Passing in front of the room's entrance, Nancy caught sight of her son.

"Dan, your supper's in the oven … again," yelled Nancy, in an attempt to prevail over the laughter of the women. Rising from her seat and nearing her son, she continued, "Where have you been all this time?"

So as not to needlessly alarm his mom on where he really was and who he was speaking with, Dan lied, "Sorry, mom; I ran into a couple of former classmates in the store who also are going to survival camp. We shopped and talked and… . ."

At that moment, Dan unearthed his scheme for a clandestine escape to the forest–survival camp. "I'm really excited about the trip," continued the teenager. His latest statement, however, wasn't totally untrue since he was excited about the upcoming trip, though it wouldn't be to survival camp.

On overhearing the budding conversation near the living room entrance, Ms. Sara Somer interjected, "Cindy's also going to survival camp." As she meticulously analyzed her newly-dealt hand of cards, Sara added, "I promised my daughter early in the school year that if she kept her grades up, survival camp would be my gift for her eighteenth birthday." After playing a seven of hearts, she continued, "I just learned the other day that many of her friends–or should I say acquaintances–are also attending camp as a final get-together before they head off to college. But even so, Cindy still doesn't seem all that interested."

Sara was a single mother who placed no person or thing before her only child. She, like Nancy Clay, was in her early forties, though the stress and demands of single parenting made her appear several years older.

"I don't think Cindy's as excited about it as much as she was earlier in the school year," continued Sara, "but it's paid for, so she's going. Kids, these days ... I don't know. One day they're excited about one thing, and practically the next day, it's something else."

Noticing Dan and Nancy step closer into the living room, Sara asked, "Dan, would you do me a favor?"

"Sure, Ms. Somer, what's that?" asked Dan.

"I understand from your mother that Jimmy's also going to survival camp," confirmed Sara. "Would you and Jimmy mind keeping an eye on Cindy? I don't want her causing any trouble; she can be a bit stubborn when it comes to taking orders–especially from park rangers."

"Sure, Ms. Somer," replied Dan, "Jimmy and I will look out for her."

Once again, Dan had no alternative but to fabricate a story. He did, however, make a mental note to make Ms. Somer's legitimate request known to Jimmy.

Turning to face her son, Nancy suggested, "Dan, why don't you get your supper and then show me and the ladies what you bought at the sportsman's store."

As Dan left the room, he overheard Mrs. Crystal Conner tell the other women that she saw the old mentally deranged man loitering around the supermarket earlier that day. Dan's face proudly displayed a grin. The gossip ensued.

Dan ate his beef stew alone in the kitchen. Knowing that he had nothing to show from his supposed visit to the sportsman's store, Dan focused on devising a plan of retreat to his bedroom unseen. Suddenly, Dan was torn from his thoughts by the telephone ring.

"I'll get it," yelled the teenager.

From the other end of the phone came, "Son, can your mother come to the phone for a minute or is she busy with the ladies?"

"Just a second, dad," replied Dan, "I'll get her."

Once Nancy entered the kitchen to accept the receiver from her son, Dan quickly bolted out of the kitchen and sought asylum in his bedroom, hoping his mother would soon be engrossed with the women for the rest of the evening and forget about his purchases ... or lack thereof. His plan worked.

The local weather forecaster, for a change, was actually right; the next morning greeted Lawton with temperatures in the low sixties and not a cloud in the sky. Coming downstairs around 8:00, Dan was met in the kitchen by both parents. On the itinerary for today: Jeff would be helping his friend, Wes Curry, move to a house in the new subdivision off Glasgow Lane and Nancy would be grocery shopping and running errands. Nothing would take precedence from her preparing the nicest and largest care package for Dan's trip. As for Dan, he'd be secretly meeting with Sam at the library.

"Good morning, son," said Jeff.

"Good morning, dad," replied Dan.

"Son," continued Jeff, "while I'm helping Mr. Curry move, I'd like you to tackle cleaning the garage. You know, the chore you promised to get to several weeks ago." After witnessing a look of frustration on his son's face, Jeff added, "Who knows, maybe you'll come across my old sleeping bag for your trip."

Reluctantly, Dan agreed to the task.

The sleeping bag jogged Nancy's memory and remarked, "Dan, last night, you forgot to show me what you bought at the sportsman's store."

Dan squirmed slightly in the kitchen chair, which caused Nancy to comment, "Don't tell me you spent the money on something frivolous."

Noticing her son look away, Nancy demanded, "Well, what are you waiting for? Go get your stuff."

Dan remained motionless, gazing at the wall clock.

"Dan," prodded Nancy, "get the stuff."

After taking a deep breath, Dan turned to face his mom and replied, "I didn't buy anything."

"What do you mean you didn't buy anything?" snapped Nancy. "You were out for nearly two hours."

"I know," replied Dan, "but . . . well, I saw a homeless man rummaging through a dumpster. He really looked down and out. Anyway, we talked–only briefly–and. . . ."

"And what?" urged Nancy.

"Well," mumbled Dan, "I gave him a few bucks."

"Are you alright?" asked an obviously worried mother, as she stepped closer to the table, bent over slightly, and took a closer look at her son.

"I'm fine," answered Dan.

Rising to an upright position, Nancy stated, "Dan, it's nice that you want to help someone, but you've got to be careful. There are a lot of crazy people out there, like the old mentally deranged man Mrs. Conner saw loitering at the supermarket yesterday."

"He's not crazy, mom," blurted Dan.

"How do you know?" asked Nancy.

The teenager knew he'd better stop while he was ahead. If she learned he'd been speaking with a homeless man for nearly two hours–not to mention sharing a meal with him–she'd needlessly worry.

Jeff entered the conversation, "Son, all we're saying is that you need to be careful."

"I am careful," replied Dan, while reaching into his pocket to pull out some money. "Here's the change," and handed it to his mom.

Nancy disappointedly took it, placed it in her apron pocket, and responded, "Well, I guess it will help with the groceries."

Even though this probably wasn't the best time to ask, he wanted to get it out of the way. "Mom," informed Dan, "after I clean the garage, I thought I'd head to the library."

"The library, on a Saturday?" questioned his mother. "What if you run into that man again?"

"I'll be careful," responded Dan.

There was a brief pause before Nancy asked, "What's up with the library? You've been visiting that place practically every afternoon for months now."

"Just research," answered Dan, "on the town and its history. There's a lot about Lawton I didn't know."

"Like what?" asked a curious Nancy.

"I don't know, just things," replied Dan.

Nancy gave a glance toward her husband as if seeking his approval. Jeff shrugged his shoulders. "Alright, but cleaning the garage comes first," warned Nancy.

"Thanks, mom," said Dan. "You won't even recognize the garage when I'm done."

After the meal, Dan set his cereal bowl in the sink and left the kitchen. With one look at the store-everything-here garage, the teenager realized that he had his work cut out for him. First on the list was to reorganize the boxes of Christmas decorations which seemed to multiply over the years. Lifting the first box, Dan noticed the marking on the carton underneath: "kids' Christmas toys." Opening the marked box, he retrieved a dancing angel treetop which he clearly remembered as a child. For a moment, he was taken eleven years back in time to the living room floor where he sat motionless for hours, mesmerized with the angel's movements. A sudden bark from Jimmy's golden retriever next door broke his concentration; he placed the divine messenger back in the designated corner of the box.

While rearranging the contents to rest the angel comfortably in the carton, Dan spotted a small stuffed reindeer which was missing one of its legs. *This is odd,* he thought, not only because he didn't remember it, but mainly since it was the most hideous stuffed animal he'd ever seen. Dan was repacking Santa's three-legged helper, when he noticed writing on the underside of the stuffed animal. As the teenager pulled the stuffed animal closer to his face, for he had left his eyeglasses resting on the kitchen table, he could vaguely read 'William,' obviously written by the hand of a child with a red marker, which had faded over the years. Dan unconsciously raised the animal to his nose, hoping that the animal had retained a faint scent of his brother; but there was nothing. Amazingly, while gazing into its brown crooked button eyes, the reindeer underwent a startling transformation for Dan. The animal was no longer hideous, but was now the most comforting stuffed animal that Dan had ever held. *This family heirloom,* thought Dan, *from this day forward will be relegated to my bedroom.* But for the moment, the stuffed animal was placed carefully in Dan's sweat shirt pocket. He then returned to his chores.

At long last, he noticed a box marked "Boy Scouts." To his delight, upon opening the tattered box, he discovered his father's old sleeping bag. It had been stored and neglected for years, as its smell confirmed. After tossing it to the workbench, Dan proceeded stacking all fifty-six boxes in the center of the garage. Then, grabbing the broom, he swept the oil-stained cement floor with all intensity and determination–determination to please his parents one final time before he left for his trip on Monday. Glancing at the clock above the workbench, Dan noticed that it was already 10:15 a.m. While thinking of his next encounter with Sam, suddenly his hands grew sweaty and his tongue stuck to his palate. Undeniably, the teenager was still uneasy in Sam's company. However, Dan's fears of Sam were quickly replaced with his resolve for answers. Was it fear of Sam or fear of the truth? Whichever it was, Dan needed critical information which only Sam could provide.

The next time Dan glanced at the clock it was 11:45 a.m. Once all of the contents of the garage were returned to their proper place, Dan dashed into the house to retrieve his glasses from the kitchen table, where his mother was unloading groceries.

"Mom," said Dan, "I'm off to the library. I finished cleaning the garage ... and oh," as he set his father's sleeping bag on the kitchen counter continued, "I found dad's old sleeping bag. But it's got a foul odor to it."

Without even nearing the counter, his mother replied, "Oh my gosh, does it ever. Leave it there and I'll wash it this afternoon."

Pulling an item from the grocery bag, Nancy remarked, "Look, Dan, I bought mix to make your favorite cookies." While emptying the contents of several bags of groceries onto the kitchen table, his mother continued, "I also bought some bottled water, chips, cereal, and orange juice for your trip on Monday."

"Thanks, mom," replied Dan, "but I really need to get to the library. I have to meet. . . ." Dan immediately stopped in his tracks.

"You have to meet who?" asked Nancy.

Dan's active imagination provided an immediate and somewhat believable answer. "I'm meeting Mike, you remember, my science lab partner during senior year; he's also going to survival camp. Anyway, we're going to meet at the library and then walk to the sportsman's store to buy supplies for the trip."

Then it dawned on Dan, his fabrications were rapidly becoming a habit and were beginning to take a toll on his healthy conscience which his parents had carefully nurtured from his childhood. He welcomed the relief he enjoyed when he reasoned that once on his trip and away from his folks, he'd feel better. After all, it was the presence of his parents, especially his mom, that made him feel increasingly guilty for the mounting lies he'd hatched.

"Supplies?" questioned his mom. "You could have bought supplies last night, but instead spent your father's hard-earned money on a meal for a homeless man."

"Mom," continued Dan, "I said I'd be more careful in the future." Glancing at the wall clock, the teenager added, "I told Mike I'd meet him at noon; I'm running late."

"Are you sure," resumed Nancy, "the garage is clean and that your father and I will be pleased with it?"

"Yes, mom," replied an anxious Dan.

"Alright," responded Nancy, "off to the library, but I want you back in this house by 4:00 this afternoon . . . no excuses."

As Dan darted for the front door, his mother yelled, "Stay out of the alleys and no talking to any homeless men."

"Alright," screamed Dan, before slamming the door behind him.

During his fast walk along Main Street to the library, Dan felt an obstruction in his sweat shirt pocket. Placing his hand inside, he felt William's reindeer toy. "Shoot," he said to himself. "I forgot to put it in the bedroom." Knowing that he was already late, Dan had no choice but to conceal it in his room after the library visit.

Walking through town at midday, Dan noticed various features of the small town, as if he was visiting it for the first time. *Funny*, he thought, *I've always wanted to flee this place and now that I'll be leaving on Monday, the town doesn't seem quite so distasteful.*

Glancing down the alley, he halfheartedly hoped to see Sam, but no one. Walking on, Dan noticed, for the first time, that the Lawton bank's lower level windows were bordered by gray shutters. He even noticed that the local grocery store, where his mother had shopped earlier in the morning, had a row of dark brown bricks near the top of its facade with off-white bricks extending below to the paved lot. These features somehow escaped Dan's observations for years.

Certainly not to be overlooked was the local Catholic Parish, Saint Augustine of Canterbury, with its exquisite stained glass windows depicting the life of Christ. The windows portraying the glorious mysteries of the rosary graced the wall above the sanctuary; the windows presenting the joyful mysteries were facing east; oddly enough, the windows illustrating the sorrowful mysteries were facing the forest. Finally, the windows representing the luminous mysteries were scheduled to be installed in the new chapel which was under construction. The church building itself was perfectly symmetrical with two matching steeples which seemed to compete for the sky. *Wow*, thought Dan, *as often as I've attended Mass here on Sundays, I never really noticed the splendor of the church.*

At last, he finally turned the final street corner. In the distance stood Lawton's public library which unapologetically commanded the view of all passers-by. The closer he got to the building, the more nervous he became. As he ascended the first library step, he seriously entertained the option of fleeing and returning home; Sam still frightened the teenager. But the idea of William possibly alone in the castle and Dan's personal quest for the truth propelled him to the second step. Sadly, his journey had only begun. Steps three through ten became Dan's mental torture, which stirred a host of feelings ranging from fear to hatred to trepidation. Finally, the library foyer was before him. Once inside the House of Learning, he ascended the grand staircase two steps at a time in an attempt to repress his unquenchable thoughts of flight.

Sitting on a beige couch near the end of the history's reading section reclined Sam with his eyes closed; possibly reliving his previous visit to the parallel world. Dan quietly approached the sofa and spoke softly, "Sam." There was no response. Again, but a little louder, "Sam." Still, there was no reaction. A middle-aged woman sitting at the opposite side of the reading section raised her nose from a romance novel as if to indicate silence. Dan lightly touched Sam's shoulder and uttered, "Sam." The sixty-year-old man slowly left his imaginary world and entered reality. Sam looked up at the teenager, inhaled slightly, and pushed himself up on the couch from his slouchy position.

"You're late," scolded Sam.

Dan's fear of Sam was confirmed.

"Sorry," replied Dan, "my parents had me do some Saturday chores around the house. Cleaning the garage took a lot longer than I expected, then I had to ... " Detecting a disinterested look on Sam's face, Dan nervously rubbed his hands while adding, "Sorry, but I'm here now." Impatient for answers, Dan asked, "Is there somewhere private we can go to continue our conversation?" After offering a backwards glance, the teenager continued, "Somewhere away from the lovesick woman reading over there."

"Yeah," responded Sam, "very few people visit the reading area in the Philosophy section. And besides, it's at the end of the room where no one can overhear us."

Once in the Philosophy section, Dan grabbed a chair and placed it opposite another chair while Sam stood peering around a bookshelf.

"What's wrong?" whispered Dan.

It was obvious that Sam was quite surprised to notice a patron visiting the Philosophy section.

Sister Mary Regina Pacis, principal of Saint Augustine of Canterbury Elementary School, stood between two rows of shelves quietly reading the back cover of a book entitled, *Philosophy for Beginners*.

When Dan spotted the nun, he informed Sam that she was once his eighth grade religion teacher at the parish school.

Sister Pacis had always taken an unwavering interest in the spiritual development of her students, especially Dan, since he had many questions about death and heaven, and had become reclusive since his brother's disappearance.

Wishing not to disturb the nun and not wanting to be overheard, Sam directed Dan to move the two chairs to the other end of the Philosophy section. Both sat on the chairs opposite each other and began their conversation, which was actually a continuation of their previous talk last night at the diner.

Dan started, "Did the drug work? What was the parallel world like? Did you run into Spiritus Malus? How long did you stay on the other side? And what did the...."

"Enough already," interrupted Sam, "just let me continue with my story." After taking a quick scan of the immediate area to verify they were still alone, Sam resumed, "Last night I told you that I took the drug. To answer your first question, yes, it worked, though I retained a little edginess until my departure from their world to ours through the oak tree the following full moon. For nearly a month, the O'Briens kept me in seclusion. Never—well, very seldom—did I venture outside their home. The doctor kept stressing the unalterable ramifications should I be seen by any of his townspeople, especially my pseudo twin, Sam White, in his world. My stay within the O'Brien's home was rather uneventful, except for one afternoon when the doctor and his wife attended their nephew's wedding at St. Jude's Parish."

Dan abruptly interjected, "You mean Saint Augustine of Canterbury Parish, you know, off Main Street."

"No, Dan," answered Sam, "like Doctor O'Brien informed me and I told you, the two worlds are virtually identical... not *totally* identical. While the laws of nature are generally constant between the two worlds, man—with his free will—has inevitably created variations between the two worlds, but these differences are only superficial. That's why here, it's Saint Augustine of Canterbury Church, but in Doctor O'Brien's world, it's St. Jude Church."

Glancing ahead, Sam ended his explanation when he noticed a man approaching the reading area. Once the man disappeared between a row of bookshelves, Sam continued, "As far as the toxin in the air, Doctor O'Brien suspected it was probably the result of unmonitored and undetected manufacturing emissions which dispersed into the atmosphere over the years. Anyway, after the O'Briens made me promise not to leave the house, with great reservation, they headed for the church. Since the O'Briens had done so much for me, I felt a sense of betrayal in breaking my promise to them. But after nearly three weeks confined indoors, I was restless and had to get out, if only for an hour or so. I imagined that the doctor and his family would be gone for at least two hours, so I took full advantage of the opportunity and ventured outdoors."

After another quick scan of the nearby area to confirm that no library patrons were nearby, Sam resumed, "I remember so vividly the afternoon when I explored the town. The temperature was absolutely perfect, about seventy-five degrees, and not a cloud in the sky. Actually, I remember thinking that the sun shone so brightly and with such intensity that I believed its sole purpose was to consume their world and anything in its path. When I escaped the house through the back door, my gaze was instinctively drawn to the forest since it was nearby; its invitation was almost overbearing. After all, I hadn't hunted in weeks. But I did keep one promise to the O'Briens, at least for awhile, that I would not enter the forest. As I walked into the heart of their town, I noticed a large crowd, about a hundred people or so, gathered around the bronze statue of the town's founder–Emmanuel Lawton. As I drew closer from the backside of the throng, being careful not to be recognized, I heard one citizen yell, 'White is delving into black magic again.' Then another irate townsperson asserted, 'He can't get away with it this time. We all know, only too well, that every time White offers demonic sacrifices, the outer limits of the dark forest encroach further upon our town. We all remember last year when the forest's darkness advanced nearly ten feet. Well, I for one won't let it happen again.'"

"Were you spotted?" asked Dan, who was now pulling his chair closer to Sam's.

Ignoring Dan's question, Sam explained, "I was standing about twenty feet behind the crowd, reflecting on the evil White's shady history and the expansion of the forest when a teenage boy, detecting the presence of someone or something behind him, spun around and spotted me. 'There he is!' exclaimed the boy. Before his word *is* reached my ears, I had already turned and was dashing down Main

Street while the crowd, quite intent on my destruction, was rapidly narrowing the distance between me and them, since my throbbing thigh prevented me from outrunning them. My attempt to flee was useless. The faster I ran, the more they gained on me and the more my thigh ached."

Sam's remarks were momentarily squelched by a loud noise. A visitor in a distant chair dozed and dropped his book to the floor.

Eventually, Sam continued, "'What to do?' I asked myself, as I felt my stride wane to a trot. With great fear, I detoured into Eldritch Forest, suspecting that the mob wouldn't follow. As I entered the woodland, near total darkness enveloped me almost immediately, as if someone had turned off the sun. Out of breath and with unbelievable pain shooting through my thigh, I fell to the forest floor. Rolling over, I glanced back and could see the crowd quite clearly in their daylight, while I suspected that they couldn't see me in my darkness. Being only a stone's throw inside the forest, I heard one oversize Lawtonian woman yell, 'You've got to come out sometime, White.' A clear and disturbing realization fell upon me: she was right. As much as I had wanted to enter the forest just minutes earlier to hunt, now that I was in the forest, I wanted nothing more than to break away."

Dan noticed that Sam was becoming increasingly uncomfortable, as Sam surveyed the area at regular intervals. The older man eventually proceeded in a lower voice, "As I tried to focus on a means of escape, a strong, biting wind echoed from the far depths of the forest to where I was resting, carrying with it the most unearthly sounds from deep within the darkness. The ominous sounds made me tremble. The fear of glimpsing something which was once confined to the inner depths of hell prodded me to rise from the ground and run as fast as I could along the forest border, always remaining about twenty feet within the darkness and out of sight of the townspeople. As I advanced along the woodland fringes, I noticed that the crowd remained motionless, staring at the area where I entered the forest. My assumption was right: they couldn't see me. I continued my journey, now limping, another two street blocks when I caught sight of my sanctuary: the O'Brien home. After taking one last sweeping view to confirm that I wasn't being followed, I darted as fast as my thigh would permit to the O'Brien's back door–to safety. Once inside the kitchen, I slowly parted

THE DOUBLE LIFE

the curtains to make sure that I wasn't followed. As I had hoped, no one was around. Once seated at the kitchen table, I rested my injured leg upon the chair which was opposite me and reasoned how I'd justify my town excursion to the doctor and his wife when they returned from the wedding. I was quite certain that the O'Briens would have heard of the incident before they reached home."

"Sam," whispered Dan.

Nothing more needed to be said, for Sam also heard the sound of approaching footsteps. Seated in the chair facing the oncoming disturbance, Sam was the first to notice Sister Pacis emerge from the bookshelf aisle and enter the reading area.

Nearing the men, the nun recognized Dan, as he turned to face the advancing visitor.

"Dan," remarked the nun, "it's been a long time. Where have you been hiding yourself?"

Dan rose and graciously responded, "Sister, good to see you. Actually, classes this past semester and summer chores have kept me pretty busy. How are you doing?"

"Very well, thank you," responded the nun. "I wanted to get a head start on my class research for this fall, so I thought I'd start at the library. How are your parents?"

"They're fine," responded Dan. "Dad landed a new job at the glass factory and mom keeps herself pretty busy helping with various charities around town."

"That's wonderful," responded Sister.

Sam squirmed in his chair.

"I'm sorry, Sister," said Dan, as he took a step closer to Sam, "this is my friend, Sam White."

"It's a pleasure, Mr. White," added Sister, as she extended her hand.

"Nice to meet you, Sister," replied Sam, as he shook her hand.

"You're doing a little research also, I assume," remarked the nun.

"Yes," responded Sam, "in a way."

"Well," added Sister, "I won't keep you from your work. It was nice meeting you, Mr. White." Glancing back at Dan, the nun added, "Dan, always a pleasure, and tell your mom and dad hello for me."

"I will," answered Dan, "and good luck with your classes, Sister."

"Thanks, Dan, and God bless," ended the nun.

As she stepped off the carpeted reading area, the annoying sound of her footsteps resumed. Once the nun turned the corner and her footsteps faded into memory, both men took a quick glance around the reading area. Realizing that they were alone again, the conversation resumed.

"Anyway," continued Sam, "the O'Briens returned home about an hour after my entry into the kitchen. And as I suspected, they had heard of the disturbance at the town square. I could tell, just by the doctor's walk, that he was furious. 'Sam,' shouted Doctor O'Brien, 'didn't I strictly forbid you to leave this house at any time, especially in broad daylight? Did I not also mention that severe consequences would befall you if you were recognized by any of the townspeople? What on earth possessed you to do such an idiotic thing ... to be seen not by one or two individuals, but by an angry mob? You've risked the safety, not only of yourself, but of my entire family. If they discover you're living here, believe me, they'll have no qualm breaking into this house and carrying you away to do who knows what to you.' The doctor stared at his wife and then continued, 'I don't know; I guess I was wrong in taking him in for a month. Maybe I was being selfish.'"

"'Selfish,' I said. The doctor immediately interrupted me, saying, 'My failure to save the life of John Schultz has been eating away at me since his death. At least once a day, every day, I relive his brief visit to my world and torture myself thinking what I failed to do and what I should have done. I assumed that maybe I could ease my sense of guilt by saving your life, especially since I've developed an experimental serum. But now, you venture to the town square in the middle of the day and practically get yourself killed.'"

Sam further explained to Dan, "I tried to reassure the physician by saying, 'Doctor, it wasn't your fault that Schultz and I entered your world. You're not culpable in any way! As a matter of fact, I think it's quite admirable–no, heroic–that you'd try to save our lives. I mean, I entered your world and you not only bandaged my wounds, but also boarded me in your house. Now doctor, I'm not a religious man either, but it sure sounds a lot like the Good Samaritan in the Bible.'"

"'Sam,' said the doctor, 'I appreciate your words of encouragement, but I'm only doing what any physician would do... nothing more.'"

"'That's where you're wrong,' I added. 'Not just any doctor would have taken genuine care of me as you have. After all, remember, I'm the deranged Sam White. Speaking of which, what's the story behind the Sam White in your world?'"

"'The Sam White in my world,' informed the doctor, 'was born into poverty. Sadly, his parents, after falling prey to the addiction of narcotics, abandoned Sam at an early age. The young boy lived on the streets until the director of Wayward Home, our local homeless shelter, discovered him one night rummaging through a dumpster. The director took Sam to Wayward Home, where he remained for several years. To say that Sam became an unruly teenager is an understatement. Anyway, the Sam in my world constantly fell into trouble with the law and was seen with increasing frequency in the company of a local gang that prided themselves in the knowledge and practice of the occult. Years ago, the gang dispersed for one reason or another, but Sam retained his obsession with black magic. Thanks to the Sam White in my world, the forest continues to expand; granted, only a few feet each year, but it's still advancing on our town. This, by the way, is another concern of mine since my house may some day be engulfed by the ever-growing forest.'"

Noticing that Dan's interest in his story hadn't waned, Sam resumed, "I interrupted the doctor, 'But can't something be done to stop Sam White? I mean there's got to be something we can do.'"

"'He's been in jail a few times,' added the doctor, 'but he's soon free–free to continue endangering our town. Anyway, that's enough about the Sam White in my world. This afternoon when you fled the forest and came here, did anyone see you?'"

"'No one,' I answered."

"'Are you absolutely sure?' re-questioned Doctor O'Brien."

"'Positive.' I answered. 'Once I entered the kitchen through the back door, I thoroughly scanned the entire area through a slit in the kitchen window curtains to make sure I wasn't followed. No one was around.'"

"'Well,' replied the doctor, 'I guess we're safe for now, but Sam you must promise me that you will never, ever venture from this house again. I mean it, Sam; your life depends on it.'"

"I gratefully and apologetically replied, 'Yes, doctor, this time I promise you.'"

"As the doctor bent over to inspect my wound," explained Sam to Dan, "Mrs. O'Brien re-entered the kitchen. I supposed that her mind was now at ease, since during my previous conversation with her husband, I noticed a shadow near the kitchen doorway; she had overheard our entire conversation. 'Sam, are you alright?' asked Mrs. O'Brien. 'Yes,' I answered; 'I'm sorry about today. I promise you both that I'll never leave your house again, until the rising of the next full moon.'"

While placing his hands into his sweat shirt pocket to clutch William's stuffed animal, Dan asked, "And did you?"

"Yes," answered Sam, "I kept my promise. I never once stepped outside the house after the mob scene. After that incident, I made it my purpose in life, at least while in their world, to be as helpful as I could. It became my self-assigned duty to cook the meals for the family and help the children with their studies. During the evening hours, once the children were asleep, Doctor O'Brien, his wife, and I would relax in the living room enjoying lengthy conversations about our two worlds. I discovered that in most cases—not all cases, of course—the same individuals between our parallel worlds shared essentially the same interests and often times possessed virtually identical psychological traits. The evening conversations also provided me with a great deal of information on their town of Lawton and their forest. But the times I pressed the doctor for the slightest description of any of their forest creatures, he remained silent. Still, I was convinced that the obvious terror of their townspeople to step only a couple feet into the forest's darkness confirmed their belief in these creatures."

Glancing at the teenager, Sam replied, "Personally, Dan, nothing would ever convince me to cross over again. That world was just too bizarre."

After a slight pause, Sam remarked, "Yesterday, you mentioned that your brother made a trip into the forest years ago. So what's that all about?"

"Well," replied Dan, "I don't know how much you know about

my family, but I have, or should I say I had, an older brother, William. Since I haven't seen him since I was five, I've only gathered bits and pieces about his early life over the last few years from my parents and relatives. It was thirteen years ago when he and I went into town with our folks when, unnoticed, we both wandered away from our parents and entered the forest. Keep in mind, Sam, that I personally don't remember any of this as I was only five and William was only seven, but this is what I've been told. Anyway, when I was found, my brother was nowhere around. Only William's stuffed animal was recovered near a tree. An exhaustive search was conducted by the police and a private investigator, but William was never found."

Dan halted his conversation and stared at another library patron until she left the reading area. The teenager continued, "When you pushed me through the tree a few months ago, not knowing that I had entered a parallel world, I headed to what I presumed was my house. While on the porch, I peeked through the living room window and saw myself and the William Clay of the other world."

Sam immediately interrupted, "You didn't make contact with the family did you?"

"Of course not," answered Dan. "I was too disoriented and, quite frankly, in shock. Actually, I thought that I was having a dream about William. Anyway, I darted back to the forest, thinking that if I fell through the tree again then I'd awake from my dream."

The two men remained silent for a moment, as if mentally registering all that had been divulged.

If the truth be known, for the past couple months, Dan had seriously entertained the idea of making another journey to the parallel world in search of William, despite the dangers beyond the tree. It was rapidly becoming an obsession for the teenager. But, he knew that Sam couldn't learn of his intentions for fear Sam would do everything within his power to prevent such an undertaking, including paying a visit to his parents.

Dan was desperate for answers. In the hope of acquiring possible lifesaving information for his future crossing, Dan attempted to ensnare Sam by asking, "Do you have any idea what dangers and what creatures exist within Eldritch Forest through the tree?"

"No, not really," responded Sam, "but I suppose ... wait a minute ... what are you getting at?"

"Just curious, that's all," responded Dan.

"Now don't get any wild ideas, boy," rebuked Sam. "I know what you're thinking. First of all, I seriously doubt that your brother fell through the oak. Has it ever occurred to you that it's just as likely he simply became disoriented on our side of the tree, wandered aimlessly, and was ultimately lost? My gosh, boy, he was only seven years old! I've seen grown adults get lost in woods half the size of Eldritch Forest. Believe me, I've seen with my own eyes the enormous distance a child can travel in only a short period of time. If you ask me, I'd say that William walked too far, and kept walking, until... ."

Dan interrupted Sam and added, "But, Sam, what I didn't tell you is... ." Dan paused briefly, thinking he may be imparting too much information.

"Didn't tell me what?" demanded Sam. "Didn't tell me what?"

With extreme reservation, Dan mumbled, "William disappeared during a full moon."

"So," said Sam.

"Don't you think that's odd?" asked Dan. "And near the oak's base."

"Dan," replied Sam, "that doesn't mean your brother's in another world."

There was another long period of silence, before Dan rose quietly from the library chair.

Strongly suspecting Dan's determination to find his brother, Sam looked up at Dan and said, "Dan, I know what you're thinking. Promise me that you won't enter the forest during a full moon ... just promise me."

Dan realized that if he revealed details of his impending trip, Sam would keep a close eye on him. So, in response to Sam's request, Dan answered, "I promise."

Knowing that he had reached a dead end in getting answers from Sam, Dan remarked, "I should probably get home."

Suspecting that continuing their conversation might only further encourage Dan to embark upon a visit to the forest, Sam responded, "Yeah, we don't want your parents needlessly worrying."

The two men shook hands; Dan thanked Sam and then turned to exit the library.

Sam remained motionless in the chair while watching the teenager approach the distant arched doorway and enter the hallway. Once out of sight, Sam experienced an undeniable feeling deep in his gut that he couldn't shake: *Dan has every intention of pursuing his adventure.* The fact that the teenager didn't ask when they could meet again further substantiated Sam's belief in the boy's imminent trip.

But what can I do to dissuade him? thought Sam. *When I left the parallel world, I vowed that I'd never return ... ever. The legends, the creatures, the death castle ... they're a great deal more than I can face, especially twenty years later. I only experienced a mad mob, a flesh wound, and edginess from the atmosphere. My gosh, I didn't even venture a thousand feet into the forest. What would Dan's chances be? Granted, I know a little of the world, but even my limited knowledge wouldn't be enough to guide him through the forest to the castle.*

As Sam rose from his chair and neared the arched doorway, an unfamiliar emotion seized him. It was a feeling he hadn't experienced in decades. Then it hit him: Sam had a friend, a good friend, and Sam feared for the boy's life.

CHAPTER FIVE

The Disturbing Confession

WALKING THROUGH TOWN ON HIS WAY HOME, DAN COULDN'T believe that he'd soon be leaving Lawton, if only for a short time. He hated to admit it, but he had mixed feelings. Each step seemed to summon thoughts of fear, followed by brief moments of elation. For as terrifying as he envisioned the journey would be, his growing determination to rescue his brother and unite his family far outweighed his trepidation. As he turned the street corner, he noticed a bright red sale sign hanging in the window of the sportsman's store. With his trip only two days away, he decided to purchase a few necessities. Unlike the items he intended to purchase last night before meeting up with Sam and visiting the diner, his new camping items were revised. This time his search for a pocketknife and flashlight were replaced with a machete and a battery-powered lantern.

After a few minutes glancing down the first three aisles, he was approached by the store manager who asked, "May I help you?"

"I hope so," replied Dan, "I'm going on a hunting trip and ... well, I was looking for a machete."

"A machete?" questioned the manager. "What exactly will you be hunting?"

Sensing disbelief in the manager's voice, Dan downplayed, "Actually, it's not really for hunting, but for whittling near the campfire."

"Oh, I see," responded the manager. "Then, perhaps I can interest you in a smaller knife ideal for whittling and with a smaller handle which would fit the size of your hand better."

THE DISTURBING CONFESSION

"Thanks," said Dan, "but I'm really looking for a machete. Do you have any?"

Reluctantly, the manager replied, "Right this way, sir."

Half of aisle six was devoted to knives and machetes of all models and sizes. Dan's eyes were immediately drawn to one of the largest machetes; the broad blade alone measured ten inches in length with a serrated edge. Taking it from the shelf, Dan responded, "This one's perfect."

"Sir," asked the clerk, "are you old enough to purchase this ... this weapon?"

"I'm eighteen," responded Dan. Pulling his wallet from his jeans, the teenager proudly displayed his picture ID to the manager.

"Very well, sir," replied the manager.

"I also need a lantern, battery powered," informed Dan.

"Let me show you our selection," suggested the manager. "They're two aisles over; follow me."

Dan selected the "No Man's Land" lantern, complete with two high-powered light beams and an accompanying flashlight.

"Is there anything else you need, sir?" asked the manager.

"No, thanks," answered Dan. "This will be fine."

Dan purchased the items with the money he stashed in his wallet from his birthday months ago. As the manager handed him his life-saving equipment, Dan thanked the store manager, stepped outside, and proceeded home.

Ominous clouds had begun to form, quite typical for late May; Dan could smell moisture in the air. He picked up his pace feverishly attempting to make it home before the heavens opened. Nearing his house, he desperately tried to think of a secret place to hide his gear. If his folks noticed the bag, they'd demand to see its contents. This was something Dan could not afford. The rain lightly fell. Glancing in all directions, while running for shelter, Dan debated on hiding the bag in the mailbox, but soon realized that the bag was far too large. *Perhaps the sandbox in the back yard would work*, he thought. A torrential downpour interrupted his thoughts of concealment. Scurrying to the front porch, Dan slowly opened the door and peered inside to see if the coast was clear, while holding the bag behind his back–just in case. As he entered the living room, he distinctly heard the mixer in the kitchen. Since he had not been heard or seen, he bolted to the staircase and into his room. Once inside, he hid his latest purchases beneath his bed, which was no small chore considering the amount of clutter which had accumulated under his bed over the years. Rising to his feet, he felt a lump in his sweat shirt pocket: the three-legged reindeer. With great care, he pulled the small stuffed animal from his pocket and placed it on his bookshelf which doubled as a headboard on his bed. Thankfully, the reindeer was only damp. After removing his soaked sweat shirt, Dan grabbed a sweater from the dresser and headed to the kitchen.

"Hi, mom," said Dan.

"Hi, honey," responded Nancy. "So, how was your visit with Mike?"

"Who?" asked Dan.

"Mike, your science lab partner, remember?" stated Nancy.

"Oh yeah … it was fine," answered Dan. "Actually, we read a couple science magazines at the library and then went to the sportsman's store; he's excited about the trip. Oh, I almost forgot, I ran into Sister Pacis at the library and she asked me to tell you and dad, hi."

"How's she doing?" asked Nancy.

"She's fine," replied Dan, "she was doing a little research for the next school year."

Taking notice of his mother opening the oven, Dan inquired, "What are you making?"

Pulling a cookie sheet from the oven, Nancy responded, "Oatmeal-raisin cookies, your favorite, for your trip on Monday. Trust me, you're not going to starve. I also set aside a few hotdogs, hamburgers, and marshmallows," as she pulled a large bag from the refrigerator.

"Wow, thanks," responded Dan in a grateful voice. "How many cookies are you baking?"

"I thought three dozen would be enough for your trip, as long as you don't make them a meal," warned Nancy.

Suspecting that hunting his meals would be difficult, at best, in the parallel world, Dan reservedly asked, "Mom, do you think I could have a couple dozen more cookies and maybe some extra non-perishable snacks?"

His mother, after placing the cookie sheet in the sink full of hot water, turned and reminded, "Dan, the camp will provide your regular meals; this is just something extra for you to enjoy."

"I know," responded Dan. "It's just that... ."

"Just what?" interrupted his mother.

There was a slight pause as Dan justified to himself that one more lie would be alright. The teenager continued, "I thought it might be a good idea to take a little extra to share with Jimmy and Cindy; it might be nice to hang out with them again."

"Honey," his mother responded, "you're always so willing to share what your father works so hard to provide. But, since they're nice kids and they are your friends, I suppose I can make another couple batches for you. But, you have to promise me that you won't replace a warm meal with these cookies."

"I won't, mom, I promise," responded Dan. The clock chiming in the hallway prompted Dan to ask, "Where's dad?"

"Remember," informed Nancy, "your father's helping his friend, Wes, move."

"Oh yeah, that's right," replied Dan.

His mother continued, "I just hope they got everything moved before the rain. I've never seen it pour this hard before for such a long period of time. It'll sure put a damper on your trip, if the sun doesn't come out tomorrow and dry things up a bit. Speaking of which, Dan, go upstairs and bring down your laundry. I'll put a load in with the sleeping bag while I make another batch of cookies. Then, when you pack, everything will be nice and clean."

"Okay," replied Dan.

While leaving the kitchen, he turned to see his mother buttering another cookie sheet; when he abruptly spun around, he bumped into his dad in the kitchen doorway who had entered the house moments earlier unheard, due to the violent downpour.

"Sorry, dad," said Dan.

"Where are you running off to in such a hurry?" asked Jeff.

"Upstairs to get the laundry for mom," answered Dan.

"Okay, but when you're done, come down here in the kitchen," ordered his dad. "Your mother and I have something we want to talk with you about."

"What's that?" asked Dan.

"Son, the laundry," reiterated his dad.

While gathering all the clothes he thought he'd need for the journey, Dan was intrigued with what his parents wanted to speak with him about. *Surely, they're not aware of my machete,* he wondered. His thoughts rambled, *Maybe somebody told them they saw me at the library today with Sam.* Filling up the hamper basket to near overflowing, Dan awkwardly walked through the doorway, down the staircase, and into the kitchen where he set the basket on the floor. Both parents were seated at the table; Jeff Clay was eating one of Dan's cookies and sipping a glass of milk.

"Son, have a seat," said Jeff. "Your mother and I've discussed it and . . ." his father set a small box on the table and continued, " . . . we'd like you to have this."

Dan anxiously reached for the small box, thinking that perhaps it was a belated birthday gift which had only recently arrived in the mail. While lifting the lid, Dan's eyes widened revealing excitement; but upon removing the lid, Dan's eyes returned to their normal size displaying slight disappointment. He removed a knife from the box and set it on the table. *A pocket knife?* Dan thought. His ungrateful thoughts continued, *This is a kid's knife; the casing's even chipped.*

The oven timer buzzed which startled everyone, including Dan who raised his eyes from the pocket knife to glimpse a tear in his mom's eye. Dan sensed that she was hurt because of his obvious disappointment; his dad also displayed signs of discontent.

In an effort to console his parents, Dan took the pocket knife in hand and said, "This is great; thanks, mom and dad; it'll come in handy at survival camp."

A small, but barely detectable smile appeared on Nancy's face while Jeff responded, "Son, this was your brother's knife; the knife he carried with him everywhere. Your mom and I gave it to him during our first camping trip as a family."

A deafening silence entered the room while his father desperately tried to conceal his emerging emotions. The boy's father eventually continued, "Funny, how time seems to slip away; why I remember giving it to William as if it was only yesterday."

Dan stared at the knife in his hand and then squeezed it. His mother, upon seeing the display, turned her head away from her son and pretended to check on the cookies in the oven which alerted the family moments earlier.

"This was William's?" asked Dan.

"Yes," responded his dad. "Now, son, please take good care of it and don't lose it."

"Thank you, thank.... I'll take good care of it," promised Dan, who didn't have to pretend anymore that he liked the knife. It was William's; that's all that mattered to him. Dan arose from the table, approached the oven, and hugged his mom from behind, saying, "This is the best gift I've ever received."

"Just do what your father said and don't lose it," politely demanded Nancy, who stepped from the oven, grabbed the laundry basket, and left the kitchen.

Upon hearing his mother in the laundry room, Dan seized the opportunity to gather more information from his father, since his departure was rapidly approaching. "Dad," asked Dan, "what was William like?"

"Son," blurted his father, "what kind of a question is that? Watching Dan's eyes drop to the floor as if he had entered forbidden territory, his father cleared his throat and apologetically began, "He was a happy child. I mean he'd laugh at just about anything and always displayed a smile which highlighted his dimples. Your mother and I made sure both of you boys went to Mass every Sunday and instilled in the two of you the importance and the habit of daily prayer. With his schoolwork, with peewee soccer ... heck, with just about everything, he always aspired to do better."

Dan's smile suggested that he was pleased with his father's response; the teenager reached for a warm cookie.

"Son," voiced his father, "I appreciate you asking me these questions about William out of your mother's earshot, but you've been more inquisitive about William these past three months than you have since his disappearance. Is there something you want to tell me?"

"Not really, dad," responded Dan. "It's just that sometimes, actually a lot of times, I wish I had an older brother to hang out with, just like the other guys. I mean, if William was here today, we'd probably both be packing for survival camp."

"One thing's for sure," responded Dan's father, "William loved the outdoors. Unfortunately, it was the great outdoors and his sense of adventure which took him from us."

Just then, Nancy re-entered the kitchen and the conversation immediately turned to the events of the day, most notably, Jeff's charitable work helping Wes move and his now aching back.

Since no one had much of an appetite that evening–the inevitable result of the half-eaten tray of cookies–Nancy opted to serve a small salad and soup. Halfway through their meal, she remarked, "After dishes, I'll make more cookies to replace the ones you and your father ate. In the meantime, Dan, why don't you go next door and ask Jimmy if he needs any help preparing for the trip; you know how he puts everything off until the last minute."

"Sure, mom," replied Dan, as he rose to clear the table. It was now 5:30 in the evening as Dan headed next door.

Before Dan even stepped foot onto the Parker's front porch, their beloved golden retriever, Max, began his relentless barking. Once on the porch, Dan realized that he hadn't been to visit the Parkers in years. *Granted, I see Jimmy every day during the school year and a lot in the summer*, thought Dan, *but never in his house with his family.* He rang the doorbell, straightened his hair, and took a deep breath. Within only seconds, the door opened revealing Mrs. Marie Parker with her ear pressed to a cell phone.

"Alright, honey," said Marie, "I'll make sure Jimmy knows. See you later tonight."

All this time, Max had been licking Dan's hand and whimpering as if to say, "Let's play." *Amazing the memory of a dog*, thought Dan, *that after all these years, Max still remembers me . . . or at least my scent.*

"I'm sorry, Dan," replied Marie, "please, come in. My goodness, it's been quite some time since you've visited us. Is everything alright?"

"Oh yeah, Mrs. Parker," responded Dan. "I thought I'd see if Jimmy needed any help for Monday's trip . . . if that's okay."

"Okay?" exclaimed Marie. "That's great! Jimmy's upstairs in his room. Go on up and surprise him."

Dan graciously replied, "Thank you, Mrs. Parker, I will."

The Parker's house was almost identical to Dan's with a few exceptions. The most notable distinction was the large library which Jimmy's parents added to the house two years ago. Being a literature professor, Mr. Tom Parker considered the addition not only an investment, but also an aid in his teaching. Max followed closely behind Dan to Jimmy's bedroom door. Dan knocked softly.

From inside came, "I'll be off the phone in a minute!"

Dan turned the doorknob and opened the door quietly, just enough to poke his head inside.

On seeing Dan, Jimmy sat up on the bed and said to his friend, Cindy, on the other end of the phone, "I'll call you tomorrow. What? Yeah, I'm excited about the trip. Aren't you? Why not? Alright, I'll call you tomorrow. Bye."

"Sorry to bother you Jimmy," started Dan, "but I wanted to see if you needed any help preparing for the trip."

"Dan," said an astonished Jimmy, "you haven't been in this house since we were... I don't know... seven or eight. Is everything alright?"

"Yeah," replied Dan. After a quick scan of the cluttered room, Dan refocused his sights on Jimmy and confessed, "Look, Jimmy, I've been meaning to tell you something for a long time now, but never quite knew how to say it. I guess what I'm trying to say is that... well, I'm sorry we've drifted over the past several years; it wasn't intentional, believe me. It's just that... well since the... you know... the incident thirteen years ago, I guess I've had a hard time adjusting. I know you tried to help, which is why I assume you kept asking me to do things with you and your family. Anyway, I'd like to start things over again, if you want to."

Jimmy remained silent, as if in a state of shock, for a few seconds but ultimately replied, "Of course I'd like to start things over." While rising from his bed, Jimmy added, "Hey, the survival camp would be a great way to get things back to how they used to be; you, me, and Cindy."

"Cindy?" asked Dan.

"Yeah," answered Jimmy, "Cindy Somer; I just got off the phone with her. Her mom's forcing her to go to camp. Can you imagine that? Someone not interested in survival camp. Sometimes, I don't understand her. You're excited, aren't you, Dan?"

"A little," answered Dan, "but, I suppose I'll be more excited once we're actually on the bus. I've never been to survival camp before; I don't know what to expect."

"Expect a lot of fun," informed Jimmy. Looking around his untidy room, Jimmy shamefully admitted, "I probably should clean first, so I can see what needs to be packed." Stepping nearer the dresser and realizing that hours of work awaited him, Jimmy gladly postponed the inevitable by stating, "But I'll do that tomorrow. Why don't you hang out here for awhile and we'll catch up on old times."

"Sure, why not," replied Dan.

The two teenagers spent the better part of three hours talking about survival camp, sports, and girls. Actually, Jimmy did most of the talking, especially when it came to sports and girls. Nonetheless, Dan could not remember the last time he enjoyed himself like that night.

It's a shame, Dan thought, *that I won't be going to camp with Jimmy; but for his own safety, Jimmy must never discover my plan to visit the forest.*

At 8:30, Dan returned home. As he closed the door to the Parker's house behind him, an undeniable sense of guilt consumed him, for he knew that in two days he'd sorely disappoint his only friend by skipping camp. But William's safety came first and nothing, absolutely nothing, would remove it from the forefront of his mind, not even the revival of an old friendship.

A guilty conscience affects one's sleep, which became painfully obvious to Dan around 1:30 a.m. amid his tossing and turning. He had hoped to have another dream about William, but this would not be the night. About an hour later, he drifted into a light sleep.

When his alarm rang at 7:00 a.m., he unknowingly hit the snooze button.

Only moments later–or so it seemed–his mom knocked on his paneled door and yelled, "Dan, it's 7:15. Get up or we'll be late for church."

Partially disoriented, Dan crawled out of bed, grabbed his clothes, and proceeded to the bathroom. Fifteen minutes later, he emerged from the bathroom groomed, dressed, and ready for church, though still not completely awake. His parents remained standing at the front door, prayer books in hand, anxiously awaiting Dan's arrival.

"Hurry up, son," yelled his father from the base of the steps.

"I'm coming," replied Dan, as he approached the top of the stairs. Descending the staircase, Dan suddenly realized that this would be one of the last times the family would be together for a month. "Hey," proposed Dan, "maybe we could go out for brunch after Mass."

"Let's see how your mother feels about it after Mass," responded his dad.

Driving to church led the family through the main part of town which Dan appreciated, since he was anxiously absorbing all the familiar sights again. Arriving in the church parking lot at about 7:40, Dan remembered that on Sunday mornings, their parish priest, Father James Roberts, heard confessions before Mass. *Maybe I should go to confession*, Dan thought, *just in case I don't return from my journey*. As difficult as the thought was to endure, he had to face the grim reality that a one-way journey was a serious possibility. After all, according to Sam's story, Doctor O'Brien said that, to his knowledge, no one ever successfully traversed between both worlds ... except Sam, of course. Thankfully, the knowledge of Sam's safe return ignited a glimmer of hope for the teenager.

The interior of the church of Saint Augustine of Canterbury was breathtaking: the high altar with the gold tabernacle, the marble altar, and the communion rail which was still intact and in use. Marked throughout the church were marble statues of angels and various saints. On the left side of the church, near a confessional, stood a massive marble statue of Saint Michael the Archangel, complete with a shield in his left hand and a massive sword firmly clenched with his right hand. Practically everywhere you looked–the tabernacle, the statues, and the stained glass windows–you were reminded of the life hereafter and the saints who now reside in heaven. What never escaped the eye of any visitor was a pristine marble statue of the Blessed Virgin Mary to the left of the sanctuary and a marble sculpture of St. Joseph to the sanctuary's right. Votive candles were strewn throughout the worship area immediately below the heavenly statues. How anyone could enter this place of worship and not be moved and filled with hope at the same time, was beyond Dan's imagination.

The loud chatter of an elderly couple two pews ahead drew Dan from his thoughts of the world to come to the thoughts of the present world. In the corner of his eye, he noticed a line of four people preparing themselves for confession. Acknowledging one's sins to oneself, not to mention a priest, was extremely difficult for Dan. *But then again*, he thought, *I guess it's not easy for anyone*. Knowing that Mass would begin in about twenty minutes, Dan called to mind his sins, while en route to the confessional box. After a few minutes of waiting without the line moving, Dan thought, *My gosh, that person's been in the confessional for nearly five minutes. What on earth has he or she done?* Just as Dan was concluding his judgmental thoughts, the confessional door opened and the next penitent entered. Dan glanced at the wall clock hanging on the rear wall of the worship area.

Finally, at 7:53, Dan entered the confessional box.

"Bless me, Father, for I have sinned," admitted Dan. "It's been one month since my last confession; these are my sins. I've entertained thoughts of revenge, I've been uncharitable, I've gossiped, and I've told a few lies against my neighbor ... namely my mother. That is all, Father."

"What caused you to lie to your mother, my son?" asked Father James.

"Well, Father," answered Dan, "she keeps asking me questions about an upcoming survival camp trip, and well, I'm ditching the camping trip and taking a trip of my own to rescue my brother."

"Why can't you be honest with your mother about this trip of yours?" questioned the priest.

"Because she'd needlessly worry for my safety," responded Dan, "and ultimately forbid me to take this journey."

"And where will this journey lead you, my son?" posed Father James.

Dan hesitated. After all, he hadn't told anyone of his forthcoming transworldly journey, not even Sam. "Father," asked Dan, "whatever I tell you here in the confessional will remain here, correct?"

"That's right, my son," responded Father James. "A priest is absolutely forbidden to divulge anything he hears in the confessional box. This is what's called the Seal of Confession."

Dan felt not only safe, but quite comfortable telling the parish priest his story. The teenager began, "I fell into a portal–a gateway, if you will–to a parallel world. Anyway, I have strong reason to believe that my older brother accidentally fell through this portal thirteen years ago. I intend to cross over to rescue him and bring him home. I need to reunite my family. That's why I can't be honest with my mom; she'll fear for my safety. But Father, I really feel called deep down that this is God's will for me."

"Hmm," mumbled the priest. Then he counseled, "My son, I can't tell you not to embark on this journey, nor can I tell you to pursue it. But, what I can tell you is to pray about it. God will lead you by the hand. Now for your penance, please pray five 'Hail Marys.'" After absolution of his sins, Dan left the confessional and joined his parents in the fifth pew; the family always sat in the fifth pew.

Even though Dan had not disclosed his identity to the priest in the confessional box, Father James knew from his story about the disappearance of his older brother thirteen years ago that it was Dan. After all, Father James made it a point to get to know all of his parishioners. Still, the priest was absolutely forbidden to mention Dan's story to anyone, not to the teenager's parents or even to Dan himself since the story was revealed in the confessional box. Father James, like Sam White, feared for Dan's safety.

At precisely 8:00 a.m., Father James entered the sanctuary and Mass began. Looking around his immediate area, Dan noticed the typical faces in their typical places. The Johnson family, with their three girls and two boys, sat immediately behind the Clays; and the Schaeffers, an elderly couple, co-claimed the fifth pew with the Clays. Around 8:30, Father James opened his homily by enlightening his congregation on the importance of a healthy and consistent prayer life, even amidst one's daily trials and chores.

For the most part, Dan attempted to maintain such a prayer life, though there were many times when he neglected his spiritual progress.

Closing the *Prayers of the Faithful*, which immediately followed the homily, Father James was heard saying, "And finally, as families prepare for their journeys on this Memorial Day weekend, let us pray for God's protection and guidance on all travelers for a safe journey home."

Dan immediately and quite vocally responded, "Lord, hear our prayer," in such a volume that even Mrs. Schaeffer offered a quick glance in the teenager's direction.

At the conclusion of Mass, it was customary for parishioners to greet Father James outside church; Nancy wouldn't have it any other way. As the Clays approached the doors, Dan became overly suspicious that the priest might divulge bits and pieces of his story in the confessional box to his parents, inadvertently, of course.

"Father," started Nancy, "that was a wonderful homily."

"Thank you, Nancy," responded Father James.

Jeff entered the conversation, "Father, we always tried to instill in our boys, at an early age, the necessity of a healthy prayer life."

Dan remained silent while noting each and every syllable that proceeded from the priest's mouth.

"Father," informed Nancy, "Dan's going to survival camp tomorrow night."

"Is he now?" asked Father James. "With your permission, may I give your son a special blessing for a safe journey?"

"Oh, Father, would you?" implored Nancy.

The priest placed both hands on the crown of Dan's head and prayed with such intensity that, unknowingly, he squeezed Dan's head to the point where the teenager tried, undetectably, to free himself from the priest's firm grasp.

Before exiting the church minutes earlier, Dan placed two dollars in the dispenser to purchase a six-inch glass votive candle. After Father James blessed Dan, the teenager asked, "Father, would you bless my candle?"

"I'd be happy to," answered the priest, as he made the sign of the cross over the candle and pronounced a few inaudible words.

After receiving the blessed candle from the priest, Dan thanked his pastor and headed to the car.

Being a teenager, one thought which continually preoccupied Dan's mind was food. For as slender as Dan was, his parents often wondered where he put it. "Can we go out for brunch?" asked Dan to whoever would respond first.

"I've got a better idea, Dan," answered his mom. "Let's go home for breakfast and we'll go out for dinner tonight."

"Okay, said Dan.

Daydreaming while he gazed out the car window during the drive home, Dan reflected, *Just think, tomorrow night I'll be off in search of William.*

His mother interrupted his thoughts of rescue and proposed, "If it's alright with you two, I'd like to visit the cemetery."

Every few weeks, following Mass, it was customary for the Clays to visit William's burial plot and offer prayers. So, his mom's suggestion came as no surprise to Dan. He was actually expecting it–no, today he was hoping to visit the site.

Saint Peter's cemetery was located on the west side of town amid beautifully landscaped surroundings. The walk to the burial plot from the dead-end road was about a hundred yards, just enough time to gather one's thoughts and prepare oneself for the meeting. Dan's parents dropped to their knees on either side of the gravestone and prayed silently. Dan, standing next to his dad, eventually knelt and whispered a silent prayer for William's safe return. The granite gravestone noted William's date of birth and presumed date of departure from this world.

How ironic, thought Dan, *William may not be dead after all, but indeed only left this world.* Immediately below the dates was etched, "Beloved Son and Beloved Brother." Finally, below this inscription was a prayer which read, "Eternal rest grant unto him, O Lord, and may perpetual light shine upon him. Amen."

Rising to their feet, the family quietly returned to the car.

Maybe this will be the last time we visit this cemetery for a long time ... assuming I'm successful and return with William, Dan thought.

Once at home, the family sat down to a warm breakfast: scrambled eggs, sausage, and bacon. This was the typical way the Clays celebrated Sundays.

"So," asked Nancy, "where would you like to go for dinner tonight, Dan?"

"Can we visit the new Italian restaurant?" suggested Dan. "You know, the one on Main Street. Jimmy said that he and his parents ate there last week and the lasagna was awesome!"

"That's fine with me," responded his mother, "assuming it's okay with your father."

"Lasagna?" questioned the man of the house. "That actually sounds pretty good."

"Then it's settled," replied Nancy, "we'll leave here at 5:00. Any plans for this afternoon, Dan?"

Feeling a little guilty leaving Jimmy's house rather early last night, Dan answered, "I thought maybe I'd visit Jimmy again."

"That sounds like a great idea," responded Nancy. "You two need to begin spending more time together, like you used to when you were younger. I think you could be a positive role model for him, especially when it comes to good manners."

Once the meal was finished, Dan rose and began clearing the table, when his mother insisted he leave the dishes for her and that he visit Jimmy.

"Are you sure?" asked Dan.

"Yes," replied his mother. "Go next door; your father will help me with the dishes."

Jeff raised his eyes from the newspaper to meet his wife's eyes and displayed a look of confusion.

"Yes, honey," said Nancy to her husband, "you'll help me clean up."

As Dan neared the back door, he glanced back at the kitchen table and saw his father affectionately grasp his mother's hand.

The back porch was at such a height that Dan could see over the fence and into the Parker's back yard where he spotted Jimmy shaking rugs. Opening the gate, Dan entered the neighbor's sanctuary, approached his friend, and asked, "What are you doing?"

"My mom," informed Jimmy, "said that if I had any notions of attending survival camp tomorrow night that my room better be thoroughly cleaned, as if the Queen of England was paying a visit. Why on earth the Queen of England would want to visit Lawton is beyond me."

Dan grinned and asked, "Do you need any help?"

"Well," replied Jimmy, "as long as you're asking, would you mind emptying the trash cans in my room?"

"Trash cans?" asked Dan. "How many trash cans are in your room?"

"I'm not sure," replied Jimmy. "The last time I checked, there were seven."

"Seven!" exclaimed Dan. "Wouldn't it be easier to have just one trash can and empty it when it's full?"

"That's what my mom asked," replied Jimmy.

Both teenagers felt good socializing again. Jimmy couldn't help thinking of tomorrow's camping trip with Dan, while Dan couldn't help thinking of tomorrow's transworld trip alone. For a brief second, Dan entertained the notion of asking Jimmy to join him on his adventure. The thought was quickly dismissed, however, when Dan realized that he'd be putting his friend in danger. Though he had briefly considered the potential dangers in the recent past, it was only now that Dan gave serious thought to the likelihood of his safe return ... or, for that matter, his return at all. Knowing that Jimmy would be extremely upset with him tomorrow night, once he discovered that his neighbor abandoned survival camp, Dan decided to make amends now.

"Jimmy, when we're finished cleaning, want to go into town?" asked Dan.

"Sure!" replied Jimmy. "What do you want to do?"

"I'm not sure," answered Dan, "we'll figure it out when we get there."

Nearly two hours later, the teenagers walked to town. Their first stop was the ice cream parlor which prided itself on being the only ice cream parlor in town to offer super size sundaes. Actually, it was the only ice cream parlor in town. Nonetheless, the dessert briefly alleviated the teenagers' hunger. Next stop was the video arcade, a place where, not surprisingly, the entire staff knew Jimmy by name. Dedicated to his studies, Dan never visited the establishment.

"Jimmy, would you teach me?" asked Dan.

"Teach you what?" replied Jimmy.

"How to play some of these video games," answered Dan.

"Sure," replied Jimmy, as he directed Dan to the racing car.

Eventually, the teenagers played practically every game in the arcade. Once out of tokens, they decided that it was best to head home. After all, it was now 4:00 in the afternoon and Dan had to clean up before visiting the Italian restaurant with his parents in an hour. During their walk home, a feeling came over both of the teenagers: their friendship, after having suffered years of non-communication, really hadn't skipped a beat. For a few moments, Dan debated internally whether or not he was making the right decision in skipping survival camp. He really enjoyed the afternoon with Jimmy; Dan, however, quickly abandoned the notion of staying behind.

Realizing that tomorrow night Jimmy would be furious with him, Dan confessed, "Jimmy, I'm sorry."

"About what?" asked his neighbor.

Knowing that his apology was ill-timed, Dan quickly fabricated another lie and replied, "Sorry about not hanging out with you a lot lately."

After kicking a rock up the sidewalk, Jimmy replied, "It's okay; I understand."

By now, their walk had taken them to the Parker's front lawn where they parted. Once inside his house, Dan bolted up the stairs to his bedroom and then into the bathroom where he remained for nearly ten minutes.

"Hurry up, son," yelled his father from the base of the steps, "we're going to be late for the restaurant."

From the second floor could be heard, "I'm coming!"

Five minutes later, Dan raced down the steps, but not before knocking a picture off the stairwell wall. "Sorry," said Dan, as he returned his graduation portrait to its hook.

"Dan," said Nancy, "since tomorrow night we'll be busy seeing you off to camp, this will be our last family outing for a month. So, let's all enjoy ourselves."

As much as Dan hated to admit it, even to himself, his thoughts immediately conjured up the possibility that, yes, this could be his last outing with the family, but not for a month . . . forever. The closer the day of his departure from this world, the more frightened he became. *I just need to make it through another day without alarming anyone or accidentally letting something slip out*, Dan thought.

CHAPTER SIX

The Invitation

THE DRIVE TO THE RESTAURANT WAS A SHORT SEVEN MINUTES. Walking down the sidewalk along Main Street, since parking in front of the Italian restaurant was scarce, and still nearly two blocks away, the Clays could smell the aroma of the homemade lasagna.

"I'm starving," informed Dan.

"I'd sure like to know where you put all the food you eat, son," said his father. "For as much as you eat, it's a wonder that you're as thin as you are."

Within twenty feet of the restaurant, Nancy noticed a line forming outside the door. "Oh no," she responded. "Do you think we should have made a reservation?"

"We'll see," responded her husband, as he advanced to the front of the line to speak with one of the hosts. Moments later, he returned with the disheartening news that there would be an hour wait.

"Should we wait or go somewhere else?" asked Nancy.

"Since we've got a big day ahead of us tomorrow," informed Jeff, "we should probably get to bed early tonight. Why don't we eat somewhere else tonight and visit this restaurant again when Dan returns from survival camp?"

Looking at Dan, his mother asked, "Where else would you like to eat?"

Glancing across the street, Dan spotted the run-down diner where he and Sam shared a meal and information only two days prior. "Can we eat at the diner across the street?" asked Dan.

"Is that alright with you, honey?" Nancy asked her husband.

"That's fine," responded Jeff.

Leaving their car parked where it was a few blocks away, the family crossed Main Street and entered the diner. Having visited the restaurant only twice in the very distant past, Jeff was quick to comment that it was as he remembered it: old plastic-ripped chairs, sticky paper napkin dispensers, and outdated wallpaper desperately clinging to the wall. Seating themselves, they selected a booth near the large window which proudly displayed a commanding view of Main Street. Within moments, the waitress arrived toting a tray of dirty dishes, noisily chewing gum, and wearing a stained off-white apron.

After setting the tray of dirty dishes on the floor immediately in front of the Clay's booth, the waitress rose to her feet and asked, "What can I get you folks?"

"Can we have a few minutes to look over the menu?" asked Nancy.

"Sure, ma'am," replied the waitress, who then quietly mumbled, "But I'd stay away from the meat loaf."

As the waitress picked up the tray of dirty dishes and proceeded to the kitchen, Jeff commented, "Well, at least she's honest."

After a few moments of silence while reviewing the one-page menu, Dan decided, "I think I'll have the burger and fries."

His father agreed, "I think I'll have the same."

Nancy, however, needed a few extra moments to decide. Eventually, she spoke up, "I think I'll try the garden salad."

Jeff motioned the waitress, who returned with a large red pencil wedged behind her left ear.

"Are you ready to order?" asked the waitress.

"Yes," responded the party of three.

After placing their orders, the family had a few minutes of uninterrupted conversation to discuss what else, but Dan's camping trip the next night.

"Dan," updated his mom, "the two chartered buses will leave tomorrow night at 7:00 in front of the fire station. Being that it's only three blocks from the house, I don't suspect we'll have to leave the house much before 6:45. Are you all packed?"

"Not yet, mom," answered Dan, "I thought I'd pack tomorrow."

"Well," replied Nancy, "your laundry's done and if I have time tomorrow, I'll make another batch of cookies while your father's at work."

"That would be great," replied Dan.

A loud noise disrupted their conversation. From over his wife's shoulder, Jeff witnessed their waitress drop a tray–loaded with fries and two hamburgers–to the floor. Knowing that all eyes within the diner were focused on her, she embarrassingly picked up the hamburgers and fries from the floor, neared the Clays, and said, "I'll bring you a new serving of fries and burgers."

Shortly before 6:00, the food was delivered safely. The Clays took a moment, bowed their heads, and said a prayer for the meal which they had received. When Dan raised his head, he sensed someone or something staring at him. As he glanced through the smeared window, he saw Sam White standing only five feet away, directly under the streetlight.

Nancy, upon noticing her son's distraction, looked in the direction of Dan's stare. "Dan, is that the man you gave money to the other night?" inquired his mother.

Attempting to trivialize his knowledge of the man and the secret they shared, Dan answered, "I'm not sure ... maybe."

"The poor man," said Nancy. "I actually feel sorry for him; I mean, most likely no family, tattered clothes, and probably hungry." While reaching for a napkin, Nancy suggested, "Dan, why don't you go out and see if he'd like to join us?"

Jeff nearly choked on his burger; he could hardly believe what he was hearing. Granted, he knew that his wife was the most charitable person he'd ever known, but he also knew that she was extremely leery of strangers, especially street people.

"Mom," answered Dan, "I'm sure he'd feel uncomfortable eating with us."

"Dan," reminded his mom, "we all need to be more charitable, especially on the Lord's Day. Now go outside and ask him if he'd like to join us."

Taking another handful of fries, Dan removed the paper napkin from his lap, slid out of the booth, exited the diner, and approached Sam.

"Hi, Sam," said the teenager in a low voice.

Sam remained silent, staring through the diner window.

"Look," informed Dan, "my folks want to know if you'd like to join us for dinner."

Redirecting his gaze to the teenager, Sam asked, "Are you sure?"

"Yeah," answered Dan, "but Sam, promise me you won't mention the conversations we had last Friday night here in this diner or the conversation yesterday in the library. It would only needlessly put my mom on edge."

"I understand," replied Sam.

Both men neared the diner's entrance; Dan held the door open. So as not to upset Nancy, Sam sat opposite her, next to Jeff; Dan sat alongside his mom.

Immediately after swallowing a mouthful of salad, Nancy said, "Sorry... hello. I'm Nancy Clay, Dan's mother, and this is my husband, Jeff."

"It's a pleasure to meet you," responded Sam. Extending his hand across the table to Nancy, Sam added, "I'm Sam White." As Nancy welcomed his handshake, Sam thanked the family for the invitation.

Attempting to raise the conversation beyond the level of pleasantries, Jeff stated, "So, I understand that our son may have given you money the other night."

"Yes, it was a noble gesture," said Sam. "We used it to buy a... ."

Dan's piercing glare directed at Sam from across the booth indicated that Sam had already gone too far.

In an effort to retract his statement, Sam reworded, "I mean, I used it to buy a meal, right here in this diner. The waitresses are pretty classy."

Just then, the waitress approached the booth asking, "Can I get you something, sir?"

"Yes," answered Sam, "I'd like a burger and fries."

"Right away," replied the waitress, who popped a bubble, spun around, and crossed the diner.

"So, Mr. White," started Nancy.

Sam immediately interrupted her, "Please, call me Sam."

"Okay, Sam," began Nancy again, "I don't mean to be rude, but

I'm curious. For years now, you've been telling the townspeople that you once visited another world in our forest."

"Honey," interjected her husband, as he set his burger to his plate, "we shouldn't meddle in his affairs."

"No," asserted Sam, "that's quite alright. To answer your question, Mrs. Clay, yes, I've visited another world, but only for a month. And, I've always stressed that this other world is not *in* our forest, but *through* our forest. After all, I don't want to needlessly alarm citizens about the forest in our world, when–in my opinion–our forest is perfectly safe." After lowering his head for a moment, Sam raised it again, looked at Mrs. Clay and declared, "It's funny how people that tell the truth are often times viewed as deranged or odd, whereas other people who tell lie after lie are viewed as normal. But, I'm happy to say that I think one person finally believes my story."

The waitress returned with Sam's meal.

"Really," inquired Nancy, "who's that?"

Looking across the table at Dan and noticing another harsh stare, Sam responded, "I don't remember his name."

"So, Sam," questioned Jeff, "what was this other world like?"

"Basically, it was a lot like our world, with only superficial differences," answered Sam.

"Why'd you leave the other world," asked Nancy, "and how'd you get back here?"

"Well, ma'am," informed Sam, "I left the other world because I was having a nervous reaction to something in the air; and how I got back here... ." Sam abruptly ended his explanation and looked at Dan again, as if seeking permission to disclose a partial secret. But once more, Dan's glare remained unchanged. "How I got back here," continued Sam, "well, it's a long story."

At last, Dan entered the conversation, but only to divert it, as the discussion was making him extremely uncomfortable. "So, today I played my first video game with Jimmy." The teenager's contribution to the conversation received only a minimal response. The rest of the meal was filled with uninteresting, but polite, pleasantries.

As the waitress arrived with the bill, Sam remarked, "Well, Mr. and Mrs. Clay, thank you for the meal." Sam shook their hands again, slid out of the booth, and walked out the door.

Without even thinking or excusing himself, Dan jumped from the booth and exited the diner to catch up with Sam. When he did, he demanded, "What were you thinking? Three times you almost spilled the beans."

"Sorry, Dan, it wasn't intentional," answered Sam, who quickly advised, "but sooner or later, your parents will discover the truth. You've got to be honest with your folks."

"I fully intend to," acknowledged Dan, "but not tonight."

The two men looked at each other, but no additional words were spoken.

Then, sensing that he was overly harsh with Sam, Dan admitted, "Look, Sam, I'm sorry. I suppose I'm a little edgy about a few things right now. But in truth, I'm glad you accepted my parents' invitation."

"I am too," responded Sam. "Your parents seem like nice folks." Still retaining his strong suspicion that Dan would be venturing to the forest the next night, Sam tried to catch the teenager off guard by commenting, "Well, I guess I'll see you later in the week."

"Yeah," replied Dan, "I'll see you soon."

Detecting no pause in the boy's response, Sam felt a little at ease. *But still, the boy is good at lying*, Sam thought. *I'll stay nearby . . . just in case.*

After shaking hands with Sam, Dan re-entered the diner. His parents had already paid the bill and were waiting for him.

"Sorry," said Dan. "I just wanted to see if there was anything else Sam . . . I mean Mr. White needed." *Dang it, another lie*, thought Dan, *and I just went to confession this morning.*

During their drive home, Nancy admitted that she felt more at ease with Sam. To her, he didn't seem half as frightening as she had imagined.

Once at home, in an effort to avoid further conversations about Sam, Dan secluded himself in his bedroom.

Whereas falling asleep that night came easily for Dan, his nightmares were difficult, at best, to endure. While in a dream state, Dan– as an onlooker–saw himself painstakingly trudging through Eldritch Forest bloody, frightened, cold, and exhausted. The next moment, the teenager had regained his former strength and witnessed himself darting through the forest attempting to outrun an unknown predator. At the climactic conclusion of his visions, Dan turned and beheld a half-man and half-serpent creature emerge from the forest's shadows. As the beast drew closer, Dan shook uncontrollably and awoke from his sleep. In sweat-drenched pajamas, he rolled over in bed and noticed that the digital clock on his nightstand displayed 2:30 a.m. While Dan usually welcomed dreams of William and his adventure, this was one that he cared not to remember. He only hoped that he'd not recall this nightmare in the morning. Before nodding off to sleep again, he entertained a puzzling thought, *Could this dream be a sign from God that He doesn't want me to embark upon this trip? Or could it simply be a warning of the perils I'll face?* Dan soon re-entered his dreamland.

CHAPTER SEVEN

Mysterious Note

THE MORNING SUN, GLARING THROUGH DAN'S BEDROOM WINdow, stirred him to life at 7:20. He climbed out of bed, grabbed his favorite jeans and shirt, and was heading for the bathroom when he abruptly stopped. It hit him: he vividly recalled his horrific dream of last night. *How I hoped I'd never remember that dream*, he thought.

On a typical morning, Dan usually planned the day ahead while cleaning and dressing. This morning, however, his thoughts were preoccupied with whether or not he should take his trip. The dream had visibly shaken him. He was ready to surrender to his haunting thoughts of peril and abandon the trip, when he looked across the bedroom and saw William's stuffed tiger resting on his brother's bed, where it had remained since his disappearance thirteen years ago. Then he glanced at William's other stuffed animal, the three-legged reindeer, which Dan had set on his headboard. These toys of William's were all Dan needed to solidify his intentions to rescue his brother.

"Good morning, mom," said Dan, as he entered the kitchen.

"Good morning, Dan," replied his mom. "Did you sleep well?"

"Yeah, I guess so," replied Dan.

"Well, we've got a busy day ahead of us," said his mom, "so, I thought I'd make you and your father a hot breakfast."

"Where is dad?" asked Dan.

"He's on the phone with Mr. Curry," answered his mom. "Apparently, the vacuum cleaner was misplaced during the move on Saturday and he's asking your father if he knows where it is. Honestly, how can you misplace a vacuum cleaner?" While pre-heating the oven, Nancy asked, "So, what's first on your to-do list today?"

Before Dan could respond, his father entered the kitchen.

"Did he find the vacuum cleaner?" asked Nancy.

"Yes," replied her husband. "Apparently, someone stored it in the garage."

"The garage?" asked Nancy. "Why would someone store a vacuum cleaner in the garage?"

While his parents continued their mind-numbing conversation about a vacuum cleaner, Dan sat at the table reviewing a mental checklist to determine if he needed anything else for his trip. Vividly recalling the injuries he suffered in his recent dream, the teenager decided that a small, but basic, first-aid kit would definitely come in handy for the trip. He interrupted his parents, "Mom, I need to walk into town this morning to pick up a few last-minute things."

"Dan, I thought you already had everything," remarked Nancy.

"Well, I thought I'd take a small first-aid kit," stated Dan, "and I'd also like to pick up a science magazine to read on the bus."

His father entered the conversation, "Dan, it'll be dark on the bus tonight; you won't be able to read anyway. And as far as the first-aid kit, I'm sure that the park rangers will have all the necessary supplies."

Nancy, however, disagreed with her husband and stated, "I think the first-aid kit's a great idea. You can never be too safe when you're out in the woods." In the midst of reaching for the plates in the cabinet, Nancy added, "Dan, take a ten dollar bill from my purse; that should be enough."

When Dan left the kitchen, Nancy admitted to her husband, "I'm sorry, but I just couldn't take it if something happened to our second son. I know it sounds crazy, but just knowing that he'll be away from us for a month scares me to death. Even a small first-aid kit will bring me a little relief."

Seeing his wife tremble slightly, Jeff conceded, "That's fine, honey. Actually, the first-aid kit's not a bad idea."

Dan re-entered the room, saying, "Mom, I couldn't find a ten, so I took a twenty."

"That's fine, honey," answered his mom, as she inconspicuously wiped a tear from her cheek. "But I expect some change."

Nearly an hour later, after the warm meal was consumed and his father had left for work, Dan headed out the door.

Passing in front of the Parker's house, Dan met Jimmy stepping onto the porch carrying a broom. "Hey, Jimmy," yelled Dan. "You're up awfully early."

"Yeah," replied Jimmy. "Can you believe my folks gave me more chores to do before tonight? They said that since I did such a good job with my room, I should be in good practice to continue with the rest of the house. I mean, come on, this is my last day in town for a month and they've got me working!"

For a brief moment, Dan mentally withdrew from Jimmy's predicament to plot how he'd secretly escape that night without his parents' knowledge. Dan abruptly changed the subject and asked, "Jimmy, are your folks driving you to the buses tonight?"

"Are you kidding?" asked Jimmy. "It's only three blocks away; I'm going to walk. Besides, they'd probably have me wash the car if we used it."

This just might work, thought Dan. "Can I walk with you tonight?" asked Dan.

"Sure, that would be fun," said Jimmy. "So, where are you off to now?"

"Into town to get a few things for the trip," replied Dan. "Want to come along?"

"Sure, I'd love to, but I can't," answered Jimmy. "If I don't get these chores done, I'm history. I'm only on number three, sweeping the front porch, and they've got nine other jobs lined up."

"Sorry," replied Dan. "So, how about I meet you on your front porch tonight about 6:45?"

"That's fine," said Jimmy, who carelessly kicked a porch chair to sweep underneath.

Realizing he had a list of things to accomplish before 6:45 that night, Dan picked up his pace into town. His first stop was the drug store to purchase a first-aid kit. Drugs and More, as the store was named, offered a large selection of first-aid kits, more than Dan could have ever imagined. Heck, there was even a kit which included a heart monitor. Glancing to the left, he noticed even more kits, but of a smaller size and price. He bent over to remove a medium-sized kit from the shelf to read its contents. "Everything seems to be here," he said to himself. Standing up, he looked to the right to see if there was anything else he might need. Noticing nothing of interest, he proceeded to the check-out counter. Two customers ahead of him stood Cindy Somer, Jimmy's friend. She casually glanced back and, upon recognizing Dan, gave a slight nod.

"May I help you?" addressed the clerk to Cindy.

Turning her head to face the clerk, Cindy responded, "Oh, I'm sorry; yes, I'm ready to check out," as she placed her items on the counter. Cindy unenthusiastically read the headlines on the tabloids while the clerk bagged her items.

"That will be $13.45," informed the clerk. Cindy paid by credit card, then took one last look at Dan and said, "See you."

Dan simply responded, "Yeah."

As long as Dan could remember, girls made him nervous. The teenager thought, *I'm not athletic, I don't have a car, and I always seem to be the target of the local bullies; so why would someone–like Cindy–ever be interested in me?*

The annoying sound of coins bouncing on the counter drew Dan's attention to the man in front of him who was purchasing cigars with loose change. After counting the coins, the clerk handed the cigars to the man, who quickly stepped away from the counter and bolted to the door. He was obviously in a hurry for someone or something.

While placing his first-aid kit on the counter, Dan noticed the rack of magazines to his right which Cindy was scanning moments earlier. He was in luck; he removed the last '*Science*' magazine from the stand and placed it on the counter next to his kit. Pulling his mom's twenty dollar bill from his pocket, he handed it to the clerk, who, moments later, said, "Here's your change, sir; thank you."

Exiting the drug store, Dan was hit by unusually warm air for late May. Setting his recent purchases on the sidewalk, Dan reached into his pocket to count the remaining change. He selfishly reasoned that his mom would approve of him buying an ice cream cone from the parlor since it was a warm day. Lifting his bag from the sidewalk, Dan headed south on Main Street a couple blocks to the parlor. He obviously wasn't the only Lawtonian craving ice cream that day; there were ten people standing in line and only one clerk. Dan shrugged his shoulders and thought, *I'll read my magazine while I'm waiting.* About ten minutes later, a lady in her mid-fifties, rather fleshy, and obviously someone who had sampled all of the ice cream flavors a number of times, asked for his order.

"Yes," responded Dan. "I'd like a double scoop chocolate cone." Dan turned to the next page in his magazine.

Moments later, Dan heard "That'll be $1.99."

Dan slipped the magazine into his bag and reached for his money.

"Thank you, sir," replied the lady. "Next!" she shouted.

The flavor and coldness of the ice cream against his palate didn't disappoint his expectations. Now that he had his first-aid kit and magazine, Dan felt he had the last remaining items needed for his trip. However, before returning home, he thought he'd walk in the direction of the fire station, three blocks from his house, to investigate the area where the chartered buses would be parked that night to map out his escape route. He took another lick from his cone. *Maybe, I should have gotten three scoops*, he thought, when quite suddenly and without warning, the plastic bag containing his kit and magazine ripped down the side, sending the contents to the sidewalk. Trying not to topple his cone while stooping to pick up his recent purchases, he failed to notice four people turning the corner, only five feet away, and heading in his direction. As Dan rose from the sidewalk, his ice cream cone was shoved to the ground. Sur and Malice, the school bullies, were also shopping with their seedy dates, Barb and Cecilia, for last-minute camping items.

"Look, girls," said Sur, "Dan's enjoying an ice cream cone by himself. No surprise there."

Malice joined in the torment and asked, "What's this?" as he pounded his fist on the first-aid kit in Dan's arm, knocking it and the magazine back to the sidewalk. "Hey guys, he's got a first-aid kit." Placing his face within inches of Dan's, he threatened, "Trust me, Clay, you'll need more than a first-aid kit when I'm finished with you!"

Noticing bystanders gathering, but without offering any assistance, Dan nervously asked, "What do you want?"

"I want you to swallow your own teeth," replied Malice, "and I'll enjoy helping you out."

"Come on, guys, let's go," interjected Barb. "He's not worth it."

"You know, Barb, you're right," responded Malice, "he's not worth it."

As the four prepared to resume their walk down Main Street, Sur deliberately reared his leg back, took aim, and kicked Dan's first-aid kit into the street, narrowly missing the bystanders. "That's what I think of your sissy first-aid kit, Clay," replied Sur.

Dan had never been more humiliated in his life. There he stood defenseless in the middle of the sidewalk, his kit crushed and resting in the street gutter, and a gathering of townspeople to witness, not deter, the incident.

Racing out of the video store, located just behind Dan, was Cindy who had witnessed the airborne kit scene from the store window. Looking at the two bullies and their dates, who were only several feet down the sidewalk, she yelled, "Hey, you creeps, leave him alone!"

The four teenagers turned and retraced their steps to Dan.

"What's this?" asked Sur. "Got a girl fighting your battles, Clay?"

Out of control, Cindy released a powerful uppercut to Sur's chin, causing him to stumble backwards a step or two.

Enraged and totally mortified, Sur regained his stance and was tempted to return the punch.

"Do it!" yelled Cindy. "Go ahead, give me a reason."

Both stood motionless.

"Come on," demanded Cecilia to Sur, "let's go!" Both Cecilia and Barb grabbed their boyfriends' arms and led them out of harm's way; after all, Cindy was still within arm's reach. As the couples walked past Dan, however, Malice purposely rammed his shoulder against Dan's shoulder, producing a sharp pain.

Dan, while trying to conceal the expression of pain on his face, heard Malice's warning from behind, "That's just a taste of what awaits you at survival camp, Clay."

Cindy took two steps forward as if to pursue the party; the four quickly picked up their pace.

"Those thugs," said Cindy, "someone needs to teach them a lesson. Are you alright, Dan?"

Embarrassingly, Dan replied, "Yeah, I'm fine." Looking about, he saw his dented box in the street gutter.

As Dan approached the curb, Cindy yelled to the bystanders, "The show's over!" One by one, the cowardly crowd dispersed.

"What's in the box?" asked Cindy.

"A first-aid kit I got for the trip," replied Dan, as he picked up the damaged carton.

"Oh, that's right," said Cindy, "you're going on the camping trip. Are you excited?"

Bending over to pick up his mangled magazine on the sidewalk's edge, Dan replied, "A little, I suppose. Are you excited?"

"Not at all," replied Cindy.

"Why not?" asked Dan.

"Well," said Cindy, "I've been on similar one-week camping excursions before–three in all–and my gosh are they boring. All the girls sit around talking about boys and complaining about the lack of amenities. What do they expect? It's a campground. Actually, I think my mom is forcing me to go because she wants some peace and quiet around the house. She says it's my birthday gift. Believe me, if I could, I'd go anywhere but survival camp."

Cindy watched Dan roll his magazine and place it in his back pocket.

"You know," informed Cindy, "I was in some of your classes this past year."

"Yeah, I know," replied Dan.

"Anyway," continued Cindy, "it's a shame that we never really got a chance to know each other. But who knows, maybe we can spend some time together at camp: you, Jimmy, and me. That might make camp bearable."

"Sure," replied Dan. "Well, thanks again, Cindy. I guess I'll see you tonight."

As he walked away, Cindy caught up with him and asked, "Where are you headed now?"

"To the park near the fire station," answered Dan, "and then home to pack."

"Would you mind if I walked with you?" asked Cindy. "I live only a block behind your house, you know."

"Sure," replied Dan.

As the two turned the corner, Cindy recounted her countless dislikes of the town and the high school from where she recently graduated. She talked the entire distance to the park! But Dan didn't mind; he actually enjoyed their conversation, though he hardly spoke a word. When they entered the park, Cindy noticed Dan's attention switch from her conversation to the park grounds. Beyond the park was the entrance to Eldritch Forest.

Dan scrupulously scanned the entire area, which prompted Cindy to ask, "What are you looking for?"

Lost in his visual search, Dan momentarily forgot that he wasn't alone, as he usually was. "Oh, um, nothing really ... just ... nothing," mumbled Dan.

"You know, Dan," said Cindy, "you've hardly said a word since we left Main Street. Are you okay? I mean, I feel like I've been doing all the talking."

"I'm fine," replied Dan.

Cindy looked at him intently and confessed, "You really are a mystery."

Exceedingly nervous, Dan suggested, "Maybe we should head home now."

"Yeah, you're probably right," answered Cindy.

Walking home, Dan, for a change, initiated two conversations that, much to his surprise, Cindy welcomed.

Saying goodbye, they parted and Dan entered his house. Knowing that his mom would want to inspect the first-aid kit, Dan quickly discarded the dented box, so as not to arouse suspicion. Hearing a noise from the living room, Nancy emerged from the kitchen and into the living area where Dan was sitting on the sofa.

"When did you get home?" asked his mom.

"Hi, mom," responded Dan, "I just now walked in."

Noticing the plastic container her son held on his lap, she asked, "Is that the first-aid kit?"

"Yes," said Dan, as he handed her the kit for inspection.

"Well, Dan, this is nice," evaluated his mom. "And, it's the perfect size for your backpack. By the way, I'm making another batch of cookies. Are you sure you'll eat all of them? I mean, I've made several dozen." Before Dan could respond, Nancy instructed, "Make sure you share some with Jimmy and Cindy. By the way, is Cindy still going on the trip?"

"Yeah," answered Dan. "As a matter of fact, I ran into her in the drug store and we walked home together. She's not too excited about camp, though."

"Well," asked his mom, "why not?"

"Apparently, she's been on three similar camping trips before," Dan explained, "and ... well ... I suspect she's getting a little bored with them."

"Three!" exclaimed his mother. "Why Sara Somer must have more money than I thought."

Since it was nearly noon, Nancy suggested that Dan take his first-aid kit upstairs and then come down for lunch.

The teenager ran upstairs, threw the kit on his bed, and proceeded to place everything else which he'd be packing on the bed, including his new lantern and machete. Viewing all the essentials, he realized that his backpack wouldn't be big enough. *Besides*, he thought, *I still need to pack all the food.* So he grabbed his dad's old army duffle bag from the hallway closet and carried it to his room. A hunch came over him. Strongly suspecting that his parents would inspect his bag to make sure he had everything, Dan decided against storing his machete in the bag for the time being.

"Lunch is ready!" yelled his mother from the base of the steps.

After saying grace, Dan and his mom enjoyed a turkey sandwich, a small salad, and chips.

Only two bites into her sandwich, Nancy stated, "This afternoon, it might be a good idea to pack everything you'll be taking to camp and then rest. Lord knows you won't get any sleep on the bus tonight."

"Sure, mom," replied Dan.

Detecting a slight choke in her voice, Dan's suspicions were confirmed that his mother would have a difficult time saying goodbye that night. The teenager realized that his mom would be deeply troubled in releasing her second son into the unknown, if only for a month. Dan was overridden with guilt. After all she had done for him in preparation for his trip–the baking, the laundry, and the purchases–he would repay her by denying her and his dad the opportunity to walk with him to the bus stop. But, he had no choice; otherwise, he'd never be able to enter Eldritch Forest undetected. Attempting to ease his aching conscience before the heartbreaking news, Dan rose from the table, thanked his mom, and gave her a slight kiss on the cheek–something he did only on rare occasions. Oh sure, Dan, like many boys his age, occasionally gave his mother a peck on the cheek, but this kiss was different and his mother sensed it.

And, as much as his mother treasured this rare sign of affection, she also knew that it was somewhat unusual, even for Dan. *Something is terribly wrong*, she thought, *but what?*

Dan left the kitchen and headed upstairs.

Everything managed to fit into the oversize army duffle bag quite nicely; everything, that is, except the food and the machete, which he would not pack until the last possible moment. Taking a pen and a piece of paper from the desk drawer, he made a capital 'M' on the paper and set it near his bag as his reminder not to forget the machete. With pen still in hand, a dreadful thought consumed the teenager. Dan remembered witnessing for years his mother's painful agony and mental torture following William's disappearance. And, even though Dan realized that he'd be out of contact in the parallel world for only a month, he knew that even this relatively short period of time would take a serious toll on her. So, he decided to write his parents a note and place it somewhere where they wouldn't discover it until after he was reported missing. After four failed attempts, Dan realized that composing the note would not be a two-minute task as he previously suspected. After several more versions, Dan ultimately penned:

> Mom and Dad,
>
> By the time you read this letter, I will undoubtedly have been reported missing. I'm fine, believe me. Please don't exhaust your time or money on trying to locate me, for I am nowhere to be found. I wish I could tell you exactly where I am, but for safety reasons, I cannot. I will return on the evening of June 30. Know that I am fine and that I love you both very much. This is something I have to do. Please keep me in your prayers.
>
> Love,
>
> Dan

Now, thought Dan, *where to hide the note so mom and dad would be sure to discover it ... but not until after a park ranger calls to report that I never arrived at survival camp during the early hours of Tuesday?* After looking about his room for a place to conceal the message and coming up clueless, Dan placed it in his jeans pocket and decided to take a nap. "I'll hide it later," he said to himself.

After removing the loaded duffle bag from his bed, Dan slipped under the covers. Overly exhausted, the teenager entered a deep sleep within minutes. For a second time, Dan saw himself–as an onlooker–searching for William. At first, he viewed a castle in the far distance; then within seconds, he saw himself standing on the sixth floor of the castle terrified beyond belief. In his dream state, he watched himself opening a door and peering in. The long narrow room housed patients who were reclining on cots under the watchful care of half-man and half-serpent creatures; resting upon a cot was William. "I know it's him!" exclaimed Dan in his dream. "It's got to... ." Suddenly, Dan jerked uncontrollably, fell from his bed, and left his dream. "What's happening?" he said to himself. Dan's entire body was shaking spastically and sweating profusely, as if a fever had broken. Oddly enough, for as frightened as he was, he was equally grateful for the dream. Grateful, for now more than ever, he was determined to make the transworld trip.

It was now 6:00 p.m. His father, home from the glass factory, and mother were quickly throwing food on the table since they had to leave in forty-five minutes.

"Hurry up, son," yelled his father from the base of the steps, "we have to eat now or we'll be late."

Within minutes, all were seated at their small kitchen table saying grace and asking God's special protection on Dan during his trip.

Immediately after the word, 'Amen' was uttered, Nancy remarked, "Dan, we'll leave at 6:45; this should give us enough time to walk the three blocks."

Now came the moment which Dan had been dreading since agreeing to walk with Jimmy to the fire station. Dan cleared his throat and said, "Mom, I thought it would be nice... ." Dan saw a lonesome look in his mother's eyes; he just couldn't do it.

"You thought it would be nice to what, son?" asked his mom.

Dan cleared his throat a second time, as if in stalling for a few seconds he'd acquire the heartless courage he desperately needed. He tried again, "I thought it would be nice if Jimmy and I walked to the fire station by ourselves tonight. I'd rather say goodbye to you and dad here, in the house, in case ... you know ... in case it gets a little emotional."

Jeff spoke up, "Son, your mother and I were looking forward to walking with you to the buses tonight."

"I know, dad, and I'm sorry," replied Dan. "But you know how I can get when it comes to saying goodbye." Switching his gaze to his mother, Dan implored, "Please understand."

His mother unconvincingly responded, "That's fine, Dan."

Dan lost his appetite.

"Son," said his father, "you may be excused. Why don't you finish your packing?"

"Yes, dad," replied Dan. The teenager rose from the table, glanced at his mother, whose head was now lowered staring at the food on her plate, and remarked, "Sorry, mom." As Dan left the kitchen and entered the living room, he felt the lowest he'd ever felt in his entire brief life, including that morning's incident downtown with Sur and Malice. The only thought which gave him any comfort was the joy his family would share in a month at seeing William again.

Before heading upstairs, however, Dan ventured into the den. Taking the note which he addressed to his folks from his pocket, Dan placed it within the pages of his mom's Sunday Prayer Book. He knew that she always carried the missal with her to Mass on Sundays. Dan opted against placing the note in her Daily Prayer Book, since he suspected she'd be reading that particular prayer book later that night before retiring. He had to make sure he was long gone before she discovered the note. The approach of footsteps startled Dan, who darted from the den. It was not until he reached his bedroom that he realized he was still carrying his mom's Sunday Prayer Book. Setting it on his dresser, he decided he'd return it to the den before leaving that night.

While in his room, Dan finalized his packing by wrapping his machete in a tee shirt and placing it at the bottom of the duffle bag. Glancing around the room, he added a few personal items: William's stuffed tiger from the bed and his Bible. Dan remembered as a child how he always looked forward to bedtime when either his dad or mom would read him stories from the Bible; even now, at eighteen, he enjoyed reading the Scriptures which offered him invaluable guidance and enlightenment. There was a knock at the door.

"Come in," replied Dan. His mother entered the room toting three plastic containers of homemade cookies and his father carrying two grocery bags filled with juice, water, chips, marshmallows, cereal, hotdogs, hamburger patties, and a collapsible camp-sized cooler with dry ice for the meat.

"Is there room in the duffle bag for these essentials?" asked his mother.

"Oh, sure," answered Dan. "And if there isn't, trust me, I'll make room."

Noticing the familiar duffle bag, his father asked, "Son, where'd you get that bag?"

"I found it in the hallway closet," replied Dan. "Can I use it, since it can hold a lot more than my school backpack?"

Lifting the bag from the bed, Jeff remarked, "This is my old army duffle bag." Returning his gaze to his son, he said, "Of course you can use it; just don't lose it."

"Thanks, dad," replied Dan. "I'll bring it back."

Refocusing his attention on the grocery bags, Jeff asked, "What about all this food?"

After unpacking and abandoning a few tee shirts and two pairs of jeans, Dan replied, "There's plenty of room."

Sensing that they wanted to talk, but didn't know what to say, Dan jokingly remarked, "Don't forget to write."

"Don't worry," replied his mother, "we will."

The ice was broken.

"Are you ready, son?" asked his dad.

"Yeah, I think so," answered Dan.

Both father and son reached for the duffle bag, as if it was an honor to carry a cumbersome bag down a flight of stairs.

Dan's father prevailed saying, "You've got to carry it three blocks, so let me at least carry it to the front door."

Dan yielded.

Taking one last look around the room, Dan viewed everything, as if he'd never see his soldier wallpapered room again. As he continued his scan, his thoughts centered on William's stuffed animal which was now missing from his brother's bed and buried in Dan's luggage.

Mom hasn't noticed that it's missing, thought Dan, *and neither she nor dad has inspected my luggage.*

Hoping to spare his mom the grief of witnessing the missing stuffed animal, Dan quickly exited the room, hoping that his parents would immediately follow; they did. Unfortunately, in his rush to leave his bedroom, Dan neglected to return the Sunday Prayer Book to the den.

Approaching the last step, the Clays heard the chiming of the three-quarter hour from the living room clock.

"Well, son," said his dad, "I guess that's your signal." Placing the duffle bag on the ground, his father extended his hand to his son for a hearty shake; his son, instead, lunged toward his father and gave him a hug. His father responded in like manner.

After a few moments, his mother, quite teary eyed by now, gave Dan the longest hug he'd ever received from anyone. "Dan, I already miss you so much," whispered his mom into his ear. "Please, please take good care of yourself."

"I will, mom," promised Dan.

Jeff placed his hand on his son's shoulder and advised, "Be careful and don't forget to write us soon."

Realizing that he could grant only one of his father's wishes, Dan said, "I'll be careful; I promise."

As Dan cleared the front door and was descending the porch steps, he heard his mother whimpering. He couldn't turn back and look; it would be too much for him to endure. He couldn't bear remembering his mother's painful goodbye on his treacherous month-long journey. As difficult as it was, Dan continued his forward pace.

Jimmy, who was already waiting near the end of the Clay's sidewalk, yelled, "Come on, Dan; we'll be late."

From behind, Dan heard the porch squeak. He turned and saw his mom dashing toward him. She ran into him, practically knocking him to the ground, in an attempt to capture one last hug. "Dan, I love you so much," she said. "Come back safely."

"I'll be home before you know it," replied Dan.

After a prolonged ten second hug, they parted.

Jimmy and Dan began their walk down the poorly lit sidewalk. As Dan's parents watched the boys turn the corner and out of sight, Nancy grabbed the fence to break her fall; she was grief stricken.

Jeff, who was standing only a few paces from the porch, dashed to her rescue not a moment too soon. Desperately trying to comfort his wife, he assured, "Honey, he'll be fine. We've raised him well. You of all people should be proud of the fine young man he's become. He'll be fine and he'll be home soon, I promise." Then, trying to fight back his own tears, he helped his wife into the house, locked the front door, and turned out the light.

The Clays' mental torment from thirteen years ago was about to replay itself.

CHAPTER EIGHT
Unwelcome Pursuers

During the teenagers' short walk to the fire station, Jimmy talked nonstop about the adventures he would have at survival camp. At the top of his list was canoeing. Jimmy was also looking forward with great anticipation to the rock-climbing excursion which the survival camp brochure prominently featured on its front cover. Throughout Jimmy's rather dull monologue, Dan was only partially listening; he spent most of the time devising a plan of escape without anyone, including Jimmy, noticing.

Sensing Dan's disinterest in his comments, Jimmy asked, "Dan, are you even listening? Dan!"

It took a few moments before Dan realized that Jimmy was speaking to him. "What?" asked Dan. "Sorry, Jimmy, I guess I was daydreaming about camp."

"Look, Dan," replied Jimmy, "you've got to stop being so distant."

With all attention focused on his getaway scheme, Dan unknowingly walked straight through an intersection, while Jimmy turned right.

"Hey, Dan," asked Jimmy, "where are you going? The fire station's this way."

Dan quickly stepped alongside his neighbor.

"I can't believe we're finally going to survival camp," remarked an excited Jimmy.

As expected, parked along the north side of the street were two chartered buses surrounded by nearly seventy teenagers and their parents. Removing the duffle bag from his aching shoulders, Dan carried it at his side the remaining twenty feet. Standing near the first bus was its driver, who was registering the passengers' names on his clipboard as they approached the bus door.

"Name?" asked the driver.

"Clay... Dan Clay," responded Dan, who watched the driver place a check mark next to his name on the roster.

The bus driver pointed to his right and said, "Set your bag at the rear of the bus and then form a line along the street curb. No one is permitted on the bus just yet."

Dan lifted his bag, which he had momentarily set upon the sidewalk, and stepped to the back of the bus pretending to set his bag with the others. Looking back, he saw Jimmy registering with the driver. Then, looking to the sidewalk, Dan noticed that everyone was engrossed in conversations and that he remained oblivious to the disorderly group. So he slipped to the opposite side of the bus and placed his bag near the rear tire, so it was out of the crowd's sight. Returning to the other side of the bus where the teenagers and parents were gathered, he saw Jimmy tossing a baseball with a few of his school buddies. Obviously, Jimmy had not noticed Dan slip out of sight for a moment or two. Now that he had registered with the bus driver, Dan knew he could grab his bag and leave anytime. He took a long look at Jimmy, who was now standing at the front of the bus.

Jimmy instinctively felt someone staring at him; he paused from tossing the baseball, turned, and spotted Dan at the rear of the bus, staring in his direction. The prodding of his friends caused Jimmy to turn around and continue tossing the ball. With Jimmy's back now facing him, Dan decided to slip out of sight permanently. In an undetected manner, he returned to the opposite side of the bus, grabbed his bag, and dodging the streetlights, bolted to the small park that adjoined Eldritch Forest. *Finally*, he thought, *I'm on my way.*

Unfortunately, in his mad scurry to the park, Dan was unaware that the baseball had rolled under the bus and onto the street. Jimmy volunteered to retrieve the ball. Crossing the street, Jimmy stopped when he spotted a man entering the park. Once the individual stepped near a streetlight, Jimmy immediately recognized the familiar shirt and the walk of the man. "Dan?" he said to himself.

Jimmy's thoughts raced, *Where's he going with his duffle bag?* Almost immediately, he began putting the pieces together. He reasoned, *Dan was acting rather oddly, even for himself, on our walk to the fire station. He didn't fool me; I know he's not excited about survival camp and just now he gave me a weird look. Something's wrong. But where's he going?* On impulse, Jimmy ran to the other side of the bus and tossed the ball to his friends. Then, when the time was right, he also crept to the back of the bus, grabbed his bag from the curb, and dashed to the park, also undetected, well almost.

Cindy, who was standing alone on the curb–since her mother had to work that night–but away from the idle chatter of her former female classmates, saw Jimmy grab his bag and dart across the street to the park. Given the loud and distracting commotion of the teenagers and their parents, Cindy also presumed she could snatch her bag and escape unnoticed. And that she did.

Jimmy followed Dan at a safe distance, though he did get closer as the darkness of the forest slowly enveloped Dan. Likewise, Cindy kept a safe distance from Jimmy. It appeared to Jimmy that Dan not only knew exactly where he was going, but what he was doing. Dan stopped; Jimmy stopped; Cindy stopped. Dan took a quick survey to make sure he wasn't being followed. Luckily, Jimmy had slipped behind a large tree before Dan turned to inspect the forest behind him. Given the darkness, Cindy was well out of Dan's sight. Seeing no intruders, Dan neared the majestic oak tree, while Jimmy stepped from the concealment of the tree and resumed his pursuit. Cindy, meanwhile, retained her fast pace. Glancing heavenward, Dan saw the full moon between the uppermost tree limbs. Now directly in front of the enchanted oak, Dan placed his hand against the tree. As he suspected and hoped, it was soft to the touch. With the large duffle bag tightly secured to his shoulders, Dan took two steps back and then lunged forward into the tree.

"What the.... !" exclaimed Jimmy, as he witnessed his neighbor penetrate the tree and suddenly disappear. Jimmy dashed to the oak tree screaming, "Dan ... Dan!"

When Jimmy's deafening and fearful scream reached Cindy's ears, she immediately advanced from a fast pace to a powerful sprint in the direction of the excitement. When she reached Jimmy, only moments later, he was on his knees behind the giant oak inspecting the forest floor for clues.

"Jimmy," asked Cindy, "what's wrong?"

Totally unconcerned that he was being followed, Jimmy replied, "Dan's gone!"

"What do you mean gone?" inquired Cindy.

"I followed him into the forest from the buses," informed Jimmy, "and then I saw him run through this tree, but he never came out the back side."

"That's completely insane," replied Cindy, "completely insane."

"Look," said Jimmy, as he rose to his feet, "I know what I saw. And I saw him vanish into the tree!"

"Maybe," suggested Cindy, "he's up ahead somewhere in the darkness."

Both teenagers began yelling for Dan, but there was no response.

Completely shocked and frightened, Jimmy rested his hand against the oak and penetrated the tree. "Oh my God," he mumbled.

Stepping from the opposite side of the oak, Cindy asked, "What's wrong?"

"The tree," said Jimmy, "it's soft."

Cindy neared her friend and asked, "What do you mean soft?," as she placed her hand against the tree. "My gosh, it is."

"I just got a weird thought," said Jimmy.

"What's that?" asked Cindy.

"You don't suppose," suggested Jimmy, "that Dan intentionally ran through the tree, do you?"

"Well," replied Cindy, "he's not anywhere around here."

There was a momentary pause before Jimmy hesitantly asked, "Should we run through it?"

"Run through it?" asked Cindy. "Are you out of your mind?"

"If you have a better idea," said Jimmy, "I'm all ears."

The two argued back and forth, which eventually escalated into a shoving match which Cindy won. Jimmy and his bag were unintentionally pushed through the tree.

Cindy stood motionless in complete panic. "What have I done?

What have I done?" she repeatedly asked herself. The growing and incessant noises from the dark distant forest startled even Cindy. With her backpack securely fastened, Cindy initially hesitated, but ultimately took two steps back and four steps forward into the oak.

In the parallel world, Dan remained motionless on his back trying to catch his breath. Within several moments, he regained enough strength to slowly lift himself to his elbows, when he was abruptly knocked flat on his back again by Jimmy crashing through the tree. Jimmy rested on Dan's chest also trying to catch his breath.

"What are you doing?" demanded Dan. "You've been following me, haven't you? Answer me!"

It took all Jimmy's strength just to nod. Jimmy, like Dan moments earlier, was out of breath. Nearly a minute later, Jimmy slowly raised himself off Dan's chest, only to be thrown down again by Cindy's graceful entrance. Now Cindy rested on Jimmy and, as Dan suspected, she was panting.

"Did you invite the whole town?" Dan angrily demanded of Jimmy. Dan lowered his chin to his chest in complete disbelief and mumbled, "Why are you two following me? This is my business and it's no concern of yours."

Able to speak now, Jimmy stammered, "What business?"

"My business is not any of your business," answered Dan, in an ever-louder voice.

With great difficulty, Cindy asked, "Where are we?"

"That's not important," answered Dan. "What *is* important–very important–is that you two return through the tree and tell no one what you saw here tonight." Quickly calling to mind Sam's story about Spiritus Malus and his sporadic patrols of the tree on full moon nights, Dan jumped to his feet, helped his friends to theirs, and was prepared to throw them back through the tree, when all three were slammed to the forest floor by Sam's crashing entrance, along with his oversize bag.

Rising to his knees, while pushing his glasses further up the bridge of his nose, Dan yelled, "Sam, what are you doing here? You told me that you'd never return to this world!"

"What do you mean this world?" interrupted Cindy. "Aren't we in Lawton?"

Dan glanced at Cindy, who was also resting on her knees, and uttered a loud, "Shush." He immediately returned his gaze to Sam ordering, "I want you to take these two trespassers with you and head back to our Lawton. I'll not have any of you risking your lives to help me rescue my brother."

"Risking our lives?" asked a nervous Jimmy, before taking a deep breath and then asking, "William ... do you think William's here?"

"Shush," rebuked Dan.

After briefly introducing herself and Jimmy to Sam, Cindy redirected her focus on Dan and firmly declared, "If I leave here now, then that means I'll have to go to survival camp. So, I'm staying."

"Cindy," said Dan, "you and Jimmy are leaving ... and you're leaving now!"

"If everyone would stop talking," interjected Sam, "I'd like to say something. You see, Dan, no one in Lawton–except you–has ever believed my story about this world. For years I've been laughed at and viewed as a lunatic. You're the first person who believed me and even spent time with me over a meal to hear my adventure. Heck, you even introduced me to your family; that meant a lot to me. You've helped me regain a sense of dignity; now I'll help you regain your family. Besides, if anything happened to you in this world ... well ... I just won't let that happen. Don't forget, I've been in this world before, not deep in the forest, of course, but at least on this side of the tree. And besides, you need my help to find Doctor O'Brien for the medication or we're all dead."

In his scrupulous review of nearly every detail of his trip, the toxic atmosphere had somehow eluded Dan, who in complete disbelief of his oversight remained silent for a moment.

Sam interrupted the brief silence and jokingly remarked, "Let's just say that once my month-long tour of duty with you is complete, my two meals with you and your family are paid in full."

"Alright," said Dan, "you can stay. But you two," pointing to Jimmy and Cindy, "have to return."

"I told you," insisted Cindy, "I'm not going to survival camp. If you have any mercy at all, you'll not throw me through the tree and into camp. Who knows, maybe I can help. I've got a pretty good uppercut, you know."

"Tell me about it," replied Dan. "I'm sorry, Cindy, but you can't stay."

Pointing to the oak tree, Cindy threatened, "If you throw me through that tree, I swear I'll have a crowd of people on this side of the tree in no time."

"Cindy," remarked Dan, "if you even think of breathing a word of this to the townspeople, then I'll.... ."

"Then it's settled. I'm staying," interrupted a confident Cindy.

Dan was enraged, but only out of safety for his stubborn friends. Realizing that he couldn't force them to return, he hung his head, as if admitting defeat.

"Dan," said Jimmy, "even though we were only five-year-old kids, I still vaguely remember playing with you and William almost every day; he was like an older brother to me, too. And I'd do just about anything to see him again. I just can't leave knowing that William may be here. I'd like to help."

A strong piercing wind did not go unnoticed by Sam who remarked in a serious and demanding voice, "Oh no, we've got to get out of here now! Spiritus Malus! Grab your bags! Run!"

Cindy, now fully recovered, asked, "Who or what is Spiritus Malus?"

"Later ... run!" yelled Dan.

Losing no time, the four transworld visitors carelessly bent down simultaneously to grab their bags resulting in a few head knocks. Sam took possession of his bag first and ran as fast as he could in the direction of town, yelling, "Hurry, our lives are at stake! Run!"

Within moments, the three teenagers caught up with Sam toting their luggage and sprinting as if the ground was collapsing behind them. Dan, having the slightest build, was right behind Sam, followed by Cindy, and finally, Jimmy. They had escaped, at least for now, what they presumed to be the arrival of Spiritus Malus.

The four travelers ran as fast as they could, considering that none of them had completely regained their strength from the crossover.

After a few minutes, Sam slowly diminished his pace. Dan suspected that given his age, he was tiring. But as Dan drew closer, he heard Sam mumble, "This isn't right; this can't be."

"What can't be right?" demanded Dan.

"The forest," answered Sam, as the two slowed to a fast walk. "The edge of the forest is supposed to be there," as Sam pointed five feet ahead, "right at that fence. I distinctly remember that fence."

As the four stepped over the rickety fence and continued their woodland escape, Dan could see that Sam was visibly distressed and somewhat confused.

Suddenly, Sam came to a complete stop. "Oh, my God," he exclaimed. Looking ahead about fifty feet into the near total darkness, Sam stared at a dilapidated structure and mumbled, "That's the O'Brien's house ... here in the forest." As tempting as it was to inspect the house, Sam knew that its appearance bore witness to abandonment; he also knew that he and his party had no choice but to move forward.

As the four advanced beyond the doctor's former residence, Sam froze again. "What the heck," said Sam, "this can't be happening." Peering ahead, he noticed that Lawton's Main Street was swallowed in darkness. Even the streetlights were unlit. A look of terror draped over the travelers' faces. Eventually, Sam spoke up, "I'll bet this is the handiwork of my evil twin, Sam, of this world."

Remembering Sam relaying the sad chapter of the other Lawton's history to him earlier, Dan rested his hand on Sam's shoulder and said, "Sam this wasn't you; it's not your fault."

Then something occurred to Dan, who enlightened, "But wait, the forest hadn't advanced this far into town when I was here four months ago."

With his head lowered, trying to conceal his emotions, Sam responded, "I don't know how this could have happened in such a short period of time." As Sam raised his sights and looked further ahead, he noticed the edge of the darkness. Knowing that he and his co-travelers were not out of danger yet, Sam regained his composure and ordered the three, "Come on. Look, there's the edge of the forest; there's safety, and we'll get some answers."

As they left the forest and Main Street behind and entered the new fringes of town, they all simultaneously, dropped to the ground in a small grassy area in pure exhaustion, barely able to speak.

After a few minutes, Sam stated, "I wonder where Doctor O'Brien lives now. The town has obviously changed quite a bit from my visit twenty years ago."

Dan, raising his head slightly, looked about. In the distance, he saw a telephone booth near the local pub. "Hey," asked Dan, "do you suppose the doctor's address is listed in the phone book?"

Sam gazed near the bar and replied, "Not a bad idea, kid. You all stay here. And by all means, stay out of sight. No one–I mean, absolutely no one–can see you. Stay low to the ground and out of sight. And whatever you do, don't re-enter the forest."

One at a time, all agreed, but Jimmy's affirmative response was followed by, "But, what's so terrible about being seen?"

"Dan," said Sam, "do your best to update the two while I'm making a phone call."

"Why?" asked Dan. "They're not staying here; they're going back tonight."

"Dan," said Cindy, "you can't tell me where I can and can't stay. You're not my mom. And even if you were, I'd still stay."

Sam cautiously rose to his feet, took a deep breath, and walked toward the phone booth which was a hundred feet into the clearing. Knowing that he, of all people, could not be detected, Sam walked as briskly as his condition would allow.

In the meantime, while the three teenagers rested near the perimeter of the forest, a quiet conversation unfolded.

"Dan," asked Jimmy, "why can't we be seen by the townspeople?"

"Alright you two," informed Dan, "in a nutshell, this is what's happened. Where we are now is a parallel world. Do you know what that means?"

Both Cindy and Jimmy nodded.

"Anyway," continued Dan, "the oak tree is a portal, or entryway, between our two worlds which is only active during a full moon. Sam visited this world twenty years ago, quite by accident. The story's told that during his visit, he was spotted by the locals who assumed he was the Sam White of this world, the one who's been performing demonic rites which enlarges the forest at the town's expense. Anyway, the bloodthirsty mob mistakenly advanced on the Sam that we know, who narrowly escaped death by seeking refuge in the forest behind us. Fearing the woods, the townspeople didn't enter, which is how Sam was able to escape the mob."

"So," asked Jimmy, "what's the deal with the forest?"

"Down through the centuries," continued Dan, "legends have been told about bizarre creatures and demonic men that inhabit the forest. It's because of these stories that the local citizens refuse to enter the forest under any condition, even in search of the evil Sam White. As Sam relayed the story to me, he managed to elude the crowd by walking the perimeter of the forest, only a short distance inside its darkness, well out of view of the mob. Sam reached the O'Brien's house, the family that took him in two to three weeks earlier to nurse the wound which he sustained during the crossover, and hid him from the mob until the next full moon."

By this time, Sam had reached the telephone booth and was scanning the phone book. "O'Brien, O'Brien, O'Brien," he mumbled to himself, as his index finger scanned the page. *Finally*, he thought, *O'Brien, Mark, MD; that's got to be him.* Grabbing a coin from his pocket, he pressed it against the coin slot when he realized it didn't fit. "You've got to be kidding," he said to himself. "Don't tell me the coins are a different size between our two worlds." He tried to shove the coin into the slot with no luck. From the nearby pub, he heard a lively crowd leaving the bar. Sam knew that he had to act fast before he was recognized. Knowing the extreme likelihood of an operator recognizing his voice, Sam nonetheless decided to place a collect call to Doctor O'Brien.

Back on the ground, Cindy asked, "Why is the portal active only during a full moon?"

"It has something to do with the beams of a full moon," answered Dan, "though no one really knows the exact cause. Since a person has to be touching the tree during a full moon to experience the phenomenon, only a few people know of the oak's powers. Apparently, only three people have crossed from our world here: Sam, a man named John Schultz, and me. It seems the residents in this world are so fearful of the forest that no one ever enters it, especially during a full moon. So you see, the portal will close tomorrow morning at sunrise and won't reopen until the next full moon, in another month, which is why you two have to leave tonight."

Picking up the receiver, Sam impatiently awaited the operator.

"This is the operator, how can I help you?"

"Yes," replied Sam. "I'd like to place a collect call to Doctor Mark O'Brien on Evans Lane."

"One moment, please," responded the operator.

Sam was still catching his breath when he heard, "This is Doctor O'Brien, who's this?"

Suspecting that the operator was listening in, Sam softly spoke, "Hello, doctor, this is Sam."

"Sam ... Sam who?" asked the doctor.

"Sam, your friend from—you know—across the way," replied Sam.

There was no response.

Trying to remain as vague as possible so as not to alert the operator, but at the same time, stir the doctor's memory, Sam continued, "Remember you took care of my hunting wound about twenty years ago."

"Oh, Sam," replied the doctor in an anxious tone. "How are you?"

"Fine," replied Sam.

Both men, on hearing voices in the background, knew that the operator was listening in on their conversation.

"Are you in town?" asked the doctor.

"Yeah, doctor," answered Sam. "I'm in for a brief visit and I brought three friends."

"Where are you?" asked the doctor. "I'll come pick you up."

"We're just outside..." Sam stared at the bar's neon sign and continued, "... O'Shea's."

"That's great," replied the doctor, "I'll be there in ten minutes to pick up you and your friends."

"Thanks," replied Sam. "We'll be across the street from the pub waiting in the grassy area near the forest's edge."

"Okay, I'll see you in ten minutes," concluded the doctor.

"See you then," said Sam.

Both said goodbye and hung up.

Still flat on the ground, Jimmy exclaimed, "Leave tonight?"

"Yes, tonight," demanded Dan.

Rolling onto her back to view the starry sky, Cindy bluntly asked, "Dan, who or what were we running from back at the tree?"

"Oh, the tree," said Dan, obviously stalling for time. "Sam said that the leader of the demonic caretakers, Spiritus Malus, patrols the entryway during most full moons trying to ensnare travelers to live with him at the castle."

"A castle... here in the forest?" asked an excited Jimmy.

"Look, guys, that's a whole other story," continued Dan, "and I don't have time to tell you now, since you're both leaving tonight!"

"And exactly how do you plan on sneaking us by this demonic man at the tree?" inquired Cindy.

In his self-absorbed thoughts to evacuate the two unwelcome travelers as quickly as possible, Dan had overlooked Spiritus Malus and the serious danger he posed to anyone near the tree. The young man of eighteen was presented with the ultimate dilemma. *If they stay, there's a good chance they'll be injured or killed... like me*, he thought. *And if they leave tonight, there's a good chance they'll encounter Spiritus Malus and end up in the castle or dead.* Dan had not only the weight of his own situation on his shoulders, but also the lives of his two friends, no, three friends. *What to do?* Dan debated internally. Just then, Sam was heard approaching.

"Alright," Sam started, "I spoke with Doctor O'Brien, and he'll be here in ten minutes to pick us up. Now remember, we must not be seen." While pointing to Jimmy and Cindy, Sam demanded, "If you two are staying with us, you have to do exactly as Dan and I say. Is that understood?"

At the same time, Cindy and Jimmy replied, "Yes."

"But, Sam," replied Dan, "for their own safety, I think they should leave."

"Dan," explained Sam, "I know you're fearful for their lives if they stay, but do you really want to send them back to the tree ... back to Spiritus Malus?"

Dan remained silent and glanced up at the stars, as if seeking divine intervention.

Sam ignored the stars and focused on the street ahead, waiting for an approaching car.

"I feel light headed," admitted Cindy.

"I'm afraid we all do, Cindy," whispered Sam. "You see, when one crosses over from our world to this world, one experiences momentary disorientation and the traveler is light headed for awhile. Eventually, if not treated, the traveler will die due to an unknown toxin in this atmosphere. That's why I looked up Doctor O'Brien right away. He developed an antidote for this toxin and gave it to me during my last visit here."

"Did it work?" asked Jimmy.

"Yeah," answered Sam, "it did. I only hope the doctor still has a supply of the medication or we'll have no choice but to walk back to the tree tonight."

Tapping Sam on the shoulder to get his attention, Dan proposed, "If Jimmy and Cindy can't approach the tree the remainder of this full moon and we don't want them endangering their lives on my personal quest, then maybe they can hide out at the O'Brien's house until the next full moon ... like you did, Sam."

Cindy, seriously objecting to Dan's suggestion, blurted, "Absolutely not! There's no way I'm staying imprisoned for a month in some stranger's house. Besides, Dan, like I said before, I could help in your search."

"She's right, Dan," concurred Jimmy. "Actually, we both could help you. Besides, if our roles were reversed, would you want to be cooped up in a house for a month?"

"The roles aren't reversed," answered Dan. "And even if they were, I'd never sink so low as to follow you around like you two followed me."

"I only followed you because I thought something was wrong," explained Jimmy, "and besides.... ."

"There he is," interrupted Sam.

Noticing the group that had only recently left the bar walk in the direction of the doctor's car, the four travelers remained on the ground near the forest, hoping for a signal from the doctor when it was safe to proceed. A few moments later, six drunkards stumbled down the sidewalk and then turned the corner.

The car's headlights flashed.

Sam, on determining that this was the doctor's signal, motioned the others to rise and quietly follow him to the car.

Once the travelers were standing next to the car, the automatic doors were unlocked and the group quickly and silently entered. As expected, Sam took the front seat, while the other three stepped into the rear. Once inside, even before greetings or introductions were exchanged, Doctor O'Brien ordered his passengers to squat as low as they could to the floor.

"You must not be seen," ordered the doctor. During the viewless drive, the doctor remarked, "Sam, it's not that I'm unhappy to see you, but why on earth did you return? You know this only means trouble for you and my family."

"Nice to see you too, doctor," replied Sam in a sarcastic tone. As Sam turned his head in the direction of the back seat, he continued, "I was following Dan because I had a hunch that he'd attempt the trip tonight."

"Who's Dan?" asked the doctor.

"He's the young man behind you with the black hair and glasses," informed Sam. "He's also been to your world before, but only for a few minutes. Anyway, he has a strong suspicion that his older brother,

William, accidentally entered your world thirteen years ago when he was a child, and now Dan's here to rescue him."

"And who," asked the doctor, "is going to rescue all of you?"

"Look, doctor," added Sam, "we won't be any trouble to you or your family; I promise. Our intention is to enter the forest first thing tomorrow morning after sunrise. We were hoping you might have a supply of your antidote for our journey."

"After your phone call," informed the doctor, "I checked my supply; there's enough for all of you. But Sam, there are more dangers in the forest than just the atmosphere."

"I know," responded Sam. "But Dan's determined to enter the forest and I won't permit him to enter it alone."

"And what about the other two?" asked Doctor O'Brien.

Sam turned slightly to rest his weight on his other knee and then answered, "The other two–Jimmy and Cindy–were following Dan and saw him enter the tree. Anyway, being teenagers, I suppose they wanted to check it out and entered the oak."

Jimmy immediately interrupted and clarified, "Not quite, Sam. Cindy pushed me through."

"It was an accident," defended Cindy.

"Anyway, doctor," resumed Sam, "whatever it was, they both ended up here with Dan and me. And I don't feel comfortable sending them back to the tree tonight for fear of Spiritus Malus."

"Well," said the doctor, "you've really got yourselves into a dilemma now."

With the passing of each approaching headlight, Sam studied the doctor's facial features. To Sam, the doctor definitely looked twenty years older, if not more. His blond hair had been replaced with no hair and his cheeks bore the resemblance of old discarded leather. Sam couldn't recall if the doctor wore glasses twenty years ago, but the pair he was wearing at the moment seemed to draw attention to his extended forehead.

"I noticed your old house in the forest," Sam hesitantly remarked.

There was a momentary pause before the doctor imparted, "For years now, the forest has been slowly encroaching upon our town, thanks to the demonic activities of your twin, Sam White. He must be doing something really sinister now, since it's only been during the past two months that the forest has advanced at a rapid rate and engulfed my house, then Main Street, and beyond. My family and I had no choice but to abandon our home. We moved as far away from the woods as we could to the opposite side of town. Actually, the entire town is spreading in our direction to escape the ever-consuming forest."

"Then that explains," said Dan, "why Main Street and the liquor store were not swallowed up by the forest when I visited this world four months ago."

"That's right," remarked the doctor. "The evil Sam must be up to some serious diabolical activities."

After a moment of silence, Sam asked, "What ever happened to my twin?"

"To this day," explained the doctor, "Sam's only been in prison once, but was soon released. Every time he's spotted, he flees into the forest sanctuary where no one else will enter. I think that the expanding forest only heightens the fear of our residents, making them even more terrified and more resolved never to enter the forest, even to capture Sam White. Now that my wife and I are getting on in years, we're seldom able to help our son, Ron, with his full moon patrols in the grassy area at the forest's edge to assist anyone who may accidentally cross over. Obviously, Ron's own growing family causes him to be late at times, which is why you never ran into him tonight, I suppose."

The car slowed and the passengers heard a garage door opening. Once inside the safety of the garage, the doctor suggested, "Okay, you can sit up now."

CHAPTER NINE

The Soul of the Beast

Stepping from the car, the passengers waited for the doctor to welcome them into his home. As Doctor O'Brien opened the door which led to the kitchen, a cat leaped from beneath the stoop, startling the four visitors.

"Sorry about that," said the doctor, "Midnight's a little frightened of strangers."

"Midnight?" asked Cindy.

"Yes," replied the doctor. "Several years ago, my youngest daughter, Alex, found him without a tag, wandering near the edge of the forest late at night. Anyway, considering the time of day she found him, and as you can see, he's completely black from ears to tail, Alex decided to name him Midnight."

Opening the door, the doctor invited his guests inside. Sitting in the living room watching television was the doctor's wife, Sharon. On hearing the door open, she yelled, "Honey, is that you?"

"Yes," replied the doctor, "and I brought a few friends."

Rising from the recliner and approaching the kitchen doorway, she noticed a familiar face. "Sam White, from the other world, is that you?"

"Yes," replied Sam.

"My gosh," continued Sharon, "it's been a long time. How have you been?"

"I assume you mean your husband's antidote," remarked Sam. "It worked like a miracle. Once I arrived back in my world, I was a little disoriented for a couple days, but then all the symptoms vanished."

Looking to Sam's left, Sharon saw the three teenagers and asked, "Are these your children?"

"Oh no," replied Sam. "These are friends of mine from the other side. It's a long story, but in a nutshell, they ... well ... actually Dan discovered the secret of the tree four months ago and decided to travel this full moon." Throughout his conversation, Sam rested his hand on Dan's shoulder as his way of introducing the teenager to Sharon.

"Dan," asked Sharon, "why on earth would you want to take such a dangerous journey? Why you can't be more than sixteen."

After clearing his throat, Dan responded, "Actually, Mrs. O'Brien, I'm eighteen and I have reason to believe that my older brother, William, is being held at the castle. I'm here to take him home."

"What makes you think he's in the castle?" asked Sharon.

Dan started, "When William was seven..."

"That, too, Sharon," interrupted Sam, "is a long story which I'm sure the kids will tell you about later."

Sensing that the travelers were still a bit tired from their crossover, Doctor O'Brien suggested, "Why don't all of you have a seat at the table while I go and gather my medicinal supplies?"

As the doctor left the kitchen, his wife motioned to Sam and the teenagers to have a seat. "Well," began Sharon, "as you already know, I'm Mrs. O'Brien, but you can call me Sharon." Looking at Jimmy, she saw a young man a bit stocky, obviously the result of high school sports, with thick wavy blond hair. "What's your name?" she asked.

"Jimmy," replied the young man. "I'm Dan's friend and was also a friend of his older brother when we were kids."

"Well, it's nice to meet you, Jimmy," responded Sharon. Finally, she glanced to Jimmy's right at an attractive young lady with brunette hair, just below the ears, and slender, but muscular. "And you are?" asked Sharon.

"I'm Cindy," answered the young lady. "I'm also a friend of Dan's and Jimmy's. Basically, I'm here to escape survival camp and to help the men when they get into trouble."

Sharon chuckled and said, "I'm happy to meet you too, Cindy."

THE SOUL OF THE BEAST

After taking another quick glance at her guests, she asked, "Now, what can I get you to eat? You have to be hungry from your journey."

All shook their heads, except Jimmy who said that a hamburger would be nice.

"Jimmy," snapped Cindy, "did you leave your manners in the tree?"

"What?" questioned Jimmy. "She asked, didn't she?"

Ever since Sharon's children had moved out of the house, she never thought she'd admit it, but she genuinely missed preparing large meals for her children and their friends. "Yes," replied Sharon, "I did ask, and I'd be only too happy to make all of you a late meal. Cindy, would you mind helping me clear the table?"

The doctor's footsteps could be heard on the wooden floor as he neared the kitchen doorway. "Alright, I've got a month's supply of the antidote for all four of you. This should last you through your journey; just remember to take one pill every day."

"That's great, doctor," replied Sam, "you're a lifesaver."

"Excuse me, Doctor O'Brien," pleaded Dan. "Would you by any chance have another month's supply?"

"Whatever for?" asked the doctor.

"For William," answered Dan.

"You're right, Dan, I forgot; sorry," said the doctor. "Let me check my supplies again."

When the doctor was just beyond the kitchen archway, Dan added, "Doctor, do you have any asthma medication?"

The doctor turned around and re-entered the kitchen, saying, "Dan, your shortness of breath is the result of your transworld travel; your symptoms will slowly pass once you begin taking the medicine."

"Not for me, doctor," replied Dan, "for my brother. My folks told me that when he was a child he suffered from severe asthma. I assume he still suffers from it."

The doctor placed his thumb and index finger on either side of his chin wondering how to tell the boy that the chances of finding his brother were slim to nil. On the other hand, the doctor admired the young man's determination and courage, especially since he suspected Sam had shared with Dan bits and pieces of what lurked in the forest. In an effort not to dash Dan's hope of finding his brother, the doctor confirmed, "Yes, I think I have something in the other room which will alleviate your brother's condition. I'll be right back."

Sharon, too, was greatly impressed with Dan's resolve, especially since she knew the Dan Clay in her world. He was the classic bully who constantly harassed other teens. As a former teacher's aide, Sharon witnessed firsthand the deplorable misdeeds of the Dan Clay from her world.

Returning her thoughts to the guests at hand, Sharon directed, "Sam, Jimmy, grab some plates and glasses in the cabinet behind you and set them on the table. Cindy and I will fry a few hamburgers."

During the preparation of the all-American meal, Sharon became ever more impressed with the loyalty and deep faith in Dan. She deciphered almost immediately that Jimmy was actually a good person who just happened to prefer sports and video games to studies. And Cindy, well Sharon sized her up as an independent and assertive young lady who was disheartened with her present young life and was searching for a change, for an adventure. *And what an adventure she and the others would undertake tomorrow at sunrise*, thought Sharon. Quite suddenly, Sharon experienced a distressing thought, *What if the children never return? Oh, my God, they're only children embarking on a grown man's odyssey.* She calmed her fears by telling herself that she'd ask her husband that night to reason with them and dissuade the group from undertaking the treacherous journey.

"Sharon," asked Jimmy, "should I pull the table away from the wall so all six of us can sit around it?"

"Oh, heavens yes," replied Sharon, "thank you."

Doctor O'Brien re-entered the kitchen to the smell of fried hamburgers and baked beans. Dan was placing the condiments on the table.

"Here, Dan," said the doctor, as he handed the teenager a small bottle of green pills. The doctor continued, "When you see William, make sure he takes one of these pills every day until you reach your own world."

Dan smiled as none had ever seen him smile before. Everyone in the room took notice. For the first time in nearly thirteen years, he finally heard someone say to him, "When you see William." Eventually, Dan not only spoke up, but gave the aging doctor a firm handshake, saying, "Thank you; I'll be sure to tell William."

On seeing this display of appreciation, Sharon was torn as she began to question her earlier notion to speak with her husband about prohibiting the group from venturing into the forest the next morning. For as much as she wanted to protect Sam and the teenagers by suggesting they stay with her, at the same time, she'd never forgive herself if the group of four was somehow able to save William but she prevented his rescue by forbidding them to enter the forest.

"The burgers are ready," informed Cindy.

"Alright then," said Sharon, "let's gather around and enjoy the meal."

The four guests took their seats, while the doctor and his wife remained standing. As the hosts bowed their heads, the transworld guests immediately rose from their seats and stared at the floor while Sharon prayed,

> "Dear Lord, we thank You for this meal before us and we pray that You safely guide our guests on their journey. Keep all harm from them and make them truly grateful for Your protection."

All responded, "Amen."

Taking his seat for a second time, Jimmy was the first to request a hamburger.

"Jimmy," chided Cindy, "where are your manners? Ladies should be served first."

"Ladies?" teasingly asked Jimmy. "I only see one lady here – Sharon."

At Jimmy's response, Doctor O'Brien glared at the teenager.

Knowing what her husband was thinking, Sharon placed her hand on her husband's and said, "Honey, I told them to call me Sharon."

"Oh, I see," said the doctor. "Well, in that case, you can call me Doctor O'Brien."

"Pay no mind to him," said Sharon, "he'll get used to it. Cindy, hand me your plate."

Within moments, all guests and the O'Briens were enjoying a

hearty meal and friendly conversation. During their talks around the table, both parties learned much about each other. For example, Sharon learned that Dan was a practicing Catholic; Cindy was thoroughly disinterested with her chatty female acquaintances, with Lawton–basically with life in general; Jimmy obviously loved his third hamburger more than the first two, and he hoped to someday play professional sports; and Sam longed to be part of a family someday. In exchange, the four visitors learned that Sharon was a devoted housewife who, despite her best efforts to conceal her feelings, was secretly terrified of the expanding forest, and Doctor O'Brien regretted not exploring deep into the forest when he was younger to confirm or deny the tales he had heard from his youth.

"So," asked Doctor O'Brien, "what time will you be leaving tomorrow morning?"

"I think we should enter the forest around 6:00," replied Sam, "so I think we should set our alarms for 4:30."

"4:30!" exclaimed Jimmy. "We've got a month for this journey and you're going to make us get up at 4:30!"

"Since we don't know how long it will take to reach the castle," explained Sam, "I think we should leave as soon as possible to give us as much time as we need." Sam glanced at the doctor and asked, "If, by chance, we return from the castle within a month, would we be able to stay with you until the next full moon?"

"Why of course," answered Sharon for her husband.

"Doctor O'Brien," asked Dan, "do the legends say how long it takes to reach the castle? And, how do you know where to look for the castle?"

The doctor set his hamburger on his plate, wiped the catsup which had lodged itself in the corner of his mouth and replied, "It's long been told that the castle is a twelve-day journey from the tree–depending of course, upon how much terrain you cover in a day–and that it sits upon a large hill which is surrounded by a moat. You know, like the castles you envision in the Middle Ages. Apparently after about a ten-day walk, one can see the colossal structure looming ahead." The doctor picked up his hamburger and took the last two bites. When the meal was finished, the conversation continued while all members pitched in cleaning the kitchen.

While returning the clean plates to the cabinet, Sam asked the doctor, "I don't mean to be presumptuous, doctor, but if Cindy and Jimmy can't return to the tree tonight for fear of Spiritus Malus, and since I tend to agree with Dan that they shouldn't put their lives at risk in the forest, would it be possible for them to stay with you and Sharon for the month? I promise they'll help around the house."

"What?" exclaimed Cindy. "Sam, I can't stay here for a whole month!" Looking at Sharon, who was now cleaning the sink, Cindy apologetically remarked, "I don't mean any disrespect, Sharon, but Sam and Dan will need my help."

"I understand," said Sharon, who quickly added, "but don't you think you two would be safer here? Besides, it would be nice having teenagers around the house again."

Sensing no reinforcement from Sharon, Cindy turned to Dan, who was returning the arrangement of artificial flowers to the table and implored, "Dan, please, you've got to take me with you!"

"I'm sorry, Cindy," answered Dan. "Look, I know you're trying to help, but put yourself in my shoes for a minute. Would you want me risking my life to save one of your family members?"

There wasn't a moment's pause before Cindy contested, "If I thought you could help, yes, I would."

"Now I know you're lying," accused Dan. "You wouldn't permit me to put my life in danger and you know it."

"Fine," responded Cindy, "if you won't take us with you, then Jimmy and I will sneak into the forest on our own the first chance we get and if we don't make it, then our deaths will be on your hands."

Jimmy nodded his head indicating agreement with Cindy's ultimatum.

Sensing that a heated argument was about to ensue, the doctor interjected, "We'll discuss this later tonight. But for now, let's see what you've packed for the trip."

The four guests grabbed their bags, which they had dropped next to the kitchen door upon their arrival. Waiting for everyone to leave the kitchen and enter the living room, Sharon remained in the doorway and turned out the kitchen light. All six walked into the living area where the television was still blaring. Doctor O'Brien was reaching for the remote control when he noticed the local news featuring a story on the notorious Sam White. Mr. White had been captured earlier that morning, but had–once again–been released on the grounds that offering rituals was an expression of free speech.

"That's garbage!" raged Doctor O'Brien, as he turned off the television. "What about the loss of our town, foot by foot. Isn't that a crime?"

Sharon, attempting to distract her husband from the latest news, placed her arm around his waist and implored, "Honey, we mustn't neglect our guests; you need to check their supplies for tomorrow's trip. Their safety may very well depend on it." Sharon's strategy worked.

The doctor set the remote on the television, turned to face his guests, and approached the coffee table where he sat on the floor for a close inspection. Opening Sam's oversize bag, the doctor was not surprised to discover a bow and arrow, a rope, four matchbooks, a lighter, and a travel clock; but he was shocked to behold a revolver and nearly a dozen lances, each spear measuring four feet in length or greater.

Before the doctor could ask, Sam defended, "They're for our safety."

"Yeah," responded the doctor, "I'm sure they are; just be careful with them."

"I will," promised Sam.

After instructing his teenage guests to open their bags and set all non-clothing items on the floor, the doctor and Sharon were surprised to see Dan place a machete alongside his Bible and a large votive candle.

Surrounding their personal possessions on the floor was a small collapsible cooler containing hamburgers, hotdogs, and dry ice. Also scattered on the living room floor were three plastic tubs of cookies, marshmallows, chips, juice boxes, small cartons of dried cereal, bottled water, a first-aid kit, a battery-powered lantern, and four mess kits.

"Good heavens," said Sharon, "where on earth did you get all this food and the machete?"

While grasping his machete, Dan informed the doctor and his wife, "I've been preparing for this trip for quite some time and since I knew that I'd be gone for a month, I convinced my mom–who thought I was going to survival camp–to pack extra food for Cindy and Jimmy, in case their parents didn't pack extra food for them." Glancing at the two teenagers, Dan continued, "Little did I know they'd actually be joining me on my trip. As far as the machete and the lamp, I bought them at a local sportsman's store since I thought they'd come in handy."

Looking directly at Sam, the doctor questioned, "Sam, do you really think you need so many lances on this trip with youngsters around?"

"Yes, doctor," answered Sam, "I do. They're for our protection. Besides, if what I suspect really exists and is waiting for us in the forest, then I'm afraid that even these primitive weapons won't be enough. But it's the best I could pull together in a short period of time."

While Sam was attempting to justify his weapons with Doctor O'Brien, Sharon was silently calculating how much food the four of them, or possibly five–if William was alive–would need for an entire month. Erring on the side of safety, Sharon eventually suggested, "I think you'll need more food, especially since we know how much Jimmy can eat."

"That's okay, Sharon," replied Jimmy, "I'll just eat a little less."

"Nonsense," said Sharon, "I'll gather some food from the kitchen and you can pack it with the rest of your belongings tomorrow morning. In the meantime, I'll cook your hamburgers and hotdogs tonight. They'll last longer in the cooler if they're already cooked. You'll just have to warm them over an open flame."

As the visitors were repacking their essentials in their bags, Cindy asked, "Sam, can Jimmy and I go with you and Dan tomorrow, please?"

Sam offered a quick glance to Dan, then to Sharon, and then to the doctor. With no outright verbal refusal from anyone, Sam stipulated, "I suppose, but you and Jimmy are to do exactly what Dan and I tell you; absolutely no exceptions. Is that understood?"

"Yes," replied Cindy, "I promise."

Jimmy, however, who had taken advantage of the contents in the candy dish on the coffee table, simply nodded.

The decision was made.

Within several minutes, the stuffed bags were returned to kitchen floor. Before retiring for bed, Sharon cooked the hamburgers and hotdogs as she had promised and stored them in Dan's cooler.

Upstairs were three bedrooms. Cindy had her own room which was tastefully decorated with early American furniture. Jimmy and Dan shared a room which contained a pair of bunk beds, while Sam slept on the living room couch. The doctor and his wife retired to their own room after giving each of their guests an alarm clock. After the goodnights were exchanged, all went to bed, hopeful for a good night's sleep.

Moments before nodding off, the doctor heard his wife mumbling. Opening his eyes slightly, he noticed Sharon kneeling at the bedside praying,

> "Dear Lord, they're good kids. Please watch over them during their journey and if it be Your will, guide them to William and lead them all to safety. If we're doing wrong by permitting Jimmy and Cindy to accompany the others, please forgive us."

As his wife climbed into bed, Doctor O'Brien whispered, "Amen."

Since the crossover had taken its toll on the travelers' strength, they fell into a deep sleep almost immediately.

For a third time, Dan saw himself as an onlooker watching himself and the other three travelers walking through the shadowy, dense forest which stretched in all directions beyond what the eye could see. The surroundings were eerie, for even though the day was graced with a cloudless blue sky, which Dan noticed periodically when a gap in the treetops displayed the heavens above, the sunlight never fully penetrated through the trees to the forest floor. Directly ahead of the group, Dan spotted an odd shaped sycamore tree which was stripped bare of all limbs, except for the very top which stood about ten feet. Looking further ahead, Dan noticed two poorly cleared paths beyond the sycamore tree—one path leading to the right and the other to the left. Before Dan could evaluate his options, he felt an invisible warm touch clutching his forearm, as though someone or something was gently directing him to the path on the left. He accepted the invitation, while the other travelers verbally questioned his irrational decision.

Looking only two feet ahead, Dan faintly detected a set of footprints which miraculously appeared on the path. Judging by the size and width of the prints, Dan presumed that they were from a being which stood over six feet, while the width of the prints led Dan to speculate that the unknown being was brawny. The remaining three travelers followed several feet behind Dan. Once the group had walked only a short distance upon the path, Dan clearly heard a rustling sound in the direction of the path not taken, which was now a few hundred feet to his right, since beyond the sycamore tree, the paths spread further and further apart as they invaded the recesses of the forest. As the waist-high undergrowth to the right began to separate, Dan remained in a trance-like state staring at a potential predator. Opening his mouth to scream, nothing came out. As the unidentified creature drew ever closer–now within a hundred feet–Dan plainly heard the sound of plants and underbrush being trampled beneath its weight. There was no doubt in the young man's mind.

The alarm rang and jolted Dan from the lower bunk to the hardwood floor of the bedroom.

Stumbling for the clock, Dan stubbed his toe on the dresser and let out a loud "Ouch." Throughout the one-minute tormenting sound of the alarm and Dan's cry of pain, Jimmy remained undisturbed. After silencing the alarm, Dan returned to the bunk bed and shook his friend. "Jimmy," said Dan in a loud voice, "get up!" There was no response. A second time, Dan shook his friend's shoulder, but this time with greater force, saying in a much louder voice, "Jimmy, time for school!" Even Dan was surprised and visibly amazed when Jimmy abruptly shuddered in the bed welcoming the new day.

The light from the full moon provided sufficient light for Dan to see the lamp on the nightstand which he switched on. Jimmy began snoring again. "Jimmy," yelled Dan, "get up now or I'll leave you here for a month." Deciding to check on Sam and Cindy, Dan opened the bedroom door and quietly crept down the poorly lit hallway toward Cindy's room. On his approach, he noticed light escaping from beneath the door. He knocked softly and asked, "Cindy, are you up?"

From behind the door came, "Yeah, I'm up. Is Jimmy?"

"Sort of," answered Dan.

From behind the door again came, "What about Sam?"

"I don't know; I'll check," answered Dan. As the young man retraced his steps down the hallway and onto the squeaky steps, he imagined that the steps made for a perfect security alarm. Four steps down, he turned and noticed the doctor and his wife–groomed and fully dressed–leaving their room.

"Good morning," they whispered to Dan.

"Good morning," Dan replied. "I'm going to check on Sam."

Like Cindy, Sam was awake and ready for the day.

"Morning, Sam," said Dan.

"Good morning, Dan," replied Sam.

From behind Dan, appeared the doctor and his wife who had followed him down the steps. Sharon greeted Sam and then entered the kitchen to prepare a hot breakfast for her guests, while Doctor O'Brien remained in the living room helping Sam and Dan collapse the sleeper sofa into its original position.

Moments later, Cindy stepped foot in the living room wearing jeans, a lightweight sweat shirt and a baseball cap. "Where's Jimmy?" she asked.

"He probably fell asleep again," replied Dan. "I'll go wake him up."

From around the corner in the kitchen, Sharon yelled, "Dan, can I see you for a minute?"

"Coming," answered Dan.

Entering the kitchen, Dan noticed that Sharon had already set the table and was frying sausage and bacon. "Wow," said Dan, "that smells great." He then jokingly added, "Maybe you should join us on our trip as our cook."

"Don't be ridiculous," responded Sharon, "I'm sure Cindy can cook." Reaching into the cabinet, Sharon continued, "Here's a few snacks; be sure to put them with the rest of your food."

"That's quite alright, Sharon," said Dan, "you've been too helpful already."

"Nonsense," said Sharon, "I want to make sure you have more than enough food for your trip. Actually, Dan, the reason I called you in here was to give you something in private. I know you're religious, as am I." From her apron pocket, Sharon removed two small bottles of water.

Since the bottles contained no markings, Dan asked, "What's this?"

"It's holy water from the Our Lady of Lourdes Shrine in France," replied Sharon. "The way I figure it, if our Blessed Mother can crush the head of the serpent, then I'm sure this Lourdes water will crush the demons' heads you'll inevitably encounter on your journey. Now take them both; put one in your pocket and store the other in your duffle bag."

"This is very generous, Sharon," said Dan, "but I can't accept it."

Sharon raised her voice demanding, "You can and you will! I'll not have your death and the deaths of your friends on my hands!"

A deathly silence followed. Even the conversation in the living room between the doctor and his guests ceased.

"I'm sorry, Dan," apologized Sharon, "I don't know what came over me. But it would mean so much to me."

"I don't know what to say," replied Dan.

"There's nothing to say," stated Sharon, "other than you'll do as I said."

With that, Dan placed one bottle in his pocket and stored the other in his duffle bag, per Sharon's request.

"Oh, my goodness," exclaimed Sharon, "the bacon's burning," as she snatched the tongs from the utility drawer. The smell of sausage and bacon emanating from the stove enticed everyone into the kitchen, including Jimmy, who was only partially dressed; he was slipping on his tattered green rugby shirt as he stepped into the kitchen. After saying grace, the household of six sat down to enjoy Sharon's appetizing meal. The guests ate as much as they could, knowing that this would be their last full meal for quite some time.

Around 5:30, as Sharon rose from her chair to begin cleaning, she ordered, "Okay, I want everyone to take one last look through their bags and make sure they have everything."

It's a good thing too, since Dan realized that he left his glasses upstairs on the nightstand. After retrieving his glasses from the second floor, Dan returned to the kitchen where he put on his green jacket. Recalling that his machete was still stored in his duffle bag, Dan lugged his bag to the living room. There, in private, he concealed his machete in a deep pocket within the jacket's lining.

At precisely 5:50, Sharon hugged her departing guests, while whispering into each traveler's ear, "God's speed."

With bags in hand, Sam, Dan, Cindy, and Jimmy followed the doctor out the kitchen door to the car. The sound of the garage door opening signaled the beginning of a trip the travelers would never forget.

Not a word was said for nearly five minutes.

Finally, Dan broke the silence by asking, "Are we sure Spiritus Malus will be gone by the time we enter the woods?"

"Yes," replied the doctor. Looking east, the doctor put the young man's fears to rest by pointing out the rising sun.

Turning the corner at the stoplight, all eyes were drawn to O'Shea's pub which was now completely tranquil; the doctor parked alongside the curb next to the bar.

"Before all of you leave," warned the doctor, "I want you to promise me that you'll watch out for each other and that you won't take any unnecessary risks. I only hope and pray that for all you're about to endure, William is alive and in the castle. If he's not, I pity you."

All guests promised the doctor that they'd do as he requested. For the first time, Jimmy and Cindy entertained the notion of returning to the safety of the house with Doctor O'Brien. But after a brief glimpse in Dan's direction—seeing him shaking slightly, rubbing his hands, and a look of fear in his eyes—Cindy and Jimmy glanced at each other, took a deep breath, and exited the car.

Eventually, the doctor also stepped from the car, shook everyone's hand, and wished them luck. The four guests thanked the doctor for his and Sharon's hospitality as he stepped back into the car. Initially, the travelers remained standing, fearful even to move; that is, until Dan took the first step toward the forest. Sam immediately trailed, followed by Cindy and then Jimmy.

As the doctor drove away, he glanced in his rearview mirror and witnessed his friends vanish into the forbidden forest. *My God*, he thought, *what have I done? I've delivered my friends into the soul of the beast!* He wept.

CHAPTER TEN
Subterranean Danger

"Wait up, Dan," yelled Sam.

It was obvious to Sam and the others that Dan had waited a long time for this moment, and not his friends, not his recurring fears, not even the dangers and mysteries of the forest were going to deter him from his personal quest. Sam finally caught up with Dan and slowed his pace by grabbing the straps on his duffle bag.

"Dan," said Sam, "we've got to wait for the others. Remember, we promised the doctor that we'd look out for each other."

"Well then, tell them to hurry up," said Dan.

The wait for Jimmy's and Cindy's arrival gave the older traveler and the teenager the opportunity to scan the forest in what little daylight penetrated the canopy. Both men simultaneously experienced feelings they'd never felt before and hoped they never would again. All at once, intense feelings of sorrow, grief, pain, and death enshrouded them. It was as if the souls that had hopelessly wandered the forest for centuries found two new hosts in which to rest. Luckily, the feelings departed as quickly as they had come.

Jimmy and Cindy came running up from behind. "Sorry," said Cindy, "I tripped over the rickety fence and dropped my bag, spilling everything, including the pills."

"The pills," said Sam, "we need to take them now. Trust me, you don't want to go a day without those lifesavers."

Since Cindy had her bottle readily available, she dropped four tablets into her hand and offered one to each of her co-travelers.

After swallowing, Jimmy asked, "So, which direction should we head?"

Despite the fact that the forest was heavily wooded with a tremendous amount of undergrowth, Dan spotted what appeared to be a poorly cleared path about fifty feet from where the group stood. Pointing ahead, Dan said, "That path–if that's what you want to call it–seems like as good of a place as any to start. Who knows, it may be the path of previous travelers searching for the castle or it could even be the tracks left by Spiritus Malus on his monthly journeys from the castle to the tree and back."

"Dan," responded Sam, "I seriously doubt this so-called path is the result of Spiritus Malus' travels. For goodness sake, if it takes twelve days or more to travel from the castle to the tree on foot, then Spiritus Malus would spend the greater portion of his unending life crossing the forest."

"Who said he travels by foot?" asked Dan.

"It was only a speculation," replied Sam. "But if I never find out how he travels, that's fine by me."

The four approached the path. With each step, they seemed to increase their speed until they were walking a brisk pace.

Nearly an hour into their hike, Cindy had a terrifying thought. "Stop," she exclaimed. The remaining travelers halted and turned in her direction. "How are we going to know our way back? I mean, the path is hardly noticeable and all these trees look the same; how will we know which way leads back to the oak tree?"

"Oh, I forgot," apologized Sam, as he reached into his bag and pulled out a can of spray paint which was rolled in a shirt. "I meant to do this as soon as we entered the forest, but ... well ... I just forgot. Look, we'll spray paint a tree with this red paint every hundred feet or so. This ought to lead us back." Stepping to the large tree directly beside him, Sam sprayed a red circle about six inches in diameter on the tree at eye level. "As far as the trees behind us," continued Sam, "we'll just use our best judgment from here back." Sam delegated this responsibility to Jimmy who was bringing up the rear.

The group walked another five hours with very few words spoken. Suddenly, Dan abruptly stopped; straight ahead was a sycamore tree.

"What's wrong?" asked Sam.

"That tree," said Dan, "I've seen it before."

"What do you mean you've seen it before?" asked Cindy. "You were never this deep in the forest during your first trip."

"I know," replied Dan, "but I've seen it somewhere; I know I have."

"Dan," said Sam, "we've only been in this world's forest several hours, how could you have seen it before?"

After a few moments, Dan remembered and shouted, "That's it. It was in my dream last night."

Stepping ahead of the group, Cindy peered beyond the sycamore and noticed that the path they were traveling on split on the distant side of the tree. "Look," she said, "the trail divides; so which path do we take?"

Knowing that he should take the path to the left, Dan stood idle for a moment waiting for the familiar invisible warm touch to clutch his forearm and lead him up the path, as it did in his dream; but nothing. Sensing that the group was becoming skeptical about his dream, Dan put his right foot forward and started up the path, passed the sycamore tree, and headed left.

"Hey, wait a minute," yelled Sam. "Shouldn't we all have a say on which path to take?"

"It's this way," said Dan, "trust me; I'm sure."

Thinking that one path was probably just as good as the other, the remaining three travelers yielded and followed Dan. With each step, Dan's heart raced faster than the previous step, for he knew what was coming next. But nothing happened.

"Hey, guys," said Jimmy from behind, "can we stop for a quick rest and maybe a snack?"

Realizing that they had already traveled several hours with no misfortunes, Sam granted Jimmy's request, though Dan rested on a log with great reluctance. Since Dan's duffle bag was the heaviest, Jimmy suggested that he lighten it a bit by removing some of his mom's homemade cookies.

Opening his bag, Dan pulled out a large plastic container which held over two dozen oatmeal-raisin cookies. "Only one cookie each," warned Dan, "these rations have to last us an entire month."

Jimmy's hunger pangs prodded him to propose, "If we run out of food, Sam can hunt us a meal."

"Jimmy," stressed Dan, "that's the rule–one cookie."

While no one was looking, Cindy slipped her cookie to Jimmy, saying, "I'm not really hungry."

"Thanks," said Jimmy, as he inhaled the cookie.

All eyes were drawn to Dan who rose from the log and stared down the path behind them.

"What's wrong, Dan?" asked Cindy.

The other travelers looked backward expecting to spot something out of the ordinary. The path behind them was just as they left it ... or was it?

"Jimmy, have you been spray painting the trees like Sam asked?" inquired Dan.

"Yeah," replied Jimmy, "as a matter of fact, I painted that tree"–while pointing to a massive elm far behind him–"minutes before we sat down for a break."

"Show me the tree," demanded Dan.

As Jimmy rose to his feet and began retracing his steps to the elm tree to proudly show off his artistic talent, all three followed him. Eventually reaching the tree, Jimmy pointed and said, "Right. . . . ," he stopped; there was no mark on the tree.

"Are you sure this was the tree?" asked Sam.

"I'm positive," replied Jimmy, "I remember painting a circle around this knot," as he ran his fingers across the natural blemish.

"But there's no paint there," remarked Cindy.

Something was wrong.

"And why is there no bark around the knot?" questioned Sam.

"You two wait here," demanded Dan of Jimmy and Cindy, "while Sam and I check out the other trees behind us."

The two men backtracked leaving Jimmy and Cindy alone near the elm. Before either teenager realized it, they were soon at Dan's heels.

"I told you two to wait back there for us," said an irritated Dan.

Trying his best to conceal his uneasiness, Jimmy explained, "I thought I should come, since I know what trees I marked." Jimmy showed Sam and Dan three other trees which he remembered spray painting, and just like the elm, they too were missing large chunks of bark and no sign of paint.

As the four travelers were returning to the rest area, Sam decided it might be a good idea to paint another tree and see what happens. Once at the rest area, Sam picked up the red spray can from the forest floor and, with lance in hand, neared another colossal elm which was only a hundred feet or so from their rest area. The remaining travelers followed.

"Alright, let's see what happens now," said Sam, as he sprayed a large circle about five feet up the tree trunk.

All eyes were glued to the tree, but nothing happened. The group waited another few minutes, but the bark and the paint remained intact. Quite suddenly, beneath their feet, the travelers felt a slight tremor, then a larger one. Almost immediately, the massive elm's roots exploded upwards rupturing the forest floor and enclosing the four travelers in a miniature Amazon-like forest. In their panic, the travelers were oblivious to the actions of the larger roots near the base of the tree; all except Dan, who remained focused and witnessed several large roots scale the massive trunk and scrape away the paint and bark.

Now surrounded by an enormous root system, the three, and eventually Dan, desperately sought a way of escape. Once the paint on the tree was eradicated by removing the bark, the roots slowly receded, but not before ensnaring and pulling anything within their reach. The four travelers were taken hostage by the roots which wrapped themselves around their trespassers. Frantically trying to release himself from the roots' grip, Sam raised his lance, which he had been carrying at his side from the time they entered the forest, and pierced the two roots which had seized his legs. Once free, he dashed five feet to his left to release Jimmy from the tree's unrelenting grip. While Sam was rescuing Jimmy from the clutches of the tree, Dan pulled the machete from his jacket and began slashing tree roots in all directions and ultimately freed himself. Throughout the ordeal, the roots continued to retreat slowly into the ground.

Cindy, nearest the tree trunk, experienced the worst strangle hold since the roots closest to the elm were the thickest—at least six inches in diameter. Cindy screamed. Having no weapon of her own, she was slowly being dragged beneath the forest floor by two massive roots. Rushing to her rescue, while being careful not to be entrapped again, the three men arrived at Cindy's side when all but her shoulders and head were underground. Sam, with his lance and Dan, with his machete thrust their weapons into the ground desperately trying to sever the roots, without injuring Cindy, who had now lost consciousness. In the frenzy, Dan's glasses fell from his face to the ground. With each stab to a root, green acidic liquid burst upwards, barely missing the men, except Dan. Not witnessing Dan's unfortunate predicament, Jimmy, who was weaponless, resumed his feverish attempt to pull Cindy to safety as Sam and Dan continued stabbing.

Then quite suddenly, and much to the surprise of the men, three massive roots, as large as the two which ensnared Cindy, reemerged from below and grabbed the legs of Cindy's would-be rescuers, dragging them away from the roots' captured prize. Calling upon reserve strengths, Sam penetrated the root which ensnared his ankle with several powerful blows from his lance, and ultimately freed himself. Dan, meanwhile, having received a direct shot of the green acid in his eyes a few moments earlier, had begun to experience obvious pain and was quickly losing his eyesight. Wasting no time, Jimmy grabbed Dan's machete, which was now resting on the ground between the two teenagers–well within Jimmy's reach–and completely severed the root from his right thigh and then proceeded to free Dan. With only Cindy's head exposed, all three men–even Dan, with his fading vision–raced to her rescue again. This time, Sam and Jimmy thrust their weapons into the ground with little or no regard to harming Cindy, knowing that she'd be dead in a few minutes without their consistent stabbings. With two powerful blows from Sam's lance, the tree eventually released its victim. The three men quickly pulled Cindy from below the soil.

After lifting the unconscious Cindy into his arms, Sam scanned the area and noticed that virtually all of the roots had re-entered their subterranean world and that the war-torn ground was supernaturally healing itself, slowly returning to its original appearance, free of all cracks and depressions. After spotting Dan's glasses slowly sliding into the earth, Jimmy leaped for the lenses and, once reclaimed, placed them in his shirt pocket.

On hearing movement and crackling noises around him, but unable to see clearly, Dan asked, "What's happening?"

Jimmy stepped to Dan's side. Noticing a green liquid flowing from his eyes and down his cheeks, Jimmy asked, "How are your eyes?"

"I'll be fine," answered Dan.

"Can you see anything?" asked Jimmy.

There was no immediate response, as Dan peered ahead attempting to decipher something, anything. Eventually, he replied, "Not really; it's too blurry."

With the constant sound of the ground healing itself nearby, Dan asked again, "What's all the noise?"

"The roots," replied Jimmy, "are receding underground and the forest floor is slowly returning to normal."

Dan listened intently and then asked, "How's Cindy?"

On overhearing his question, Sam, who was only several feet away replied, "She's unconscious, but she's alive."

Grabbing Dan by the arm, Jimmy led his friend back to the rest area, followed by Sam carrying Cindy. As Sam set Cindy on the ground next to her backpack, she slowly regained consciousness.

Before even catching her breath, Cindy asked, "What happened?"

"Well," replied Sam, "as you were being pulled underground, you lost consciousness. We eventually freed you from the roots' grip and carried you back here."

While Sam was bringing Cindy up-to-date, Jimmy assisted Dan to the ground while telling him his glasses were safe. Tilting Dan's head back and resting it on Jimmy's knee, Jimmy rinsed Dan's eyes with bottled water. Dan squirmed a bit and then rubbed his eyes.

"How's that?" asked Jimmy. "Can you see anything?"

Not really," replied Dan.

Raising three fingers, Jimmy asked Dan, "How many fingers am I holding up?"

"It's too blurry," replied Dan.

With this unwelcome response, Jimmy poured another dose of water into his friend's eyes.

Overhearing their conversation, Cindy asked, "What happened to Dan?"

"In stabbing the roots to release you," explained Sam, "Dan was sprayed by a green fluid–probably acidic–which shot from the roots. Right now, his vision is pretty blurred."

"Is he going to be alright?" asked Cindy.

"I hope so," answered Sam, "but we'll probably know better tomorrow."

After a third rinsing of his eyes, Dan looked up at Jimmy and admitted, "I guess I was wrong."

"Wrong?" asked Jimmy. "Wrong about what?"

"I suppose I do need your help," confessed Dan.

Since Jimmy didn't know what to say, he simply grinned, though Dan couldn't make it out.

Cindy crawled in Dan's direction and sat next to him. "You'll be fine," she said. "After a good night's sleep, I'm sure you'll be fine."

Sam cleared his throat to grab the group's attention for an announcement. "Since we've traveled a fair distance today, I suggest that we camp here tonight." Glancing at the only non-injured traveler, Sam added, "Jimmy, watch your friends while I gather some timber for a fire."

Jimmy nodded in agreement.

With Sam away, Cindy and Jimmy painfully admitted to Dan that they were terrified at the elm. But, at the same time, this encounter with the tree only strengthened Cindy's and Jimmy's resolve to help Dan find William. *After all*, thought Cindy, *Dan and Jimmy put their lives on the line to save mine.*

Dan shamefacedly admitted to his teenage friends that he was wrong in demanding they return to their home world. Even he had underestimated the dangers which lurked in the forest. Sadly, they all knew that this was only the first of thirty days.

Nearly fifteen minutes later, Sam returned carrying an armful of timber. "Who would have thought finding fallen limbs in a forest would be so difficult?" he asked. After dropping the wood to the footpath, Sam posed, "So, what'll it be tonight? Hotdogs or hamburgers?" With a vote of three to one, Sam pulled the hotdogs from Dan's cooler, while Cindy took Jimmy's water bottle, since he agreed to help Sam with the meal preparations.

After a fourth rinsing of his eyes, Dan sadly conceded that he didn't notice any change. "How can I rescue William if I can't see him?" he asked.

"Hey," demanded Sam, "stop that kind of talk right now, boy! It's only been an hour; you need to give it some time. I'm sure you'll be fine tomorrow."

Dan appreciated Sam's optimism, but the teenager had serious doubts about his recovery, since he purposely withheld from his traveling companions the excruciating pain he was enduring.

"Hey, Dan," asked Jimmy, "can I get your lantern? I thought it was pretty dark all day, but now it's really dark."

"Sure, Jimmy," responded Dan.

On spotting Jimmy removing the lantern which was strapped to the side of Dan's duffle bag, Sam warned, "Jimmy, don't waste the batteries on that lantern; we may need it in the days ahead. I'll have a campfire roaring soon enough."

With great disappointment, Jimmy reattached the lantern to the duffle bag.

Sam was right. Within five minutes, all travelers were enjoying an illuminating fire. Even though he was famished, and he suspected Jimmy was too, Sam placed only four hotdogs on the mess kit pan; he knew that the food rations were extremely limited. Jimmy sadly noticed this too, but said nothing.

While the hotdogs were warming, Sam remarked, "So I guess we'll never know what happened to the painted circles on the tree."

"What do you mean we'll never know?" asked Dan. "Didn't you see it?"

"See what?" inquired Jimmy.

"The tree roots," replied Dan.

"Oh yeah," said Sam, "we definitely saw the tree roots."

"No," remarked Dan. "Didn't you see the large roots scale the tree trunk and scrape the paint? Didn't you see it?"

There was a moment of silence which was broken by Jimmy softly admitting, "I guess in all the commotion, we missed it."

"Well," said Sam, "if that's the case, then I guess these spray cans are useless."

Knowing that the so-called path was poorly cleared and that the darkness of the forest would hinder their return trip, Cindy asked, "But then how will we find our way back?"

"Yeah, Sam," inquired Jimmy, "how will we find our way back to the oak tree?"

After another period of silence, Dan suggested, "I'm sure it sounds a little strange coming from me, since I can't see too clearly, but maybe you three–and hopefully me, in time–should commit forest anomalies and the terrain to memory. Right now, that's probably the best we can do."

"I suppose it's as good of an idea as any," responded Sam.

Glancing into the mess kit pan atop the fire, Cindy remarked, "Sam, I think the hotdogs are done."

"I think you're right," replied Sam, as he removed the pan from the flame.

Reaching for the spare mess kits, Jimmy handed the open kits to Sam, who placed the warm hotdogs on the metal plates. Reaching into Dan's duffle bag, Sam pulled out only two juices while informing his friends that even the juice had to be rationed. Next, Cindy retrieved a container of cookies and chips from the bag, all the makings of a meal fit for a king. Before eating, Dan offered a brief prayer, but no one joined in, not even to say "Amen."

Once the solo prayer had concluded, the travelers picked up their warm bunless hotdogs and indulged. Even Dan, who had trouble deciphering some of the contents of his plate, recognized the long slender meat product and consumed it in three bites. A conversation developed.

"After today's adventure," said Sam, "I think it's clear that we've entered a strange world with weird plant species... and probably creatures as well. Having said that, I propose that we each take turns at night watch." Walking a few feet to his bag, and then back to the three teenagers, Sam displayed his travel alarm clock while remarking, "This will help us on our shifts. When you go on duty, it's your responsibility to set the alarm for the next shift and place it beside the person who'll be relieving you. If you forget, then you're stuck with two consecutive shifts. The three of us–Jimmy, Cindy, and I–will watch for two hour increments." Looking at Dan, Sam added, "Sorry,

Dan. Maybe tomorrow you can assume night watch; but for now, you need your rest."

"I understand," replied Dan. "I couldn't see anything anyway."

Looking back to Jimmy and Cindy, Sam added, "So, here's the schedule. I'll take the first watch, then Jimmy, and then Cindy. If you hear any movement in the forest, I mean any movement whatsoever, you're not to investigate; you're to wake up everyone. Any questions?"

"No," replied Cindy and Jimmy, "we understand."

Not knowing what creatures, if any, crawled the forest at night, Sam handed a lance to Jimmy and Cindy for their patrols while sternly warning them to handle the weapons with extreme caution.

By now, the travelers were enjoying an oatmeal-raisin cookie that, due to the constant jostling in Dan's duffle bag, was actually several smaller pieces instead of a whole cookie. Nonetheless, the dessert was welcomed by all.

"One other thing," added Sam. "Cindy, can I place you in charge of logging our days in the forest? We need to make sure we arrive back at the oak in thirty days."

"Sure," replied Cindy, as she took a pen from her bag and put one check mark on the inside back cover of the novel she packed for reading at survival camp.

"Dan," asked Jimmy, "how are your eyes?"

"About the same," responded Dan.

After taking the empty plate from his friend and setting it on the ground, Jimmy grabbed the half-empty water bottle, tilted Dan's head back, and rinsed his eyes another time. "I'll wake you during my watch to rinse them again," offered Jimmy.

"That's alright," replied Dan. "I'll be fine."

"Tough. I'm going to anyway," said Jimmy.

As his friend walked away, Dan was grateful for Jimmy's genuine interest in his recovery. He only hoped that sometime he'd be able to return the favor, preferably in their own world.

Due to the near total darkness and the enormous height of the trees, none of the visitors to the forest could tell when the sun set, so they relied on Sam's wrist watch and their own weariness to decide when to retire. Given the stress of their first day, most notably the last few hours, the teenagers fell asleep rather quickly, but none before Dan.

While Sam patrolled the area near the campground and slightly beyond, he was surprised to hear nothing, absolutely nothing, not even the sound of insects. He was becoming increasingly concerned that the stillness of the forest was actually too quiet, too quiet for a place which legends say was roaming with bizarre and bloodthirsty creatures. Nonetheless, Sam had no intention of purposely scurrying a creature from the underbrush. Looking at his wrist watch, Sam realized that he had only thirty more minutes of duty. The campfire was slowly losing out to the darkness of the forest which permitted the dampness of the wooded area to penetrate the bones more quickly. For his friends' comfort and safety, Sam approached the campground area and quietly placed another timber on the fading flames; he then returned to his post.

Shortly thereafter, the alarm rang next to Jimmy, who quickly turned it off and rolled out of his sleeping bag. Before relieving Sam, however, Jimmy approached Dan's side and woke him, saying, "Let me rinse your eyes and then you can go back to sleep." Jimmy put his hand under Dan's neck and raised it slightly. Reaching for the water bottle on the opposite side of Dan's sleeping bag, furthest away from the fire, Jimmy poured a liberal amount into Dan's eyes. By the patient's reaction, Jimmy knew that the water was cold. "Sorry, buddy," apologized Jimmy, who then gently set Dan's head back upon the sleeping bag. Dan immediately fell asleep. Rising to his feet, Jimmy neared Sam, who was still tending his post.

"Any activity?" asked Jimmy.

"Absolutely nothing," replied Sam.

"Great," said Jimmy, "I can only hope that my watch is as uneventful."

"Remember," warned Sam, "any noise or movement–anything at all–wake me up immediately; don't try to be a hero."

"Believe me," replied Jimmy, "I have no plans on being a hero."

Sam shook his head as he walked away.

With Sam gone, an intense feeling of cowardliness overcame Jimmy; he wasn't as brave as he thought he'd be. *Still*, he thought, *I have to remain vigilant for the others, especially Dan who wouldn't be able to see an approaching predator.* Trying to think of something to dislodge his overpowering feelings of fear, Jimmy thought about sports. *Maybe,* he wondered, *I should apply for a college football scholarship, assuming it's not too late.*

Suddenly, Jimmy detected a rapid flash of light from the corner of his eye high in the forest canopy. He glanced, but just as quickly as he raised his head, it was gone. *What was that?* he thought. *It looked like a large glowing insect zipping about the treetops.* Starting to yawn, Jimmy dismissed the apparent illusion while attributing it to his interrupted sleep.

Again, a brilliant flash of light appeared at the treetops. This time, Jimmy definitely saw it, but only for a brief second. With no detectable trace anymore, Jimmy reasoned, *It's probably just the moon's beams struggling to reach the forest floor.*

Approaching the camp area, Jimmy knelt next to Sam who was sleeping with his hands outside the sleeping bag. Looking at his wrist watch, Jimmy noticed that his tour of duty elapsed thirty minutes ago. "Dang it," said Jimmy, "I forgot to place the clock next to Cindy." Totally disregarding the rule that if someone forgets to reset the clock and move it to their successor, then he or she is stuck with two consecutive watches, Jimmy approached patrolman number three. After quietly waking Cindy from a deep sleep, Cindy expressed surprise that it was already time and that she hadn't heard the alarm.

Looking about, Cindy asked, "Where's the alarm clock?"

Sadly, Jimmy realized that he also forgot to move the clock moments earlier from his sleeping area to Cindy's, as he was hoping to convince her that she just didn't hear it.

Glancing to Jimmy's sleeping area about ten feet away, Cindy remarked, "Oh, there it is."

"Please, Cindy, I'm tired," implored Jimmy.

"Alright," said Cindy, "but you owe me one."

"Thanks," said Jimmy. "But I want to show you something first."

As the two left the camp area and walked toward the outer post, Jimmy pointed to the canopy where he saw a flicker of light on two occasions during his watch. "It's probably nothing," said Jimmy, "but you may want to keep an eye out for it."

Cindy yawned and then nodded.

Returning to the campground, Jimmy decided that he'd wake Dan once again to rinse his eyes. However, stirring Dan from his sleep this time, proved a little more difficult than before, since Dan was slow in reacting to Jimmy's shakings. Eventually, Jimmy's persistent nudges paid off and Dan awoke. Unfortunately, Dan was so tired, that he had trouble keeping his eyes open for the rinsing. Noticing his friend's difficulty, Jimmy opened one of Dan's eyelids with his index finger, while he doused the patient's eye with water using his other hand. Before falling back to sleep, Dan noticed that for the first time since the elm tree skirmish, he could vaguely make out Jimmy's facial features.

The third watch proved as uneventful as the first two, as far as the forest floor area around the campgrounds. Keeping a watchful eye on the treetops as Jimmy suggested, Cindy failed to notice that the oddly shaped flicker of light was hovering over the campsite. Near the end of her watch, a loud and persistent cough from Sam drew Cindy's attention to the camping area where she spotted the glowing object. Cindy screamed in an effort to awaken the men and draw their attention to the hovering object. Unfortunately, as soon as she screamed and the men awoke, the object darted out of sight to the canopy.

Sam and Jimmy ran to Cindy.

"What is it?" yelled Sam.

"Didn't you see it?" asked Cindy.

"See what?" demanded Sam.

"The light hovering over the camping area," answered Cindy.

"You saw it too?" asked Jimmy.

"Yes," answered Cindy, "it was really there, Jimmy; it wasn't your imagination."

Sam looked sternly at Jimmy and asked, "Were you planning on telling me about this incident sometime?"

"Yeah," replied Jimmy, "but since I didn't see it until after your watch–that is, when you were asleep–I thought I'd tell you in the morning."

"Alright, you two," warned Sam, "from now on, I want you to wake me whenever you see something out of the ordinary. I don't care if it's an ant blowing its nose. I want you to wake me. Is that understood?"

"Yes, Sam," responded Cindy and Jimmy in unison.

Though the forest was still dark, it wasn't as dark as it was before they retired for bed, so all assumed that the morning sun had risen ... at least somewhere.

Glancing at his wrist watch, Sam remarked, "Well, since it's already 6:00, I suggest we roll up our sleeping gear and have some breakfast."

In their race to Cindy's scream, Sam and Jimmy suddenly realized that they had unintentionally left Dan alone at the campground where the unknown glow was last seen. All three travelers dashed toward the campfire; Jimmy reached the area first.

Dan, although wide awake in response to Cindy's shriek, remained nestled in his sleeping bag. As the three drew closer to the patient, Dan was overjoyed to discover that his eyesight had nearly returned to normal.

"Jimmy," he exclaimed, "ask me how many fingers you're holding up!"

Knowing exactly what his friend was asking, Jimmy displayed two fingers near Dan's face.

"Two," responded Dan.

A great yoke was lifted from the shoulders of the four travelers, as a feeling of great relief overtook them.

With renewed vigor, the three travelers helped Dan out of his sleeping bag and proceeded to the dying fire. After setting their nearly recovered patient on a log, Sam walked off the footpath to the forest beyond and gathered a few more timbers to resurrect the fire. While Sam was rummaging through the undergrowth and while Jimmy was rinsing Dan's eyes one more time, Cindy stepped from the fire to survey their provisions. Since they just enjoyed hotdogs the night before, and since hamburgers were probably not the best choice for breakfast, she had no alternative but to serve juice and marshmallows, roasted marshmallows, that is.

"Hey, Jimmy," said Cindy, "let me know when the fire's roaring again. I'll need it for the marshmallows."

Jimmy's thoughts immediately switched from Dan's improving condition to sausage and bacon, just like Mrs. O'Brien served yesterday morning before the travelers entered the forest. As hungry as Cindy was, the mere sight of the marshmallows made her stomach turn. Desperate for something else to eat, she dumped the contents of Dan's duffle bag to the forest floor. She shook and shook the bag until several small boxes of dried cereal dislodged themselves and fell to the ground. *Of course,* she thought, *I remember seeing these the other night on the O'Brien's living room floor.* For such a modest find, Cindy was on top of the world; she couldn't bear the thought of roasted marshmallows for breakfast for the next twenty-nine days.

By now, Sam had returned from the forest and placed two large timbers atop the fire. At Sam's suggestion, the three men left the fire and walked to their sleeping areas to pack their bedding, while Cindy resumed the meal preparations. Cindy watched, as the men awkwardly rolled up their sleeping bags and collected their clutter from the previous night. She was pleased to see Jimmy helping Dan, whom she suspected was still not totally healed from his eye injury.

Once the men were finished and neared the campfire where Cindy was now roasting the marshmallows, Jimmy jokingly remarked, "Looks appetizing. Are we permitted only half a marshmallow per the ration ranger?"

"No," answered Cindy, "you can have a whole marshmallow!" After offering a grin to Jimmy, who was standing directly above her, Cindy continued, "Look over there," as she pointed to the left, behind Dan's battery-powered lantern.

Jimmy took four steps to the left and discovered the boxes of cereal. "Oh, wow!" he exclaimed. "We could have been enjoying this last night with our one bunless hotdog, five chips, one cookie, and three ounces of juice."

Since Jimmy was genuinely excited with his discovery of the cereal, Cindy thought that now would be the best time to inform him that he had to eat the cereal without milk. To her surprise, Jimmy offered no complaint.

Placing his hand on Dan's shoulder, Jimmy asked, "Are you feeling better?"

"Yeah," replied Dan, "actually a lot better. Things are finally coming into focus and aren't nearly as blurred as they were last night, thanks to your rinsing routine."

"Happy to do it," replied Jimmy.

"Alright," informed Cindy, "everyone grab a roasted marshmallow from the fire—Jimmy, you can have mine—and then come sit over here for a bowl of milkless cereal of your choice and a little juice... all compliments of Mrs. Clay."

My mom, Dan thought. *I wonder if she's heard the news. I hope she's alright.*

Dan's thoughts of home were interrupted by Sam asking, "So, Dan, are you up for hiking today?"

There was no immediate response, for Dan was mentally vacillating between answering Sam and thinking of his parents' well-being.

Sam tried again, "Dan... Dan."

Sam's persistence forced Dan to return to the present world.

"Sorry," replied Dan, "I was just thinking about...." Another short pause ensued before Dan gave Sam his undivided attention. The teenager continued, "I was just thinking about my injury and how I can't let it slow us down."

"I'll tell you what," suggested Sam, "we'll walk today, but if your eyes begin to ache, tell me and we'll take a break. How's that sound?"

"That's fine," answered Dan.

The four enjoyed their first breakfast in the forest together. As meager as the meal was, the deepening bonds of friendship between the four and the lively conversations more than made up for it.

CHAPTER ELEVEN

Nightmare Revisited

At precisely 9:15 a.m., through the oak tree in the other world where the four travelers had only recently departed, the telephone rang in Jeff Clay's small cubicle at the glass factory. Jeff, on hearing the distinctive ring of his phone, raced down the carpeted corridor, balancing a cup of coffee, and reached his cubicle on the sixth ring. "Jeff Clay," he said, as he pressed the speaker button.

From the other end came, "Is this Jeff Clay of 5709 Beacon Lane?"

"Yes, it is," answered Jeff, "but this is my office number."

Again, from the other end, "Mr. Clay, this is Park Ranger, Celeste Roman. I'm the Director of Operations for the survival camp."

Jeff hastily picked up the receiver, sensing that something was wrong; he knew that a call like this was not normal. Testing his suspicions, Jeff stuttered while asking, "Is everything alright?"

"I tried calling your home number," continued Ranger Roman, "but there was no answer; so I called this number which was listed on your son's survival camp enrollment form."

"That's fine," replied Jeff. "Is there a problem?"

"This may sound a little odd," said Ranger Roman, "but did your son decide to skip survival camp?"

"No," responded Jeff in a stern voice, as if he knew what was coming next. "He walked to the buses on Monday night with his friend, Jimmy Parker."

From the other end of the phone, Jeff heard a prolonged exhale;

Ranger Roman was obviously having trouble deciding on how to say what had to be said. After a few moments, Ms. Roman resumed, "Mr. Clay, I'm afraid that neither your son, nor Jimmy Parker, ever made it to survival camp."

"There's got to be some mistake," insisted Jeff.

"I'm sorry, Mr. Clay," said Ranger Roman, "but we've looked everywhere; and even though both Dan and Jimmy were registered as having entered the bus Monday night, no one–absolutely no one–ever remembered seeing the teenagers on any of the buses or at camp. As a matter of fact, it's standard procedure that the moment the buses arrive on the campgrounds, every person is checked off the list as they exit the buses. The boys simply never arrived."

Jeff's mind wandered; he was obviously concerned for his son's safety, but he was also troubled thinking of his wife's reaction upon hearing the news.

"Mr. Clay ... Mr. Clay...." the park ranger continued.

"Yes, I'm here," replied Jeff, now in a quiet voice, as he set his coffee cup down and raised his hand to rub his forehead.

"Mr. Clay," said Ranger Roman, "in my sixteen years on this job, I've seen many cases like this where the teenagers, for one reason or another, skip survival camp, elude their parents, and spend the time with friends. They almost always show up."

"What do you mean almost always?" asked Jeff.

Attempting to dodge the question, Ms. Roman informed, "Mr. Clay, our park guidelines mandate that after I notify the family or next of kin, I contact the police to report a missing person."

The words "missing person" threw Jeff back thirteen years; Jeff collapsed into his chair.

On hearing the loud noise of Jeff falling into his seat, and fearing the worst, Ranger Roman exclaimed, "Mr. Clay ... Mr. Clay...."

Putting his head between his knees, gasping for air, Jeff finally responded, "Yes, I understand. You have to contact the police."

Though she obviously couldn't see Jeff, the park ranger knew that he was emotionally spent; she offered words of comfort saying, "Mr. Clay, I'm sure your son is fine and that he'll show up any day now." After giving Jeff her direct telephone number for any future questions he or his wife may have, she ended by stating, "Pardon me, Mr.

Clay, but one last question. Did your son or Jimmy know a young lady named Cindy Somer?"

Clearing his throat, Jeff answered, "Yes, she was a friend of Dan's and a good friend of Jimmy's. Why?"

"I'm afraid she's missing too," replied Ranger Roman. "If they're good friends like you said, maybe they're hanging out somewhere nearby for a few days. I'm sure they'll be home soon. But in the meantime, I must contact the police department."

"Of course," responded Jeff. "Thank you for calling."

After goodbyes were exchanged, Jeff very slowly, as if in slow motion and in complete disbelief, returned the receiver to its holder. "Oh God, no," Jeff said to himself. "How do I tell Nancy? How can I... oh, my God... how can I ask her to relive a second never-ending nightmare?"

Grabbing his jacket, Jeff raced out of the cubicle and to the parking garage intent on making it home before the police placed a call or made a visit. As much as he dreaded the thought of telling Nancy, he knew that it would be best coming from him. Arriving home, he was grateful that Nancy had not returned home from wherever she was. While changing his clothes upstairs, he heard the rattling of keys and then the front door slam; Jeff raced downstairs only partially dressed, wearing his dress slacks and a white tee shirt.

As Nancy glanced up and saw her husband descending the staircase, she asked in bewilderment, "What are you doing home so early; it's only 9:45?" As if not caring to hear his answer, she proceeded to carry three bags of groceries into the kitchen.

Jeff followed his wife into the kitchen where he revealed, "I need to talk to you about something. You see, I got a call at work...."

His wife interrupted saying, "Look at these postcards I bought at the supermarket." Showing them to her husband, she added, "Here's one of Lawton Public Library and here's one of the covered bridge. I thought that you and I should each send one to Dan. Knowing him, he's probably homesick by now."

At that moment, it dawned on Jeff that this was the first time his wife was in a pleasant disposition since Dan left for camp–or wherever he was–last Monday, which made what Jeff had to say next to impossible. Pulling one of the kitchen chairs from under the table,

Jeff told his wife that he had something very important to tell her and asked her to sit down. "This morning," started Jeff, "I got a phone call at work from Park Ranger Celeste Roman at the survival camp. Anyway, it seems that.... ." Jeff couldn't go on.

Nancy immediately rose from the chair and neared the kitchen window over the sink. Peering into their back yard, she knew that something was wrong.

Jeff had seen this reaction from his wife thirteen years ago and he knew that she suspected something dreadful had happened.

"Go on," prodded Nancy, in a soft voice.

For as often as Jeff had rehearsed his monologue on his drive home from work, his mind went completely blank. Unrehearsed, he blurted, "Apparently, Dan, Jimmy, and Cindy never made it to camp."

There was no reaction from Nancy–nothing. She continued to stare out the window, but this time in another direction, as if she was looking for something.

Noticing that his wife was accepting the tragic news unpredictably well, Jeff continued. "Park Ranger Celeste Roman, the Director of Operations, called me to see if Dan was here. When I told her that he wasn't, she told me not to worry, since she's seen this scenario played out many times before. She suspected that Dan, Jimmy, and Cindy skipped survival camp to spend some time by themselves and that they'd return home soon."

Nancy finally spoke up, "So, Dan's missing?"

I'm sorry," replied her husband, "I'm afraid so."

Nancy slowly turned her gaze from the tranquil backyard–tearless and unemotional–and walked across the tiled kitchen floor toward the doorway which adjoined the living room. She paused near the entryway, reached for the refrigerator door handle, and passed out cold. Jeff leaped to catch her, just like he did near the fence last Monday night when Dan left. But this time, he was too late. While plunging to the kitchen floor, Nancy gashed her forehead on the corner of a bottom kitchen cabinet. Lifting her in his arms, Jeff noticed that she was bleeding, but only slightly. He carried his wife to the living room, placed her on the couch, and then ran upstairs to the bathroom medicine cabinet to retrieve tape, bandage, and antiseptic ointment. While racing down the steps, the telephone rang. Jeff knew he had to tend to his wife, but, *What if it's the police*, he thought. He dashed to the kitchen.

"Hello," said Jeff. There was a momentary pause. Then, "Yes, officer, I know," replied Jeff, "Park Ranger Celeste Roman called and informed me. Actually, my wife has taken the news rather poorly, so I wonder if you might instead come by the house later today." Another pause ensued. Finally, Jeff replied, "Thank you, officer." The conversation ended; Jeff returned the receiver to its holder.

Darting to the living room sofa, Jeff noticed that Nancy was beginning to stir. Resting his hand across her shoulder, he implored, "Easy, honey, stay still until I bandage your cut."

Acting as if she didn't hear her husband or wasn't the slightest bit concerned about her bleeding forehead, she quietly mumbled, "Dan." With her left hand, she reached for her husband who was kneeling beside the couch, pressed her face into his tee shirt and began to weep uncontrollably.

After a few moments, she uttered something, but her intense sobbing prevented Jeff from understanding what she was saying. He simply held her and said, "Shush. It'll be alright; I promise."

Minutes later, Jeff was able to interpret what she was murmuring.

"I can't endure another hell; I just can't," forewarned Nancy. "I'll not survive this one. I can't . . . I just can't." Nancy slowly dozed off.

CHAPTER TWELVE

Predator of Dreams

In the eerie world, by 10:00 a.m., the four travelers had already hiked a few miles.

"Dan, how are your eyes?" yelled Jimmy from behind.

"Better," answered Dan.

Surprisingly, the effects of the tree acid, while incredibly painful initially, had subsided literally overnight, thanks to Jimmy.

A gentle breeze was felt and could be seen rustling the limbs overhead. Stopping for a brief moment, the travelers took advantage of the cool breeze against their faces, since the four-mile walk had warmed them up considerably.

"Dan," asked Sam, "are you strong enough to go on?"

"Sure," replied Dan.

Looking back at Cindy, Sam asked, "And you, Cindy, are you feeling alright?"

"Yeah, I'm fine," replied Cindy.

With that, the four resumed their journey up the left path at a brisk pace with Dan and Sam in the lead, Cindy in the middle, and Jimmy at the rear. Dan was just telling Sam that he felt well enough to assume patrol duty that night, when branch-crushing movements were heard in the distant trees to their right.

"I forgot," said Dan to Sam, "my dream."

Partially knowing what to expect–though not totally–Dan ordered Sam to grab his revolver.

"What for?" asked Sam.

"I'm not sure," replied Dan, "but we'll need it!"

All travelers gazed to the right and trembled as they witnessed the separation of the low-lying tree limbs . . . just as Dan had witnessed in his dream. Unfortunately, the thick foliage and the relative darkness prevented anyone from making out what was approaching. The four explorers remained standing, clenching their weapons, not knowing what to expect. Even Cindy, who only yesterday was weaponless at the aggressive elm, was now clenching one of Sam's lances, as were Dan and Jimmy. Sam reached for his revolver. The anticipation was unbearable.

Suddenly, the movement stopped. All was quiet–too quiet, as far as the group was concerned.

"Was this in a dream you had?" Sam whispered to Dan.

"Yeah," returned Dan in a whisper.

"What happened?" asked Sam.

"I don't know," replied Dan, "the alarm went off."

The noise and movement returned. The lower branches separated again, but this time at an increased speed until it seemed that the object was nearly in front of them. Instinctively stepping back a few steps, the travelers were awestruck to see a three-headed saber-toothed tiger leaping from the woods, nearly ten feet in the air, and headed directly for the group on the footpath. The body of the beast was massive: at least seven feet long and weighing well over four hundred pounds, while each of its three heads prominently displayed two 7-inch fangs. All three heads were identical: maggot-infested fur, two large black eyes, and two oversize ears diseased with worms.

The appearance of the beast and its sudden onslaught happened so quickly that none of the travelers had time to release their weapons for the kill. The beast pounced on Sam, throwing him to the ground, causing the others to fall backwards and become disoriented for a moment. The creature sunk two of its fangs into Sam's shoulder; but hitting bone, the fangs penetrated only slightly. Sam screamed, while trying to divert the other oncoming fangs of the other heads with his bare hands. Dan, rolling onto his knees and reaching for his lance which he had dropped during his fall, jumped to his feet and plunged the weapon with incredible force into the beast's right front paw. A great roar was heard from the three heads, causing all life forms in the canopy to scurry. Upon impact of Dan lancing its paw, the prehistoric predator released its bite on Sam's shoulder only momentarily, but then took another bite–this time into Sam's upper arm. The right head of the beast, which was on Dan's left side, forcefully attempted to use its mouth and fangs to dislodge the lance from its paw. The creature was unsuccessful.

Seeing Sam's revolver only two feet away, Jimmy reached for it, but pulled back sharply, as the tiger's left head snapped at Jimmy's hand. Jimmy, still sitting on the ground, instinctively pushed himself backwards narrowly missing the fangs' penetration. With great trepidation, Cindy stealthily reached for her lance beside her and crawled behind Jimmy and around the tiger. Trying to avoid contact with its left head, Cindy managed to get a clear shot, but inflicted only a flesh wound on one of the beast's hind legs. Another roar was heard. With the monster momentarily distracted, Dan quickly bent down, grabbed his duffle bag, and struck the beast's right head which had resumed its attempt to remove the lance from its front paw. With a sharp blow from the heavy duffle bag, the head was knocked back far enough and long enough for Dan to reach in and dislodge the lance from the beast's foot. The unbearable pain upon removing the spear caused another mighty roar, but not as loud as the earsplitting roar which was heard when Dan plunged the same lance through the neck of the tiger's right head and then withdrew the weapon. The numbing pain of the tiger compelled it to release its death grip on Sam's upper arm. The creature slowly backed off, turned, and headed to the thick of the forest, while dangling a lifeless head near its lower limbs.

Even though the teenagers had miraculously escaped an encounter with the fangs, Dan and Jimmy were determined to kill the creature, lest it return during their journey to inflict more injuries, or even worse, somehow communicate the travelers' presence to creatures of its own kind. This was not out of the realm of possibility, for they now knew that anything was possible in this world. With his lance in hand, Dan trailed the beast which was now retreating into the dense forest. Jimmy grabbed his lance and joined Dan. The hunter had now become the hunted. As the beast slowly limped away, but still at a rather fast pace, the young men pursued it at a relatively safe distance through the brush, hoping for one fatal blow.

Cindy remained behind, gathering whatever clothing she could from her backpack to apply to Sam's shoulder and arm.

"Sam, don't move," ordered Cindy, "you'll only make it worse."

Somewhat delirious, Sam asked, "What was that?"

"You mustn't talk," demanded Cindy.

After glancing about, Sam painfully continued, "Where are Dan and Jimmy?"

"Shush," said Cindy, as she applied pressure to his wounds and then proceeded to search for the first-aid kit.

Dan and Jimmy, now nearly a hundred feet into the dimly lit forest, closed in on their weakening prey. Dan glanced at Jimmy and motioned that the moment had arrived. Dan took careful aim and thrust his lance into the beast's backside. The beast, with as much strength as its ailing body would allow, spun around with great force to face the teenagers, as if signaling one final attack. Dan silently, but quickly, took advantage of the beast's sightless right side and crept through the thick brush, while Jimmy remained facing the tiger's front side, trying to distract the beast with aerial movements of his lance. Jimmy's diversion allowed Dan to reach successfully the backside of the beast unnoticed.

Unaware, the wounded creature was now surrounded. Jimmy continued his aerial distractions, while Dan sneaked up from behind in an attempt to reclaim his weapon which he thrust into the creature's backside only moments earlier. Unfortunately, Dan got too close to the animal. Detecting movement from behind, the tiger whipped its serrated tail, striking Dan's ankle and throwing him several feet away. The wounded creature turned and slowly approached Dan, who was now confined to the ground, unable to stand, due to the deep gash in his right ankle. Amid great pain, Dan rapidly slid backwards on the forest floor trying to put as much distance as possible between himself and the approaching predator.

Focused on his escape, Dan was oblivious that behind him, in the darkness, was the entrance to the Great Chasm. Jimmy began yelling, trying to avert the tiger's attention from Dan. The beast, obviously familiar with the forest terrain, mustered its waning strength and charged at Dan, who unknowingly edged even closer and ever faster to the gorge, until he found himself slipping into its outer fringes, but not before grabbing a partially decayed tree limb near the surface of the Great Chasm. With no success at deterring the beast from its advance on Dan, Jimmy took careful aim and threw the lance, lodging the weapon in the beast's shoulder, in the exact spot where the three necks converged. A death roar was heard for miles. The beast fell forward and would have landed directly atop Dan, if the teenager hadn't quickly swung to the right allowing the tiger to narrowly miss him and fall to its death in the gorge.

While watching the beast plunge, Dan distinctly noticed a rather peculiar looking plant about fifty feet away that was adorned with lengthy tentacles which stretched from the darkness of the chasm below and up onto another footpath. Dan's attention was drawn from the massive plant form, when suddenly, he felt and heard his lifesaving branch snap. Jimmy heard it too. Then it happened again. An invisible warmth clutched Dan's wrists keeping him suspended until Jimmy came racing to the edge of the abyss. Jimmy fell to the ground and grabbed Dan's forearms. The moment Jimmy made contact with his teenage friend, the invisible touch vanished.

Even though Dan was relatively thin and Jimmy was rather husky, gravity was working against them. In desperation, Jimmy yelled, "Cindy! Cindy! Help ... hurry!"

Hearing the screams, Cindy sprang to her feet, while ordering, "Sam, don't move; I'll be right back," and then ran in the direction of the cries for help. The safety of her friends quickly dispelled her fears of the forest; she was on a mission. Once off the footpath and within the darkened woods, Cindy detected what she thought was Jimmy flat on the ground, twenty feet ahead. As she drew closer, she saw Jimmy grasping Dan's forearms; Dan's head was still visible above the gorge. Cindy dashed in their direction, only to witness Dan's arms slipping from Jimmy. Once at the scene, Cindy dropped to her knees alongside Jimmy and together, they pulled Dan to solid ground. Dan lay on the ground trying to catch his breath, while Jimmy and Cindy did the same.

"Thanks, guys," said Dan.

"That's two. . . . ." said Jimmy, and then paused to catch his breath. "That's two you owe me: rinsing your eyes and now this."

After a few moments of gazing about, Cindy admitted, "You were right, Dan."

"About what?" asked Dan.

"The path," replied Cindy. "I know it's hard to believe after what we've just been through, but the left path which we took was the correct one." Pointing to another footpath that fell directly into the gorge, she continued, "If we'd taken the path on the right, that's where we would have ended up." Noticing the sharp decline of the path into the chasm, Cindy ended by saying, "And we'd probably be in the gorge right now."

After inspecting the footpath not taken, Dan agreed, "I think you're right."

While pausing to catch his breath again, Dan recalled the warm invisible touch. *What or who could it be?* he thought.

Dan's thoughts were abandoned by Jimmy asking Cindy, "How's Sam?"

"Oh my gosh," replied Cindy, "I left him back on the footpath."

Seeing Dan struggle to stand, it was only then that Cindy noticed blood on his pant leg. In a hurry to return to Sam, Cindy and Jimmy quickly helped Dan to his feet, placed his arms across their shoulders, and helped him to the path where they found Sam safe, semiconscious, but in a great deal of pain. The two teenagers carefully lowered Dan to the footpath.

Cindy approached Sam and knelt next to him to further inspect his wounds.

Glancing at Dan, who was stretched out on the footpath, Sam painfully asked Cindy, "What happened to Dan?"

Jimmy immediately interrupted Cindy's attempted response and said, "The tiger's sharp tail yanked a chunk of flesh from his ankle."

While Jimmy was graphically detailing the encounter, Cindy rose to her feet and resumed her search for the first-aid kit. Upon discovery, she was shocked to discover that there was no antiseptic ointment. "What kind of a first-aid kit doesn't have ointment?" asked a frantic Cindy. While rummaging through the backpacks, she continued, "There's got to be something here that will act as a disinfectant."

"Hey," exclaimed Jimmy, "what about this?" as he grabbed a bottle of whiskey on the ground which had rolled from Sam's bag during the recent attack.

"Yeah, I suppose that'll work," replied Cindy, who took the bottle from Jimmy, broke its seal, and poured a liberal amount on Sam's shoulder and upper arm wounds. Sam gasped and then began to jerk uncontrollably from the intense pain. He eventually lost consciousness.

"Sam!" yelled Cindy.

The older traveler remained motionless.

"What have I done?" screamed Cindy.

"Cindy!" yelled Jimmy, as he grabbed her shoulders. "Get a hold of yourself. Obviously, the pain was too intense that he lost consciousness. He was already half out of it anyway, long before you poured the whiskey. But it's something you had to do." Looking down at Sam, Jimmy knew that he wasn't experiencing the severe pain now. "Actually, Cindy, this may be the best thing for him," continued Jimmy. "Now, he can rest without the pain."

Knowing that Dan had sustained a severe ankle injury, Cindy was now fearful of applying the liquor, in the event he ended up like Sam.

Watching Cindy glance at Dan and suspecting her hesitation, Jimmy whispered, "Cindy, we have to do it. If we don't treat his ankle, it'll become infected, and then ... well, we just have to do it."

With that, Cindy neared Dan and mumbled, "Dan, let me see your ankle."

Sensing Cindy's unwarranted guilt regarding Sam, Dan offered no resistance as she and Jimmy knelt next to him and slowly raised his pant leg. There was no need to lower Dan's sock, for it was already ripped to shreds and hanging down the side of his boot. Cindy softly gasped; she was shocked that the wound was as bad as it was.

"Dan, this looks horrible!" exclaimed Cindy.

"Thanks, Cindy," answered Dan. "Great bedside manners."

"Sorry," said Cindy.

Grabbing the bottle, Cindy continued, "This may sting a little."

As she poured a healthy dose on Dan's ankle, he painfully screamed, "A little?"

Dan did his best to suppress further screams for fear of upsetting Cindy, but the pain was so intense that he, like Sam, eventually passed out.

Only two days into their journey, two of the four travelers were unconscious on the forest floor. After bandaging their wounds with strips of cloth ripped from tee shirts and then covering their patients with sleeping bags, Cindy and Jimmy patiently waited, hoping against hope that their friends would re-enter the conscious world. Knowing they had to do something to keep themselves occupied, Cindy and Jimmy gathered the strewn mess of clothes and objects which fell from their bags during the tiger's charge. The two panic-stricken teenagers waited nervously for their co-travelers to arouse, while plagued with fears of another attack.

Back in the world which the travelers left on Monday night, the doorbell awoke Nancy Clay from a deep sleep on the couch.

"Lie still, honey," said her husband, "it's probably the police."

Opening the front door, Jeff welcomed two police officers into their living room. Nancy sat up.

"Mr. and Mrs. Clay," said one of the officers, "I'm Officer Moore and this is Officer Nelson."

"Thank you for coming, officers," said Jeff, "this is my wife, Nancy."

Officer Moore continued, "I understand that you've been notified by park personnel of your son's disappearance."

"Yes," responded the Clays.

"Well," replied Officer Moore, "we're here to let you know that we'll do everything within our means to locate your son. Statistics show that the highest probability of locating a missing person is with an extensive search conducted within ninety-six hours of the disappearance."

Officer Nelson entered the conversation, "Do you have a recent picture of Dan that we can circulate at the station?"

"Yes," replied Jeff, as he approached the bookshelf to grab a family photo album. Quite unintentionally, Jeff handed Officer Nelson a photo of William.

"I thought he was eighteen," replied Officer Nelson, "he looks no more than seven or eight."

While Officer Nelson was returning the photo to the boy's father for confirmation, Jeff replied, "I'm sorry; this is an old picture of Dan's older brother, William."

It was painfully obvious to the Clays that the officers were new to the force and had not researched the case thoroughly when Officer Nelson remarked, "Maybe your son, William, knows where Dan and his friends might be."

Nancy did her best to conceal her emotions, but failed.

"I'm sorry," said Officer Nelson, "did I say something wrong?"

"It's quite alright, officer," said Jeff. "You see, William was also listed as a missing person thirteen years ago."

Officer Nelson hung her head in shame, or possibly in disbelief. Then, dropping to her knees, directly in front of Nancy upon the sofa, Officer Nelson implored, "Forgive me, I'm sorry. I'll personally do all I can to find Dan. That I can promise you."

As Officer Nelson rose to her feet, Jeff supplied her with a photo of Dan at his recent birthday celebration.

"Thank you, Mr. Clay," replied Officer Nelson.

As the officers walked to the front door, Officer Moore suggested, "Mr. and Mrs. Clay, it might be a good idea if you, the Parkers, and Ms. Somer get together for mutual support and compare notes. Who knows, maybe you'll unearth something."

"Thank you, officer," replied Jeff, "we will."

When the door closed behind them, Nancy knew beyond the shadow of a doubt, that the police would have no luck in finding Dan, just as they came up empty-handed thirteen years ago.

In the newly discovered parallel world, Dan slowly awoke after being unconscious for three hours; Sam remained unconscious. Despite the fact that they had taken Doctor O'Brien's medication that morning, the three teenagers were jittery the entire day never knowing when or from what direction the next attack would occur. Even though they had killed the saber-toothed tiger themselves, they missed Sam's protective paternal-like presence which offered them a sense of genuine security. The afternoon passed very slowly. Fearing the forest inhabitants with such intensity, no one dared step away from the group, except to go to the bathroom, and even this was postponed as long as humanly possible. The teenagers filled the afternoon with frequent checks on Sam, who remained unconscious, and frequent applications of the spirituous medication to both patients. Around 5:00, Cindy suggested that Jimmy start a fire for warmth, protection, and dinner preparations. Even though none of them felt like eating, including Jimmy, Cindy insisted that everyone eat something to maintain their strength. Once a glowing fire was built, Jimmy grabbed a semi-crusty mess kit and handed it to Cindy who placed three of the precooked hamburgers in it to warm, and set it atop a log on the fire. While Cindy carefully removed the hot pan from the fire a few minutes later, she and Dan were astounded to see Jimmy taking only one juice and pouring it into three cups.

Noticing that all eyes were upon him, Jimmy asked, "What? We have to conserve our rations like Sam said."

Of all times for Sam to be unconscious, thought Dan.

After grace, but before his first bite, Dan asserted, "I'll take the first patrol shift tonight."

"Dan, you need your rest," said Jimmy. "I'll take the first shift, Cindy can take the second, and I'll assume another shift after her."

"Jimmy, that's ridiculous," blurted Dan. "It's only my ankle; I can sit while on night watch." Sensing that Jimmy and Cindy were not convinced, Dan proposed, "If it'll make you feel better, I'll take the first shift, then I can have a period of uninterrupted sleep."

Against their better judgment, Jimmy and Cindy cautiously agreed.

"Alright, Dan," replied Jimmy, "you can take the first shift, I'll sit the second, and Cindy will take the last patrol."

Nodding in agreement, Dan added, "One other thing; at the start of each shift, we need to disinfect Sam's wounds."

"And your wound," interjected Cindy, while staring at Dan.

"I'll be fine," said Dan, "leave the whiskey for Sam."

"Hey," said Jimmy, "if we agree to let you patrol, then you have to agree to Cindy's suggestion."

Dan halfheartedly agreed to the terms.

Over the next few hours, carefree and meaningless conversations developed which, for a brief time, eased the travelers' minds of the dangers which lurked in the forest around them. At about 10:00 p.m., after checking off another day on the inside back cover of her novel, Cindy unrolled her sleeping bag, climbed inside, and glanced at Dan limping to a nearby mound for his night watch, carrying a lance and pocketing Sam's revolver. Jimmy, meanwhile, walked in Sam's direction toting a bottle of booze.

About fifty feet away from the camp, Dan sat on a patch of raised ground with the greatest of care. Even though the short walk from the campfire sent his ankle throbbing, he kept his personal agony secret for two reasons. First, not to unduly alarm his friends and second, if he could convince the group that his ankle was improving, they'd continue their trek in the morning... assuming that Sam was conscious and well enough to hike. Resuming their march was important to Dan, since no one knew for certain how many days it would take to reach the castle. Dan was determined not to let his ankle hold back the group. If, by chance, they arrived at the castle and returned to the oak tree before the next full moon, that would be fine. They'd simply wait it out at the O'Brien's house.

Dan wrinkled his nose; he could smell the liquor on his ankle that Cindy had applied only minutes earlier. *Maybe pouring some whiskey inside me would be more helpful than pouring it outside me*, Dan thought.

To pass the time on his first night watch, the teenager tried to memorize, as best he could, the layout of that particular section of the forest. *This could make the difference between arriving at the great oak in time and not arriving at all*, he thought. To his right, he noticed two separate trees that oddly enough, had grown from the same trunk. *This*, he thought, *would be an ideal marker to commit to memory*.

Straight ahead, he spotted an unusually large clump of underbrush supporting an array of wild flowers. Dan squinted his eyes and bit his lip; the pain in his ankle was exacerbating. Dan leaned back on his elbows, but not before taking both hands and carefully lifting his injured ankle onto a large stump in front of him. "Ah," he said to himself, "that feels better."

Now resting a little more comfortably, Dan continued his examination of the area. Glancing upwards, he was still amazed at the vast density of the canopy. Occasionally, the wind blew long enough and strong enough to separate the massive limbs, revealing the night sky. Dan was taken back several years, to a time when he spent countless summer nights sitting in his back yard staring at the stars and memorizing the heavenly constellations. Suddenly, from the corner of his eye, he spotted a quick flash of light in the uppermost tree limbs. Dan rose off his elbows, as if a couple feet higher, he'd be able to identify the flash. But as quickly as it lit up the treetops, it disappeared. Then, only moments later, he saw a second flash of light; but this time, about five hundred feet from the first sighting. Even though Dan had never witnessed this phenomenon before–he only heard about it from Jimmy and Cindy–he wasn't startled. It was peaceful; it was tranquil. Once again, it vanished. Sensing that the object may reappear, Dan painfully rose to his feet and hobbled back to the campsite to retrieve his flashlight which was magnetically secured to the side of his lantern. While at the campground, Dan took a quick look around and noticed that Sam was still unconscious–or sleeping–and Cindy was tossing and turning, probably due to Jimmy's incessant snoring. After grabbing the flashlight, Dan returned to his post. Only five minutes had elapsed before the brilliant figure reappeared and seemed to dance at the treetops. Completely at ease and unafraid, Dan switched on the flashlight and aimed the beam in the direction of the dancing light. With the beam landing upon several large branches as a backdrop, Dan slowly rotated the beam in small circles, as if the beam was dancing. First, he rolled the beam in a circle from left to right, paused, and then continued with a right to left movement. The fiery object mimicked the beam. When Dan rotated the light from right to left, the illuminated creature also moved in a circle from right to left. Dan reversed the direction and the object followed accordingly. It was as if the beam and the illuminated creature were synchronized. This was the first real enjoyment Dan had experienced in the forest.

Suddenly, and without warning, Dan dropped the flashlight and grabbed his ankle. *Something's horribly wrong*, he thought, *oh, my God, it's unbearable*. Dan passed out with the flashlight resting at his side with its beam aimed into the darkened forest.

A short time later, he awoke to the familiar warm invisible touch which he experienced earlier that day while hanging above the abyss, but this time the touch penetrated his jeans to his ankle. Dan sat up on his elbows again to look down at his legs. Even though the sensation was still present and most therapeutic, he couldn't see anything or anyone. Dan leaned forward and waved his hand in all directions around his wounded ankle expecting to hit an obstruction, but nothing. With the pain subsiding, Dan reclined back on the ground. Looking heavenwards, he spotted the sparkling light of the tree dancer descend from the canopy and float several yards in front of him, gazing in the direction of his ankle. If he didn't know better, Dan could have sworn that the illuminated creature could see something or someone clutching his ankle. Unfortunately, the fiery object remained at such a distance from Dan that he couldn't determine what sort of creature it was. Dan's eyesight had not yet completely returned to normal. Suddenly, the invisible touch lifted from Dan's ankle and at once, the fiery object scurried to the canopy. Out of curiosity, Dan reached down to pull up the pant leg on his jeans; Dan let out a gasp, his ankle was completely healed. He twisted his leg around to inspect the whole area, but there were absolutely no marks or scars. He even went so far as to check his other ankle, just in case. As he suspected, there were no marks of injury on it either. Looking at Sam's wrist watch, which Dan borrowed earlier, he noticed that his shift ended thirty minutes ago. Since Dan vividly remembered Cindy setting the alarm clock next to Jimmy's sleeping area after she treated his ankle, Dan deduced that Jimmy had obviously hit the snooze button. Completely healed, Dan was debating on whether or not to take the next shift and leave Jimmy snoring, that is until he realized it was past time to treat Sam's wounds. Dan literally jumped to his feet, as if checking out his healed ankle. There was absolutely no pain. Grabbing the flashlight, the lance, and the revolver, he neared the campfire.

At the campsite, Dan approached Sam's side and cleansed his wounds. Sam stirred rather spastically, but didn't open his eyes. "Sam," Dan said softly, so as not to wake the others. "Sam," he said again, but there was no answer. As Dan was replacing the cap to the bottle, a thought crossed his mind, *Why did this person or thing that healed me, not heal Sam?* Dan racked his brain, but the most logical explanation he could imagine was that this person or thing wanted the group to move forward–for some reason–and that even though Sam's injuries were obviously painful, they weren't life threatening anymore and they wouldn't impede the group's hike, like a wounded ankle. *But that's ridiculous*, Dan's thoughts continued, *there's got to be a logical explanation.* Before replacing the bandages over his friend's wounds, Dan leaned forward and took a closer look at Sam's injuries. He wasn't completely sure, but it appeared to him that Sam's wounds were healing rather quickly and nicely. They didn't appear as severe as they were, even just several hours earlier. He took a second look and then covered Sam's shoulder and upper arm with the homemade bandages.

Rising to his feet, he quietly approached Jimmy to awaken him. "Jimmy," he whispered, "you're up."

Very slowly, as if rising from the dead, Jimmy climbed from his sleeping bag, took his lance and revolver from Dan, and walked to his post. Obviously still half asleep, Jimmy failed to recognize that Dan was standing without any pain.

"I'll tell the group in the morning," Dan said to himself.

Within moments, Jimmy disappeared into the haunting darkness.

While unrolling his sleeping bag near Sam, Dan glanced at Cindy, who was closer to the campfire; he was pleased that she had finally fallen asleep. Before closing his eyes, Dan, as was typical for him, began his evening prayers saying,

> "Saint Michael, the Archangel, defend us in the day of battle. Be our safeguard against the wickedness and snares of the devil. May God rebuke him, we humbly pray, and do thou, O Prince of the Heavenly Host, by the divine power of God, cast into hell Satan, and all the

evil spirits who prowl about the world seeking the ruin of souls. Amen." [1]

Dan was in the middle of making the sign of the cross, when from behind came, "You honestly don't think that's going to help, do you?" asked a groggy Sam.

"Sam," said Dan in a quiet but excited voice, "how are you feeling?"

"Not great," replied Sam, "considering I was mauled."

"You really gave us quite a scare," admitted Dan.

"Did I, now?" asked Sam.

"Yeah," answered Dan. Leaning closer to Sam, he teased, "Don't do it again."

"I'll do my best," replied Sam.

Dan gave Sam a slight pat on his chest indicating that he was glad Sam was back.

"So," asked Sam, "what's that prayer you were just reciting?"

"It's the Prayer to Saint Michael the Archangel," answered Dan.

"Look, boy," said Sam, "I know you're religious and all, and that's great. But there's no way in hell–or in heaven for that matter–that Saint Michael would ever enter this Godforsaken world; trust me." While pulling his sleeping bag over his shoulders with his uninjured arm, Sam continued, "Heck, I seriously doubt that our so-called Guardian Angels ventured through the oak tree with us. Personally, I think the angels would rather take a guided tour of hell itself than visit this place."

"You're wrong, Sam," insisted Dan. "Saint Michael is the most powerful of all the heavenly spirits. I know that he'd do anything and everything within his power to help us, but we have to pray for his guidance and protection... every day. And, as far as our Guardian Angels are concerned, well, I know they're here with us. I mean, not more than fifteen minutes ago, I felt... ." Dan stopped.

"You felt what?" questioned Sam.

Suspecting that Sam would probably ridicule him for his spiritual convictions, Dan replied, "Nothing... forget it." Hoping for a few answers concerning Sam's beliefs, or lack thereof, Dan asked, "Sam, were you ever a religious man?"

"Well," acknowledged Sam, "I was raised a Catholic, like you, but unlike you, I quit practicing the faith because my prayers were never answered. No matter how often I prayed, they went unheeded. Even selfless prayers for someone else's benefit, not my own, were left unanswered."

"Did you ever stop to think that maybe they were answered," posed Dan, "but just not how you expected? I've always been told, and I believe, that when we reach heaven, then we'll clearly understand why certain prayers were answered and why others were delayed or never answered."

"You can continue praying for our safety," said Sam, "but don't expect me to join in."

While glancing about the darkened forest and upon hearing a sudden shriek in the far distance, Dan replied, "Something tells me that before this journey of ours is over, you'll be praying ... and praying like you've never prayed before."

"No way, kid," replied Sam.

It was obvious to Dan that his older companion was quickly losing strength, so Dan concluded, "Sam, let's get some sleep." Now nestled in his sleeping bag, Dan whispered, "Good night."

"Good night, boy," replied Sam.

Within a few moments, Sam was sound asleep, while Dan remained awake several minutes longer wondering what was hindering Sam's complete healing. While wrestling with his thoughts, he nodded off.

CHAPTER THIRTEEN

The Deluge

THE NEXT THING DAN REMEMBERED WAS BEING TOUCHED ON his right ankle by Cindy, who was starting her night patrol and had just administered a treatment to Sam's injuries and was prepping her second patient. Seeing no wound, she switched to his left ankle, rolled up his pant leg, and pulled down his sock. Nothing was there either. By this time, Dan was wide awake.

Noticing him stir and his eyes open, Cindy asked, "Where's your wound?"

"It's a long story, Cindy," answered Dan, "but suffice it to say, it's healed."

"What? How?" asked Cindy.

"I'll tell you at breakfast," whispered Dan.

Dan could see in her eyes that she thought either he or the situation was outright weird. Wanting nothing more than to discontinue the conversation, Dan closed his eyes and pretended to fall asleep. As Cindy stood up and walked away, Dan opened his eyes a slit to witness Cindy glancing back at him totally baffled.

At sunrise, or what one would consider sunrise in the darkened forest, Jimmy and Dan slowly stirred and headed toward the campfire, which was quickly fading. Dan volunteered to gather more kindling wood. With Dan out of earshot, Cindy–who had just ended her shift–struck up a conversation with Jimmy, who still appeared half asleep, sitting on a log near the pitiful fire.

"Jimmy," said Cindy in a low voice, "a couple hours ago before

I began my watch, I sterilized Sam's injuries and was ready to treat Dan..."

"So," interrupted Jimmy, with a yawn.

"But when I got to Dan," continued Cindy, "there was no wound!"

"What do you mean there was no wound?" asked Jimmy.

"That's exactly what I mean," replied Cindy. "His gash was completely healed. And just now, when he went off to gather wood, didn't you notice that he wasn't limping?"

"I guess I wasn't paying attention," answered Jimmy. "I suppose I was resting my eyes."

Then it occurred to Cindy, who asked, "Wait a minute. Didn't you notice that there was no wound when you tended to Dan last night when you and he switched watches?"

Jimmy looked away; he was ashamed to admit that during his watch, he failed to administer the treatments. "About a half-hour into my patrol," explained Jimmy, "I remembered the therapy. Then, I noticed that the campfire was nearly out, so I thought I'd gather timber to revive the blaze before tending to Dan and Sam. Anyway, the fire took longer to restore than I expected and... well... I guess I forgot about the patients, and instead returned to the lookout post. I didn't mean to forget, Cindy, honestly."

From behind, Cindy heard Dan approaching. From Jimmy's vantage point, he noticed Dan was carrying a large armful of wood and, as Cindy accurately noted earlier, he wasn't limping.

Once Dan was within vocal range, Jimmy yelled, "Hey, Dan, you're not limping!"

"Oh yeah," replied Dan, "I've been meaning to tell you about that."

By this time, Sam was climbing out of his sleeping bag, but with great difficulty. Jimmy and Cindy, who didn't know that their co-traveler had regained consciousness several hours earlier, rushed to his aid.

"Sam," yelled Cindy, "you're awake!" After giving him a hug, Cindy continued, "Don't you ever give us another scare like that!"

Sam remained silent.

However, the silence didn't faze Cindy who cautioned, "You

shouldn't be up and about. Get back in your sleeping bag and I'll bring breakfast to you."

"You'll do no such thing," demanded Sam, as he neared the campfire. "I'm perfectly capable of walking, unlike my friend here," while glancing at Dan.

Sam noticed it too. Dan was squatting near the fire, without any visible sign of pain, placing two logs on top.

"Hey," asked Sam, "what gives? Before I lost consciousness, Cindy and Jimmy told me that you were struck in the ankle by the tiger and that you had a pretty nasty gash to prove it."

Dan put a third log on the fire, sat back on the forest floor, and admitted, "I haven't been totally honest with you."

"What do you mean?" demanded Cindy in a raised voice.

"Well, it's not like everything that happens to me has to become public knowledge," responded Dan in a defensive tone. A moment of silence followed. "Sorry, Cindy," apologized Dan. Looking in Jimmy's direction, Dan continued, "Remember when I slipped into the perimeter of the gorge and was hanging on to a branch?"

"Yeah," answered Jimmy, "how could I forget?"

"Well," continued Dan, "don't you think it was a bit odd that a small branch, and one which was pretty rotten, was suspending me?"

"No offense, Dan," said Jimmy, "but I really didn't look at the branch all that closely. I was focused on saving you."

"Anyway," explained Dan, "what I didn't tell you was that I felt an invisible warm touch grasping my wrists and holding me up until Jimmy arrived. It's the same touch I felt in my dream the night at the O'Brien's house."

"You mean you had a dream about a warm invisible touch," asked Sam, who decided to enter the unearthly conversation, "and then you felt the same touch while hanging from the abyss?"

"Yeah," answered Dan, "and that's also how I knew to take the path to the left."

"What do you mean you knew to take the left path?" asked Cindy.

"Because in my dream," explained Dan, "the warm touch led me down the left path."

"Wait a minute," interrupted Jimmy, "you decided to lead us up an unknown path because of a dream you had?"

"Well," said Dan, "the way I figured it, one path was probably as good as the other and besides, I know that the warm touch is here to help all of us."

"So," asked Cindy, "what's this got to do with your overnight healing?"

"Last night," clarified Dan, "while on patrol duty, I passed out, only for a few minutes, from the intense pain. I regained consciousness again when I felt that same warm touch clutching my ankle. When the person or thing removed its grasp, I looked at my ankle, and ... well ... the wound was gone."

"So," asked Sam, "who or what do you think it was?"

"I don't know," answered Dan, "but, like I said, I know it's here to help us on our journey."

Dan lowered his head, then raised it, took a deep breath, and said, "Since I'm being honest, there's something else you should know."

"Oh, this ought to be good," said Jimmy in a disbelieving voice.

"What's that?" asked Cindy.

"I also saw the illuminated object in the treetops last night," admitted Dan. "But what was strange is that when the warm invisible touch was grasping my ankle, the lit object descended from the trees and hovered behind the invisible being, as if it could see the being or thing that was healing me."

"Did you get a good look at the flashy object?" asked Sam.

"No," replied Dan, "it was still too far away from me. I guess my eyesight hasn't returned totally yet."

Sam, Jimmy, and Cindy looked at each other as if to pass judgment on Dan.

Knowing what they were thinking, Dan remarked, "Look, I know it sounds strange, but you two," Dan stared at Cindy and Jimmy, "can't deny the existence of the illuminated object since you saw it with your own eyes and you can't deny that my ankle is healed. You got to believe me that this invisible being is here to help us."

"If the object or being is here to help us," inquired Sam, "then why didn't it help us against the tiger; and why didn't it heal me, as it healed you?"

"I don't know," answered Dan. "But I do know that if we took the path to the right, we'd all be at the bottom of the gorge." Looking at Cindy, Dan resumed, "You admitted yourself that we'd be in the belly of the chasm if we'd taken the path to the right. And as far as your wounds," said Dan to Sam, "well, I don't know."

After a momentary pause, Sam snidely asked, "You think this is a spiritual being, don't you?"

"Maybe," replied Dan.

"Oh my gosh," exclaimed Sam. "Would you listen to yourself? You actually think this being is your guardian angel helping you ... don't you?"

Glancing at Jimmy and Cindy, Dan detected a growing sense of disbelief. "Look, you guys can think what you want," said Dan, "but as far as I'm concerned, I'll take any being's help, especially in this strange world."

While reaching for a box of cereal, Jimmy remarked, "What I don't get is why this being hasn't helped anyone else. I mean, why didn't it help Cindy when she was attacked by the tree roots or Sam when he was mauled by the saber-toothed tiger?"

"I wish I knew," answered Dan.

Before long, the cereal box had made its rounds and all four travelers were enjoying their breakfast beside the roaring fire.

In between his mouthfuls of dried cereal, Jimmy asked, "So, should we walk a little today or stay put until Sam's wounds heal a little more?"

"I think it'd be best if we move on," replied Sam. "After all, I'd rather be a moving target than a sitting target."

"Sam," said Cindy, "we appreciate your valor, but I think we should stay here a day."

Knowing that Sam's health and safety should take priority over reaching the castle, and recalling that just late yesterday afternoon while the three teenagers were waiting for Sam to awaken from his unconsciousness they discovered a lake just beyond a little knoll during rest room breaks, Dan suggested, "We could spend part of the day washing our clothes in the lake, mending a few clothes which were ripped during our run-ins with the tree and the tiger and maybe even re-inventory our rations. Besides, Sam, a day of rest wouldn't hurt you, either."

"I'm fine," replied Sam, "it's my shoulder and arm that are sore, not my legs. I can walk." Sam was raising a spoonful of cereal to his mouth, when he set the spoon down and asked, "What lake?"

"A lake we discovered yesterday," informed Cindy. "Just over there," as she pointed to her left.

Fearing for their safety, Sam ordered, "I don't want any of you adventuring into the wilderness alone. It's just not safe."

"But, Sam... ." pleaded Jimmy.

"No buts, Jimmy," interrupted Sam, "it's far too dangerous."

The four travelers continued their cereal in relative silence, though the lack of milk made the chewing somewhat noisy.

Eventually, Dan spoke up extending a compromise to Sam concerning their proposed hike that day. "Tell you what, Sam, we'll walk a little today, but as soon as you feel tired, or if your shoulder or arm starts aching, we'll end the hike."

After offering his proposition, Dan looked at Cindy and Jimmy who both offered a nod of approval.

"That sounds fair to me," replied Sam.

"And I'll carry your bag," offered Dan.

"I can carry my own bag, boy," snapped Sam.

"Then we stay here," said Dan.

"Alright, alright," yielded Sam, "you can carry my bag, but stop being such a mother hen."

While handing Sam a cup of juice Cindy asked, "Sam, what's the deal with the whiskey?"

Sam cleared his throat trying to stall for time while also trying to concoct a believable lie. "I brought it along ... you know ... in case we needed it for medicinal purposes."

"Yeah, right," replied Jimmy, "you old lush. And what about the other two bottles in your bag? Exactly how much 'medicine' did you think we'd need for our journey?"

"Have you been going through my bag?" accused Sam.

"No way," replied Jimmy. "They rolled from your bag when the tiger knocked us over."

"Hey, wait a minute," interjected Cindy. "How come we never saw the alcohol when we emptied our bags at the O'Briens?"

Before Sam could hatch another story, Jimmy correctly stated, "Because he had them rolled up in his shirts. Remember, the O'Briens only asked to inspect our non-clothing items."

"Look," admitted Sam, "I occasionally enjoy a bit of whiskey. Is that so bad?"

"Not really," replied Dan, "but since it has come in handy for our injuries, I think you should set aside some of it–no, all of it–for medicinal purposes."

Sam was placed in a delicate situation. He really wasn't a drunk, but he did, like he said, enjoy a little liquid refreshment on occasion. However, there was no denying the fact that Sam was quickly developing a real likeness for the teenagers. He also knew that he couldn't live with himself if something dreadful happened to any of them and there wasn't whiskey to bathe their wounds. Sam stretched his legs near the fire and consented, "Fine, I won't sip any for the rest of the trip." Then glaring at Jimmy, he concluded, "But, I'm not a lush."

"Thanks, Sam," replied Dan.

When the meal was finished and the camping gear packed up, the four embarked upon another day's hike. From what little the travelers could see above, it appeared to be a relatively cloudless day. Dan volunteered to take the lead, and no one questioned him, since he seemed to have the protection of an invisible being. The teenager was followed by Sam, Cindy, and finally, Jimmy. Throughout their morning hike, Sam periodically reminded his co-travelers to make mental notes of their surroundings, so that between the four of them, hopefully something would look familiar upon their return.

"So," asked Sam, "have you three known each other a long time?"

Since Dan was directly ahead in the direction of Sam's voice, he turned slightly and responded, "Well, Jimmy's been my neighbor since we were kids. He, my brother, and I were pretty close, always hanging out together, especially on the weekends."

From the rear of the line, Jimmy yelled, "What are you guys talking about?"

Sam spun around and answered, "I asked if you've all been friends for awhile."

"Oh," replied Jimmy, "yeah, we've been friends for quite a few years."

"But when William disappeared," continued Dan, "things changed, not right away, of course, but gradually. I guess I was trying to come to terms with his disappearance. When I reached my early teen years, that's when ... well ... my parents said I was becoming somewhat of an introvert. They didn't understand that I really missed William and that the times I spent alone were when I'd think about him."

Detecting a feeling of loss in Dan's voice, Sam quickly changed the subject and asked, "What was school like?"

"We already graduated," informed Jimmy.

"Actually," said Sam, "I figured that. But what was school like before you graduated?"

"Unlike most guys," volunteered Dan, "I enjoyed school. I mean the learning part. What I didn't enjoy was the constant harassment from the school bullies. I suppose being a straight 'A' student didn't help my situation with Sur and Malice."

"Sur and Malice?" inquired Sam.

"Yeah," replied Dan, "they were the bullies who succeeded in making my school life miserable. And it never failed; the more I tried to avoid them, the more they seemed to be lurking around the corner just waiting for me."

"So," asked Sam, "why didn't you stand up to them?"

"Stand up to them?" questioned Dan. "Are you crazy? They were football players. Look at me; I'm 5'7" and weigh 135 pounds. And in case you hadn't noticed, Sam, I'm not too muscular or athletic. Heck, I don't really mind not being athletically inclined, but I wouldn't mind being a little more coordinated."

Cindy and Jimmy increased their stride and were now walking alongside Sam, listening and adding to the conversation.

"Why do guys make such a big deal about sports anyway?" asked Cindy.

"Why not?" interjected Jimmy. "Sports are what keeps us in shape, and let's face it, most girls like a guy who plays sports. I also suspect that being on the football team kept bullies, like Sur and Malice, at a safe distance."

"Well," said Cindy, "I think it's ridiculous. I mean, I'd rather spend time with a guy who's honest and charming."

"Charming?" chuckled Jimmy. "If you want charming, read a romance novel."

Cindy delivered a look of disgust toward Jimmy, as Sam rejoined the conversation, "Dan," remarked Sam, "I wouldn't waste my time worrying about those bullies. They'll have their reckoning in due time. As a matter of fact, if any of these so-called bullies saw you battling the raging tree roots and the saber-toothed tiger like you did, I think–no, I know–they'd have a whole new attitude toward you."

Hearing an owl screech above, all eyes gazed upward, while a mighty gale separated the tree limbs, revealing a storm front moving in from the west.

"Looks like a storm's heading our way," informed Sam. "Let's try to get a few more miles in today before it hits."

Sam resumed his previous conversation. "So, getting back to school, were all of you in the same year?"

"Yeah," answered Dan, "but we weren't all in the same classes. Jimmy and I shared most classes, except algebra; Cindy was only in my chemistry and English classes."

"And," raised Sam, "what about your families?" Looking at Dan, Sam acknowledged, "I know you're one of two children and I've obviously met your parents, who by the way, seemed like a really nice couple."

Cindy was the first traveler to volunteer information. "I'm an only child. My dad died in a skiing accident when I was five and my mom's raised me alone ever since. It's obvious she loved my dad very much, which is why, to this day, she says that she'll never remarry. I don't remember much about my dad; but I do remember him reading me bedtime stories every night. Mythological stories were my favorite, because my dad always portrayed the creatures. My mom, Sara, is also my best friend. I mean, we do a lot of things together, partially because I enjoy it, but mainly because it's my way of easing her burden. As a single mom, her job at the real estate office and everything else she does around the house consumes all her time. She doesn't have a lot of free time for the two of us to do many things together, but when we do, we always have a great time. And, well actually, that's the main reason why I didn't want to attend survival camp. I wanted to spend my last summer doing things with her before going to college."

"Cindy," interjected Sam, "if you wanted to spend more time with your mom this summer instead of going to survival camp, why didn't you just tell her?"

"I don't know," replied Cindy, "I guess I wasn't sure if she wanted to spend the summer with me. I've actually thought about taking a year off before entering college, just to help her out and, let's face it, I'm not all that excited about going back to school anytime soon. High school was horrible. I had great teachers and all, but my gosh, the girls. All they ever seemed to talk about was boys and"–looking at Jimmy–"sports. I think I need a break from school."

"And what's your story, Jimmy?" asked Sam.

"My story?" inquired the teenager.

"Haven't you been listening, Jimmy?" rebuked Cindy. "Sam wants to know a little about us."

"Oh," said Jimmy, "well, like Cindy, I'm also an only child. There's really not much to say. My dad's a literature professor and my mom works for an employment agency. We live next door to Dan, and"–pausing to think of what to add–"I like sports."

"Yeah," replied Sam, "I gathered that. What about school?"

"It was okay, I guess," stated Jimmy, "it's just that the grades didn't come too easily for me. I studied, probably not as much as I should have, but I always seemed to fall below, way below, the mark. Sometimes, I wish I was more like Dan."

"More like me?" exclaimed Dan. "Are you nuts?"

"Dan," replied Jimmy, "you're smart and you're levelheaded. There's no question that you'll make something of your life. But me, I have serious doubts about a future career."

For the first time in years, Jimmy paid Dan a compliment.

"There are a lot of things I've done in my life," admitted Jimmy, "that I'm ashamed of and I wish I could do over again." Looking at Dan, Jimmy recalled, "For example, remember last school year when Sur and Malice dropped your lunch on your lap in the cafeteria?"

"Yeah," replied Dan, "how could I forget? I was humiliated in front of the whole school."

"Well," said Jimmy, "when you walked out of the cafeteria, I stood up and was prepared to follow you to see if you were okay, but... ." Jimmy abruptly ended his story.

"You stood up?" questioned Dan.

"Yeah, he did," answered Cindy.

"But, why didn't you check on me?" asked Dan.

Jimmy halted his hike, allowing his co-travelers to pull in front of him. Realizing that Jimmy had stopped, the three likewise ended their march and turned to face Jimmy.

"What's wrong, Jimmy?" asked Dan.

"I'm sorry, Dan," replied Jimmy. "I didn't check on you in the cafeteria because ...."–an ominous silence befell the nearby forest–" ... because I was afraid that Richard and Ken, who were eating at my table, would give me a hard time about being your friend."

Dan was wounded to the core. But at the same time, he knew it took great courage for Jimmy to admit it.

Standing only a few feet from Jimmy, Dan walked over, placed his hand on his neighbor's shoulder, and remarked, "Thanks for being honest. I have to admit, I noticed that there were many times when we were talking at school and the next moment you were gone. I always wondered why and suspected the reason was because you didn't want to be seen with me. But then again, Jimmy, you've proven your friendship to me over the last couple of days like no one's ever done before. Not many people would rinse my eyes or risk their own lives over an abyss to save mine." Removing his hand from Jimmy's shoulder, Dan hesitated momentarily and then remarked, "You don't need to show any signs of our friendship in public; I'll understand."

Only now realizing that his self-centered act months ago in the school cafeteria hurt his friend more deeply than he suspected, Jimmy responded, "Dan, you're my friend and we've been friends for a long time. I'm glad you're my friend, actually one of the best."

Cindy took two steps closer to Jimmy and remarked, "Even though what you did–or should I say, didn't do in the cafeteria–was totally spineless, I'm proud of what you just admitted."

Feeling another strong gust of wind, Sam ordered, "Come on; we better keep moving if we want to get as much time in today before the storm."

As Cindy left Jimmy's side and moved ahead, Jimmy thought, *With all that Dan's been through in his life—the loss of his brother, the constant harassment from bullies, the lack of support from friends like me, and most of all, his determination in the face of danger over the last couple days—he's the one with the courage and the conviction to get us all home safely.*

The four resumed their trek to the castle.

About a mile up the poorly cleared and poorly lit path, Cindy remarked, "Hey, Sam, I think I should take a look at your..."

"I'm fine," interrupted Sam.

"Sam," said Dan, indicating his agreement with Cindy's suggestion.

"Okay," yielded Sam, "but we're losing valuable hiking time."

"What's the point in setting a new hiking record," asked Cindy, "if you die along the way?"

"It's a flesh wound," snapped Sam, "I'm not at death's door."

"Nevertheless, when it comes to your wounds," stated Cindy, "you'll do as I say."

After Sam seated himself on a large rock and lowered his shirt, Cindy removed his homemade bandages and leaned in for a closer look at his injuries.

"That's amazing," said Cindy.

"What's that?" asked Sam.

"Well," informed Cindy, "considering you've had these wounds for just a little more than twenty-four hours, you're healing abnormally quickly."

"It must be the marshmallows," Sam jokingly responded.

Dan opened the bottle and handed it to Cindy, who poured another liberal amount on Sam's wounds. Though his injuries were healing rapidly and rather nicely, the cure-all still carried a punch, causing Sam to jolt and fall off the rock. Cindy set the bottle to the ground and helped Dan lift their companion to the boulder. While in a squat position, Dan glanced behind and saw Jimmy rummaging through Dan's duffle bag. Obviously, Jimmy's thoughts had reverted to his stomach.

Dan was about to verbally chastise Jimmy when Sam also noticed his friend's piracy and remarked to Dan, "It's alright; we all should probably grab a bite to eat anyway."

For good measure, Cindy doused Sam's wounds a second time while the patient was engrossed with Jimmy's antic.

"Great Scott," yelled Sam, as he jolted a second time. "Are you in that much of a hurry to get rid of the whiskey?"

"Sam, it's either that or we'll bury you in this Godforsaken world," replied Cindy.

"Grab the shovel," replied Sam in a sarcastic voice.

Sam took a deep breath and rose to his feet. As the three quietly neared Jimmy from behind, the pilfering teenager was startled when he heard their untimely approach. Attempting to conceal one of Mrs. Clay's cookies, Jimmy remained sitting on his heels, as if inspecting the bag, while shoving the rest of the cookie into his mouth.

"What are you doing, Jimmy?" asked Dan.

There was no response; the cookie was quite large.

Knowing only too well that Jimmy was trying to swallow the evidence, but up for a little enjoyment, Dan prodded, "Jimmy, what are you doing?"

In a failed effort to throw his friends off, who were now standing directly over his shoulders, Jimmy muttered, "Nothing," and then choked on the cookie, spewing its chewy ingredients upon Dan's duffle bag.

"Jimmy," exclaimed Dan, "not on my bag!"

Sam and Cindy did their best to restrain their amusement at the situation.

While laughing, Sam remarked, "It's alright, Jimmy. I think we all could use a light snack."

Once everyone had a cookie and water in hand, Cindy asked, "So, Sam, what's your story?"

"My story?" asked Sam. "Well, I'm sixty, but as you know, I visited this strange world twenty years ago."

"Have you ever been married?" asked Dan.

"No," replied Sam, "my studies took up all my time."

"Your studies?" questioned Jimmy.

"Yes," admitted Sam. "I used to be a philosophy professor at Saint

Mary's College in Pleasantville—you know, about thirty miles southeast of Lawton."

"You ... a professor?" asked a stunned Jimmy.

"Yes, Jimmy," responded Sam. "Anyway, I, much like Dan, enjoyed the academic circles. Looking back, I suppose that I probably enjoyed my career too much, since it left virtually no time in my life for anything else. Anyway, one day, a colleague of mine—and a good friend—convinced me that I needed to get out and enjoy life. I remember him telling me once, 'The entire world is a library, so why restrict yourself to one book?' He suggested, and I agreed, that I join him one morning for rabbit hunting. I must admit that at first I was reluctant about killing an animal, but I slowly suppressed, and eventually overcame, the feeling. To make a long story short, hunting soon became my favorite pastime, though I never let it interfere with my class preparations or with my students' enrichment. Several months into my newly discovered hobby, another avid hunter informed me that Eldritch Forest in Lawton presented the best conditions for rabbit hunting. Apparently, its lack of visitors and hikers, on account of its shrouded mystery, enabled the rabbits to breed ... well ... like rabbits. I remember the weekend clearly. It was Presidents' Day. Being a three-day weekend, I rose early in the morning to allow travel time and still have a few hours of early morning hunting. My friend was right; the conditions were perfect."

Looking at Dan, Sam remarked, "Dan, I know you've heard this story before, but for the sake of your friends...."

"No," interrupted Dan, "I'd like to hear it again."

Sam continued with his story. "Near the end of my two-hour hunt, I spotted movement in the brush. I pulled back and released my arrow, but missed the rabbit, thanks to a sudden noise which shook me. I did notice, though, that the arrow went straight through a tree. Well, you probably know the rest of the story: I crossed over, met the O'Briens, lived with the O'Briens, alarmed the O'Briens, and finally left the O'Briens. Anyway, when I arrived back in our world through the tree, I did my best to refocus on my studies. However, the need for someone to listen to my story and believe my story slowly took a toll on my lesson preparations, until I was eventually relieved of my position at the college. With no job, I took the remainder of my savings and moved to Lawton, where I told just about everyone I met about the strange and bizarre world I discovered through their forest. But, I always stressed that the strange world was not *in* their forest, but *through* their forest. Fortunately, I never went so far as to tell anyone about the oak tree, fearing that someone might attempt the suicidal–I mean risky–journey into the dangerous parallel world. Deep down, I wanted people to believe me and my story, but I didn't want anyone crossing over and endangering their own lives."

"Thanks," said Jimmy sarcastically, "for making us feel so much safer."

Sam ignored Jimmy's comment and continued, "With no luck at finding a job in Lawton, probably because all Lawtonians soon viewed me as a lunatic, I had no choice but to live on the streets; though during the past couple years, I have stayed at the local homeless shelter and have frequented Lawton's soup kitchen."

"Wait a minute," interjected Jimmy. "If you were living at the homeless shelter like you say, where did you get the lances and the revolver?"

"Just because I was homeless," answered Sam, "doesn't mean I abandoned hunting. To answer your question, I hid my bag which contained my weapons, rope, and clothing within the deeper recesses of the Eldritch Forest in our world." Sam paused to take a large gulp of water and then resumed, "But my obsession to have someone–anyone–believe my story caused me to do something that will haunt me for the rest of my life."

"What's that?" asked Cindy.

"A few months ago," explained Sam, "I saw Dan aimlessly wandering the forest one early evening; a full moon was rising. Dan seemed distraught about something, because ... well everyone knows that the forest is off limits, especially at dusk. Anyway, Dan approached the majestic oak and remained motionless for a few minutes, just staring at the tree."

As Sam took a break from his story to take another bite of his cookie, Dan informed his teenage friends that he was staring at the tree because he knew he had seen it before, but he couldn't remember where or when.

Sam resumed, "Eventually, Dan placed his hand inside the tree.

So, I quietly crept up behind him and—against my better judgment—pushed him through the tree."

Looking at his co-travelers, Sam noticed that Cindy and Jimmy had a look of disbelief in their eyes.

Suddenly, the group felt another strong gust of wind force itself through the canopy to the forest floor.

"I'm sorry," said Sam, "but that's how bad my compulsion had become. I stepped back about twenty feet and hid behind some shrubs, waiting for Dan to re-emerge from the tree. A short while later, Dan came darting through the oak. As tempting as it was to approach him and confirm that he visited the other world, I remained out of sight."

Taking another glance at Cindy and Jimmy, Sam still detected a look of discontent on their faces.

"I know what I did was wrong," admitted Sam, "which is why I'm here now."

"What do you mean?" asked Cindy.

"Well, I guess you could say I'm trying to redeem myself," replied Sam. "When I left this strange world twenty years ago, I swore that I'd never return. And that remained my conviction until just recently. You see, after I shamed myself by pushing Dan through the oak, from that point on, I had a loathing of myself and my actions. After meeting with Dan a couple times to recount my month-long journey to this world, I became highly suspicious that he'd be attempting his second transworld journey soon. So, the night of the next full moon—the night of your departure for survival camp—I remained hidden in the periphery of the forest, hoping against hope not to see Dan enter the forest. Anyway, once Dan made his appearance and embarked upon the first leg of his journey—and then seeing the two of you follow him—I knew what I had to do; I had to revisit my personal nightmare. It was my self-appointed mission to save Dan, and now you two," as he looked at Cindy and Jimmy, "to make amends for my heartless and selfish act of pushing him through the tree."

"So," replied Cindy, "you had no desire to return to this place, yet you did for Dan's safety and ours?"

"Cindy," corrected Sam, "don't make me out to be a martyr. I just did what I had to do, nothing more."

"I'm sorry," admitted Cindy, "that I misjudged you."

Before taking another sip of water, Cindy added, "Sam, I think it took a lot of courage to re-enter the portal, especially knowing partially what awaited you within this world's forest."

Sam looked at Dan, as if seeking forgiveness.

Dan had a blank look on his face. The recounting of Sam's story resurfaced momentary feelings of exploitation and manipulation.

But after realizing the great risks Sam had undertaken to accompany him and hopefully rescue his brother, Dan ultimately responded, "Sam, I don't hold it against you. Actually, the more I think about it, your memorable shove a few months ago may end up being the catalyst which saves William."

By this time, the four had more than finished their one cookie and water and were ready to resume their hike. The wind grew stronger and louder as they gathered their belongings and headed out, but not before making a mental picture of their surroundings. The group was just approaching a small mound on the footpath when Cindy commented that she'd never encountered winds of such strength in all her life.

"Cindy," said Dan, "remember, we're not in our world."

Just then, the rain softly fell, barely making it to the ground through the treetops. All at once, the sky let out a mighty roar, as all experienced the loudest thunder they'd ever heard, which caused even the ground to shake. The four instinctively covered their ears. Through the swaying limbs, the travelers witnessed an awesome light show, as the lightning filled the air with electric particles.

"Dan," yelled Sam, "I thought it was dark in the forest before, but now it's ... my gosh, I can barely see your face. Grab your lantern."

Dan set his duffle bag on the moist ground and removed his 'No Man's Land' lantern. The forest, in the midst of the storm, seemed even more menacing than before, if that was possible. The travelers scanned the nearby area in agitation. Dan, with his lantern in hand, walked ahead of the group scanning for any would-be predators which might be foolish enough to adventure from their dry dwellings into the drenching conditions; Cindy accompanied Dan at the lead. Without warning, the skies opened and released such a deluge that not even the dense foliage could deter the rain from smashing to the forest floor. Cindy and Dan, now about twenty feet ahead of Sam and

Jimmy, lifted their bags to cover their heads from the downpour; Sam and Jimmy did likewise.

From the corner of her eye, Cindy witnessed something drop from a nearby tree. Wanting to look, but fearful at the same time, she slowly glanced to her right and saw an enormous frog, about the size of a small cat, sitting at the edge of the trail. Cindy, who typically wasn't fearful of frogs, turtles, and the like, let out a scream once the purple frog opened its mouth displaying its teeth in the lantern's indirect light.

Her scream caused Dan, who was standing beside her, to jump. Another crash of thunder filled the air. Dan turned in Cindy's direction and–in order to be heard over the clap of thunder and the torrential rain–yelled, "What's wrong?"

Cindy only pointed.

Dan glanced to Cindy's right and saw the frog at a safe distance away. With the absence of the thunder's roar, Dan calmly stated, "It's only a frog. Granted, it's a little larger than we're used to seeing and the color's a bit odd, but... ."

The frog took a leap in the direction of Cindy and Dan and revealed its teeth. "Oh my gosh!" yelled Dan.

By this time, Sam and Jimmy were approaching Cindy and Dan, thanks to her scream moments earlier.

As the frog advanced a little closer toward the group, Dan extended his lantern in its direction to expose the frog's teeth to Sam and Jimmy. To the group's astonishment, as soon as the lantern's intense beam hit the frog, it immediately retreated.

"I guess after living in relative darkness all its life," speculated Dan, "it's probably fearful of the light."

Suddenly, hundreds of frogs fell from the trees, as the heavy rains forced them to take shelter on the forest floor. The frogs advanced quickly toward the travelers. Several frogs leaped within only a few feet of Jimmy and then abruptly stopped, which puzzled the teenager.

Why'd they stop, Jimmy thought, *I'm not holding a lantern.*

Instantly, one of the frogs opened its mouth and unfurled its six-foot tongue at Jimmy, making contact with his bare arm. The tongue remained attached to Jimmy for a brief second and then was reeled back into the frog's mouth. Jimmy instinctively looked at his arm and discovered that the frog had deposited a tadpole which was savagely burrowing itself into his skin. Jimmy jerked and let out a cry of disbelief, commanding the attention of his friends who witnessed the oddity of a tadpole using a human as a host.

Sam grabbed the small tadpole as quickly as he could–it was slippery and slimy–and pulled, releasing its life grip on Jimmy. Throwing it to the ground, Sam crushed it with his hiking boot. Sam had just exterminated the unwelcome guest, when several more frogs advanced upon the group. While the tadpoles didn't have the ability to attach themselves to clothing, a few managed to latch onto the travelers' arms and one even embedded itself on Sam's face. Cindy, who was trying desperately to catch her breath in order to continue her screaming recital, received two tadpoles on her arm, directly below the elbow.

In the midst of ripping the tadpoles from their arms and face, Sam recalled the first frog's reaction to the light. "Dan," ordered Sam, "hand me the lantern!"

Without hesitation, Dan complied.

"Follow me," demanded Sam, "off the path to the large red shrub ahead. The frogs are afraid of the light; we need to build a fire ... now!"

Huddled together in a circle facing one another with their clothed backs facing the oncoming frogs' tongues, Sam held the lantern out from the inner circle in the direction of the red shrub, while all four walked in unison slightly beyond the trail's edge. During their short ten-foot journey, the group experienced the bombardment of tongues slapping against their backs and backpacks, and gratefully felt the tadpoles slip off their clothing to the muddy ground.

Once at the shrub, Sam handed the lantern to Dan, who held it over Sam's shoulder as the older traveler bent over to gather kindling wood near the base of the shrub. While on his knees, Sam received a tadpole to the wrist from a frog perfectly concealed in the shrub's shadow which was cast by the light beam. Putting the safety of his friends first, Sam decided not to dislodge the tadpole, but continued searching for timber. Putting his bare hands even deeper into the thicket, Sam retrieved what he was looking for: wood that was still relatively dry. He gathered as much as he could manage and then ordered his co-travelers to reverse their direction to the center of the path. Although he preferred to start the fire somewhere far from the frogs, he saw that the amphibious creatures were everywhere. Literally hundreds, if not thousands, blanketed the nearby footpath and the forest fringes.

Once in the middle of the path, Dan raised the lantern above the group's heads and ceaselessly swung it in the air unleashing a broad band of light in all directions, while Sam squatted to the ground–still with his back toward the oncoming tongues–and attempted to start a fire. With the frogs now at a relatively safe distance away, thanks to Dan's light show, Cindy and Jimmy removed their backpacks and held them over Sam's head to deter as many of the raindrops as possible. Unfortunately, the heavy rains proved Cindy and Jimmy's efforts ineffective. Unable to ignite a fire, primarily due to the rain, but partially due to the growing pain in his injured wrist, Sam asked for anything combustible for fuel. Instinctively, Cindy reached for the novel in her backpack and handed it to Sam, but not before ripping off her daily log on the back cover and stuffing it in her pants pocket. Within minutes, a spark was seen, then a flame, and finally a warm glow which sent the frogs even further away, hopping deeper into the safety of the dark woods.

While sitting on her heels near the warm fire, Cindy noticed Sam's wrist. "Dan," said Cindy, "give me your machete; Jimmy, get the alcohol from the bag." Without questioning, the young men did as they were told; Cindy was now in command.

Falling to her knees upon the muddy ground, Cindy ordered Sam to place his injured wrist firmly and squarely between her knees. The female traveler sterilized the knife with whiskey. Sam closed his eyes and tightened his lips, as the tip of the machete punctured his wrist. Cindy knew she had to enter his wrist with precision to avoid rupturing a vein. Sam jerked, but luckily only after the machete and tadpole were successfully removed. The repulsive parasite dropped to the ground. Only now totally disgusted, Cindy pierced the burrowing creature with the blade. Reaching for the liquor bottle again, Cindy soaked Sam's newest wound and then took a quick swig of the moonshine to soothe her nerves. Throughout the entire surgical ordeal, the three men were genuinely impressed with Cindy's eventual mastery of the situation, who only minutes earlier, was shouting in terror. Before returning the cap to the bottle, Cindy treated her own tadpole-inflicted wounds and those of her co-travelers.

CHAPTER FOURTEEN

The Priestly Visit

IN THE OTHER WORLD, THROUGH THE OAK TREE, NANCY CLAY remained in bed for nearly three days only getting up to use the restroom which was adjacent to her bedroom. Understandably, Jeff took off work to aid his grieving wife and assist the police. The only time Nancy ventured downstairs was to meet the Parkers and Ms. Somer when they visited Wednesday night to give and receive moral support. During their evening conversation, only two things were unearthed: no one in town had seen the teenagers in days and that, in addition to the youths, Sam White was also reported missing, since he had not frequented the soup kitchen, as was his daily ritual for nearly two years. The only other time Nancy left her room was when Father James Roberts, the Clays' parish priest, paid a visit.

Father James was in his late thirties, a little less than six feet tall, with sandy-colored wavy hair. He was a holy man of God who strived to instill hope in the lives of his parishioners. The priest arrived Thursday morning around 9:30. Knocking on the door, he was greeted by Jeff, who was clutching a cup of coffee.

"Good morning, Jeff," said Father James.

"Good morning, Father," replied Jeff. "Please, come in."

Jeff took Father James' lightweight, black jacket and hung it in the front closet.

"I'm sorry, Jeff," said Father James, "that I'm only now getting around to making a visit, but I've spent most of the last two days consoling the Parkers–who arrived at the rectory Tuesday morning and

THE PRIESTLY VISIT

stayed until late evening–and comforting Ms. Somer. I placed several calls to you and Nancy upon hearing the news, but no one answered the phone."

"I've taken off work," informed Jeff, "but I guess your calls arrived when I was running errands or meeting the police; and Nancy ... well, she's secluded herself upstairs where there's no phone."

Overly concerned that he hadn't made contact with the Clays, Father James added, "I know there's no excuse for my delay, but ... well ... please forgive me."

Knowing the intense agony that the Parkers and Ms. Somer must be experiencing, for Jeff vividly recalled the dreadful ordeal which he and Nancy endured the first few years after William's disappearance, Jeff replied, "Father, there's no reason for you to apologize. Granted, Dan's missing, but at this point in time, I think you should spend most of your time with the other families."

"Thank you, Jeff," responded the priest, "you're far too kind." After glancing at the staircase, Father James asked, "How's Nancy taking the news?"

"Not too well, I'm afraid," answered Jeff. "Other than visiting very briefly with the Parkers and Ms. Somer last night, she hasn't left her room in nearly three days. She won't eat, she won't bathe, and since both of our boys are now missing–and William presumed dead–she's beginning to question her faith."

"I see," said the priest. "But her reaction is perfectly normal."

"May I offer you a cup of coffee?" asked Jeff.

"If it's not too much trouble," responded Father James, "that would be nice."

As Jeff walked toward the kitchen, the priest followed, asking, "Do you think I could speak with Nancy?"

"I'd like that, Father," replied Jeff, "but anymore, it's an emotional and physical struggle for her to talk with anyone about Dan. She wouldn't even leave her room on Tuesday afternoon to visit some of the townspeople who stopped by to offer their condolences."

Handing Father James a cup of coffee over the kitchen counter, Jeff asked if he'd like cream and sugar. After Father's negative response, Jeff said, "Excuse me, Father, let me go upstairs and see if Nancy would like to speak with you."

"Very well," responded Father James.

As Jeff left the kitchen and headed for the staircase, the priest followed behind as far as the living room. Being a relatively newly ordained priest, Father James was not a resident of Lawton during William's disappearance, though he had heard of the misfortune from his parishioners. Looking around the living room, Father James took notice of three photographs hanging above the mantel. Setting his coffee cup on the living room table, Father James approached the fireplace where he glimpsed a picture of, who he supposed was, William when he was about seven, most probably the last picture taken of William; a graduation picture of Dan; and a family portrait which, by the look and size of the boys, must have been taken shortly before the first family tragedy. Father James was impressed to see a picture of the Sacred Heart of Jesus and the Immaculate Heart of Mary proudly hanging in close proximity to the other three framed photographs. Though he didn't know the Clays personally, he knew that they were religious people who never missed Sunday Mass and who occasionally attended weekday Mass.

Mumbling was heard from behind the priest, followed by a loud creak from the staircase; Jeff and Nancy were descending the steps. Nancy was wrapped in a long flannel robe and since she wasn't groomed, Father James suspected that she did not intend on leaving the house that day, or any day in the near future for that matter.

"Good morning, Nancy," said the priest, as he neared the steps.

"Good morning, Father," replied Nancy, who was now approaching the base of the staircase.

Instinctively, Father stepped forward and gave her a hug, while saying, "I'm so sorry to hear of the news."

"Thank you, Father," replied Nancy with tears welling in her eyes.

Jeff escorted his pastor and Nancy to the couch.

Once all were seated, the priest remarked to Nancy, "I was just apologizing to Jeff for my delay in paying you a visit, and I'd also like to extend my apologies and condolences to you personally."

Nancy took a tissue from her bathrobe and wiped her nose. Placing the tissue back in her pocket, she responded, "Thank you, Father. I appreciate your coming by, but I think it's best that you spend most

THE PRIESTLY VISIT

of your time with the Parkers and Ms. Somer. They were obviously devastated last night. Believe me, I know from personal experience that one never totally rises from a tragedy like this, but Jeff and I remember the counseling which your predecessor provided us, so we'll be okay. I guess what I'm trying to say is that this tragedy is a first for the other families and they need your spiritual direction now more than Jeff and I do."

"I understand, Nancy," replied the priest.

"Father," asked Nancy, "I have to be honest with you."

"Yes," replied Father James.

"I'm really beginning to question my faith," admitted Nancy.

"Go on," prodded the priest.

"I just don't understand," continued Nancy, "why God would permit such a horrible thing to happen to a young man like Dan. I'm sure you know that Dan was a religious person who'd never harm anyone. He was kind, thoughtful, and ... why just the other day, he gave some money to a homeless man. He even befriended Sam White, the one who the entire town views as a lunatic." Nancy leaned forward to remove a couch cushion, which was aching her back, and then asked, "Is it true that Sam White is also missing?"

"It appears so," answered the priest.

"I remember," relayed Nancy, "meeting Sam White just a few nights ago when we invited him to join Dan, Jeff, and me for a meal at the diner. He seemed like a nice man–and as far as being deranged–heck, I'm closer to insanity than he is. Anyway, practically the whole town looked down on Sam, or at least looked away, but not Dan. Dan had a unique gift of seeing through superficialities and glimpsing the interior qualities of a person. That's exactly what he did with Sam White."

Nancy reached for her tissue again, while Jeff, who was sitting on the couch beside his wife, put his arm around her for emotional support.

"Mr. White's poor family," continued Nancy. "Come to think of it, does he have a family?"

"I'm not sure," answered Father James. "Nancy, getting back to your issue about faith and the works of God, no one, not even a priest like me, can completely comprehend the purpose and will of God and what He ordains. We do know, however, that once in heaven, we'll clearly understand why He ordained certain things."

"That's exactly what we told Dan a few years back," interjected Jeff, "when he asked us why God permitted William to go ... you know ... missing."

"But, Father," asked Nancy, "why would God permit a second tragedy? Wasn't the loss of one son enough?"

"Nancy," replied Father James, "please don't torture yourself. We must pray for patience, understanding, and the insight to know the will of God, not just in this particular tragedy, but in all things."

"I know you're right, Father," said Nancy, "and I try to accept His will; but deep down, I don't. I just can't."

"It'll take time," admitted the priest, "but we must persevere in our prayers." After taking another sip of his coffee, Father James continued, "Since the news, I've prayed continually and even offered several Masses for the group's protection, for their safe return, and for their families. You must also pray."

Nancy rose from the couch, neared the pictures hanging above the mantel, and while staring at the recent graduation portrait, asked, "Where can Dan be? Why hasn't he called?" With all her effort, Nancy tried to conceal her emotions, but she hadn't the strength. Jeff sprang from the couch to comfort his ailing wife.

The sight of Nancy was extremely difficult for Father James to endure, especially since he strongly suspected that Dan, while indeed missing, had not been abducted; he freely embarked upon a trip. Being careful not to mention anything audibly, Father James plunged deep into his thoughts, *I'm fairly certain it was Dan in the confessional box last Sunday morning telling me that he'd found a portal to a parallel world and that he had every intention of following through with his plan to visit this world and bring his older brother home. But Church rules are perfectly clear: under no circumstances, is a priest permitted to disclose what is heard in the confessional. Certainly, I'd tell a penitent to return stolen property, but Dan wasn't guilty of anything of this nature. Dan was only guilty of telling falsehoods to his mother. By my solemn vow as a priest, I certainly will not disclose what Dan revealed to me; but even if I wanted to comfort Nancy, what would I say? After all, Dan never told me the location of the*

THE PRIESTLY VISIT

portal. The only thing I can do is what I've been doing all along: console the grieving families.

After allowing a few minutes for Nancy to compose herself, Father James eventually remarked, "Nancy, I'm sure that the children and Sam White are fine. Let's do our best to keep our hopes alive and pray for them."

Without removing her gaze from Dan's graduation portrait, Nancy replied, "Father, I've been praying and I'll continue to pray. But my prayers over the past thirteen years have still gone unanswered."

After taking a final sip of his now lukewarm coffee, Father James rose from the couch and said, "Well, I should pay another visit to Sara Somer. She was beside herself when I spoke with her earlier this morning on the telephone."

Realizing that it would be beneficial for Nancy and Jeff–not to mention the four travelers–Father James offered a suggestion, "One more thing: start attending Mass on weekdays and after the service the three of us will pray at the kneeler directly below the marble statue of Saint Michael the Archangel. If I remember correctly, that's one of Dan's favorite statues in the church."

"Thank you, Father," replied Jeff, "we'll do our best to be there."

Nancy remained staring at Dan's graduation portrait while Jeff accompanied Father James to the front door. Once at the entry, Jeff handed the priest his jacket, while Father James reached for his wallet and removed his business card. Handing it to Jeff, he said, "Here's my private number; call me anytime you or Nancy want to talk."

"Thank you, Father," replied Jeff, "and thank you for coming."

After closing the door, Jeff rested his forehead against the doorjamb and whispered, "God, watch over Dan."

His brief, but sincere, prayer was interrupted by a loud creak; Nancy ascended the staircase.

CHAPTER FIFTEEN

Lakeshore Discoveries

IN THE STRANGE WORLD, THE FOUR TRAVELERS OVERSLEPT, partially due to the physically draining attack of the amphibians the night before and partly due to the constant rain and wind which kept the travelers awake until five in the morning. Night watch was suspended the previous evening since Sam rightly assumed that no predator would be wandering in the torrential rains.

Sam was the first to rise. Pulling his head from his sleeping bag, since the rainfall forced the explorers to sleep with their heads inside their sleeping gear, he turned his arm to glance at his wrist watch. After experiencing a sharp pain in his wrist from last night's surgery, he noticed it was 9:00 a.m.. *Oh my gosh*, he thought, *the day's half over*. Ultimately, however, he decided to let the teenagers sleep a little longer to regain their strength.

Sam quietly crawled out of his sleeping bag. He was amazed that, considering he set his sleeping bag on a river of mud last night, the ground was nearly dry. He surmised that the constant howling wind during the night dried the forest floor. Noticing that the overnight rainfall had extinguished the fire, Sam quietly and cautiously ventured off the footpath and into the forest to gather fallen timber, but not before looking up and down the trail for any lingering frogs. Upon his return to the campsite, he unintentionally knocked his foot against the lantern which caused Cindy to stir.

Pulling her head from the sleeping bag and seeing Sam standing several feet away holding an armful of wood, she asked, "What time is it?"

"Shush," voiced Sam, "not so loud; you'll wake the others. Go back to sleep. We'll spend the day here resting and reorganizing our gear."

"What?" yelled Cindy. "Are you crazy? We need to get as far away from this frog-infested cesspool as soon as possible."

"Shush," warned Sam again, "you'll wake up... ."

It was too late; Dan popped his head from his sleeping bag.

"Good morning, Sam; morning, Cindy," said Dan, while yawning. Rubbing his eyes and then looking about, Dan asked, "Where are the frogs?"

"I'm happy to say they're nowhere in sight," answered Cindy, who was still scanning the footpath to confirm her reply.

"Would you two keep quiet," demanded Sam, "you'll wake up... ."

Again, it was too late; Jimmy's feet emerged from the sleeping bag. All three looked in amazement.

"How on earth," Dan asked Sam and Cindy, "did he turn around in his sleeping bag last night?"

"Who knows?" replied Cindy. "It's Jimmy."

"Well," said Sam, while positioning the timbers and trying to restart the fire, "since we're all up, I suggest that we stay here today to rest up and clean up ... if there aren't any objections."

Immediately, Jimmy responded, "Sounds great to me."

Cindy remained silent, while she continued surveying the footpath. She was obviously concerned that the frogs might return for round two. Seeing no frogs, she eventually responded, "Okay."

Then there was Dan, who also remained suspiciously quiet. He absolutely abhorred the idea of losing an entire day of hiking, since it meant that William would have to endure another day at the castle. But at the same time, he suspected that maybe Sam was making this suggestion because his wounds were troubling him but was too proud to admit it. Whatever the reason, there was no denying the fact that Sam had been invaluable on the trip. After all, Sam had taken many wounds that, were he not there, could very easily have been inflicted upon someone else–perhaps even himself.

Sam approached Dan, knelt on the ground next to his sleeping bag, and asked, "Dan, what's your answer?"

"Sorry," replied Dan, "yeah, let's rest here today."

"Now, wait a minute," reminded Sam, "we're not here to rest the entire day; we're also going to do some cleaning and mending."

"Cleaning?" asked Jimmy. "Cleaning what?"

Walking back to the fire, Sam lifted the pan which was resting on the ground and pointed to its inside while saying, "There are pieces of burned hamburgers and hotdogs stuck to the pan, for one. As far as mending, well let's see, there are Dan's jeans which were torn by the tiger's tail; my shirt, also from the tiger; Cindy's jeans from the tree roots; and your ... wait a minute." Sam looked directly at Jimmy and asked, "Haven't you been attacked by anything yet?"

"Very funny," replied Jimmy. "I'll have you know that I was thrown by the roots, pushed to the ground by the tiger, and received three tadpoles last night."

Dan joined in on the amusing conversation and asked, "Yeah, Jimmy, but did you shed any blood?"

There was a momentary pause while Jimmy prepared a response. Eventually, he answered, "As a matter of fact, I did. I noticed a few drops of blood on my arm last night, thanks to those creepy frogs."

While scraping the dried mud off her sleeping bag with her fingernails, Cindy added, "Well at least you weren't pulled underground by that possessed tree."

"No," replied Jimmy, "but I was thrown pretty far and pretty hard; and besides... ."

Still standing near the fire, Sam lightly tapped a metal spoon against the filthy pan to capture everyone's attention and said, "Alright, that's enough. My gosh, with as much bickering as you three do, it's a wonder you're not related. Come over to the fire and get some breakfast; then we'll assign chores."

As the three teenagers neared the fire, Sam explained, "The way I figure it is that since Cindy's prepared all our meals, it's about time we cooked for her. Who knows, maybe after a few days of the men's cooking, she'll volunteer to cook again."

"Cooking?" asked Jimmy. "I can't cook."

Tossing a bag of marshmallows to Jimmy, Sam declared, "Then consider this your first lesson."

All four huddled around the fire, warming themselves from the cold, damp air which had lingered from last night's storm, while also protecting themselves from a possible stray purple frog or two.

After piercing the marshmallows with a stick, Jimmy reached for the cereal boxes. Even though it's nearly impossible to mess up cereal, especially without milk, Jimmy somehow managed to accomplish the impossible. While pouring the dried cereal into the four bowls, his foot inadvertently struck the wobbly log which he had set the bowls upon. The bowls and the cereal fell to the forest floor.

"Jimmy!" yelled Cindy.

"Alright," said Sam. "Don't panic. During this trip, we can't afford to waste any food; absolutely nothing. So everyone pick up the cereal, brush it off, and place it back in the bowls."

While detecting a look of revenge on Dan and Cindy's faces, Jimmy confessed, "I'm sorry; it was an accident."

The two teenagers offered no response, as they knelt on the ground and dusted off their breakfast.

While picking up his cereal from the soil, Dan whispered to Cindy, "I already miss your cooking."

"Jimmy's got to sleep sometime," reminded Cindy.

Several minutes later, as the travelers were eating their abnormally crunchy cereal and roasted marshmallows, Sam delegated himself to assign chores. He began, "Now, since we're spending the day in this location, let's take advantage of our respite from the hike. As I mentioned earlier, we'll do a few chores that we've postponed over the last couple of days. We need to clean the mess kits, mend and wash a few clothes, consolidate our belongings, redistribute the weight of our supplies between the four bags, clean our muddy sleeping bags, and clean Dan's lantern, which, after last night, is also covered with mud. Who knows, we may need that lantern again soon."

"Not too soon, I hope," interjected Cindy.

While glancing at their disinterested faces, Sam continued, "Now, before I assign tasks, does anyone want to volunteer for any of the chores I've mentioned?"

"Not especially," answered Jimmy, "but didn't you say we were going to rest today?"

"I did," answered Sam, "once the chores are done."

Looking at Cindy who had finished her cereal and returned to her sleeping area several feet away to resume her earlier obsession of scraping the dried mud off her sleeping bag, Sam asked, "Cindy, do you, by any chance, have a mending kit?"

"Actually," responded Cindy, "since my mom packed my bag, yes, I have a mending kit. But there's not much thread."

"Whatever you have will have to do," replied Sam. "Would you mind mending a few tattered clothes?"

"That's fine," said Cindy.

Placing his empty bowl next to Cindy's on the forest floor for cleaning, Jimmy remarked, "Cindy, are you serious?"

"About what?" asked Cindy.

"You actually have a sewing kit in you backpack?" continued Jimmy.

"I told you, Jimmy," replied Cindy, "my mom packed it."

Jimmy shook his head in complete amazement.

"Dan ... Jimmy," said Sam, "which one of you wants to clean the mess kits?"

Thinking the only other option was washing clothes, Jimmy quickly volunteered.

"Dan," said Sam, "that leaves only you and me. Would you rather clean the four sleeping bags and your lantern or consolidate and redistribute our belongings?"

Jimmy slapped his hand against his thigh in disappointment, thinking, *Dang it, I forgot about the consolidation chore and now I'm stuck with the dishes.*

It took Dan no time to opt on cleaning the sleeping bags and his lantern. After all, Dan thought Sam's shoulder and wrist were probably still sore and he shouldn't be on his hands and knees cleaning sleeping bags.

"Very well then," said Sam, "I'll go through our bags and pitch what we don't need and then repack our bags equally. But before I do, is there anything in them that's personal which you'd rather I not see?"

One at a time, the three travelers responded, "No."

All of a sudden, it dawned on Cindy that no one had been selected, or forced, to clean the clothes. "What about our clothes?" asked Cindy.

"Our clothes?" asked Sam. "Oh yeah, our clothes. Well, maybe that's a chore we all could enjoy together."

"Why can't we just wear what we've got on for the next month?" asked Jimmy.

"If you even think about it," replied Cindy, "then you're walking downwind of me."

"Now, shush you two," ordered Sam. "The reason why we should do it together is simple: it's far too dangerous. While gathering wood this morning, I noticed a lake a few hundred feet from here. But I won't have anyone wandering off to the lakeshore alone. It's not safe."

None of the teenagers objected.

"Sam," asked Jimmy, "then how should I wash the mess kits if I can't go to the lake? Should I use the bottled water?"

"Absolutely not," demanded Sam. "We need that for drinking." Without skipping a beat, Sam recommended, "Tell you what Jimmy; you help Dan scrape the dirt off the sleeping bags and his lantern and we'll all wash the dishes together at the lake this afternoon while we're cleaning clothes."

Walking over to Dan, who had already begun cleaning the sleeping bags, Jimmy mumbled, "What's everybody's obsession with cleaning. First my parents force me to clean my room before leaving for survival camp and now I'm stuck cleaning sleeping bags in another world."

The remaining two hours of the morning flew by quickly, once the group put their noses to the tasks at hand. Cindy was so meticulous in mending Sam's shirt that it looked practically new. Repairing her and Dan's jeans took less time than Sam's shirt, though the tough denim caused her to poke herself with the needle several times. As for the young men, after much complaining from Jimmy, two of the four sleeping bags were fairly clean, considering they had to scrape the dried mud with their eating utensils and pull off countless burs with their bare hands. Sam suggested that once all four bags had most of the dried mud and burs removed from them the group would carry them to the lakeshore for a final washing. Dan proposed that they go to the lake sooner rather than later, to allow as much time for the sleeping bags to dry before using them that night. Sam wholeheartedly agreed.

Taking a break from the sleeping bags, Dan began cleaning his lantern, which was a relatively easy task, once he grabbed his machete and started scraping. The final chore–redistribution of their supplies–was also accomplished with minimal effort. By cramming the remaining cookies from three containers into two, Sam was able to empty one container for an inevitable future use, though the cookies were now basically glorified crumbs.

After emptying the contents of Dan's duffle bag to the ground, Sam noticed something rather peculiar. "Hey, Dan," yelled Sam, "got a minute?"

Dan set the lantern aside and neared Sam.

"Yeah, Sam," said Dan, "what's wrong?"

"Well," began Sam, "I wasn't snooping, but when I emptied your bag this fell out." Sam was holding a stuffed animal. "Now, it's not any of my business," continued Sam, "but we can't afford to carry any frivolous things. I know it doesn't seem like much, but trust me, after climbing a few hills, even this small toy will add to your load."

Dan lowered his eyes and said, "Please, Sam, I packed it because it was William's favorite stuffed animal when he was a child. I figure if he doesn't recognize me after all these years, maybe he'll remember the stuffed animal. Unlike me, it hasn't changed."

Even Sam, an unemotional sixty-year-old, was moved. "I'm sorry, Dan," replied Sam, "I didn't know. It'll be our little secret."

"Thanks, Sam," responded Dan, as he turned and retraced his steps to his half-cleaned lantern.

To Sam's surprise, Jimmy's bag was in order with nothing to discard and nothing out of the ordinary.

"Cindy," yelled Sam, "can I see you for a minute?"

The teenager approached Sam while carrying a shirt which she was in the process of reattaching a button.

"Look," said Sam, "it's not right for me to go through your personal belongings. So, why don't you look through your bag yourself? Remember, pitch anything that won't be of use on our trip."

"Sure," answered Cindy.

Once their belongings were consolidated and the weight was evenly distributed between the four bags, Sam called the group together for lunch.

By noon, the light breeze had subsided, the ground was completely dry, and the temperature had climbed to the mid-seventies. There was no need for a fire now, but the travelers kept it alive for an added sense of protection and also to prepare their lunch. The four gathered about five feet distant from the fire to avoid its excessive heat and made themselves comfortable on the ground. About a half-hour earlier, knowing that the cooking pan would not be thoroughly cleaned until the afternoon when the group adventured to the lake, Sam did his best to remove the dried hamburger and hotdog remains with a knife. On today's menu were hotdogs, chips, water, and a smashed cookie.

It was unmistakably clear to Sam that his friends were exhausted, not so much from the morning's chores, but mainly from too little sleep the night before. "I think," complimented Sam, "we've all done a great job with this morning's chores. And to celebrate, I'm lifting my ration rule—just this one time—on the cookies. For lunch, we can each have a cookie and a half."

Looking at the two containers of cookies which were sitting on the ground next to the mess kits, Jimmy asked, "How can we tell how much is a cookie and a half? They're all smashed."

"I'll put what I think is appropriate on each plate," responded Sam, while he reached for a semi-clean pan and handed it to Dan.

After wrapping a towel around its handle to avoid a burn, Dan held the pan with the four hotdogs over the fire. When the meat products were warmed and all plates were partially filled, Dan bowed his head and said grace, but only mumbled, since he knew his friends wouldn't join in. Midway through his prayer, Dan raised his eyes and was surprised to see that all three travelers–including Sam–had their heads lowered; this was a first. Dan thought, *When was the last time, if ever, a prayer was echoed from this dismal place?* As he ended his prayer and the travelers responded "Amen," a deafening noise was heard instantly from the treetops by rapidly fleeing creatures. *Obviously,* thought Dan, *invoking God's name instills such fear in the creatures that they flee in fright.* With everyone now staring at the canopy, Dan sensed a definite feeling of fear among the group.

Once the noise overhead subsided, the topic of religion naturally ensued.

"I know Dan's a Catholic," recognized Sam, "but what about you, Jimmy?"

"Yeah, I'm a Catholic," responded Jimmy, "but an occasional Catholic. I mean I go to Mass, just not every Sunday."

"And you, Cindy?" asked Sam.

"No, I'm not a Catholic," replied Cindy. "Actually, I'm not sure what I am. Several times when I was in grade school though, my mom and I attended a Baptist service."

Sam placed another chip into his mouth.

"And," asked Cindy of Sam, "what religion are you?"

After swallowing, Sam answered, "Well, nothing now, though many years ago, I used to be a Catholic."

The talk of religion reminded Dan that he had recently stored both bottles of the holy water in his duffle bag. Recalling his promise to Sharon O'Brien that he would carry one bottle in his pocket at all times, Dan made a mental note to grab a bottle from his bag after lunch.

Noticing that his friends had nearly finished their meals, Sam asked, "Has everyone had enough to eat?"

"Not really," replied Jimmy, "can I have another hotdog?"

"Absolutely not," reproved Sam, "we need to conserve our food supply."

"Then why'd you ask?" remarked Jimmy.

Sam had no answer; he simply looked upwards as if imploring strength.

Once the meal was consumed, Sam gathered the mess kits and utensils while asking the others to collect the sleeping bags and clothes for a hike to the lakeshore.

Fifteen minutes later, but before leaving the campsite, Sam established a few ground rules, "Now look, we've never been to a lake in this world before and if this forest has taught us anything, it's that anything can, and most probably will, happen. So I want two of you to carry the items to be cleaned and one of you to bear a lance with me for our protection. I'll lead the way and the person carrying the other lance will follow behind the group."

The mood in the camp had drastically changed instantaneously. The lighthearted conversations over their meal were now replaced with feelings of anxiety, fear, and tension.

Understandably, Dan volunteered to protect the party from the backside, since none of his friends would be stranded in the savage world if it wasn't for his personal quest.

With his lance ready, Sam took the first step in the direction of the lake while warning, "Remember, be as quiet as possible and"–looking at Jimmy–"no talking."

With great effort, Jimmy lugged the four sleeping bags, while Cindy carried the clothing and mess kits. Dan stationed himself at the rear poised to spear anything that dared to cross their path. When the lake was within sight, the travelers breathed a sigh of relief that no creature was encountered. Sam thought maybe the beasts slept during the early afternoon.

Within minutes, the group was standing on the shore of the lake.

The body of water was so immense that no one could see the opposite side. The surface was also shrouded in a thick mist creating an invisible vastness. Nevertheless, the group was grateful to be in the open air and sunshine.

"Alright," whispered Sam, "I want Jimmy and Cindy to rinse the dishes, sleeping bags, and clothes in the water–but only on the extreme edges of the lake. We don't know what lurks beneath the surface, so don't make any loud noises or splash the water which may draw attention to us. Understood?"

Completely terrified, not of the water, but of what may exist below, Jimmy and Cindy whispered, "Yeah."

"Dan," commanded Sam in a soft tone, "stand next to Jimmy with your lance raised, ready for release and I'll stand beside Cindy."

The first sleeping bag was spread gently atop the lake, while Jimmy and Cindy were careful to dip only their fingertips into the cold water. Dan and Sam stood over their friends' shoulders clutching their lances ready to release their deadly weapons at the first sign of disturbance. Very slowly, the two washers pulled the sleeping bag in their direction at two foot increments, gently rubbing their hands against the bag to remove the remaining embedded dirt. Within five minutes, the first sleeping bag was cleaned.

Rising to his feet with the drenched, but clean, sleeping bag, Jimmy paused and looked at Sam in a puzzled manner, as if asking where he should hang the sleeping bag so it would dry and remain clean.

Sam, sensing Jimmy's predicament, whispered, "Drape it on that rock over there."

About thirty feet behind and slightly to the left of the group rested a large gray boulder near the forest's edge which was covered with thick undergrowth and dangling tree limbs. The boulder towered nearly six feet and was riddled with unusual holes symmetrically dispersed throughout its hard texture. Jimmy thought it looked a bit odd, but dismissed his overactive imagination by reminding himself that so far, everything in the forest appeared out of the ordinary. The teenager draped the first sleeping bag over the boulder, while Cindy slowly unraveled the second sleeping bag atop the lake.

Feeling his arm going numb from the several minute suspension, Dan switched his lance to his other hand and assumed his earlier posture; Sam did likewise.

The second sleeping bag–Jimmy's–was filthy.

"What'd you do, Jimmy," whispered Cindy, "drag this through the forest?"

"No," replied Jimmy, in a low voice, "I just move a lot when I sleep."

"Hey, you two," said Sam softly, "shush."

After ten minutes of intense scrubbing, the bag was fairly clean as Jimmy placed it atop the boulder alongside the first sleeping bag.

For a change in routine, Cindy reached for the clothes and the mess kits, but not before accidentally clanging a metal knife against the pan, causing the loudest noise that anyone had made since their arrival at the lake. All paused and remained motionless, scanning the lake's surface and its rapidly evaporating mist to detect any possible movement in response to Cindy's pan and knife recital. Sensing nothing, Cindy and Jimmy continued with their cleaning. The clothing and the eating utensils were relatively easy and quick to clean, but the pan was another story.

Jimmy bravely submerged the pan and used a knife to gently scrape the dried food particles.

Sam and Dan leaned in even closer, directly over Jimmy, fearful that something might sense vibrations below the surface, but there was nothing.

Even though cleaning the cooking utensils and the clothes took only several minutes, to the fearful travelers, it seemed more like an hour.

As Jimmy draped the clothes on the boulder and placed the clean utensils at its base, Cindy, who was still at the lakeshore, reached behind and grabbed the third sleeping bag; it too was clean in about five minutes.

As with the others, the fourth sleeping bag was quietly unfurled atop the water. Once the initial two feet of the bag were cleaned, Cindy and Jimmy extended their hands further out and reeled in another two feet of the sleeping bag when suddenly, a large protuberance shot upwards from below the bag. Cindy screamed and fell back on the ground supporting herself with her elbows. Jimmy, however, sprang to his feet, darted behind Cindy and dragged her on the ground until they were several feet from the lakeshore. Sam and Dan released their spears at the unknown entity which was veiling itself in the water beneath the sleeping bag. Since the creature's appearance was masked below Dan's sleeping bag, no one knew what it was or if the lances had inflicted an injury. One thing was for certain though, Dan's sleeping bag now bore two souvenirs of their trip to the lake. The protuberance sank to the lake bottom.

All was quiet on the lakeshore as the travelers remained motionless. The only discernible noise was the water striking the small rocks on the shoreline. Cindy remained seated on the ground with Jimmy crouched behind her, while Sam and Dan slowly retraced their steps to the two teenagers without removing their stare from the sleeping bag floating atop the lake.

Within a matter of seconds, two red eyes emerged from underneath the fringes of the sleeping bag at the water's edge. All remained silent, except Cindy, who let out a light gasp at the sight of the creature's eyes. Hoping that whatever the creature might be was responsive only to motion, the four remained perfectly still. Their plan appeared to work, at least initially, until the creature slithered to the shoreline approaching the group, revealing its identity. The water snake was massive, displaying a circumference of at least two feet and a long red tongue which rolled around its deadly fangs.

For his friends' safety, Dan bolted in the direction of the boulder, hoping to draw the snake's attention away from the group and to him. The snake hesitated momentarily, but then changed its course and slunk in Dan's direction. Dan had every intention of luring the snake further from the group, when he tripped on the dense undergrowth near the base of the gray rock. Jumping to his feet, he felt a sharp pain; Dan's previously healed ankle had twisted during the stumble. He leaned against the rock for leverage, attempting to take the weight off his right ankle. Glancing over his shoulder, he noticed that the snake, while a good ten feet long, was still fifteen feet away, but was rapidly gaining on his lead. The teenager's gaze was instinctively drawn to the movements of Sam and Jimmy, who were fearlessly plunging into the lake to retrieve the lances–which were now several feet from the shore–while Cindy returned to the waterside to snatch the last sleeping bag. Suspecting he couldn't outrun the serpent with his twisted ankle, Dan's only alternative was to hop around the massive boulder and into the forest, directly behind the rock, to lose the serpent in the dense woods.

Back in the lake, Sam retrieved both lances and tossed one to Jimmy. The two men ran from the water and advanced toward the snake, but with great caution.

Leaning against the rock on the side opposite the approaching serpent and his friends, Dan remained out of view.

"What the heck?" Dan asked himself, as he felt the boulder stir.

The teenager hopped two feet away from the rock. In the end, much like his initial encounter with the oak tree, curiosity got the better of him. Dan slowly extended his hand and touched the rock. First he detected warmth, and then he felt the rock budge. Dan quickly withdrew his hand. Glancing to the front side of the boulder, he saw the serpent's long slender tongue clear the massive rock.

Without warning, the tree limbs overhead shook.

Sam and Jimmy, while not yet upon the snake, were close enough to witness an amazing one-sided battle. From the dense tree limbs above the gray rock, emerged a large head with two antennae.

"Oh my gosh," exclaimed Sam, "is that a ... ?"

Jimmy stood with his mouth gaped.

Cindy screamed.

Eventually, Jimmy replied, "I don't know; but whatever it is, let's not make it mad," as he and Sam slowly withdrew three steps.

The beast lowered its head from the tree limbs and targeted the serpent with a clear liquid from its antennae. Within only seconds, the snake was paralyzed, while the spray of digestive enzymes immediately started decomposing the serpent for an easy digestion by the toothless giant snail.

In the commotion, Dan fell to his knees.

Moments later, the snail rested its massive head on the lakeshore and began devouring the partially decomposed snake.

Unsure of the snail's intentions, Sam and Jimmy, who had only recently spotted Dan on his knees poking his head around the backside of the snail, motioned Dan to enter slowly the forest behind him.

While all in the group were grateful for the snail's timely appearance, they made sure to keep a safe distance between themselves and the spray from the antennae, just in case the creature was interested in a second course. After gathering what little gear remained on the lakeshore, the three travelers left the water's edge and headed to the forest, while keeping a close eye on Dan and his attempt to escape undetected into the woods behind.

Dan thought that his best chance to steal away was while the snail was consuming its meal. Suspecting he'd make less noise crawling than limping from tree to tree, not to mention the fact that he was already on his knees, he quietly raised his right knee and moved it several inches closer to the forest border before gently setting it upon the ground. He did the same with his left knee. But upon contact with the ground, a snap was heard from a crushed twig beneath his knee. Dan froze.

The king snail, on hearing the snap, extended its long neck backwards toward Dan. The beast grabbed Dan by the legs with its powerful jaws and gently swung him in midair, setting him on the ground in front of itself, only a few feet from the dead serpent. Amazingly, Dan was unharmed, as if the snail had no intention of devouring the teenager.

On witnessing the incident, Sam and Jimmy raised their lances and ran to the beast. Cindy followed behind.

Looking up, Dan was terrified at the beast's enormous head, now in full view. As the giant snail slowly lowered itself in Dan's direction, two lances were launched at the beast. One slightly nicked the shell of the creature, while the other pierced the lakeshore no more than five feet from Dan. The beast continued lowering its head. Dan crossed his arms over his face, while the king snail rubbed the side of its head against Dan's chest, leaving a sticky film on the teenager's shirt. Dan remained motionless, terrified to move a muscle. Again, the massive snail gently touched Dan's chest. Cautiously, Dan uncovered his face for an up-and-personal look at the beast. Seeing no teeth, his fears were eased somewhat. A third time, the king snail rubbed the side of its massive head against Dan's chest, being careful not to make contact with its antennae. Drawing on reserve strengths and courage, Dan raised his hand and touched the snail's face. The snail let out a humming sound, as if to indicate delight. Dan sat up and then struggled to stand. With the snail's head still lowered, Dan gently placed his hand on the creature's head for support; a slimy film was transferred to the teenager's hand. Now stabilized on his feet and sensing little, if any, fear, Dan limped to grab the two lances from the ground and started his walk toward the group that was now close by.

Sam and Jimmy reached Dan first with Cindy only a few feet behind.

While placing Dan's arm across his shoulder, Sam asked, "Are you alright?"

"I think so," answered Dan. "I don't think it meant me any harm."

"Nonetheless," advised Sam, "we'll not take any chances," as he took the two lances from his friend.

Dan looked over his shoulder and witnessed the giant snail feasting on its rapidly rotting serpent meal.

Jimmy, meanwhile, warily neared the giant snail to gather the cooking utensils, sleeping bags, and clothing which had fallen from the creature to the lakeshore. With Cindy's help, the two carried the gear to the campsite while Sam assisted Dan to the footpath.

Arriving at the campground, Sam gently lowered Dan to the ground, while Cindy and Jimmy unloaded the supplies. Heading for Dan's duffle bag, Cindy opened the first-aid kit and pulled out strapping cloth to wrap Dan's sprained ankle.

Once seated on the ground next to Dan, she asked, "What's the deal with you and your right ankle?"

In slight pain, Dan responded, "Just lucky, I guess."

Jimmy now joined Cindy and Sam at Dan's side, interested to learn of his adventure.

"There's not much to say," reported Dan. "The snail grabbed me by its mouth and then set me down. I know it sounds insane, but after a few moments, I didn't feel like I was in any real danger. Sure, I covered my face at first, but deep down, I never thought it intentionally wanted to harm me. After all, it could have very easily sprayed me, but it didn't."

After securing the strapping cloth with a fastener, Cindy rose, glared at Sam, and asked, "When can we leave this campsite?"

"I'm not sure," replied Sam. "Dan's in no condition to walk."

"But this place," replied Cindy, "the frogs ... and now the giant snail nearby ... I just don't feel safe."

Aware of Cindy's heightened anxiety, Sam replied, "I'll tell you what. Even though it's only"–Sam looked at his wrist watch–"3:00 in the afternoon, I'll relight the fire for our protection, have an early dinner, and then get a good night's sleep. If Dan's ankle is better in the morning, then we'll walk part of the day."

"Sam," suggested Jimmy, "even if Dan's ankle isn't better tomorrow, I'll help him along. I'm with Cindy; I'd like to move on."

Dan was torn. For as much as he wanted to move on and rescue William, he didn't want to be a burden to Jimmy and Sam who would, most likely, have to help him along the path the next day. In an effort to ease Cindy and Jimmy's anxieties, Dan predicted, "I'm sure my ankle will be better tomorrow. Actually, it doesn't hurt all that much right now."

Having seen Dan's partially swollen ankle before Cindy applied the strapping cloth, Sam knew that his young friend wouldn't be better the next day and that he was belittling his pain. While stepping to the path's border to gather firewood, Sam simply stated, "Let's start the fire and have a meal."

Since Dan was out of commission, Jimmy assumed the early dinner preparations.

After watching Jimmy drop a precooked hamburger to the ground, then covertly pick it up and throw it in the pan, Cindy remarked, "I'm really not that hungry."

"Nonsense," replied Sam, "we all have to eat to keep up our strength."

"May I have cereal instead of a hamburger?" pleaded Cindy.

"I suppose so, Cindy," replied Sam, "but I think you should reconsider a hamburger since there's not a lot left in our supplies. In a few days, you'll wish you had a hamburger."

In ten minutes, the meal was prepared. Heeding Sam's advice, but also hoping not to be offered the hamburger which fell to the ground, Cindy unwillingly handed her plate to Jimmy. Taking a bite of the warmed bunless burger, Cindy was actually surprised that it tasted pretty good. Dan's preoccupation in picking a pine needle from his hamburger distracted Cindy's thoughts of what may be hidden in the deeper forest.

After the meal, Sam jokingly asked, "Who'd like to clean the dishes at the lake?"

"Cindy will," replied Jimmy.

"Maybe Jimmy should," replied Cindy, "since he hasn't been injured yet."

"This conversation," informed Jimmy in a raised voice, "is injury enough for me."

"Alright, you two," said Sam. "If you keep making noises like that you'll attract the beasts of the forest." Just as Sam suspected and hoped, the two teenagers immediately ended their bickering.

The travelers spent the rest of the late afternoon and early evening hours reveling in light conversations. At 10:00, Sam suggested that everyone retire early, since the natural darkness of the forest was conducive to sleep. Sam volunteered to assume the first watch until midnight. After glancing at Dan, Sam approached the teenager and helped his young friend to his sleeping area.

"Thanks, Sam," said Dan.

"No problem," replied Sam.

As Sam was walking away, Dan blurted, "Hey, Sam, would you mind grabbing my Bible from my duffle bag and my lantern? I feel like reading a little tonight."

"Sure," answered Sam. Seconds later, Sam returned with the two items. "Don't read too long," cautioned Sam, "we don't want to drain the batteries; we may need the lantern in the days ahead."

"I packed extra batteries," informed Dan, "but no, I won't be long. Good night, Sam."

"Good night," replied Sam.

After resting his Bible on his chest, Dan surveyed the campsite. Jimmy had already nestled into his clean dry sleeping bag, Cindy was updating her daily log, and Sam was throwing extra timber on the fire. While lifting the Bible, Dan's index finger poked through one of the two lance holes in his sleeping bag. Suddenly it occurred to Dan that the four travelers were becoming a family away from home. He knew that any of his three friends would willingly risk their lives to save another member and that he would do the same for any and all of them. *What would my journey have been like alone?* Dan thought. *What was I thinking in attempting a solo trip? There's absolutely no way I would have made it even this far without any of them: Cindy, the surgeon and cook; Sam, the protective father figure; and Jimmy, the risk taker. But is it right to endanger their lives any further?* Dan shook his head, as if to dispel his rambling thoughts, and opened the Bible. He began reading silently, "There is no greater love than this: to lay down one's life for one's friends." After a few minutes reflecting on the verse, Dan struggled to read another passage, but eventually fatigue won out and the Bible fell to his side.

CHAPTER SIXTEEN
The Female Warrior

AT 5:00 A.M., SAM AND DAN WERE AWAKENED BY CINDY'S scream. Twenty feet in front of her and resting alongside Dan was the giant snail. Dan also was surprised and jolted when he opened his eyes and spotted the creature. Though Dan was startled, he wasn't frightened. Seeing the teenager stir, the snail lowered and rubbed its head against Dan, who returned the sign of friendship by patting its head. Jimmy ran from his patrol station, while Sam jumped from his sleeping bag and clutched his weapon which was resting beside him.

"No!" yelled Dan to Sam. "He's not here to harm us. Trust me, I know."

Slowly lowering his lance, Sam asked, "How do you know?"

"I don't know," answered Dan, "I just do."

Testing Dan's theory, Jimmy, who was now standing near the fire, lowered his lance to the forest floor and slowly advanced toward Dan and the snail.

"Jimmy," yelled Sam, "get back!"

The teenager continued his slow approach.

Sam raised his weapon again, while keeping an eye on Jimmy—just in case. Once within arm's reach of the snail, the beast very slowly and gently moved its head in Jimmy's direction. Jimmy carefully extended his hand and rubbed the beast's head. Again, the snail let out a slight purr. Jimmy was surprised how much slime was on his hand when he removed it from the creature. On seeing a successful exchange between Jimmy and the snail, Sam, once again, lowered his weapon and approached the snail.

"Go ahead, Sam," said Dan, "pet it."

"I don't know," replied Sam, "it's awfully slimy."

"Sam," said Jimmy, "this is the first friendly beast we've encountered in the forest. Who knows? It may end up saving our lives again in the future."

Sam extended his hand near the snail's head, but then quickly withdrew it. He attempted a second time, but again, failed to follow through. Finally, a third time he stuck out his hand. This time though, Jimmy grabbed Sam's arm and drew it to the snail that let out another faint purr.

"Well I'll be," said Sam, "it is a gentle creature."

By this time, Cindy had climbed out of her sleeping bag, but remained a distance away. After witnessing Jimmy and Sam touching the beast, she also tried to approach the snail, but only advanced a couple feet, and even this was with great trepidation. After several more failed attempts to approach the giant creature, the snail slowly advanced toward her. When the beast was within several feet of Cindy, the snail made a mighty grunt which frightened her. Cindy turned and was prepared to run from the creature, when she spotted a three-headed saber-toothed tiger on a sizeable slope to her right, crouched for an attack. Upon seeing the dreaded tiger, Sam raised his lance, while Jimmy snatched Dan's weapon at his feet and joined Sam in a sprint to Cindy's rescue. Dan did his best to hobble on his sprained ankle in Cindy's direction. Unlike the previous tiger, this beast showed no signs of hesitation. The tiger immediately sprang into the air toward Cindy, when quite suddenly, the snail aimed and released its deadly spray covering the large cat from its three noses to its tail. The effect was so instantaneous that by the time the tiger hit the ground only feet from Cindy, its life had expired and was rapidly decomposing.

Catching her breath, Cindy turned back around to witness the giant snail gently lowering its head to her. Without delay, Cindy advanced the few feet which were impossible only moments earlier, reached out to pet the gentle beast, and mumbled, "Thank you."

Sam and Jimmy ran the remaining steps to Cindy; Dan finished the last few feet on his knees. Not one at a time, but all at once, the travelers caressed the tame beast. There was no doubt in anyone's mind now that the snail did not intend to harm the group.

"Alright now," said Sam, "let's not spoil the creature," as he walked away and stepped off the path into the forest fringes to gather firewood.

Slowly removing his hand from the snail's face, Jimmy exclaimed, "My gosh, I can't get over the slime. Look... ." as he held his hand two feet away from the snail displaying a solid sheet of slime between his hand and the creature's face.

"Quit making fun of it," reprimanded Cindy.

"I'm not making fun of it," replied Jimmy, "I'm only telling ... I mean ... showing it like it is."

Sam had gathered a few timbers and was passing near the group when Dan asked, "Sam, can we keep it?"

Sam stopped in his tracks, turned to face Dan, and replied, "No; I think it'd be happier roaming the forest by itself than embarking on a mission with us four." Sam resumed his walk to the campfire.

Pretending that she didn't hear Sam's decisive no, Cindy asked, "Hey, what shall we name it?"

After a few seconds, Dan suggested, "How about Toby?"

"No," replied Cindy, "that's a guy's name and we don't even know if it's a male or a female."

"Then how about Slimy?" suggested Jimmy. "That's not a girl's or a guy's name."

Cindy thought, *I guess Slimy could be a guy's or girl's name and... well... it does fit its description.* Nodding her head, Cindy replied, "Alright, Slimy it is." While still petting the creature, Cindy looked up into the giant snail's face and asked, "How about Slimy?" To everyone's surprise, the snail lowered its head again; the three teenagers attributed this as a yes.

From the campfire was heard, "Come on you guys, let's get some breakfast," yelled Sam.

Jimmy and Cindy made for a fast walk to the fire, leaving Dan to limp alone.

"Hey," remarked Sam. "Would one of you help Dan?"

Cindy and Jimmy abruptly stopped in their tracks and glanced back at Dan.

"Sorry, Dan," confessed Cindy, "I guess I got all worked up with the snail and forgot about ... sorry."

Now standing on either side of Dan, Cindy and Jimmy helped their friend to the fire.

"So," asked Cindy, "how's your ankle today?"

"A little better," answered Dan.

"It doesn't look like you'll be able to walk on it today," voiced Jimmy.

"Well," replied Dan, "maybe not the whole day, but at least part of the day."

As the two lowered Dan to the forest floor near the fire, Sam overheard their conversation and added, "If your heart's set on walking, Dan, then after breakfast, I'll see if I can find a sturdy branch in the forest, whittle the top a bit, and see if it'll work as a crutch."

"Sam, that'd be great," replied Dan in a hopeful voice, "but do you think you can do it?"

"What kind of a question is that?" asked Sam. "If I didn't think I could do it, would I have volunteered?"

"I suppose not," answered Dan.

"But," admitted Sam, "since it will probably take a couple hours, we won't leave until later this morning."

"That's okay, Sam," replied Dan, "a late start is better than no start."

While pointing to the cereal boxes, Sam directed the group, "Grab your breakfast, while I continue working with this fire. It's purposely being difficult this morning."

The three teenagers filled their bowls with milkless cereal and began their meal. Glancing over her shoulder, Cindy noticed that Slimy hadn't moved. "Sam," asked Cindy, "why isn't Slimy eating its meal?"

"Slimy?" asked Sam. "Who's Slimy?"

"That's what we named the snail," replied Cindy.

"And that's the best you three could come up with?" inquired Sam.

"Actually," continued Cindy, "that was Jimmy's suggestion."

"Now," remarked Sam, "why doesn't that surprise me?" Sam tried one more time to resurrect the fire while saying, "I suppose that the snail isn't eating its kill because it has no teeth."

"Then why'd it kill the tiger?" asked Cindy.

"I'd suppose that the snail killed it to save you," replied Sam.

"Do you really think so?" asked Cindy.

"Well," remarked Sam, "I don't know why else it would have killed the tiger if it knew it couldn't eat a carcass with bones."

"But it ate the snake at the lakeshore," remarked Cindy, "and it had bones."

"But snake bones are flexible and much smaller," informed Sam, "which I suppose the snail can ingest; tiger bones are far too large and dense."

Cindy glanced back at Slimy.

With a gentle blow from Sam, the kindling eventually caught fire. "There, now we can have roasted marshmallows," said Sam.

The teenagers rolled their eyes.

Glancing across the reborn fire at Sam, Cindy asked, "Sam, what about something for Slimy?"

"Cindy, we don't have any food to spare," apprised Sam. "And besides, even if we gave it something, I can promise you that it wouldn't be enough. I mean, you saw it gorge that snake yesterday."

"Gross, Sam," said Jimmy, "not while we're eating."

"Sorry, boy," said Sam. "Anyway, Cindy, Slimy will head back to the lakefront when it's hungry."

By now, the fire was a roaring blaze. Jimmy leaned forward to grab four marshmallows from Dan's bag and lanced the second course of their meal.

"Wait a minute," blurted Sam.

Jimmy stopped, as if he'd done something wrong.

"With all the commotion this morning," alerted Sam, "we forgot to take our pills."

"Sam," said Jimmy, "what's the big deal if we miss a day?"

"Look, everyone," replied Sam, "we've been good so far at taking our pills everyday; but trust me, you don't want to experience the uncontrollable jitters like I did twenty years ago."

Cindy reached into her bag, pulled out four pills, and distributed them to her friends. After swallowing, Sam asked, "Dan, how'd you sleep last night?"

"Alright, I suppose," replied the teenager.

Just then, the memory of the invisible warm touch crossed Dan's mind. *Why didn't the invisible being pay me a visit last night?* thought Dan. He couldn't arrive at a logical explanation, other than perhaps the being didn't think the sprain was bad enough for a healing. *After all*, reasoned Dan, *it's only a sprain; I can still hike a short distance today.*

Once the meal was finished, the three teenagers cleaned the area, while Sam ventured into the woods to find a large branch worthy to become a crutch. Returning to the campsite thirty minutes later, Sam was surprised that no one was around. Looking at the dead saber-toothed tiger, his mind wandered and he feared the worst. Sam dropped the would-be crutch and yelled, "Dan ... Cindy ... Jimmy!" He checked the fringes of the footpath; but nothing. Surveying the forest floor at the edge of camp, he spotted a trail of slime leading in the direction of the lake. *After yesterday, surely they wouldn't follow Slimy back to the lake*, thought Sam. The older traveler grabbed his lance and followed the slime trail.

Even though the lake was not far from camp, it took Sam some time to reach the shore, since he diligently scanned the entire area of the forest with each footstep. Just as he was losing hope, he heard noises. Sam raced in the direction of the clamor. *Why*, thought Sam, *that sounds like laughter*. As he left the forest and touched foot on the lakeshore, he spotted the three teenagers riding the giant snail! Darting in their direction, he yelled, "What on earth are you doing? Get off that snail right now!" Sam's back was facing the water.

Eventually hearing Sam's command over their laughter, Dan, who was sitting atop the snail behind Cindy and Jimmy, turned and on seeing his co-traveler exclaimed, "Sam, get on!"

"I'll do no such thing," yelled Sam.

While still glancing in Sam's direction, Dan spotted several tentacles floating atop the lake and rapidly extending onto the shoreline.

"Sam!" yelled Dan. "Run!"

"I'm not falling for that, boy," responded an irate Sam. "Get off that beast now!"

Hearing Dan yelling near her ear, Cindy turned and also noticed

Sam; then she spotted an octopus-like creature's head resting on the water's surface near the shore revealing two bulging eyes on either side of its gray taut forehead. *That's weird for such a creature to inhabit fresh water*, thought Cindy, *but then again, this isn't home*. Noticing the encroaching tentacles, Cindy yelled, "Sam ... run!"

"Alright you three," yelled Sam, "you've had your...."

Sam couldn't get the word 'fun' out, before one of the tentacles wrapped itself around his waist with such force that he dropped his lance and fell face forward to the ground. The tentacles were unearthly enormous; a quick estimate led Dan to speculate that each feeler measured forty feet. Sam's attempts to stand were in vain; the beast was reeling in its next meal.

Cindy screamed, while Dan jumped from the snail, totally oblivious to his aching ankle. Fortunately, the teenage men were armed. Dan raced toward Sam, who was slowly being dragged to the water's edge, while Cindy snatched Jimmy's lance from his hand and leaped to the lakeshore.

Immediately, Jimmy glanced to his side and saw his two friends racing on the shore toward Sam. "Oh, my God," said Jimmy, as he spotted the lake creature and jumped from the gentle giant.

Dan, who arrived at Sam's side first, was violently spearing the tentacle wrapped around Sam's waist, but with only minimal results.

Cindy approached from behind and joined Dan in lancing the weakening limb.

Dan had only sunk his lance into the tentacle several times, when a second feeler raised itself from the lakeshore, ensnared Dan's neck, and dragged him several feet away, shooting his glasses into the air and his lance to the ground. While gasping for air and hopelessly attempting to release the beast's death grip, Dan felt another tentacle grab his right ankle. Quite unexpectedly, the two tentacles savagely pulled against each other; the beast was attempting to rip the teenager in half. Dan tried to scream, but it was all he could do to barely breathe. Although unable to yell for help, Dan's pain was excruciating. His rib cage was being twisted from side to side, while his intestines ultimately discovered unfamiliar areas within their cavity wall.

While trying to free Sam, Cindy glanced behind and witnessed Dan's fatal predicament. Without knowing from where her strength came, Cindy delivered one powerful thrust of the lance into the feeler, completely severing it and releasing Sam.

The powerful and pursuing tentacles prevented Jimmy from arriving until only now.

Cindy, while rushing to Dan's aid, yelled to Jimmy, "Pull Sam into the forest ... now!"

Jimmy grabbed an unconscious Sam by the arms and pulled him to safety next to Slimy. Racing back to the shore only a few minutes later, Jimmy stopped in his tracks and was astounded. Cindy, who was already clutching one lance, picked up Dan's spear from the ground and was wielding both weapons simultaneously: one at the tentacle around Dan's neck and the other at the beast's limb around his ankle, while also dodging an oncoming tentacle which was determined to capture the female warrior. With four mighty blows, she dismembered the tentacle around her friend's neck; Dan gasped for air, but wasn't free yet. The feeler around his ankle, while severely mangled from Cindy's precise and persistent thrusts, was still deadly. The moment Dan's neck was free, the second tentacle began dragging the teenager by the ankle nearer and nearer the waterfront.

Seeing Jimmy approach from delivering Sam to safety, Cindy tossed him one of her weapons to repel a wandering tentacle which was heading in his direction; Cindy dashed to the shore after Dan.

The gray, penetrating eyes from the beast just above the water's surface, only feet out, sensing peril with Cindy, summoned its remaining limbs to distract and attack the merciless slayer on the shore, until its already-captured prey was successfully submerged beneath the cold waters.

Cindy was enraged.

While successfully avoiding the oncoming tentacles' ruthless pursuit to ensnare her, she eventually reached Dan the moment his boots touched the water's edge. Now on her knees and with both hands firmly gripping her weapon, Cindy raised her arms over her head and came down on the gripping tentacle with such force, that her lance pinned the feeler to the bed of the lake. The tentacle surrendered its victim.

Several feet back, Jimmy had successfully deterred the advance of an approaching tentacle and was now dashing to his friends at the shoreline. At Cindy's order, Jimmy quickly pulled Dan from the water's edge and dragged him next to Sam, well out of the deadly tentacles' reach.

Cindy rose to her feet and glared into the gray, cold eyes of the beast floating above the water. The tentacles receded from the shore as the head submerged below the still waters.

As she turned to leave the shoreline, Cindy spotted Dan's glasses partially buried in the moist soil from the struggle. Bending over to unearth them, she hoped that they were still in one piece, since she knew that without them in this world, Dan would be an easy target. Miraculously, they were intact. While clutching her lance, Cindy glanced to the forest's edge and saw Jimmy standing watch over Sam and Dan. *The lance*, thought Cindy. She scanned up and down the shoreline visually searching for Sam's lost weapon. *We can't afford to lose a single lance*, her thoughts continued, *they're crucial to our safety.* At last, she discovered Sam's lance a fair distance ahead. Upon retrieving the weapon, she raced to the group. En route, Cindy noticed that Slimy, obviously hungry, was inching itself away from the three men to its familiar camouflage spot.

Sam remained unconscious. Dan was awake and alert, but in severe pain from neck to ankle.

Looking at her injured teenage friend, Cindy asked, "How're you feeling?"

"I've felt better," replied Dan, with great effort.

Cindy handed him his glasses. As he raised his arm to accept his lenses, Cindy knew by the expression on his face that even this small task was extremely painful for him. With just one look at Dan's shredded pant leg, which she had only recently mended, Cindy realized that the battle was worse than even she suspected. "Let's get back to the campsite," urged Cindy.

"Yeah," replied Jimmy, "I think that's a good idea."

While resting on the ground, Dan asked with labored breaths, "How's Sam?"

"He's unconscious," answered Cindy, "but I think he'll be alright. Time will tell."

Looking at Jimmy, Cindy proposed, "Let's see if we can carry Sam back to camp."

"Okay," replied Jimmy, as he bent over to lift Sam.

Even though Sam weighed approximately 175 pounds, it was 175 pounds of dead weight, which would explain Cindy and Jimmy's arduous task of raising Sam to his feet. After several unsuccessful attempts, they finally managed to secure one of Sam's arms across Cindy's shoulder and his other arm around Jimmy's shoulder.

"Dan," asked Cindy, "are you able to hop?"

"Sure," replied Dan, as he grabbed Jimmy's waist to pull himself up and began hobbling alongside the group, while maintaining a firm grip on Jimmy's arm for balance.

As the four hiked through the brief, but dense, forest to the campsite, two parallel furrows were etched into the semi-moist soil from Sam's boots as he was dragged through the woods.

Along the path to safety, Jimmy commented, "The way I figure it, if Sam's okay, then the three of us are dead."

"Yeah," replied Dan, while still breathing with difficulty. "When Sam comes to and realizes that this was all our fault, we're all dead."

Cindy voiced the same sentiments.

"Cindy," asked Dan, "where on earth did you learn to wield a lance like that? I mean, I kind of felt sorry for the octopus—or whatever it was."

"Yeah," seconded Jimmy, "it's like the lances became an extension of your arm. What's up with that?"

"I don't know," admitted Cindy. "I've never taken a self-defense class or anything like that. Heck, the only sport I ever played was volleyball, and that was in grade school. I guess when I saw Sam fighting for his life and then Dan being twisted by that thing, my blood boiled and I got enraged. I remember saying to myself, 'How dare you threaten me and my friends.' Or who knows, maybe it was just my adrenaline kicking into overdrive."

Jimmy turned his head slightly to make eye contact with Cindy and conceded, "I'm glad you're on our side."

Arriving at the campsite, Cindy and Jimmy paused briefly to let Dan switch his hand from Jimmy's arm to a low-hanging branch. Once the first passenger was released, Cindy and Jimmy dragged Sam to his sleeping area and gently set him alongside his sleeping bag. Jimmy unzipped the bag and placed Sam inside.

"Cindy," said Jimmy, "it might be a good idea to get a fire started, maybe cook a meal, and ... well, clean up the campsite a bit. Then, maybe Sam won't be as upset when he wakes up."

"Actually, that's not a bad idea," replied Cindy, "but first, I need to sterilize Sam's waist."

On overhearing their conversation, Dan–who was now sitting on the ground–crawled near Sam's backpack and rolled the alcohol bottle in Cindy's direction.

"Jimmy," said Cindy, "can you remove his shirt?"

"What?" asked Jimmy. "Oh, sure."

As Cindy feared, the powerful suction cups on the underside of the beast's tentacle had torn flesh, leaving the area prone to severe infection. As she poured the medication, Sam twitched, but did not awaken. Curiously, when she applied the alcohol to his shoulder and upper arm–the trophies of the saber-toothed tiger encounter–Sam didn't squirm. His upper torso was well on the road to recovery. Cindy was just about to return the cap to the bottle when she remembered Dan. Rising to her feet, she approached her friend, who had only recently crawled to his area and was resting comfortably–or so he let on–in his sleeping bag. Seeing her near him from the corner of his eye, and carrying the bottle, Dan closed his eyes.

Strongly suspecting a charade, Cindy knelt on the ground beside him and said, "Dan, it doesn't matter to me; sleeping or not, you and the bottle have a date."

Dan opened his eyes and reluctantly removed his right leg from the sleeping bag. The lower half of his pant leg was so mangled that Cindy didn't need to pull it up. Rather, she tore what few threads remained. Even Dan's white tube sock was twisted to shreds, much like his earlier sock from the tiger's tail.

Dan's injuries were far worse than Sam's. Perhaps it was because the creature had a grip on Dan for a longer period of time or possibly because Dan was yanked to the water's edge by his ankle. Whatever the reason, skin was brutally ripped from his mid-calf to his ankle. Cindy dreaded what she knew she had to do. There was no doubt in her mind that the pain would be so intense that Dan would lose consciousness. For a brief moment, she thought, *My gosh, if the school bullies could see Dan right now–completely calm, but yet in obvious pain–they* wouldn't believe their eyes. He's got more guts and courage than anyone I've ever known. If only Malice and Sur could see him now.* Dan's sudden cough drew Cindy from her thoughts to the patient below her.

"Let's take a look at your neck," said Cindy. After removing his mangled shirt, Cindy noticed, once again, a severe loss of skin, though not as bad as his leg. She hesitated, for Cindy knew that if she didn't administer the cure-all, he'd most probably die of infection before the next full moon. At the same time, she also knew that once she disinfected his injuries it was highly likely that he'd slip into unconsciousness or even worse, a coma. While Cindy was debating her course of action, Jimmy was attempting to re-ignite the campfire. Cindy yelled for Jimmy.

From the corner of his eye, the fire keeper noticed Cindy motioning him to her side. The teenager jumped to his feet and approached, but not before taking a close look at Sam, who remained unconscious.

Once Jimmy was standing over Cindy and her patient, she rose, grabbed Jimmy's arm and led him away a few feet out of Dan's earshot. "Find a thick piece of wood about six inches long for Dan to bite on," ordered Cindy.

A look of terror invaded Dan's eyes; he overheard and he knew that he was in for a wild ride. Within minutes, Jimmy returned with a sturdy branch which was far too long, but the perfect diameter. Jimmy broke off a six-inch piece against his knee and handed it to Cindy. However, before accepting the teeth grinder, Cindy straightened Dan's sleeping bag and fluffed his small pillow. She strongly suspected that shortly after the regimen, he'd pass out and she wanted him to be as comfortable as possible.

After accepting the wooden mouthpiece from Jimmy, Cindy held it near her patient's mouth and instructed, "Dan, this may sting a bit, so I want you to bite down on this. Understand?"

Amid his waning strength, Dan admitted, "Last time you said it might hurt ... well ... it hurt like hell."

Looking into Dan's eyes, Cindy acknowledged, "Yeah, you're right; I'm not going to lie. It's going to hurt like hell again. But we have to do it; I'm sorry."

Knowing that Cindy was only trying to save his life, Dan honestly and boldly ordered, "Go ahead; do it."

The mouthpiece was inserted. Cindy gestured Jimmy to slip behind Dan and then directed him to press both hands on Dan's shoulders. Cindy held the bottle directly over Dan's calf, nearly parallel to the ground, but intentionally did not pour. She looked directly overhead, as if something was lurking in the trees. Instinctively, Dan looked heavenward. While keeping her chin reaching for the sky, Cindy's eyes glanced downwards. Noticing that Dan's gaze and mind were lost in the trees, she tilted her hand and released the cleansing agent. Even with the timber in his mouth, a deafening sound of agony echoed through the murky forest, as Dan overpowered Jimmy's grip on his shoulders and rose slightly off his back. The cry of anguish lasted several seconds. Then, all was quiet as Dan's eyes shut and he dropped to his sleeping bag. Putting his hand over Dan's heart, Jimmy was relieved to feel a soft beat. While removing the timber from his mouth, Cindy and Jimmy were awestruck: the branch had been bitten in two. With the patient unconscious, Cindy soaked Dan's entire leg and neck, and then covered the wounds with a new supply of homemade bandages. Glancing over her shoulder, Cindy was amazed that even after Dan's loud cry of pain, Sam had not stirred. Once Jimmy left Dan's side, Cindy brushed back Dan's hair on his forehead and whispered, "I'm sorry."

Slowly rising to her feet, Cindy stared at the brave young man for a moment and then walked toward the soon-to-be campfire, once Jimmy perfected his technique.

"Jimmy," blurted Cindy, once she was standing over him, "you need to start the fire with kindling wood, not that big stump."

"I thought I'd take a short cut," defended Jimmy.

"You and your short cuts," warned Cindy, "will get us all killed one day."

Cindy didn't even wait for a response as she walked to the edge of the trail and gathered dried leaves and small decaying twigs for the fire. Returning to her friend, she set her collection on the ground inside the stones which bordered the previous fire, took the lighter from Jimmy, and in no time, a roaring fire was ablaze.

"You're determined to be the best at everything, aren't you?" asked Jimmy.

Ignoring Jimmy's accusation, Cindy uttered, "I wonder if Dan will pull through."

"Pull through?" asked Jimmy. "Of course he'll pull through; he's a fighter. Anyway, you shouldn't be talking like that."

"I know," admitted Cindy, "but I've never seen so much skin ripped off a person's body, at least not as much as Dan's missing on his leg. It took everything in me to disinfect it. I don't think I could do it again, especially after seeing the pain he endured."

"Cindy," replied Jimmy, "if we don't treat his leg again, it'll get infected, and then what?"

Attempting to dismiss the inevitable next dousing from her mind, Cindy suggested, "I'll start cleaning up the area, so at least we'll have a bit of good news for Sam when he wakes up. While I'm cleaning, why don't you make a little lunch?"

"Sure," joked Jimmy, "maybe I'll eat Sam and Dan's portion."

"Absolutely not," snapped Cindy. "This food has to last us a long time."

Opening the bag which contained the rations, Cindy realized that the time was rapidly approaching when someone would have to hunt. The mere thought of advancing deeper into the woods made her tremble.

Noticing Cindy taking inventory, Jimmy asked, "What about the juice and water? Are we running low?"

"I'm afraid so," answered Cindy. "But after seeing what lives in the lake, I don't think we should drink any of that water anyway."

"But we have to drink something," said Jimmy, "we've got a long time in this world before the next full moon."

Thinking back to her Girl Scout days, Cindy proposed, "Well, I guess we could boil the water; but who in their right mind would put their hand in the lake? Let's wait until Sam wakes up and ask him, maybe he'll have a solution."

For thirty minutes or so, Cindy busied herself tidying up the sleep areas and reorganizing the backpacks, while periodically checking on her two patients. In the midst of her chores, she neared Jimmy who was warming two hotdogs and asked, "What are we going to do with that decaying tiger? It's already beginning to smell."

"I don't know," answered Jimmy. "Hopefully, Sam and Dan will regain consciousness tomorrow. And when they do, we'll probably leave the campsite, assuming they're able to walk. So, let's just leave it alone for now," ended Jimmy.

"I only hope the tiger's relatives don't discover that it's missing until we're long gone," declared Cindy.

Resuming her tasks, Cindy took two of the last few water bottles and placed one next to Sam and the other beside Dan. She surmised that when they awoke, they'd be dehydrated. Cindy hoped that Sam would awaken that afternoon and not tomorrow as Jimmy suspected; and Dan ... well ... she hoped he'd wake up sometime. Looking at her teenage friend, she thought, *Dan was–and still is–prepared to suffer and sacrifice virtually anything to rescue William; and he never seems to get a break. Out of the four of us, he's probably suffered the worst.*

From behind was heard, "Cindy, lunch is ready." Cindy bent down to pull Dan's sleeping bag over his shoulders; a damp wind had arrived.

The lunch was consumed in near complete silence. During the meal, it became painfully obvious to Cindy and Jimmy that no one would survive the perilous journey without the help of the others. Each person complemented the other.

While swallowing the last bite of hotdog, Cindy nearly choked when Jimmy volunteered to clean the dishes as best he could without water. Knowing that Cindy was completely exhausted, Jimmy suggested, "Why don't you take a nap? We're obviously not going any further today and your patients will still be where they are when you awake."

"I suppose you're right," responded Cindy, "just promise to wake me if either Sam or Dan stirs."

"I promise," said Jimmy.

Cindy handed her dirty plate to Jimmy and then proceeded to her sleeping area. After the mess kits were cleaned, Jimmy opted on watching the two patients while stretched out upon his sleeping bag. Unfortunately, his eyelids proved too heavy as he–like Cindy only minutes earlier–fell into a deep sleep.

Overly fatigued, Jimmy slept until 3:00 in the afternoon, when he was jolted from his nap by loud and continuous growling noises. Sitting up in his sleeping bag, his eyes were drawn to an uproar at the corner of the campsite, roughly twenty feet away. *What the heck?* he thought.

Fighting for the free tiger meat were … two … three … five… six forest moles, each obviously cursed with a ferocious appetite, each measuring four feet in length, and each displaying razor-sharp incisors, as Jimmy witnessed the barbaric mammals effortlessly rip the carcass of the saber-toothed tiger to shreds.

With the forest's perpetual darkness, the moles never ventured underground except to escape a larger predator or to avoid the torrential rains.

While staring at the six moles, Jimmy noticed one of the rodents rotate its furry neck and glare at him. Taking no chances at surrendering its portion of the meal, the mole charged five feet in Jimmy's direction, displayed its bloody teeth and then inched its way backwards to the group. The sounds of tearing and growling caused Cindy to stir. Looking to the edge of camp, she also spotted the scavengers and let out a slight gasp, but didn't scream.

While remaining motionless, Jimmy whispered, "Shush."

For creatures with underdeveloped eyes and covered in fur, thought Cindy, *they can obviously see the slightest movement and hear the faintest noise.*

Knowing that his lance was at arm's reach, Jimmy attempted to snatch the weapon, in the event the predators became territorial. Jimmy had barely extended his hand, when the mole that first threatened him, came charging full speed. Jimmy grabbed the lance just in time to repel the advancing creature. Fortunately for Jimmy, the other five moles were engrossed in their meal. As much as Cindy wanted to help Jimmy, she knew that if she did, the remaining burrowing mammals would be upon her and the sleeping patients. Nevertheless, while remaining motionless for Dan and Sam's sake, she scanned the area, strategizing her line of attack to help Jimmy. As she moved her eyes–not her head–to the group of moles, she noticed that all five were indulging themselves, oblivious to the stray mole. Returning her gaze to Jimmy, she was surprised at the stamina and determination of the rodent. Its persistent offensive movements, however, had forced Jimmy to slide backwards on the seat of his pants little by little, until he was trapped between the rushing mole and two massive trees directly behind. There was no retreat. When the mole swung its head in Cindy's direction–caused by a sharp blow to its face from Jimmy's lance–she got a clear glimpse of its long teeth and pointed snout. After backtracking several feet, the mole–amid a loud and violent snarl–made one final charge at Jimmy.

Cindy bolted from her sleeping bag and was diving for her lance when a shot was heard.

Sam had awakened and decided to end the ceaseless uproar with a shot from his revolver. With the rodent still painfully struggling toward Jimmy, another shot was fired. As the creature collapsed to the soil only feet from Jimmy, the five remaining moles took notice. But sensing no immediate threat to their carcass, they redirected their attention to the dead tiger and resumed their feast.

So as not to startle the moles, Cindy and Jimmy cautiously neared Sam who was sitting up in his sleeping bag with his revolver aimed at the five rodents.

"Sam," whispered Jimmy, "you're awake!"

Sam remained silent, as he was still focused on the moles. Eventually, he replied, "Yeah, thanks to the noise you two have been making."

"Sorry," said Cindy.

Jimmy and Cindy looked at each other, both hoping the other would start the dreaded conversation. After a second long stare, Cindy spoke up, "Sam, we owe you an apology."

"Go on," replied Sam, without removing his sights or aim from the deadly rodents.

"Well," explained Cindy, "we didn't mean to run off with Slimy ... it just sort of happened. But, I promise, it'll never happen again."

"Yeah," replied Jimmy, "never."

At that moment, Sam was more furious than he was in pain. Finally removing his stare from the moles which were scurrying into the forest, Sam lowered his revolver, looked at the two teenagers, and reproved, "Don't you know what could have happened to you? You put your own lives at risk."

"Sam," said Cindy, "we're really sorry."

Sam thought it was best not to continue the conversation any further. After all, his point was made and hopefully heeded. Noticing Dan in his sleeping bag and recalling his heroic act at the lakeshore, Sam asked, "How's Dan?"

"Not good, I'm afraid," replied Cindy, who was now looking at Dan.

"How bad is he?" continued Sam.

Cindy took a deep breath and explained, "Virtually all the skin from his mid-calf to his ankle has been ripped off, as well as a large amount of flesh around his neck. I had no choice but to disinfect it, and the pain was so excruciating that he slipped into unconsciousness."

"Do you think he'll pull through?" asked Sam.

"I hope so," answered Cindy, "but I'm just not sure when. We need to keep a close eye on him. When he does wake up, he probably should stay off his feet for a couple days."

Sam rubbed the palm of his long slender hand against his cheek while thinking of Dan's situation and then commented, "When he wakes up, he's not going to like the idea of losing valuable hiking days; but what's the point in risking his life to save William's, who may or may not be in the castle?" After offering a passing glance at the tiger's defleshed bones and the lifeless mole, Sam continued, "You know, we wouldn't be in this predicament if you three hadn't wandered off."

Attempting to prevent a further admonishment from Sam, Jimmy interjected, "We cleaned the campsite."

Cindy looked at Jimmy in complete disgust.

CHAPTER SEVENTEEN
Dual Hunt

BY 5:00 THAT AFTERNOON, CINDY HAD, FOR THE THIRD TIME that day, disinfected Dan's wounds and reapplied the homemade bandages; and Jimmy and Sam had successfully relocated the expired mole to the woods. Noticing the time, Sam suggested that they prepare dinner.

"Speaking of dinner," said Jimmy, "I think we're running low on food."

"Yeah," replied Sam, "I noticed that the other day."

While watching Jimmy throw another log atop the fire, Sam suggested, "Since we won't be hiking tomorrow, maybe I should go hunting."

"Yeah," replied Jimmy, "and maybe I should join you."

"Absolutely not," insisted Sam, "you're to remain at camp to protect Dan and Cindy."

"But, Sam," pleaded Jimmy, "I could ... "

"I said no," interrupted Sam.

Knowing that the likelihood of encountering a creature in the deeper forest was greater than at the campsite, Cindy, who was sitting at Dan's side several feet behind Sam, turned and remarked, "Sam, Dan and I will be fine near the fire; I think you should take Jimmy along."

With great reluctance, Sam asked, "Are you sure, Cindy?"

"We'll be fine," replied Cindy.

"This will be fun!" exclaimed Jimmy.

"Fun?" contested Sam. "I hardly call putting our lives in danger in an unknown forest 'fun'."

After putting the finishing touches on Dan's bandages, Cindy glanced over her shoulder again and added, "Sam, I also noticed that we're running low on water." Although fearful of the lake's creatures, Cindy knew that the group would not survive long without water. She proposed, "Sam, should I gather some water from the lake tomorrow while you and Jimmy are hunting?"

Sam immediately spun around and yelled, "I never want you or anyone near that lake again! Is that understood?"

Both Jimmy and Cindy froze; they never heard Sam use that tone of voice. Regretting his tone, but not his message, Sam confessed, "Sorry, I didn't mean to yell. I just don't want anything harmful happening to any of you. I couldn't live with myself, because … well … you're kind of like family now, and besides, Dan and I need your help to make it to the castle."

Jimmy, knowing that it was difficult for Sam to admit what he just did, reconfirmed, "We're like family?"

Sam paused, shook his head, and corrected, "I said kind of," as he wandered to his sleeping area. Away from the teenagers, Sam was now free to reveal the intense pain he was experiencing from his injury at the lake. He closed his eyes and gritted his teeth. Upon opening his eyes, he glanced back at Dan resting near the fire and couldn't imagine the pain he would endure once he awoke. Sam remained hopeful, however, that slumber would speed Dan's recovery and that a good night's sleep would ease his own pain before tomorrow's hunt.

Within fifteen minutes, Jimmy yelled, "Dinner's ready."

Hotdogs, chips, cookies, and the last of the juice were on the night's menu. In Dan's absence, Cindy led the group in prayer. After the blessing, the conversation about supplies resumed.

"Sam," said Cindy, "I know you don't want us near the lake, but we'll need water soon."

"I know," acknowledged Sam.

"So," continued Cindy, "how are we going to get water from the lake without getting near it?"

Sam surveyed the area; his eyes lit up. "See that plastic cookie container over there?" as he pointed near Dan's duffle bag.

"Yeah," replied Cindy.

"Well," proposed Sam, "I could rope two lances together, end to end, and then run the lance through the handle of the container. Granted, I'd still be near the water, but at least not directly above it."

"That might work," replied Cindy.

"Might?" questioned Sam. "Of course it'll work."

After the meal, Sam was surprised, like Cindy earlier, when Jimmy volunteered to clean up. Sam observed, as he initially did a couple days earlier, that Jimmy was slowly coming around and becoming a team player.

After a few hours of story telling around the campfire and updating Sam on the group's skirmishes at the lake, Sam remarked, "I suggest we all get a good night's sleep and then tomorrow we'll restock our food and water supplies. And who knows, maybe tomorrow Dan will awake. One more thing; since we're near the lake, I think we should resume our night patrols and treat Dan's wounds at the beginning of each shift."

"And your injuries," interjected Cindy.

Sam reluctantly agreed to the teenager's suggestion.

Cindy accepted the first two and a half-hour duty, followed by Jimmy, and then Sam. Throughout the watches of the night and early morning, not a single unusual incident occurred, which Sam suspected was rather peculiar for the forest. The only newsworthy item occurred during the second shift. As Jimmy poured whiskey on Dan's neck and leg, the patient stirred momentarily. Dan, though still in much pain, was going to be okay. Jimmy slept easier knowing that his friend would recover.

The following morning, the three travelers gathered around the campfire by 8:00 where Jimmy updated his friends on Dan's progress. Unfortunately, Dan had not stirred since the second shift. First on the menu were the pills, which the three travelers washed down with their rapidly depleting water supply. Even to Jimmy, the dry cereal was becoming boring, but at least it quelled his hunger pangs.

Before finishing her meager meal, Cindy left the campfire and neared Dan's sleeping area. Sensing her uneasiness, Sam followed.

"Cindy," said Sam, "what's wrong?"

"Nothing," snapped Cindy, as she knelt at Dan's side.

DUAL HUNT

"Cindy," prodded Sam, "what's wrong?"

"It's just..." mumbled Cindy. While staring at the motionless Dan, she nervously asked, "How long do you think you'll be hunting today?"

"I'm not really sure," replied Sam. "Why?"

"No reason," said Cindy, "curiosity, I suppose." Glancing up at Sam, she warned, "Just be careful."

Detecting a look of fear building in her eyes, Sam asked, "Cindy, would you rather Jimmy stay here with you?"

"No, Sam," replied Cindy, "you'll have better luck at the hunt with an extra man."

"Cindy," comforted Sam, "after the story Jimmy told me last night over the campfire on how the lake creature retreated once you mangled a few of its tentacles, I don't think you have anything to worry about."

Wanting not to unduly alarm Sam, Cindy confidently replied, "I'll be okay. Just don't be gone too long."

Picking up the crutch which Sam had whittled for Dan the previous night, Jimmy left the campfire and approached the group using the wooden support. "Hey, not bad," admitted Jimmy, "but it's pretty painful under the arm."

Reaching for a torn shirt which she hadn't had time to mend, Cindy wrapped it atop the crutch. "Now try it," she said.

"Wow," replied Jimmy, "that's a lot better."

After taking the crutch from Jimmy and setting it beside Dan's sleeping bag, Sam advised, "Jimmy, we'll be leaving on our hunting expedition in a few minutes, so gather your things. But first, there's something I need to do."

The sixty-year-old traveler walked to his sleeping area and pulled a cord of rope from his oversize backpack. After snatching two lances from the forest floor next to his sleeping bag, he returned to the campfire. Sitting upon a log, Sam created his water collection bucket in no time at all. "There," he said to himself, "this ought to work out nicely. I'll try it out after the hunt."

During Sam's construction project, Jimmy had crawled back into his sleeping bag. Glancing at the teenager, an irritated Sam yelled, "Come on boy, let's go."

Jimmy dragged himself from his sleeping gear and grabbed his lance, while Sam grabbed a lance, his revolver, and his bow and quiver.

"Alright, Cindy," said Sam, "we'll be back as soon as we can. Wish us luck on the hunt."

"Be careful," warned Cindy.

"We will," said Jimmy, as he turned and tripped over his lance.

Cindy silently watched the two men depart, until the thick darkness in the distance surrounded them. She then focused her attention on Dan, who remained motionless but, thankfully, was breathing. Thinking it would be best to keep busy and not dwell on what inhabited the nearby woods, Cindy decided to clean the dishes with a knife and no water, but not before grabbing her lance from her sleeping area and keeping it at arm's reach until the two hunters returned.

It was Sunday morning in both worlds. In one world, a hunt for food was taking place, while in the other world, a hunt of another kind had begun. Jeff Clay was hunting for his wife's Sunday Prayer Book. After thoroughly searching the den, where Nancy usually stored the missal, Jeff decided to check their bedroom. *Maybe she's been reading it during the week*, he thought.

Entering their bedroom, he was surprised to see his wife still in bed. "Honey," said Jeff, "get up or we'll be late for Mass."

"Jeff," replied Nancy, "I'm not going to church today." Not wanting to alarm her husband, she never told him that yesterday morning, a little before noon, she had begun to experience acute pain in her neck and lower right leg.

"Honey," implored Jeff, "please, for Dan; he needs our prayers."

Jeff had taken Father James' advice to attend weekday Mass. Actually, he had not missed Friday or Saturday's daily Mass since the good priest's suggestion on Thursday morning. Nancy, however, never left her bed.

"Do you think I haven't been praying for Dan?" asked Nancy. "I've been praying for him nonstop, ever since I learned of his disappearance. It's just that I've been praying from bed."

Jeff took a moment to quickly scan the top of the dresser and desk for the Prayer Book, but discovered nothing.

Doing his best not to unduly upset his wife, Jeff asked again, but in a softer voice, "Nancy, for Dan, will you come to Mass?" Sensing that an approval might be forthcoming, Jeff quickly added, "Tell you what; you get cleaned up and dressed and I'll look for your Prayer Book."

"Alright," conceded Nancy. Sitting up in bed, she informed, "My Prayer Book's in the den."

"No, it's not," replied Jeff, "I already looked and it's not there."

Climbing out of bed, Nancy stated, "Well, that's odd; I always store my Prayer Book on the first bookshelf in the den. Why don't you look again?"

Since his wife had agreed to go to Mass, he figured the least he could do was check the den again. "Alright," said Jeff, "I'll check again while you're cleaning up."

Nancy entered the bathroom, while Jeff entered the hallway en route to the den downstairs for one last look. As he expected, there was no trace of the Prayer Book. Perplexed, Jeff returned to the bedroom.

At 9:45, Nancy was nearly ready for church. As she was brushing her hair, she asked, "Jeff, did you find my missal?"

"No," replied her husband, "it's just not there."

"I wonder where it could be?" she asked.

"Well," said Jeff, "we're running late; I'll search later today."

Just then, both jumped when a loud clap of thunder was heard.

"Honey," suggested Nancy, "you better get the umbrellas."

Opening their closet door, Jeff discovered his wife's yellow umbrella, but then asked, "Where's my umbrella?"

"Oh," replied his wife, "it's probably in... ." Nancy stopped short.

"It's probably where?" asked Jeff.

Stepping two feet back to sit on the unmade bed, Nancy continued, "It's probably in Dan's closet."

"What's it doing in there?" asked Jeff.

"He borrowed it a couple weeks ago during a thunderstorm," informed Nancy. "He probably threw it in his closet."

Jeff walked from their closet to the bed, sat beside his wife, and while putting his arm around her waist, said, "I'm sure he'll be home soon."

Nancy blew her nose and then reassured, "I'm fine; go get your umbrella."

Jeff hesitated, but eventually left his wife's side and entered Dan's room. After discovering his umbrella in the closet, Jeff glanced to his left and spotted Nancy's Prayer Book on Dan's dresser. "I wonder what it's doing in here," Jeff said to himself. Picking up the missal, he stepped into the hallway to meet his wife who was standing outside their bedroom door with her purse in hand. "Honey," said Jeff, while displaying his wife's missal, "look what I found on Dan's dresser."

Nancy took the book from Jeff, saying, "How did it end up there?"

Jeff shrugged his shoulders and then escorted his wife down the stairs to the garage.

The short drive to church proved to be mental torture for Nancy. Passing the library, she recalled how often in the past few months Dan had frequented the House of Learning. Around the corner was the high school, bringing to mind Dan's disappointment in not receiving the scholarship. Then the diner slowly came into view, as Nancy recalled eating there with Jeff, Dan, and Sam White just last Sunday. For Nancy, arriving at the church could not have come any sooner.

While helping his wife from the car, Jeff remarked, "Remember, after Mass we'll pray with Father James below the statue of Saint Michael the Archangel for Dan and the others' safe return."

Nancy only nodded.

As they entered the church, a great relief came over Nancy. In God's house, she felt a peace she hadn't experienced since before last week's heartbreaking news. Walking down the aisle, the Clays stopped, genuflected, and entered the fifth pew–as was customary. Kneeling to offer prayers, Nancy, for the first time, was at a loss for words. She desperately wanted to pray, but couldn't. Nancy rose from her knees and sat in the pew, while Jeff remained on his knees beseeching God to shield Dan and the others and to lead them home safely.

Jeff's silent prayer was interrupted by Father James, who was walking down the aisle from the back of the church. On spotting the Clays, the priest stopped briefly and rested his hand upon Jeff's shoulder.

"I'm so glad you're both here," remarked Father James.

"Thank you, Father," replied Jeff.

Nancy greeted the priest with a simple nod; no words were spoken.

"I want you to know that I'll remember Dan in a special way during this Mass," added Father James.

Again, "Thank you, Father," voiced Jeff.

"I'll meet you after Mass at the statue of Saint Michael," ended the priest.

"We'll be there," replied Jeff.

Father James proceeded to the altar.

Knowing that she should pray, but unable to compose her own personal prayer, Nancy opened her Prayer Book to the section entitled, 'Common Prayers' and began reciting the 'Memorare' to herself. As Nancy was silently pronouncing the words,

> "Remember, O most gracious Virgin Mary, that never was it known that anyone who fled to thy protection, implored thy help, or sought thy intercession was left unaided," [2]

she noticed an unusual bookmark. Flipping to the page which held the small piece of paper, Nancy unfolded it. As she began to read the message, she fell forward against the shoulder of her husband, who was still kneeling.

Concerned for his wife's safety and mental health, Jeff clasped her wrist and asked, "Are you alright?"

There was no response; Nancy was reading the note. Jeff glimpsed the brief letter and nearly fell out of the pew. Together, they silently read Dan's message penned several days earlier:

Mom and Dad,

By the time you read this letter, I will undoubtedly have been

> reported missing. I'm fine, believe me. Please don't exhaust your time or money on trying to locate me, for I am nowhere to be found. I wish I could tell you exactly where I am, but for safety reasons, I cannot. I will return on the evening of June 30. Know that I am fine and that I love you both very much. This is something I have to do. Please keep me in your prayers.
>
> Love,
>
> Dan

Nancy dropped to the kneeler and without any effort, prayerful thoughts flooded her mind. Now, there were not enough hours in the day to implore God's help for all that she was absorbing. Jeff, likewise, was supported by the kneeler imploring the Almighty's protection upon their son. Within moments, music was heard and the assembly rose to begin their Sunday worship. Throughout the Mass, Nancy clenched Dan's note in her hand, opening it every few minutes to read it, again and again. Before the homily, Nancy had committed her son's last written words to memory.

During his homily, Father James emphasized the importance and the power of daily prayer. "Prayer," he reminded his congregation, "doesn't have to be verbal; it can be mental. And it shouldn't be recited only during certain times of the day. We should develop the habit of praying at every moment of the day, whether we're engaged in work or at rest. Offer your thoughts to God."

Nancy nodded in agreement.

After Mass, Nancy and Jeff stepped into the side aisle, where the statue of Saint Michael the Archangel adorned an area between two rows of pews, with a railing and a kneeler immediately below. Gazing upwards, Nancy marveled at the sword and shield grasped by the hands of the Archangel and at the grace displayed by the mighty messenger of God. From behind the Clays, Father James approached and motioned that they kneel below the statue.

Before kneeling, an excited Nancy shared, "Father, Jeff and I just received the most incredible news."

Seeing the joy in her eyes, Father asked, "What news?"

Unable to put her emotions into words, Nancy handed Dan's handwritten note to the priest.

While reading the message, Father James suffered a knot in his stomach like he never knew before. His strong suspicions were finally confirmed. The priest thought, *Oh God, Dan was serious about an upcoming trip which he divulged in the confessional; the teenager had embarked upon his unearthly adventure.* While refolding the note and returning it to Nancy, Father James prayed to himself, *God, be with him.*

While accepting the paper, Nancy exclaimed, "Isn't it wonderful, Father? Dan's fine and he'll return soon."

"Yes," responded the priest. Believing that hidden dangers most likely exist where Dan had traveled, and not wanting Nancy to cease praying for her son's return, Father James pleaded, "But we mustn't let this note preclude us from praying for his safety. We must pray constantly."

"Oh yes, Father," replied Nancy.

As the three knelt below the heavenly statue, but before offering their prayers, it occurred to the priest that there was no mention of the other teenagers or Sam White in the written message. *Could it be*, Father James thought, *that the four are separately lost?*

A light tap on the priest's shoulder drew him from his thoughts.

"Father," asked Nancy, "should we begin now?"

"I'm sorry," replied Father James, "yes, let's begin. In the name of the Father, and the Son, and the Holy Spirit. Amen." After a litany of prayers, the priest reasoned it quite appropriate that they conclude with the Prayer to Saint Michael the Archangel whose marble depiction loomed overhead.

Father James accompanied the Clays to the back doors of the church where he promised them his continued prayers and reminded Nancy specifically about weekday Mass. After all, the priest strongly suspected that her son would most likely encounter danger, but he couldn't relate his additional knowledge of Dan's whereabouts to Nancy or Jeff. Instead, Father James stressed daily Mass attendance to the Clays for their son's safe return.

"Thank you, Father," replied Nancy, "I'll be here tomorrow morning and every morning thereafter."

As the days passed by, Nancy was true to her word. Not only that, but she faithfully put into action the priest's suggestion to pray without ceasing. In this, she discovered great inner strength and peace.

•

In the parallel world through the oak tree, Sam and Jimmy prowled the shadowy forest while constantly scanning the area, not just for game, but also for predators which might consider them game. In the darkness ahead, Sam could barely make out what appeared to be a rabbit. He stopped and stared, hoping that the tree limbs above would separate, if only for a moment, to shed minimal light on the movement ahead. But there was no wind. Taking a chance, Sam strung his bow, took aim, and released his weapon. Considering the lack of light, he did fairly well, though the arrow missed the long-eared mammal by a few feet and pierced a tree behind. Walking to the maple tree to remove his arrow, Sam was slightly embarrassed, since days earlier he had made himself out to be the excellent huntsman.

In an effort to soothe his aching pride, he explained to Jimmy, "I was seeing if the tree was a portal."

"Yeah, right," responded Jimmy, while watching his companion dislodge the arrow from the tree.

"Well then," said Sam, after clearing his throat, "let's move on."

Hiking up a relatively steep hill, both men paused for a moment to catch their breath; the atmosphere and the uphill climb were taking a toll on the hunters. Reaching the top, both men were overjoyed at spotting several deer at the base of the hill. Concealing themselves behind two trees, Sam aimed his arrow through a fork in one of the trees and released. Again, the arrow missed the deer which quickly fled the scene. Descending the hill, the men naturally picked up speed. Upon reaching level ground, the search for the missing arrow began. Within minutes, it was located in another tree.

"Sam," teased Jimmy, "none of these trees are portals."

"Look, Jimmy," explained Sam, "the light is so poor in these woods it's a wonder I'm even able to hit a tree."

Frustration and disappointment gradually weighed on the hunters as they ventured another hour's hike deeper into the unknown forest without spotting prey.

"We better head back to camp," suggested Sam. "I don't want to leave Cindy and Dan alone too long. We'll try again tomorrow."

Bored, due to the lack of potential prey, Jimmy wholeheartedly agreed. Much to the men's delight, they recognized many of the trees and the topography on their return trip. *We may find our way back to the oak tree at the end of the journey after all*, thought Sam.

After a two-hour return trip and realizing that they were closing in on the campground, Sam returned his arrow to his quiver.

"Sam," whispered Jimmy, "look!"

About fifty feet ahead in a small clearing were six rabbits feasting on low rising undergrowth. Sam quietly grabbed another arrow, took aim, and released. The arrow narrowly missed a tree and embedded itself in one of the rabbits.

"Good shot," said Jimmy.

"Thanks," replied Sam.

With their energy and excitement renewed, the hunters walked to retrieve their prize. Once within twenty feet of the dead rabbit, however, the men heard a loud shuffling noise amidst the dense trees to their right. The hunters halted and stared into the dimly lit forest. A spider, which easily measured three feet in length, emerged from the darkened woods and entered the small clearing where the men stood. The eight-legged predator rapidly closed in on the lifeless rabbit. Sam, very quietly and very slowly, retrieved another arrow from his quiver in the event the spider was foolish enough to advance upon them. Sensing danger, but still intent on stealing its prey, the colossal spider slowed its pace and inched the last few feet toward the rabbit, while keeping the men in view. Once directly over its prize, the spider lunged its fangs into the rabbit's neck, raised it from the ground, slowly turned, and then dashed from the clearing to the cover of the forest trees. Sam kept his arrow elevated for a few moments longer.

"Man, that thing was huge!" exclaimed Jimmy.

"Yeah," replied Sam, "but that thief better hope it never crosses my path again or it'll get a taste of this arrow."

Detecting hurt pride, Jimmy placed his hand on Sam's shoulder and said, "Come on, let's get back to camp."

The two hunters left the small clearing and stepped into the forest behind them, far from the spider's entry. Little did they know that a short distance ahead, luck would finally be on their side. As they began their initial descent of a small knoll, Sam spotted another rabbit munching on the leaves of a small shrub completely unaware of the approaching hunters. Again, Sam aimed and released. This time, the dead prey was theirs. The two men paraded the remaining ten-minute trek back to camp, as if they were heroes.

At the campsite, Cindy was gently pulling Dan closer to the campfire for their protection, when she heard movement in the forest behind. Cindy quickly snatched her lance and turned to confront her assailant. Then, in the same direction of the commotion, she heard voices. Eventually, the so-called attackers appeared: Sam and Jimmy. Cindy lowered her weapon.

"Cindy," yelled Jimmy, "we got a rabbit."

Sam held his prize near the fire for Cindy's inspection.

"That looks great!" replied Cindy. "Finally, something to eat besides hamburgers and hotdogs."

Glancing down at Dan, Sam asked, "How's he doing?"

"About the same," replied Cindy. "I treated his wounds once since you left. He stirred, but only slightly and only briefly. I'm really getting concerned."

In an attempt to reassure her, Sam replied, "You're doing fine. I'll look after him now; why don't you take a nap?"

"Thanks, Sam," said Cindy, "I think I will." As she walked to her sleeping area, Sam admitted to himself that he also was overly concerned for Dan, but refused to make his fears known. *After all*, he thought, *it would only upset Cindy even more.*

While Cindy and Dan slept, Sam and Jimmy debated on a quick trip to the lake to test the new water contraption. Rationalizing that the lake was only a short distance away and that they wouldn't be gone too long, Sam grabbed his two lances, which he roped together earlier, while Jimmy crammed the remaining cookies into one container. Toting his lance and two empty containers for water, Jimmy joined Sam on his trek to the waterfront.

The lake was quiet and no movement was detected on its surface. Attempting to make as little noise and movement as possible, Sam carefully placed one of the empty containers at the end of his two-length lance and lowered it into the water. Once submerged, he gently lifted it and extended the precious cargo to Jimmy, who removed the container from the lance and replaced it with the second empty container. The same procedure was followed. Even though the two men were away from the camp only ten minutes, Sam was concerned for Cindy and Dan. Supplied with water, the two men hiked back to camp. Noticing that Cindy and Dan were still asleep, Sam quietly ordered Jimmy to remove the empty water bottles from the backpacks and line them on the ground, while he poured part of the lake water into a mess kit pan and set it directly atop the campfire. Within fifteen minutes, the water was boiling. After setting the pan on the forest floor to cool, Sam covered it with a cloth to protect the purified water from thirsty bugs, which were plentiful.

"Now," whispered Sam to Jimmy, "once it's cooled off, we'll pour it into the bottles.

The two men repeated this procedure four times, until all the water was boiled, cooled, and transferred into the travelers' portable water bottles. Taking advantage of the roaring fire, Sam readied the rabbit for lunch. The unintentional sound of metal clanging against metal awakened Cindy, who eyed Sam and Jimmy heating their prize catch.

Climbing out of her sleeping bag, Cindy advanced to the enticing smell.

"How'd you sleep?" asked Sam.

"Fine," replied Cindy, who quickly added, "wow, that smells good."

"Now there's only one rabbit, so we can't feast like kings," informed Sam, "but it's enough for a small treat."

During the meal, the expressions on the faces of the three explorers confirmed that the rabbit was delicious.

Halfway through the meal, Jimmy–from the corner of his eye–noticed Dan stir. "Hey," Jimmy blurted, "I think Dan just moved."

Sam and Cindy immediately turned with a mouthful of food and stared at Dan. The patient moved again. The three diners dashed to Dan's sleeping area, several feet away, to witness Dan roll onto his side.

In a soft voice, Cindy said, "Dan ... Dan, are you awake?"

Only heavy breathing was heard.

Putting her hand on Dan's shoulder and lightly shaking, she said again, "Dan ... Dan, wake up."

Rolling onto his back, Dan slowly opened his eyes. Blurred at first, his three friends slowly came into focus. With unbearable difficulty, Dan asked, "What happened?"

His two male co-travelers let out a sigh of relief; Cindy tried to fight back a tear.

"Well," explained Jimmy, "after you limped back to the campsite from the lakeshore, Madame Nightingale here," Jimmy glimpsed Cindy, "sterilized your leg and you just passed out."

"How long have I been out?" asked Dan.

"A little more than twenty-four hours," answered Cindy.

Dan attempted to climb from his sleeping back, but all three companions lightly penned him down.

"Oh no," ordered Sam. "You're to remain in that sleeping bag for quite some time."

"Hey, Sam," suggested Cindy, "since we're having a special meal, maybe we could carry Dan closer to the fire for a bite."

"Special meal?" questioned Dan.

"Yeah," replied Jimmy, "I got a rabbit today."

"*You* got a rabbit?" interjected Sam.

"I mean," clarified Jimmy, "we got a rabbit."

Sam rolled his eyes at Jimmy's apparent clarification, while stepping to the top of Dan's sleeping bag to raise his teenage friend to a seated position. Cindy and Jimmy opened the sleeping bag and helped Dan to his feet, being careful not to rest any of his weight on his injured leg. Placing Dan's arm across his shoulder, Sam assisted his young companion to the campfire. Once at the dining area, the three gently lowered Dan to the ground, and then propped his wounded leg on a pillow, which Cindy borrowed from her sleeping bag. Jimmy grabbed the last morsel of rabbit from the pan, placed it on a plate, and handed it to Dan.

"Thanks," said Dan, "it smells great."

The remaining travelers reached for their plates and resumed their meal.

Between bites, Dan asked, "Was the rabbit hard to catch?"

"Well..." started Sam.

"A giant spider stole our first kill," interrupted Jimmy.

"A giant spider?" asked Cindy, as she dropped her fork to the ground.

"Yeah," answered Jimmy, "it must have been three feet long and stood probably the same in height."

"What happened?" asked Dan.

"What do you mean what happened?" asked Jimmy. "We let the spider take the rabbit. Wouldn't you?"

"Do you think it's near camp?" asked an open-eyed Cindy.

"No," replied Sam, "it was much deeper in the forest."

Cindy's fears were calmed for the moment.

After the meal, the travelers relaxed by the warmth and protection of the fire catching up on the day's activities. At one point, Sam rose, walked to his sleeping area, and returned to the campfire moments later carrying a homemade crutch.

"Here, Dan," replied Sam as he handed the injured teenager the newly hewed crutch from a tree limb. "I thought this might come in handy until your leg heals."

Accepting the gift, Dan could only say, "Thanks."

All eyes were on Dan and his primitive crutch, when he ultimately asked, "Can I use it tomorrow for our hike?"

"Hike... tomorrow?" questioned Sam. "I don't think we'll be doing any hiking for at least a couple days, until your leg's better. Your sprained ankle is one thing, but the gash on your leg will take quite a bit longer to heal."

"Sam," replied Dan, "I know I'll be slow and we won't cover much ground, but even a little progress is better than none. We can't afford to lose any more days or this trip so far will have been pointless."

Sam threw another log on the fire while remarking, "Look, the worst case scenario is that we're late in returning and we have to wait at the O'Brien's house until the next full moon."

"Sam, I promise," pleaded Dan, "if we walk tomorrow, I'll let you know the first sign my leg starts to hurt. Then, even if it's only noon, we'll camp for the day. Please, Sam."

The sixty-year-old man stared into the fire.

"And besides," added Dan, "it wouldn't be right to let our parents needlessly worry until another full moon."

The teenagers' parents—Sam had forgotten about them. *How they must be worried out of their minds*, thought Sam. As much as Sam hated to admit it, Dan had a point. With great reservations, Sam conceded, "Okay, tomorrow we'll move on. But the first sign—and I mean the very first sign of pain—we stop."

The teenagers agreed to the terms.

After the meal, since a hike was out of the question for the rest of the day, the travelers spent the afternoon cleaning a few items and resting. Since the rabbit was consumed at lunch, the evening meal consisted of precooked hamburgers, chips, their newly acquired water, and conversation. The four engaged in lively talks until nearly 11:00, at which time Sam suggested that everyone retire.

Cindy reached for the nearly empty whiskey bottle and asked, "Sam, you've still got more whiskey in your bag, don't you?"

"Heck yeah," informed Jimmy, "he's got two more bottles."

Looking at Dan, Cindy said, "Sorry, Dan, but you know the drill."

Knowing that it was for his own good, Dan, while still sitting on a log near the fire, reluctantly exposed his calf and ankle. Sam and Jimmy were still amazed at Dan's injury.

Oh my gosh, thought Sam, *there's hardly any skin*!

Sam and Jimmy immediately sprang to their feet to restrain a spastic patient as the treatment was administered.

With moisture in his eyes from the extreme pain, Dan softly, but with great difficulty said, "I'll be fine." He knew he had to downplay his condition or tomorrow's hike would be canceled.

After allowing a few minutes of recovery time, Sam reached for Dan's crutch, while Cindy and Jimmy attempted to help Dan to his feet.

Wanting to prove that he could endure the hike tomorrow, Dan politely refused Cindy and Jimmy's help saying, "No thanks; I can make it to the sleeping area myself." Dan accepted the crutch from Sam and slowly rose from the log.

With his arms positioned to catch Dan should he stumble, Sam remarked, "Now remember, take it slowly and don't put any weight on your injured leg."

"I won't," replied Dan, as he cautiously tested his crutch en route to his sleeping bag. With all eyes focused on Dan, he eventually dropped to his knees, crawled into his sleeping bag, and reached for his Bible.

Amazing, thought Sam, *after all that boy's been through, he continues to pray.*

Once the campsite was in order, Cindy volunteered to take the first watch. With lance and lantern in hand, she marched to her lookout post, while Sam and Jimmy snuggled into their sleeping bags. Dan nodded off, dropping his Bible to the forest floor.

Throughout Cindy's vigil, nothing unusual was witnessed. Concluding her shift, she stepped to the campfire, threw two more logs on the dying flame, and reached for the bottle. However, before treating her patient, she woke Jimmy to prevent the alarm from ringing and waking Sam. "Jimmy," she whispered, "it's your turn." As she suspected, she had to shake him several times. Finally he stirred, only to roll onto his side. Again, "Jimmy, wake up." Rolling flat on his back, he opened his eyes to Cindy's face only inches from his. "Come on," she demanded, "you're on duty." As Jimmy slowly emerged from his sleeping bag, Cindy continued, "I may need your help with Dan. Would you hold him down if he starts jerking?"

"Sure," mumbled Jimmy.

Once at Dan's side, Jimmy unzipped the sleeping bag and gently removed Dan's leg, while hoping not to rouse him. During the medicinal procedure, Dan jolted to severe pain and sustained uncontrollable shaking. Within a few minutes, the spasms ended and Dan remained wide-awake staring at the darkened treetops. Within a half-hour, he returned to his dreams.

Jimmy's patrol, while initially uneventful, was soon graced with the reappearance of the illuminated object in the treetops. Though the being never flew near Jimmy, for a brief moment it descended from the canopy and hovered over Dan. Jimmy rose to his feet and neared the light. Unfortunately, before he was within ten feet of Dan, the lit creature soared to the canopy. *I wonder who or what that is*, Jimmy thought.

Glancing at Sam's wrist watch, which Jimmy was wearing, he noticed that his shift was nearly over. Walking to Sam's sleeping area, he awoke him before the alarm rang. "Sam," said Jimmy, "you're on patrol."

Unlike Jimmy's exit from slumber, Sam climbed out of his sleeping bag immediately.

While reaching for his lance, Jimmy informed his older companion that he had, once again, seen the brilliant light in the treetops.

"What did it do?" asked a slightly concerned Sam.

"Nothing," replied Jimmy, "though it did descend from the canopy and hover over Dan for a few seconds."

"Is Dan okay?" asked Sam, as he and Jimmy neared Dan's sleeping area.

"Oh sure," answered Jimmy, "the object just floated above him."

"Nonetheless," said Sam, "let's check on him anyway."

By now, the two men had reached their injured co-traveler. After an inspection of Dan's wounds, Jimmy bid his evening farewells to Sam and headed in the direction of his own sleeping area.

"Good night," replied Sam, as he marched to his post.

Throughout his tour of duty, Sam constantly scanned the treetops, hoping to capture a momentary glimpse of the fleeting creature. Unfortunately, the object never materialized. In the distance, Sam noticed Cindy rise from her sleeping bag and near the fire's warmth. Since the flame was quickly fading, Cindy reached for a nearby log and dropped it atop the fire. Within moments, she returned to her sleeping area.

CHAPTER EIGHTEEN
The Formidable Footstep

WHILE GATHERING THE DRY CEREAL AND MARSHMALLOWS FOR breakfast, Cindy asked, "Sam, how much farther ahead is the castle?"

Sam grabbed his cereal bowl and replied, "According to Doctor O'Brien, within ten days' walk, one should be able to spot the castle in the distance–depending on the traveler's pace and assuming there's enough light in the forest to see the castle–and reach the fortress in twelve days."

"We've been walking several days already," informed a weary Cindy. "Do you think the doctor may have been wrong and that we could come across it any day now?"

In an attempt to dispel any feelings of hopelessness, not to mention that the group suffered a sizeable setback in travel time due to unavoidable injuries, Sam replied, "I'm sure we'll come upon it soon."

"I hope so," responded Cindy.

"Morning," said Jimmy to Sam and Cindy, as he neared the fire.

"Good morning, Jimmy" said the two travelers.

"So, Sam," asked Jimmy, "did you see the lit object last night?"

"No," answered Sam, "but one of these nights I'm bound to."

"You know," proposed Jimmy, "if I didn't know any better, I'd say the object is following us." After dropping a nearly-stale marshmallow into his mouth, he poorly articulated, "And what's its preoccupation with Dan? I mean, Dan said that several nights ago it hovered in the near distance while the warm invisible touch clasped his ankle; and then last night I saw it again hovering over Dan."

"I wish I knew," replied Sam, "but I doubt it's out to harm us. If so, let's just say it's had plenty of opportunities to do so."

Dan approached, upon his crutch, from behind. For the first time since his attack at the lakeshore, he was showing signs of improvement.

"Good morning," said Dan.

"Morning," said all three.

"Dan," said Sam, "before you eat any breakfast, you need to take one of your pills. After all, since we forgot about it last night over the fire, you haven't taken one in two days."

Holding out his hand, he received a pill from Cindy, who then distributed the medication to the other travelers. Jimmy, who remained standing, helped Dan seat himself upon a log. After grace, the travelers enjoyed their meal while discussing who would do what chores in closing down the campsite. It was obvious that everyone was excited to be finally leaving the area. Eager to get started, Jimmy took everyone's empty bowls and began cleaning; Sam doused the campfire while Cindy repacked their supplies equally among three bags. Dan's bag was purposely left empty, since he was in no condition to lug supplies. After closing down their sleeping areas and cleansing Dan's injuries and Sam's waist, the travelers were on their way.

The somewhat warm weather beckoned Jimmy to wear his favorite short-sleeved shirt and jeans; Cindy also wore jeans, a green top, and her baseball cap; and Sam wore his tattered tan pants and a faded white short-sleeved shirt. Even though the temperature was mild, Dan opted on his gray sweat shirt, with his holy water secured in its pocket, and his ripped jeans. Sam took the lead, while Dan hobbled immediately behind. Several feet behind the men lagged Cindy and Jimmy. With an occasional strong gale, the group witnessed a clear blue sky overhead when the forest spread its limbs, but this was only rare.

After an hour's walk, Sam asked Dan, "How are you doing?"

"Fine," answered Dan.

"Remember," added Sam, "let me know when you want to take a break."

"Sure," said Dan, "but I'm fine right now."

In an effort to provide Dan with a momentary respite, Sam halted, turned, and looked behind. Sam noticed that Cindy had picked up her pace, but Jimmy was quickly losing ground, as he paused periodically to scan the sides of the footpaths.

"Come on, Jimmy," yelled Sam, "let's get a move on."

Somewhat startled by the yell, Jimmy looked ahead. Noticing that he had fallen a fair distance behind, he picked up his stride until he reached Cindy's side. With that, Sam and Dan turned forward and resumed their hike.

"So," asked Sam, "do you think you'll recognize William if you see him?"

"I think so," replied Dan. "Remember, the first time I crossed over—not knowing where I was, of course—I walked to my folks' house in this world and saw William through the living room window. He stood about 5'8" with dark black straight hair, kind of like mine." Dan halted briefly to reposition the crutch under his arm and then confirmed, "Yeah, I'm sure I'll recognize him."

Nearly two hours further into their hike, Sam decided to take a ten-minute break. Stopping, he looked behind to see Cindy walking, though slower than her earlier pace, and Jimmy still a hundred feet or so behind Cindy. *What's wrong with that boy?* Sam thought, as he shook his head. "Listen up, everyone," yelled Sam, "we'll take a ten-minute break."

As the four reclined on the forest floor, everyone knew what was on the other person's mind.

Finally, Cindy asked the piercing question, "How much longer to the castle?"

"I'm not sure," responded Sam, "but it can't be too much further ahead," in an attempt to lessen the group's anxiety.

"Do we even know we're walking in the right direction?" questioned Jimmy.

Sam remained silent.

Detecting frustration on his friends' faces, Dan remarked, "Listen, this is my personal odyssey. There's no reason why any of you should continue on. I'll be fine."

"No one is continuing this trip alone," blurted Sam, "it's far too dangerous. Either we all proceed ahead or we all return to the O'Brien's house."

Cindy and Jimmy looked at Dan, who had grabbed his crutch and was struggling to his feet. Knowing that in the near future Dan would return to the forest alone if the group headed back now, Cindy declared, "I'll stay here with Dan."

"And," added Jimmy, "I'll stay here with Cindy and Dan."

"Please guys," implored Dan, "you must go back now. Like Sam said, it's too dangerous."

"Dan," said Cindy in a teasing way, "don't tell me what I should do. I'm staying and that's final."

Jimmy seconded her decision.

"Well then," said Sam, "I guess we're off to the castle."

Before the other three travelers rose to their feet, Dan said, "I don't know what to say, other than thanks."

The three nodded as if to say we're all in this together.

The explorers took up their old positions and marched on. Shortly before noon, Sam was quite impressed that Dan had been keeping up and the group had traveled a fair distance that day. If Sam had to guess, he'd estimate they hiked about seven miles. As was typical, Jimmy remained about a hundred feet behind Cindy surveying the terrain. No sooner had Cindy ascended a modest incline on the path, descended its opposite side, and was out of Jimmy's sight when a plot of low-growing weeds—no more than three inches high and about twenty feet in diameter—mobilized itself and scurried onto the footpath, as Jimmy was turned scanning the forest behind. Unaware that the Undalon Crawler—as the deadly weed was known—had replanted itself immediately in front of him, Jimmy turned and placed a few steps onto the weed. Instantly, the Undalon Crawler jolted in the opposite direction of Jimmy's stride, collapsing the teenager to his back upon the weed. Immediately, long runners exploded from the patch of weeds and wrapped themselves around Jimmy's ankles, wrists, waist, and neck.

Jimmy let out a scream as the weed tightened itself around his body and released a burning chemical. The teenager hopelessly tried to free himself from the plant's powerful grip, but the more he did, the tighter the grasp became. Jimmy could feel the weed's secretion burning his skin. The teenager screamed a second time. At once, several creeping stems extended themselves over his mouth, sealing it shut.

Luckily, his second cry for help reached the ears of his co-travelers. Looking back and seeing no one behind Cindy, Sam raced to the area where he heard the scream only seconds earlier. Being closest to the teenager, Cindy was the first to reach Jimmy. Even with his limited mobility, Dan hobbled as fast as he could, trying to keep pace with Sam and Cindy.

By the time they reached Jimmy, nearly thirty seconds later, the Undalon Crawler had enveloped Jimmy's entire body; the teenager had experienced significant burns. With lance in hand, Sam savagely attempted to sever the plant's runners from Jimmy, while Cindy stomped on the deadly weed hoping to remove its strangle hold. The plant runners instinctively wrapped themselves around the would-be rescuers' ankles. With his lance, Sam stabbed and dislodged the runners from his ankles and then Cindy's. But no sooner had he freed themselves, when other aggressive stems secured another tightening grip on the two travelers. Even Dan, who had just arrived, stood over Jimmy violently striking his crutch upon the weeds, but with no success. It was a losing battle. For as fiercely as the three fought to unravel the Undalon Crawler from their friend, the tighter the grip became on Jimmy and his supposed liberators. Dan took another jab at the plant with such force, that he lost his balance and toppled to the ground. Before Cindy could bend over and help Dan to his feet, the Undalon Crawler captured Dan. He squirmed with his reserved strengths to free himself, but his struggles were to no avail. With one final push to escape the weed's entrapment, Dan noticed that almost immediately, all was still. The deadly plant not only released its grip on Jimmy, Dan, and the others, but the group distinctly felt the plant beneath them budge slightly. The predatory plant was attempting to flee into the safety of the forest. Within moments, the weed smoldered, turned brown, and then died. The travelers were free.

Sam helped Jimmy to his feet, while Cindy helped Dan to his. All eyes were drawn to the spot on the Undalon Crawler where Dan had collapsed moments earlier. There on the dead plant rested a bottle of holy water. During the struggle, the holy water had tumbled from Dan's sweat shirt pocket and leaked onto the lethal weed. No one knew what to think, or what to say for that matter.

Dan, however, with great difficulty, bent over and grabbed his holy water bottle while stating, "Sharon O'Brien said this would come in handy; I guess she was right."

After stabilizing Dan on his feet again and handing him his crutch, Sam and Cindy placed Jimmy's arms across their shoulders and walked him up the path to the area where the travelers had dropped their bags before darting to his rescue; Dan followed on his crutch. Setting Jimmy to the ground, Sam removed the teenager's shirt to examine his injuries. Sam was rather amazed at the damage which was inflicted in the relatively short period of time. But as bad as they were, he'd live. Even Dan, who collapsed upon the Undalon Crawler was more or less unscathed, thanks to his long-sleeved sweat shirt and the fact that he was in the grip of the organism for a briefer time. Sam and Cindy's ankle burns were scarcely noticeable.

Sam knew that the best treatment for burns was water. But since there was no uncontaminated water source readily available, Sam removed the water bottles from the travelers' backpacks and poured the precious liquid on Jimmy's face, arms, wrists, and chest. Noticing that the burns were worse on his wrists, Sam ripped two sleeves off one of his own shirts from his backpack, saturated them with water, and then tied them around Jimmy's wrists.

"Cindy," instructed Sam, "turn around while I remove Jimmy's pants to treat his legs."

Cindy did as Sam requested.

The burn marks on Jimmy's thighs and ankles were not nearly as bad as those on his arms, wrists, and neck. Obviously, the clothing provided some layer of protection, which also explained why his chest burns were not as severe either. After pouring a moderate amount of water on his legs, Sam replaced Jimmy's pants. There was nothing else Sam could do. Time would ultimately restore him to health.

While resting on the forest floor, Jimmy gazed up at Cindy and said, "Hey, Cindy, I finally got nabbed. Does this count as an injury even though no blood was drawn?"

Deeply regretting her earlier comment about his lack of injuries sustained during their journey, Cindy simply stated, "Yeah, Jimmy, that's an injury–but you'll live."

Noticing fatigue in the eyes of his co-travelers, Sam suggested the group camp there for the day. The teenagers heartily agreed.

Cindy organized the campsite, while Sam rummaged the nearby forest for kindling wood. Coming back into view five minutes later carrying an armful of timber, Sam dropped the heavy load to the ground which startled the two male patients resting on the forest floor nearby. Once the timbers were ablaze, Cindy gathered the mess kits and four hotdogs and set the pan on the open flame.

Looking into the collapsible cooler and counting, Cindy raised her head and informed, "Sam, we've only got twelve hotdogs and four hamburgers left and there's not a drop of juice."

"Actually," said Sam, "that's more food than I thought we had."

Overhearing their conversation, Jimmy gently rolled onto his side and asked, "Are there any cookies left?"

"Yes," replied Cindy, "but only one container."

While Sam and Cindy prepared lunch, Jimmy asked Dan, "So, you really think William's in the castle?"

"I'm sure of it," answered Dan.

"How do you know?" questioned Jimmy.

"Because I had a dream about it," replied Dan.

"A dream?" asked Jimmy. "Are you serious?"

"Yeah, Jimmy," responded Dan. "Remember the dream I had about the sycamore tree and then how we came upon it shortly thereafter?"

"Yeah," replied Jimmy.

"Well," added Dan, "I also had a dream that I saw William resting on a cot in a long narrow room in a castle. If one dream becomes a reality, who's to say that the second one won't also?"

"I suppose," said Jimmy. "But you have to consider the possibility that William isn't there, so if it turns out he's not, you've already prepared yourself."

"I don't need to prepare myself," snapped Dan in a sharp tone, "I know he's there; he's just got to be."

Trying not to overexcite his friend, Jimmy replied, "Yeah, you're right; he's probably there."

Sam approached the young men resting on the ground. "Are you two able to join us nearer the fire?"

"Sure," responded Jimmy and Dan in unison.

Sam lifted Dan to his feet. Handing Dan the crutch, the teenager stood on his own. Sam sat on his heels and positioned Jimmy's arm across his shoulder and raised him to his feet.

As Sam was assisting his young friend to the campfire, Jimmy remarked, "Sam, I appreciate it; but I'm sure I can walk on my own; they're only burns."

Sam suspected that Jimmy probably could manage the short distance himself, but didn't want to take the chance of a stumble. "It's best not to overexert yourself right now," advised Sam.

Once closer to the fire, the three men settled on a log and enjoyed a warm meal with Cindy. Even though he thought he'd never admit it in his entire life, Jimmy was tiring of hotdogs.

"Sam," asked Cindy, "do you think we'll be able to hike tomorrow?"

Looking at the two teenage men, Sam replied, "I guess we'll just have to wait and see how Jimmy and Dan feel tomorrow."

"I'll be fine," said Jimmy.

"I'm sure I'll feel better tomorrow, too," predicted Dan.

"Nonetheless," replied Sam, "we'll wait until tomorrow."

During the meal, the Undalon Crawler, its unheard-of locomotive ability, and its untimely demise were discussed at great length. Dan commented that he wouldn't be surprised if the enormous vine he witnessed over a week ago stretching from the inner depths of the Great Chasm and onto a neighboring footpath also possessed unearthly qualities.

After the meal, Sam and Cindy occupied their time cleaning the area, while the young male patients enjoyed a much-needed nap.

At 6:00 p.m., Sam began the dinner preparations. Chips, cookie crumbs, water, and the last of the hamburgers were served promptly at 6:30. Calling Dan and Jimmy to the fire, Sam was encouraged to see Dan stand on his own and near the campfire with relative ease. Jimmy was also recovering nicely. In-depth conversations on the castle and the Reclaimers consumed the dinner hour.

After cleaning the area, but before preparing for bed, Cindy reached for the whiskey bottle. While applying the alcohol to Dan's leg and neck, he shook again, but only slightly. When treating Sam's wounds on his waist, which were inflicted by the octopus-like creature, he experienced only minimal discomfort, indicating that his injuries were also healing nicely. Finally, Jimmy's blistering burns received a drenching of water from the depleting stockpile.

Even though the day was quite warm, the evening proved unusually chilly. For added warmth and protection, Sam and Cindy moved the four sleeping bags closer to the campfire. Since Sam knew that Dan and Jimmy were in no condition to patrol that night, he and Cindy agreed that they'd each assume a four-hour shift. They realized that if the young men were to recover from their injuries sooner rather than later, they needed uninterrupted sleep.

CHAPTER NINETEEN
Ceremonia

THE FOLLOWING MORNING, SAM AND CINDY WERE PLEASED to report that nothing unnatural wandered into the campsite during their patrols; not even the illuminative being made an appearance. After taking their pills, the group sat down to a bowl of cereal which–like their water supply–was rapidly depleting. Cindy suggested that everyone take smaller portions so the cereal would last longer.

To Jimmy's surprise, Sam blurted, "No; we need to eat our regular portions to keep our strength up and"–Sam looked at the young men–"to allow our bodies to heal."

On overhearing Sam's pronouncement, Jimmy immediately interjected, "A second bowl sounds great."

"Absolutely not," replied Sam. "I said our regular portions, not larger portions."

Jimmy rolled his eyes.

Attempting to distract Jimmy's thoughts from food, Dan asked, "So, Jimmy, how are you feeling today?"

"Actually," answered Jimmy, "pretty good."

Sam reached for Jimmy's right wrist which had suffered the most severe burns, removed the shirt sleeve bandage which was still tied around his wrist, and after a close inspection diagnosed, "Not bad; you're lucky the plant's chemical burns didn't penetrate deeper into your skin." Feeling that the bandage was dry, Sam reached for his cup of water, saturated the homemade bandage, and then retied the fabric to Jimmy's wrist. The same procedure was followed with the left bandage.

"No ... please ... no," implored Dan, as he eyed Cindy gripping the neck of the whiskey bottle.

"Dan," demanded Cindy, "you'll endure this treatment until you experience no pain or until I say you've had enough." As she sterilized Dan's leg and neck, Cindy was pleased that her friend experienced only a slight discomfort.

Bending over for a closer look at Dan's leg, Sam was pleasantly surprised that a scab was already forming–the first sign of recovery.

"Well," said Sam, "what's the verdict? Do we move on today or rest here?"

Cindy remained silent letting the young men decide the day's fate, since they knew best if they could handle the hike. It was unanimous; the young men felt well enough to put in a few miles. Once the campfire was extinguished, the area was cleaned, and the gear was packed away, the four set out.

In the world through the majestic oak tree, the Parkers and Ms. Somer–who arrived at the Clay's house thirty minutes prematurely–were waiting on the front porch. Nancy, who was just returning from weekday Mass and prayers, greeted them at the porch steps.

"Good morning," said Nancy.

"Good morning," replied the guests.

Removing her house key from her purse, Nancy asked, "Won't you come in?"

"Thank you," said Marie Parker, "that would be nice."

Once inside, Nancy asked her guests to have a seat.

Before Sara Somer even sat upon the sofa, she blurted, "Is it true?"

"Is what true?" asked Nancy.

"The note," continued Sara. "Did you find a note from Dan?"

Marie rose from the sofa and informed a baffled Nancy that

Father James had mentioned the discovery of the note to them. "Was there any mention of Jimmy in the message?" asked Marie.

"I'm sorry," replied Nancy. "Would you please excuse me for a moment?"

"Surely," replied the guests.

Nancy left the living room and walked into the den, only to return a few moments later carrying her Sunday Prayer Book. Removing Dan's note, she presented it to her guests, who read it intently, hoping to detect a hidden message concerning the whereabouts of their missing children.

"It says here that Dan will return on the thirtieth," remarked Tom Parker.

"If our children are with Dan," voiced a hopeful Sara, "then they will also return then."

"I don't know what to tell you," said Nancy. "I honestly don't know if Dan's alone or with them."

Recognizing a dead end in their personal investigation, Tom graciously stated, "We appreciate your time, Nancy," as he escorted his wife across the living room floor.

"We'll remain hopeful that the children are together," expressed Marie, "and that they'll return together."

"If they're together, I'm sure they will," replied Nancy, as she accompanied her guests to the front door.

Before the door was opened, however, Sara pleaded, "You will let us know if you receive any more notes, won't you?"

"Of course I will," assured Nancy.

Nancy had just closed the door behind her guests when she sensed that the families needed moral support, much like they tried to offer her last week. Tormented with guilt, Nancy threw open the door and urged, "Please, you must stop by again soon; we could all use the support of each other." Nancy took two steps onto the porch and apologized, "I'm sorry if I haven't been gracious–it's not intentional, of course–but ... "

"We understand," interrupted Tom.

"Nancy," admitted Sara, "it would be nice to visit again–one-on-one–without the other bridge ladies."

The Parkers expressed similar sentiments.

"We'll call on you soon," promised Marie, as she and Tom crossed the lawn to their house.

"Thank you," replied Nancy.

After offering a brief wave to Sara, once she stepped into her car, Nancy crossed the porch and entered her quiet, childless home.

In the parallel world, the four travelers started up the path on another day's journey in pursuit of the legendary castle. Considering Dan's semi-healed leg and Jimmy's plant burns, the four covered a large amount of ground that day, greater than anyone would have expected. Finally, the group got a break: throughout the entire day's trek, not a single creature was spotted. Over the hotdog meal that night, the topic about food and the lack of it, dominated the conversation. It was decided that the next day, the three teenagers would join Sam on a hunting expedition. Sam only recommended a group hunt thinking it would probably be safer if everyone stayed together. Cindy assumed the first patrol shift that night. For the first time in days, all four travelers felt up to the task of night watch.

The following morning, once breakfast and pills were consumed, the group geared up for a day of hunting. After easily consolidating the diminishing food supply and contents of the four backpacks into Dan's and Cindy's bags–which were purposely left at the campsite–Sam's and Jimmy's empty backpacks were carried on the hunt, along with Sam's bow and arrow, his revolver, Dan's machete, and four lances. Dan, not feeling the need to use the crutch anymore, half-heartedly carried it along at Sam's suggestion. The group left camp at such an early hour that the early morning dew was still dripping from the tree limbs above. After nearly three hours of hiking, while grateful they hadn't crossed the path of any predators, the travelers were quite discouraged that their two converted carcass bags remained empty.

Sam was just telling his three companions that they should head back to camp, when faint movement was heard in the thick brush ahead. Motioning with his right hand for the three teenagers behind him to halt, Sam rested on one knee. Moments later, the four witnessed a deer emerge from the thicket. Raising his bow and pulling the string, Sam launched an arrow. The buck received a fatal wound three inches below its neck. Cheering and a lengthy applause were heard from behind Sam; the teenagers couldn't stomach another hotdog. With the utmost caution, the four advanced to the brush to claim their prize. During their approach, Sam and Jimmy were especially watchful; they didn't want to encounter another greedy spider.

Arriving at the thicket safely, Sam opened his bag, pulled out Dan's machete, and for the next two hours, the group carefully dismembered their latest kill in pieces manageable to carry. After all, the travelers had a long hike back to the campsite. Once everyone was loaded up, Sam felt rather guilty leaving part of the carcass behind, but he was sure that the forest predators wouldn't let the beautiful creature go to waste. During their return trek to camp, the four travelers–including the two recovering patients–took turns relieving each other of the two backpacks which were loaded with venison. This was the first day the group actually enjoyed walking through the forest.

As they neared the campsite, Sam gestured his three companions to halt and remain quiet. All four sets of eyes were fixed upon Dan's duffle bag, which was sitting on the forest floor ahead near the extinguished campfire; its contents shifted as the bag swayed slightly.

"What do you suppose is in your bag?" whispered Cindy to Dan.

"I don't know," admitted Dan, "but I'm going to find out."

The explorers quietly placed the venison on the ground and inched their way along the path. Dan dropped his lance and crutch and, on all fours, reached his spirited backpack first. Once beside his open bag, Dan reached out quickly and folded the top flap over. With firm pressure applied, he denied a safe retreat to whatever was inside. Immediately, the bag shook uncontrollably, as Dan tried to maintain his grip. Suddenly, the movement stopped.

Sam, Jimmy, and Cindy stood above the bag with their lances raised.

Putting his face next to the bag, Dan warned, "I don't know what you are or even if you can understand me, but there are three spears pointed in your direction."

No response or movement came from the bag.

"I'm going to open the bag," continued Dan. "Come out slowly and you won't get hurt." The teenager removed one hand from the top of the bag and then the other. He then unfolded the top flap, revealing its contents. Suddenly, an object flew from the bag at such an incredible speed that it escaped the notice of Sam, who was now resting on his knees alongside Dan.

Noticing Dan instantly stare to the canopy, Sam asked, "What just happened?"

"Didn't you see it?" asked Jimmy, from only two feet away.

"See what?" demanded Sam.

"Something just bolted from the bag so fast," informed Dan, "that you must have missed it, Sam."

Upon a closer inspection of the bag's contents, Dan noticed that the cookie container was open. "That's odd," he said, "I know I closed the lid on the cookies when we were consolidating this morning." Dan held up half a cookie, which miraculously was not smashed from the earlier repackaging efforts. Within seconds, it was swiped from his hand.

"Did you see it?" asked Cindy.

"Yeah," said Dan.

"See what?" asked Sam.

Suspecting that the being was still in the area, Dan made himself comfortable on the forest floor, set a second cookie fragment on the ground, quickly covered it with a mess kit, and then rested his foot atop the pan. The remaining travelers also reclined on the path to watch Dan humiliate himself again. Within the blink of an eye, the being was hovering in front of Dan's face.

Startled at first, Dan eventually exclaimed, "Hey, it's the fiery object that's been soaring in the canopy."

The being–which was a woman only six inches tall with rapidly beating wings–only nodded.

"Can you speak?" asked Dan.

Again, the little woman only nodded.

"Well," pleaded Dan, "say something."

This time, the glowing being shook her head.

Watching Dan, Cindy teased, "Well, aren't you the great communicator?"

Staring at the small woman, Dan continued, "Tell me your name and you can have the cookie under my foot." Seeing no reaction from the luminescent life form, Dan prodded, "Do we have a deal?"

Eventually, the being unwillingly nodded.

"Well," asked Dan, "what's your name?"

From the tiny woman came a faint voice.

"What did she say?" asked Cindy.

"I think she said Ceremonia," answered Dan.

The small woman decreased her wing speed and gradually lowered herself to the forest floor, alongside the mess kit, expecting to receive her reward.

Dan was prepared to lift his foot, but postponed the being's prize by asking, "Ceremonia, what are you?"

"Dan!" yelled Cindy. "You promised her the cookie after your first question; now give it to her!"

The tiny woman looked up at Cindy, folded her arms, and nodded.

"Sorry, Ceremonia," replied Dan, "but before I give you the cookie, I want you to know that we mean you no harm. We're your friends, assuming you know what friend means."

Again, the small woman only nodded.

"Dan," ordered Cindy, "give her the cookie!"

The teenager raised his leg, lifted the pan, and then offered the cookie to Ceremonia; the glowing being snatched the dessert and then flashed to the canopy.

Looking upwards, Cindy yelled, "Ceremonia, come back!"

"Wow," replied Jimmy, "if we had her speed we'd be at the castle in no time."

"What do you think she is?" asked Sam.

"I have no idea," answered Dan. "Hey, I just thought of something. If she lives in the forest, maybe she knows the way to the castle."

"I'm sure she does," replied Cindy, "but after the way you treated her, I doubt we'll ever see her again."

"What do you mean the way I treated her?" asked an annoyed Dan.

"Oh, come on, Dan," rebuked Cindy, "you wouldn't give her the cookie after she told you her name."

Sam entered the conversation, "Alright you two, enough bickering; let's get our bags of meat picked up and start a fire."

The four travelers retraced their steps to their bags, while constantly looking overhead for a sign of Ceremonia.

Knowing that the venison would last longer if it was cooked versus raw, Sam spent the remainder of the afternoon heating the meat.

By 5:00 p.m., the travelers were enjoying a venison meal with chips, water, and cookie fragments. In between bites, the topic of the day's trek was discussed in great detail. After taking a vote, it was decided that the group should advance a few more miles before retiring. Within an hour, the group was back on the trail. Unfortunately, no one in the group saw Ceremonia throughout their three-hour evening hike, though everyone constantly scanned the canopy for any clue of the lit being.

At 9:00 p.m., the group ended their hike and pitched camp. Once the campfire was aglow, the travelers enjoyed another venison meal.

"How long do you think this cooked meat will last?" asked Cindy.

"Well," said Sam, "it'll probably last a few days."

After filling her plate with a second course, Cindy glanced at Dan, who was reaching for another slab of meat, and asked, "How are your leg and neck feeling?"

"Not bad," replied Dan. "There's a scab forming, so no amount of booze can bother me now."

"You can joke about it now, Dan," replied Cindy, "but if it wasn't for Sam's alcohol, you'd still be in a lot of pain." Looking at Jimmy, Cindy questioned, "How are you doing?"

"Great," answered Jimmy, "especially on a full stomach."

"I guess this means tonight will be the first night in a long time that we won't have to break open the whiskey bottle," reminded Sam.

When the meal was finished and the dishes cleaned, Sam, Jimmy, and Cindy talked near the warmth of the fire, while Dan read from his Bible by the flame's glow. After an hour of light conversation and spiritual reading, Sam suggested that Cindy take the first watch, followed by Jimmy, Sam, and Dan. Jimmy walked to his sleeping area, while Cindy headed to her post. Setting his Bible on the ground, Dan rose to his feet, with minimal difficulty, and helped Sam gather timber from the woods to store near the campfire for fuel throughout the night.

Once the two men returned to the campsite, each carrying an armful of wood, Sam remarked, "Thanks, boy; now off to bed."

As Dan left the area, Sam watched him while thinking, *He's a good kid. He's considerate, he's helpful, and he's ... so help me, if I ever set eyes on those school bullies.* Bending over to place another log on the fire, Sam noticed that Dan had forgotten his Bible. Sam debated on returning it, but then realized that Dan wouldn't read from it again until the next night. Sam rested upon a log near the fire with the Bible face down on the forest floor beside him.

After years of unanswered prayers, Sam promised himself long ago that he would never again pray or read from the Good Book. As curious as he was to open the Bible, he remained true to his word. Admittedly, while he occasionally mumbled an amen during grace on their journey, it was only to appease Dan; Sam's heart remained distant.

Sam felt as though he had just nodded off near the fire, when Cindy approached from behind.

"Sam," asked Cindy, "since you're already up, do you want to take the next shift?"

"My gosh," replied Sam, after a prolonged yawn, "is it that time already?"

"Actually, it's Jimmy's shift," reminded Cindy, "but I thought since you were already up ..." Cindy paused when she noticed the book resting on the ground near Sam and asked, "What were you reading?"

"Nothing," answered Sam.

After lifting the book from the soil, Cindy questioned, "The Bible? You were actually reading the Bible?"

"No," replied Sam in a defensive tone.

Sensing uneasiness and perhaps a falsehood from her companion, Cindy confided, "Don't worry, Sam, I won't tell anyone. Heck, I should probably read it myself. After all, what better place to read the Bible for strength and comfort than in this miserable place where every creature seems to have fangs?"

"I wasn't reading it," reiterated Sam. While staring at the Bible in Cindy's hand, Sam quickly added, "I'm on duty," and marched away.

Before heading to his post, however, Sam approached Jimmy's sleeping area and reset the alarm for two hours ahead. As Sam hastened to the lookout post, he glanced back at Cindy and witnessed her sitting by the campfire reading the Bible. Sam reached his post.

Sam and Jimmy's shifts were uneventful. As a matter of fact, it was so uninteresting that the men had trouble keeping awake; but they managed.

At 4:00 a.m., the alarm rang and Dan assumed patrol. He, too, was bored. "If only I could see the stars," he said to himself, "like I used to do from my back porch, I could pass the time relearning the constellations. Heck, all I can see are dark trees and limbs above." Dan glanced to the campsite where his three friends were sound asleep. Returning his gaze to the forest at hand, he glimpsed Ceremonia dancing in the limbs above. Dan thought about yelling to her, but didn't want to wake his co-travelers, since they were exhausted after yesterday's extended hike. On the other hand, he wanted to get Ceremonia's attention.

A dishonorable idea crossed Dan's mind. "What the heck," he said to himself, "there's been no activity tonight." He rose to his feet, walked the short distance to camp, and snatched a cookie. Returning to his post, he momentarily displayed the cookie in Ceremonia's view–but only briefly, because he knew from experience that she could snatch it from his hand in a heartbeat–and then placed it under his lantern. He hadn't had time to return to his log from placing the cookie under the lantern, when Ceremonia was hovering above the lantern. Startled at first, Dan eventually said, "Hey, Ceremonia, looking for something?" As he suspected, the small lady offered no response. "Come on, Ceremonia," pleaded Dan, "say something."

Ceremonia remained silent, but continued hovering atop the lantern.

"There's something I wanted to ask you earlier," added Dan, "but not in front of the others. Several days ago when my wound from the tiger was healed, I felt a warm invisible touch. Anyway, I also saw you floating nearby looking at the being or creature that was healing me."

Ceremonia offered no response.

"For the cookie under the lantern," continued Dan, "who or what healed me? Please, I need to know."

Ceremonia flashed to the canopy.

Looking heavenwards for her light, Dan saw nothing. Knowing he'd been had again, he tilted the lantern, reached down to grab the cookie and was opening his mouth to take a bite, when the cookie fragment vanished. The only thing Dan saw was a flash of light ascend to the canopy. Dan stepped from the lantern and raised his voice, "You're nothing but a thief!"

Ceremonia ignored his accusation and reclined in a small fork of a tree limb enjoying a cookie which was nearly half her size. The remainder of Dan's watch passed without incident.

After a good night sleep and a full meal the night before, the remaining travelers were completely refreshed at Dan's awakening. While eating breakfast at the campfire, all related that nothing out of the ordinary occurred during their watches; even Dan reported nothing. Thinking back to his patrol, Dan felt slightly ashamed that he tried to trick Ceremonia into answering a question. However, he had no intention of telling the group that he saw the little lady again only an hour or so earlier.

"I wonder if we'll see Ceremonia today?" asked Jimmy.

"Probably not," replied Cindy, "thanks to Dan."

Dan remained silent.

"I wonder how long she's lived in the forest and if she'd be willing to help us?" asked Jimmy.

"Alright, guys," interjected Sam, "enough of these questions. We must focus on our objective of reaching the castle, as if we'd never met the miniature lady. Now come on, let's clean up this mess, pack our bags, and move on."

In the midst of cleaning the campsite area, Ceremonia instantly appeared and hovered near the fire. Her rapid arrival took everyone by surprise, including Jimmy, who reacted by dropping his mess kit to the ground.

"Good morning, Ceremonia," said Cindy.

The little lady said nothing.

"I'm sorry," continued Cindy, "for the way Dan treated you yesterday."

"Sorry?" yelled Dan.

Ceremonia drifted a few feet from the fire and in an instant, a brilliant beam of light emanated from her and encircled her small body. The light gradually expanded as Ceremonia also grew in size, corresponding to the enlarging circle of light, until Ceremonia stood about five and a half feet tall. The travelers, understandably, took a few cautious steps back. Once Ceremonia's feet touched the ground, the encircling light vanished. Red shoulder-length hair, blue eyes, and a pair of semitransparent wings graced the being, who wore a light blue garment which covered her from neck to ankles. The four travelers remained quiet and motionless for nearly a minute.

Finally, Cindy spoke up and asked, "What just happened?"

"Don't be frightened," said Ceremonia.

For once, all heard her clearly.

"Don't look so astonished," replied Ceremonia, "the sound of my voice corresponds to the size of my body."

"You're beautiful!" slipped from Jimmy's mouth.

"Why, thank you, Jimmy," replied Ceremonia.

Looking at Dan, Ceremonia asked, "Nothing to say? Why just yesterday and earlier this morning during your watch you were full of questions."

Sam entered the conversation. "Wait a minute, Dan. You said that nothing happened during your shift."

"Well," admitted Dan, "I guess I forgot to mention Ceremonia."

Cindy took two steps closer to Dan, looked him straight in the eyes, and blurted, "You tried to trick her again this morning with a cookie, didn't you?"

Dan stared at the ground in humiliation.

"That's quite alright," said Ceremonia, "I got the cookie."

"Excuse me, ma'am," said Sam, "my name is Sam White."

"Yes," interrupted Ceremonia, "I know."

While glancing at Jimmy, who was now resting upon a fallen tree, and then at Cindy, Ceremonia added, "And you're Jimmy and you're Cindy."

"How do you know our names?" asked Jimmy.

"Well you see," said Ceremonia, "I've been watching and overhearing your conversations since you entered the forest a number of days ago."

Dan finally raised his head and accused, "So, you've been spying on us."

"No," replied Ceremonia, "not spying, just curious, I suppose. You see, this forest doesn't receive many visitors of your kind. Oh sure, over the centuries, other humans have ventured into the forest for its hunting or to seek out the castle, but I always seemed to be at the wrong place at the wrong time and only rarely have I encountered humans. Actually, the last humans I saw were a family that entered the forest in the 1600's."

"1600's!" exclaimed Jimmy, as he fell from the fallen tree. "How old are you?"

"Jimmy," reprimanded Cindy, "that's rude. You never ask a lady how old she is."

"Sorry," mumbled Jimmy.

"That's quite alright," replied Ceremonia. "In two years, I'll be 800 of your years."

Jimmy, who was now picking himself up from the ground and plunking himself upon the downed elm complimented, "You look pretty good for 800."

"Jimmy," said Cindy, "shush."

Ceremonia walked closer to the group and joined Jimmy on the fallen tree. "So," asked Ceremonia, "why are you visiting the forest?"

As the three remaining travelers joined Ceremonia and Jimmy on the toppled elm, Sam suggested that Dan tell the story.

Nearly fifteen minutes later, once Ceremonia was updated, she asked, "Dan, do you really believe that William is being held in the castle?"

In a firm and determined tone, Dan answered, "Yes, I do." After a moment's pause, the teenager added, "Ceremonia, since you've lived in this forest for centuries, do you know if William is in the castle?"

"Please, Dan," stated Ceremonia, "you make 800 sound like it's old; my parents lived more than twice my age. Anyway, to answer your question, I don't know. Just because I've lived in the forest for a time doesn't, and shouldn't, imply that I know everything that goes on or see everyone that travels on the forest's many paths. It's a vast forest. And to be honest, I haven't flown near the castle in decades."

"Why?" asked Jimmy. "Are you afraid of the Reclaimers?"

"Oh heavens no," replied Ceremonia. "You see, the will power of the Reclaimers is far inferior to the will power of the tree nymphs. In the quest for mental domination, the size of the body is immaterial."

"So," asked Sam, "you're a tree nymph?"

"Yes," answered Ceremonia.

"What's a tree nymph?" inquired Jimmy.

"Tree nymphs," explained Ceremonia, "are gentle beings that care for the woodland, mainly the trees, to ensure the forest's beauty. Eons ago, the forest was adorned with literally thousands of tree nymphs whose illumination lit up the canopy. Unfortunately, the few that remain today–only sixteen–are still hunted by the hideous centaurs which roam the forest."

"What's a centaur?" interrupted Jimmy.

"A centaur," answered Ceremonia, "is a dreadful creature which has the arms, head, and trunk of a man, but the legs and body of a horse. At last count, there were thirteen in the forest." After pausing for a moment, Ceremonia nervously asked, "Have you seen any?"

"No," replied Cindy, "and I hope we never do."

Continuing her story, Ceremonia explained, "We tree nymphs are hunted by the centaurs because, once they consume a tree nymph, the centaurs have the ability to change themselves into any person or thing they wish for three days and three nights. So, please be wary of what or who you see along your journey; it may be a centaur in disguise."

The travelers instinctively scanned the immediate area.

Ceremonia interjected another word of caution to the travelers, saying, "The most feared creature in the forest–not to the tree nymphs, of course–is the Oswagi Bird. Whenever, if ever, you come upon a forest clearing, be sure to scan the skies. These birds typically hunt on the fringes of these grasslands."

Fearing for the safety of the teenagers, Sam interrupted and asked, "What's an Oswagi Bird?"

"They are large birds of prey," described Ceremonia, "so massive, in fact, that they've been known to lift an adult saber-toothed tiger into the air with only minimal effort. Just promise me you'll be careful."

"Oh," replied Sam, "that I can promise you." Obviously intrigued with the lady and her vast knowledge, Sam inquired, "So, Ceremonia, do you have a family?"

"Not an immediate family," replied the tree nymph. "My parents met their end 500 years ago at the hands of a centaur. And now, with only a few of my species left, we live in small communities at the treetops."

Dan turned slightly upon the fallen tree to face Ceremonia and asked, "Since you know the layout of the forest better than anyone, would you lead us to the castle?"

"I could," replied Ceremonia, "but this is a mission which you should accomplish yourselves. I'm sorry Dan."

The teenager turned and stared into the campfire in complete disappointment, while Sam quickly changed the subject by asking, "Why do you alter your size?"

"Basically, it's for our protection from the centaurs," answered Ceremonia. "During the day, we grace the forest by walking in our large size or by flying in our small size, whatever it takes to tend the forest. But at twilight–typically the time when the centaurs hunt, though they've been known to stalk prey during the daylight hours– we purposely transform ourselves into our smaller dimensions so the leaves of the canopy can support us. This way, we're out of the range of the beastly centaurs while we sleep. And, if by chance during the day we spot a centaur, we can quickly alter our sizes or even become invisible."

Dan made another attempt to continue his conversation from his earlier patrol, despite his friends' presence, asking, "When I was being healed by the warm invisible touch several days ago, I saw you hovering behind the being or creature that was curing me. Can you tell me what or who it was?"

"I'm sorry, Dan," responded Ceremonia, "I cannot say."

"Please," prodded Dan, "I need to know."

"Isn't it enough," replied Ceremonia, "just to know that someone or something is watching over you?"

Just as Dan was opening his mouth to respond, Cindy interrupted,

"If you're fearful of the centaurs, then why do you glow at night? I mean, I'd think that would only draw attention to you."

"It's quite simple," replied Ceremonia, "we glow at night to light our path when we're flying."

"Well, Ceremonia," said Sam, "this has been an enlightening conversation, and as much as I'd like you to join us, I understand that you have your reasons. But if you ever change your mind, we'd appreciate your company."

"Thank you, Sam," replied Ceremonia.

As the tree nymph rose from the dead elm and was preparing to leave, Jimmy blurted, "One last question. If Spiritus Malus patrols the oak tree during full moons to lure potential stray travelers from our world, or even residents from this world's town of Lawton, why doesn't your species intervene and protect the travelers–if the tree nymphs aren't fearful of the Reclaimers as you say?"

Ceremonia paused for a moment and then responded, "That's a very good question, Jimmy. I'm actually somewhat ashamed to answer it, but the truth of the matter is that where there are Reclaimers, there are often–though not always–centaurs nearby. Centuries ago, we tree nymphs used to do just that–protect the occasional incoming transworld traveler and citizens of this world. Sadly, many tree nymphs lost their lives at the powerful arms of the centaurs while trying to protect the humans. For once in the grip of a centaur, the tree nymph is powerless to transform itself, since to do so requires his or her total strength and concentration. As it is now, with only sixteen tree nymphs remaining, it's well within the realm of possibility that with only a few visits to the oak tree, our species could be annihilated. Granted, centaurs are not always present with the Reclaimers, but our dwindling numbers preclude us from taking even those slim chances."

Ceremonia walked away with her head lowered, mortified at what her species had become. When she was only several feet from the group, suddenly another beam of brilliant light emanated from her, encircled the tree nymph, and slowly diminished around her shrinking body, until she was only six inches tall. Then, with the speed of light, she vanished in the canopy.

After Ceremonia's swift departure, the four travelers stared into the failing fire for several minutes processing the information Ceremonia had relayed; no words were exchanged. A log on the blaze rolled forward which snapped the group from their daze. Sam smacked his hands against his knees, rose from the toppled elm, and remarked, "Alright, troops, we need to finish cleaning the area and hit the trail. After all, we're still on a deadline."

Knowing the urgency of reaching the castle and returning to the oak before the next full moon, Dan was the first of the teenagers to stand.

"Come on you two," said Sam to Cindy and Jimmy. Sensing how they were feeling, or more precisely, suspecting who they were thinking about, Sam added, "I'm sure we'll meet her again."

"Do you think so?" asked a hopeful Cindy.

"Yeah," answered Sam, "I'm sure."

After Sam planted the seed of hope in their minds, Jimmy and Cindy jumped to their feet and joined Sam and Dan in cleaning the campsite, since the chore was abruptly interrupted by Ceremonia's dramatic appearance an hour earlier. In less than thirty minutes, the group had cleaned up, packed up, and was ready to press forward.

Dan felt strong enough to leave the crutch behind, though Sam persuaded him to bring it along one more day in case his limp returned.

"After all," reminded Sam, "it's not that heavy."

CHAPTER TWENTY

Calamity in the Clearing

FROM WHAT LITTLE THE TRAVELERS OCCASIONALLY GLIMPSED through the canopy, they suspected it was another cloudless day, though it was only a guess since the sun's rays barely penetrated to the forest floor. Throughout their morning hike, the group periodically scanned the canopy in search of Ceremonia. Determined to get answers, Dan was a bit more intent than the rest of his party on spotting the tree nymph. In addition to surveying the treetops like everyone else in his party, Dan had a hunch that Ceremonia was nearby, even though he couldn't see her. He couldn't prove it, of course, but somehow he knew it. *Anyway*, thought Dan, *she did say she could become invisible; she could go unseen.*

As the group broke for lunch, Sam estimated that they had traveled eight miles thus far. "At this rate," speculated Sam, "we could set a new hiking record today."

"Great," said Cindy unenthusiastically, as she removed the precooked venison from the cooler and pulled out the mess kits.

The lunch was consumed in record time, mainly because few words were exchanged. After the meal, and with no appearance from Ceremonia, the rather disappointed travelers embarked upon the second leg of the day's journey. It was painfully obvious to Sam that the teenagers were genuinely impressed with Ceremonia and that they'd hoped she'd join the group. Sam, too, enjoyed the tree nymph's company and remained optimistic that she would pay them another visit in the near future.

When camp was pitched at 5:30 in the evening, Sam was proud of their new record: seventeen miles on rugged, dangerous terrain. Even more impressive was the fact that no indigenous creatures were spotted during their arduous hike. That night, as was routine, the four friends alternated night watch patrols. Nothing, not even Ceremonia, visited the camp area.

The following morning, the teenagers overslept due to complete exhaustion from the previous day's hike. Sam, ending his watch, decided to let his friends sleep in a bit. But, at precisely 7:00, Sam roused his friends to the new day. Around the fire, the morning ritual began: Cindy distributed Doctor O'Brien's pills, Dan skewered the marshmallows, and Jimmy unpacked the mess kits and the dwindling dry cereal, while Sam resurrected the fire.

Hoping that the day's journey wouldn't be like yesterday's hike where the teenagers hardly spoke a word, Sam found himself admitting silently, *Heck, I'd take the bickering of Jimmy and Cindy over this dead silence.* While strategically placing another timber on the fire, Sam raised his voice and said, "Alright, listen up, everyone."

The three teenagers looked at Sam expecting him to congratulate them again on yesterday's record hike. The young travelers were surprised when Sam remarked, "Look, I enjoyed Ceremonia's company too and, yes, I wish she would have agreed to join us, but the fact of the matter is she didn't. We must respect her decision; I'm sure she had her reasons. And, Dan,"–Sam turned to face the young man–"this is our journey, not hers; we can't expect her to risk her life for our personal quest."

Ashamed of his selfish acts in attempting to coerce the tree nymph for answers, Dan remained silent.

Sam redirected his gaze to Cindy and Jimmy and warned, "I'm sure we'll see her again, but we must continue our journey, not in disheartened moods and being inattentive, but with vigor and guarding one another like we did when we started this journey. These sullen and unenthusiastic attitudes will end up getting one of us critically injured. We've got to snap out of it before one of us gets seriously hurt or worse."

The group could see that Sam was visibly upset with yesterday's prolonged silence and that he genuinely feared for their safety.

"That's all I've got to say," concluded Sam, as he turned and began his initial approach to his sleeping area.

He halted when Cindy admitted, "I'm sorry, Sam, you're right."

Sam turned to face the group.

"It's not only that I wished Ceremonia had joined us," continued Cindy, "but I'm also tired, and ... I'll admit it ... I'm terrified of what may await us in the castle. But I'll do my best to remain watchful; like you said, our lack of vigilance may get someone injured or even killed."

"I agree with Cindy," replied Jimmy, "today will be better."

All eyes focused on Dan, who was now roasting the marshmallows. Sensing he was in the spotlight, he struggled to admit what he knew he should, and ultimately did, "Look, I know I was wrong in trying to trick an answer or two from Ceremonia and that I was wrong in asking her to help us...."

"No," interrupted Sam, "you weren't wrong in asking her to help us, but you were wrong in not respecting her decision. No one should pressure someone into doing something they can't or shouldn't do."

"Maybe I'm being selfish," conceded Dan, "but I just thought we'd have a better chance finding William if she came along." The teenager stepped away from the fire, placed his back toward his friends, and admitted, "I'd also like to see Ceremonia again, if only to apologize."

"Dan," said Sam, "I'm sure she understands why you acted the way you did, but when you do see her again, an apology would be a nice gesture."

A strong wind blew, catching the attention of the travelers.

"I hope that's not another storm approaching," voiced an uneasy Cindy. "If I never see another one of those hideous purple frogs, even then would be too soon."

"Cindy," replied Jimmy, "they were just frogs."

"Yeah," confirmed Cindy, "frogs with disgusting tadpoles which acted more like leeches."

"If you think they're so bad," said Jimmy, "then why wasn't that counted as an injury for me?"

While the two continued to bicker, Sam thought, *What have I unleashed?* Sam raised his voice to interrupt Cindy and Jimmy and suggested, "Okay, you two, let's gather around the fire for some breakfast."

After Dan said a brief prayer to bless the limited food which they were about to receive, he also asked for a special blessing on the day's journey and upon Ceremonia.

Immediately after the prayer, even before her first mouthful, Cindy said, "Jimmy, what I meant is that the tadpoles didn't draw a lot of blood from you."

Sam let the two bicker it out since he figured it would keep them attentive during their hike.

After a rather boisterous breakfast, the four cleaned the area, packed their bags, and were off, renewed with energy. While Cindy and Jimmy resumed their debate about who had lost the most blood and sustained the worst injuries, Sam asked Dan, "What'd you think of Ceremonia?"

There was a slight pause before Dan's answer, not because he was trying to hatch a lie, but because he didn't know how to verbalize what he felt. Eventually, Dan answered, "Well, she seemed nice. Actually, I got the impression, at least at first, that she wanted to help us which is why I don't understand why she ultimately refused."

"Who knows?" responded Sam. "Maybe she wanted to help us but knew that it would be better for us if we accomplished our objective ourselves. It's kind of like a mother who holds back in helping her child tie its shoes. Initially, the child is slow in doing it and the mother wants to help, but knows that if she does, the child will never learn to do it alone. Do you understand, Dan?"

"Yeah, I think so," replied Dan.

Suspecting that Dan was withholding something, Sam prodded, "What aren't you telling me?"

"Promise not to laugh?" asked Dan.

"Of course," replied Sam.

"Well," admitted Dan, "I kind of enjoyed tricking her into swiping the cookies. It was kind of like two kids squabbling."

"You mean like those two behind us?" asked Sam.

"Yeah," said Dan, "something like that."

"If you asked me," joked Sam, "I think Ceremonia enjoyed humiliating you."

Sam put his hand on Dan's shoulder, indicating things would be fine.

The explorers enjoyed a brief respite from their hike around mid-morning and then a longer break for lunch. Throughout the entire morning's trek, during which each hiker diligently scanned the nearby forest fringes for potential predators, only occasional glances were directed to the canopy for Ceremonia. After a venison lunch, the group resumed their quest.

At 5:00 in the evening, Sam and Dan suddenly ended their conversation about the castle when they noticed that the woods were alit a couple hundred feet ahead; they halted. Cindy and Jimmy also stopped–both their steps and their bickering–when they saw the light ahead. The group had been in the dark forest for such a long time, they were transfixed on the glow before them. The four proceeded, but with an added ounce of caution, for each traveler knew that daylight in the darkened forest was unnatural. As they neared the lit area, they beheld a clearing in the woods. The area was completely free of trees, supported an abundance of prairie grass, and welcomed the blinding sunlight. Being an avid sportsman, Jimmy dashed to the clearing as if he had intercepted a football and was dashing to the end zone.

"Jimmy, don't!" yelled Sam. "It could be dangerous!"

Cindy and Dan joined in the loud warning as the three darted ahead trying to reach and restrain Jimmy. But, being the athlete that he was, there was no catching him.

When Jimmy reached the clearing, the pure exhilaration from the open air and sunshine compelled him to run even faster and deeper into the open field, totally ignoring Sam's first rule of the dark forest: always scan the area before advancing. By the time the group of three reached the edge of the clearing, Jimmy was at least three hundred feet into the enticing grassland.

Oh no, thought Sam, as he witnessed a large shadow crossing the meadow a hundred feet or so behind Jimmy, but rapidly closing the gap. As the three looked upward, they instinctively raised their hands to protect their unaccustomed eyes from the bright sunlight. As their eyes slowly focused, they saw an enormous bird closing in on its potential victim.

The Oswagi Bird–as Ceremonia called it–was indeed a massive

prehistoric bird of prey nearly thirteen feet in length. Four pairs of powerful legs supported the bulky beast; each leg was adorned with four six-inch talons. Its entire body was covered in black feathers, where thousands of burrowing stinkbugs had taken up residence. To raise the enormous predator to the skies, its gray-spotted black wings easily spanned thirty feet from tip to tip. The face of the creature was that of an aggressive wart hog, complete with a pair of four-foot tusks which proved remarkably useful when goring fellow Oswagis during aerial battles. Even when sleeping, the tusks deterred any suicidal would-be predators. Countless razor-edged teeth graced its spacious mouth for ease in ripping flesh from its prey. Finally, the six-foot tail–also covered in black feathers–bore numerous cavities capable of oozing droplets of poison when engaged in rearward combat.

The three travelers darted into the clearing–putting their own lives in danger–screaming to Jimmy, hoping that he'd spot the creature silently gliding above and attempt erratic movements to disorient the beast. Unfortunately, by the time Jimmy noticed the ominous shadow which was now within his side-view vision, it was too late. Within seconds, the bird plunged, sunk its front talons into Jimmy's shoulders, and effortlessly snatched him from the ground, as if lifting a small rodent. Jimmy screamed violently, as he was taken aloft and further from his distant rescuers. The teenager vainly struggled, hoping that the creature would release its deadly talons from his shoulders, thinking that if he was dropped, the pain of impact would be less severe than what he was presently experiencing. Unfortunately, the more he resisted, the deeper the talons penetrated his shoulders. Having lost a great deal of blood in only a short time, Jimmy's body soon became limp, mirroring the sways of flight of his captor.

As the three travelers looked on in complete horror, they witnessed the bird release Jimmy into her nest atop a hundred-foot rock formation, which adjoined a nearby hill, and then fly off, but not before two smaller heads of the same hideous creature popped from the side of the nest. Jimmy was scheduled to be a meal, not for the mother, but for her two nestlings. Before waiting until the mother Oswagi was completely out of sight, the three travelers ran along the perimeter of the clearing toward the nest, only to race deep into the forest, at a much faster pace, when the mother Oswagi took an unexpected change in her flight path and headed in their direction. The Oswagi glided several feet into the forest and made an ungraceful landing. Thankfully, the density of the forest and its low limbs prevented the creature from flying deeper into the woods. The bird immediately unrolled her long, black tongue, attempting to locate her additional victims by their scent. The three explorers took cover on the opposite side of a large fallen walnut tree which, judging from the plentiful moss and other plant life covering it, had toppled several years ago. The three remained motionless, trying not to even breathe.

Once the Oswagi was within feet of the walnut tree, it rotated its head 180 degrees to the direction of singing in the clearing. Instantly, the bird spotted a centaur in the distant grassland. Malignus, the neighborhood centaur, was obviously drunk, as centaurs were known to spend most of their lives, and shambling about the grassy area on the far side of the clearing. The Oswagi performed a quick turnabout, scampered from the forest–picking up speed as she did so–rose in the air at the clearing, and soared in the direction of the boisterous Malignus. The centaur, not yet totally intoxicated, heard the dreaded sound of massive wings whipping overhead, looked with terror at the approaching bird, and dashed in the direction of the forest on the opposite side of the clearing from the travelers. Sam, Dan, and Cindy cautiously neared the periphery of the forest on their side of the clearing to witness not only the centaur entering the protection of the remote forest, but also the Oswagi gliding into the wooded area and closing in on Malignus.

With the mother Oswagi distracted, the travelers made a second mad dash to the massive boulder.

After several nerve-racking minutes, the group reached the rock formation; Dan set his backpack to the ground.

"What are you doing?" asked Sam.

"I'm going to save Jimmy," answered Dan.

"Not on that leg, you're not!" demanded Sam.

"Look, Sam," said Dan in a domineering voice, "no offense, but I'm younger and my leg's fine."

"Are you implying," responded Sam, "that I can't.... ."

"Sam!" interrupted Cindy. "Let him do it!"

Realizing that he was outnumbered and that the teenagers were probably right, Sam yielded, "Okay." Looking at Dan, he advised, "But go up the back side. Use the hill which adjoins the boulder; it'll cut your climb nearly in half, not to mention that the back side is out of the Oswagi's view."

"Thanks," said Dan.

As Dan took one step forward, Sam yanked the teenager by his shoulder and blurted, "Wait!" Sam bent over, pulled the rope from his bag, and handed it to Dan.

"What's this for?" asked the bewildered teenager.

"What do you mean what's this for?" questioned Sam. "You weren't planning on carrying Jimmy down, were you?"

In his haste to save Jimmy before the bird's return, Dan had overlooked the obvious detail. "I'm sure I could carry him down," claimed Dan.

"Don't be absurd," said Sam, "that's far too dangerous. Lower him down on the rope and Cindy and I will be here to catch and untie him."

"Alright," replied Dan, "we'll try it your way," as he secured the rope around his shoulders.

Looking up at the enormous boulder from the adjoining hill, Dan was grateful that the rock was very irregular–plenty of fractures in which to secure his hands and feet. As Dan began his initial ascent, he was equally amazed and disgusted at the size of the Oswagi droppings that to him resembled cow dung. Trying his best to breathe through his mouth, he made gradual progress.

On the ground, Cindy nervously watched Dan ascend, while Sam anxiously watched for the bird's return from the forest beyond. Only twenty feet into his climb, Cindy witnessed Dan's foot slip. A patch of moist moss, concealed within a crevice on the rock face, caused Dan to falter and lose his foothold.

Cindy gasped.

While focusing on securing his dangling leg into another niche, he inadvertently lost the footing of his other leg. Now, with only his hands secure within a crevice, Dan hopelessly searched with both feet to locate another cleft for support.

Forgetting that any loud noise might draw the attention of the bird, Cindy yelled, "Hang on!"

Sam raised his sights to the misfortune overhead.

Dan made several attempts to anchor his feet against the boulder, but with each effort, his feet slipped from the rock. With his arms tiring and his feet still suspended in midair, he was slowly surrendering to gravity, when he suddenly felt the familiar invisible warm touch grasp his ankles and bolster him. Dan took a great leap of faith and released his hands from the rock crevice. As he did so, the invisible touch lifted him three feet, well within the grasp of several niches for his hands, and more importantly, crevices to secure his feet. Then, nearly as soon as the touch arrived, it was gone.

At the base of the rock, Sam was surprised that Cindy didn't scream when Dan released his hands; Sam feared that his friend would plummet to his death. Astonishingly, in the midst of the unseen rescue, Sam and Cindy somehow knew that Dan's invisible friend was paying him another visit.

Meanwhile, Jimmy, who was semiconscious, felt and vaguely saw two smaller versions of the mother Oswagi pecking at his left ankle. While the nestlings had not yet grown tusks, their teeth were sufficiently developed to puncture Jimmy's skin. Still losing blood from his shoulder wounds, Jimmy's strength and eyesight continued to wane. With great effort, he pulled his left leg from the birds, drew his knee to his chest, and with fading vision, aimed his foot at the two blurry objects. Amazingly, Jimmy booted one of the junior beasts into the air and beyond the nest, tumbling it down the side of the boulder and knocking against Dan's shoulder; Dan lost the grip of his right hand from the sudden impact.

Cindy gasped again.

But this time, the climber quickly and easily reestablished his hold. Dan glanced between his feet and witnessed the baby Oswagi bash against the rock several times during its descent to its death. Now only a couple feet from the base of the nest, Dan paused and listened attentively to determine if the mother Oswagi was approaching from the opposite side of the boulder. On hearing nothing, except for Jimmy and the last baby Oswagi fighting it out, Dan resumed his ascent.

Once inside the nest, Dan took a quick scan of the vile surroundings. The nest consisted of large tree limbs and mud. The teenager correctly assumed that the tremendous weight of the flying species obviously required something more durable than twigs; it also explained why the nest was constructed atop a boulder and not in a tree near the edge of the clearing. For as enormous as some of the trees were in the forest, not even the sturdiest tree could support a bird of such mass.

The aerial dwelling was almost perfectly round, roughly fifteen feet from edge to edge, and blanketed with decaying bones and a thick layer of regurgitated food. The smell was revolting. Dan quickly covered his nose and breathed through his mouth. The sole surviving bird was now striking Jimmy's thigh, while the ailing teenager did his best with his fading eyesight, strength, and consciousness to repel the miniature flesh-eating beast, but with only minimal success. While Jimmy sustained deep cuts on his ankle and thigh, they paled in comparison to his shoulders' injuries. Dan approached the young bird of prey from behind and kicked it to the opposite end of the nest. Since the nestling wasn't yet able to fly, Dan positioned the rope around his friend before the baby Oswagi made its return trip. Once the chick was within range, Dan booted it again, this time knocking it out cold.

With no sign of the mother bird, Sam placed his hands on either side of his mouth and yelled from the ground, "Is he alive?"

After double-checking that the mother Oswagi was not on her return flight, Dan leaned over the nest's edge and yelled, "Yeah, but he's lost a lot of blood."

On hearing the diagnosis, Cindy approached the adjacent hill and dropped her backpack.

Sam followed her to the mound and demanded, "What are you doing?"

Ignoring Sam, Cindy raised her head and yelled, "Dan, I'm coming up!"

"No, you can't!" yelled Dan from the rock.

Jimmy shook briefly.

"He's got thirty pounds on you, Dan," reminded Cindy. "You won't be able to lower him."

As much as Dan hated to admit it, Cindy was right. Unwillingly, he agreed to Cindy's offer of assistance. As he awaited her arrival, Dan neared Jimmy's side again and applied pressure to his friend's wounds with a handkerchief from his pocket.

Sam grabbed Cindy by the shoulder to steal her attention and warned, "It's far too dangerous."

"Sam, don't start," snapped Cindy, "we don't have time."

Again, Sam knew that this was an argument he'd certainly lose. Eventually conceding, Sam suggested, "I'll continue watching for the mother bird down here and yell if I see her approaching."

With that, Cindy ascended the hill and put her feet to the rock.

Occasionally rising from his patient, Dan scanned the skies over the grassland for the return of the mother Oswagi and then glanced down the side of the boulder to chart Cindy's progress. On his second downward glance, Dan was surprised at the speed with which Cindy was scaling the rock. He had no reservations admitting to himself that she was a better climber than he was; not a single misstep! In his descending gaze, Dan also noticed that Sam was meticulously watching Cindy ascend the rock while periodically scanning the nearby forest and skies for the mother Oswagi. With his eyes focused below, Dan suddenly heard a loud clattering noise behind and quickly spun around; he exhaled forcefully at the sight of a lone squirrel rummaging through the nest. Even though Cindy was ascending the face of the boulder rather quickly, the wait proved exceedingly difficult for Dan to endure.

To ease his mind and pass the time, Dan surveyed the surrounding area with the hundred-foot aerial advantage. Looking east over the grassland, Dan saw no sign of the mother Oswagi. Looking north and south, the teenager saw only trees. Turning to look west, Dan momentarily froze and then whispered, "Oh my God, there it is!"

In the distance, rising higher than the treetops and upon a large highland stood the enormous ghastly castle! In a trance-like state, Dan thought, *We could easily make that hike to the castle in a matter of hours.*

Dan left his dream-like condition and glanced down at Jimmy. "I can't think about the castle now," he told himself, as he dropped to his knees to tend his friend. "Come on, Cindy, hurry," he mumbled to himself. Rising to his feet again, he quickly scanned the skies; thankfully, there was still no sign of the ravenous bird. Then he peered down the side of the rock; Cindy was now only several feet below the nest. Approaching Jimmy one final time, Dan applied more pressure with the already saturated handkerchief to his friend's shoulder wounds. Rising and walking to the nest's border, he saw Cindy's hand reach over the edge. Dan promptly pulled her to safety.

While Dan quickly tied a double-loop knot in the rope directly under Jimmy's armpits, Cindy took a quick inspection of the nest. Had she looked beyond the aerial shelter to the west, she would have spotted the castle. Instead, her eyes were drawn to the baby Oswagi that was still out cold.

"What happened to the chick?" asked Cindy.

"It got in the way of my foot," answered Dan, as he struggled to lift Jimmy to his feet. Looking over his shoulder at Cindy, who was now squatting to get a closer view of the baby beast, Dan implored, "Cindy, help me raise Jimmy to his feet."

Cindy stepped to the opposite side of Jimmy and together, she and Dan gently lifted their friend. Since Jimmy was barely conscious and didn't have the strength to stand on his own, the two teenagers supported him by wrapping their arms around his waist.

With the rescuers standing on either side of Jimmy, Dan advised, "Press one hand against his back for support, put your other hand under his knee, and lift with me. While carrying Jimmy to the nest's edge in a seated position, Dan was admittedly grateful for Cindy's rescue effort; he realized that Jimmy would have been far too heavy for him to lift alone. With great caution, Cindy and Dan set Jimmy on the edge of the branches which fashioned the nest. While Cindy balanced Jimmy, Dan secured a firm grip on the rope. For added leverage, Dan braced one foot against the wall of the nest where it met the floor of the airy dwelling. After motioning that he was ready, Cindy slowly slipped Jimmy over the edge.

"Oh my gosh, he's. . . ." yelled Dan.

Before Dan could utter the word 'heavy,' Cindy was on the rope with Dan. Together, the two stabilized Jimmy's momentary free fall and then gradually lowered the rope. Within minutes and after strenuous efforts, the wounded traveler was in the arms of Sam, who immediately untied his ailing companion and placed him on the ground.

Knowing that there was no time to rest, since the mother Oswagi could return at any moment, Dan reeled in the rope and wrapped it around Cindy, who asked, "What are you doing?"

"I'm going to lower you down," replied Dan.

"No you're not," insisted Cindy. "I'll get down the way I came up."

"Cindy," said Dan, "don't be a martyr; this will be faster."

Peering over the edge, Cindy nervously asked, "Are you sure you can support me?"

"Of course," replied Dan, "you weigh less than I do."

With great reluctance, Cindy tightened the rope around her waist and perched herself on the rim of the nest.

"Ready?" asked Dan.

Cindy remained silent, while staring down the side of the rock.

"Go!" yelled Dan. "We're wasting time!"

With Dan's foot firmly planted against the side of the nest, Cindy slid off the edge. The relative ease with which Dan lowered Cindy surprised even him. Suddenly, Dan experienced a sharp pain in his ankle; he let the rope slip through his hands for a brief second, dropping Cindy fifteen feet, before he resecured his grip. The baby Oswagi was awake and pecking at Dan's ankle. To prevent Cindy from plummeting, Dan had no choice but to keep his leg braced against the nest and endure the affliction. Glancing at his hands, Dan saw blood drip upon the nest's limbs. Apparently, the rope burns were more severe than even he imagined. A few minutes later, Cindy safely touched ground.

Before even removing the rope, Cindy looked overhead and yelled, "What happened?"

"Sorry," yelled Dan, "the baby's awake."

The Oswagi nestling was, once again, kicked to the far side of the nest.

Even with his bleeding hands, Dan knew he couldn't rest, since the mother Oswagi could return at any moment. Dan dropped the rope to the grassland floor and swung one leg over the nest's edge searching for a crevice. After securing his foot in a niche, Dan sought another; success was achieved. As Dan descended, he was amazed that the crevices were easier to locate than during his ascent. Unfortunately, with each downward step, the pain in his hands grew in intensity. Within several minutes, he too was standing on the adjoining hill.

Immediately noticing his bloody hands, Cindy exclaimed, "Oh my gosh, Dan, what happened?"

"I'm fine," replied Dan, "let's get Jimmy to the cover of the forest."

Sam and Dan raised Jimmy to his feet, placed him between their shoulders, and darted for the woods as fast as they could. Cindy grabbed the rope and bags from the ground and trailed the men.

To the surprise of the group, Jimmy was still slightly conscious. After everything the four had endured in the forest since their odyssey began, none of them ever dreamed they'd view the woods as a sanctuary; but at that moment, it was. Once a safe distance into the forest, Dan and Sam rested Jimmy upon the ground, while Cindy dropped the men's bags, opened her own, and grabbed the liquid cure-all. The same horror which plagued her when she treated Dan after his attack by the lake creature tormented her again.

Sam, on seeing her hesitation and suspecting her quandary, remarked, "Cindy, I'm sure he'll pass out, but if we don't treat him, he'll die. I can't even begin to imagine what microorganisms infest that beast's talons."

Sam bared Jimmy's ankles while Dan removed what was left of his friend's shirt. Cindy released the alcohol on the patient's injuries. At the precise moment Jimmy screamed in sheer agony, an overpowering screech was heard from the clearing at such a volume that the birds of the canopy scattered. The mother Oswagi had discovered her dead chick at the base of the rock. Jimmy lost consciousness.

"Dan," said Cindy in a hesitant voice, "give me your hands."

Knowing that the forthcoming act of mercy would be extremely difficult for Cindy to withstand, Dan offered no resistance and extended his hands. While excruciatingly painful, Dan gritted his teeth and remained silent for Cindy's sake.

With the patient out cold and Cindy's face turned, Sam sterilized Jimmy's wounded thigh.

CHAPTER TWENTY-ONE

The Three-Foot Prognosticator

IT WAS NOW 7:00 IN THE EVENING AND EVEN THOUGH SAM WAS completely exhausted from the day's hike and the group's fortunate escape from the Oswagi Bird, he stepped into the nearby woods to gather timber for a fire. Sam correctly assumed that since the group was a safe distance into the forest and the Oswagi Bird could only venture into the inner woods with great difficulty, a small campfire would go unnoticed by the prehistoric bird and would be beneficial for the group's safety and warmth. Upon his return fifteen minutes later, he found Cindy and Dan asleep. Nevertheless, he built a protective fire. About an hour later, Dan awoke and silently approached Sam from behind. Once within a couple feet of Sam, the teenager cleared his throat; Sam jumped.

"Dan," reprimanded Sam, "don't sneak up on me like that."

"Sorry," replied Dan, "I was just coming to warm myself and to keep you company." In the midst of scanning the nearby footpath, the teenager continued, "Any sign of the Oswagi Bird?"

After taking a quick visual survey himself, Sam responded, "No, nothing. It's almost too quiet." Returning his attention to the immediate area, Sam focused on the teenager's hands that Cindy had wrapped with ripped shirts before nodding off. "How are your hands?"

"The bleeding has stopped," updated Dan, "but they're still a little sore."

"Yeah," confirmed Sam, "I imagine they'll be sore for quite some time." Concerned for his other companion, Sam asked, "Any movement from Jimmy?"

"No," replied Dan, who immediately turned to face Jimmy's sleeping area and added, "I just wish he'd make some movement . . . anything."

"And Cindy," asked Sam, "is she still sleeping?"

"Yeah," answered Dan, "I think so."

Dan wanted to tell Sam about his discovery of the castle from the heights of the nest, but seeing the bags under Sam's eyes, he decided that the news could wait until later. *After all*, thought Dan, *we're not hiking anytime soon*. Instead the teenager proposed, "Sam, why don't you rest for an hour or so? I'll get dinner ready."

"Thanks," answered Sam, "but I'm fine."

"Sam," implored Dan in a louder tone, "go. I'll wake you up in an hour."

To the teenager's surprise, Sam ultimately accepted his offer and headed for his sleeping area, but not before placing another log on the fire.

While gathering the cooking utensils from the backpack and the venison from the collapsible cooler, Dan occasionally glanced west, even though he couldn't see much beyond several feet in front of him, thinking that William may be so close–probably only a five-hour hike away. While daydreaming, he accidentally dropped the pan in the fire; Cindy stirred. Luckily, the precooked venison didn't fall into the flame.

Within minutes, Cindy was sitting on a log next to Dan discussing the day's adventure and what possibly awaited them at the castle.

"Jimmy really scared me today," admitted Cindy.

"Yeah," replied Dan, "me too," as he removed one of the few remaining bags of chips from the backpack. Dan rested on his knees and wrapped a piece of torn clothing around the pan's handle while asking, "Why, Cindy?"

"Why, what?" replied Cindy.

Dan returned to the log and took a few moments to collect his thoughts, while gazing into the flames.

Cindy placed her hand on Dan's shoulder and again asked, "Why, what?"

Without removing his sights from the fire, Dan admitted, "Jimmy could have died today."

"But he didn't," consoled Cindy, "thanks to your bravery and quick thinking."

"Why did you and Jimmy take this trip with me?" blurted Dan. "My God, if something horrible happens to either one of you, and you . . ." Dan couldn't bring himself to pronounce the death sentence. The young man glanced at his bandaged hands and asked, "Why'd you come?"

"Dan," answered Cindy, "I could have gone to survival camp, but I don't know. Something inside told me that you might need my help. Actually, come to think of it, that's not totally true; I wanted to help you. Throughout high school, I've watched you being bullied by those class thugs and I've always admired the way you never cowered. Let's face it, you're going to be somebody special someday and I want to make sure that I'm there to help you become that person. Besides, we'll make it back, all of us; I promise."

Dan offered a weak smile to Cindy as if agreeing that the group–including William–would return safely to their world.

Dan grabbed a fork, turned the venison, and then returned to his log. "With all the commotion in the nest," continued Dan, "I forgot to point something out to you."

"What's that?" asked Cindy.

"Well," explained Dan, "as I was scanning the sky for the bird, I looked west and I saw. . . ." Dan abruptly ended his sentence.

A rustling sound was heard in the undergrowth off the footpath to the teenagers' right. Both travelers automatically reached for their lances on the ground near the fire. Since their arrival in the forest, a lance had become another appendage to the travelers. Both jumped to their feet and quickly turned to face the direction of the noise. Peering into the brush, Dan swore he saw a yellow eye staring at him, which was reflected from the campfire's glow. When the unknown entity turned its head slightly, Cindy also took note. Keeping their lower bodies completely motionless, they slowly raised their spears to shoulder height and prepared for release.

As Dan turned his head slowly toward Cindy, only for a moment, the being sprang from the undergrowth, landed three feet in front of

Dan, and then–without pausing–took its final lunge upward to Dan's face, wrapping its four-clawed hands around Dan's neck and its four-clawed feet around his waist. The whole ambush happened so quickly that neither Dan nor Cindy had time to release their weapons. The impact propelled Dan backwards to the ground, narrowly missing the fire, as the creature vigorously tried to sink its fangs into Dan's neck. Even with his wounded hands, Dan feverishly fought to repel the creature's advance. Only three feet tall, the beast had unbelievable strength. Face to face with the creature, Dan couldn't help but notice its remaining offensive facial features: one yellow eye in the center of its forehead, a forked tongue, an elongated nose, jagged fangs dripping with saliva, and grass growing from the top of its head and chin. *It's a troll!* Dan thought, while trying to dodge the incoming fangs.

Throughout the ordeal, Cindy valiantly tried to pierce the creature from behind, but the troll's scaly tail, which bore its second eye, fearlessly lashed at Cindy, preventing her from a clear shot. The tail's whipping was so powerful and constant that on more than one occasion, Cindy was knocked to the ground.

Suddenly, a shot was heard; Sam stood several feet away clenching his revolver. In the glow of the campfire, a faint trace of smoke was seen rising from the gun's barrel.

Dan shoved the beast off his chest and quickly scooted back on the ground to place a safe distance between himself and the dying troll. Luckily, Dan had not been bitten, though he sustained minor flesh wounds around his neck and waist from the creature's claws. The troll squirmed and attempted to speak.

As Sam aimed his revolver again, Cindy raised her hand in Sam's direction and screamed, "No, wait!"

"I know who you are," spoke the troll with growing difficulty, "and I know why you search where no one or no thing dares to enter." Swallowing with great effort, the creature feebly added, "Since I can prophesy the future, I know that you will all suffer near the castle and within its cold stony walls." Looking directly at Cindy, the troll predicted, "And in the days ahead, you will be transformed into a... ."

Another shot was fired.

Once the troll expelled its last breath, its body instantly decomposed into hundreds of red worms with black stripes which quickly burrowed themselves into the forest floor. After a brief moment of silence, brought on by disbelief, Cindy glared at Sam and demanded, "Why'd you shoot it? The troll was telling me what I was going to become."

Sam lowered his revolver and explained, "Cindy, whether or not that thing could see into the future doesn't matter. If you knew the future, then you'd spend the rest of this trip worrying about something which will probably never happen. When a person delves into the future, they are inevitably tormented by the present."

"But, Sam," reasoned Cindy, "if we knew the future, we'd have a better chance returning to the oak."

Dan rose from the forest floor and stomped on the ground to seal the holes where the troll worms had entered.

"Cindy," said Dan, "Sam's right. The troll probably couldn't tell the future anyway, but only wanted to frighten you."

"What's a troll anyway?" asked Sam.

Having taken a mythology course last semester, not to mention her father's stories when she was a child, Cindy explained, "Trolls are mischievous dwarfs that live under bridges."

"That's it!" exclaimed Dan. "The troll must have been living under the castle's drawbridge which is only a few hours hike from here."

Sam took a step closer to the young man while asking, "How do you know the castle is nearby?"

"That's what I was starting to tell Cindy," explained Dan, "when the troll ambushed us. When I was in the Oswagi's nest waiting for Cindy to climb the rock, I scanned the area and to the west I saw the castle."

"Are you sure?" asked a doubtful Sam.

"I'm positive," answered Dan.

"And when," continued Sam, "were you planning on telling me?"

"Well," replied Dan, "once I got down from the nest, we had to race to the forest's safety, so I couldn't tell you then. Later, I meant to tell you when you returned from gathering the firewood, but I fell asleep. So I decided I'd tell you later over dinner."

"Dan," pleaded Sam, "I wish you'd tell me these things right away."

"Sorry, Sam," said Dan, "but I didn't think it would make any difference if I told you an hour or so later, since we were already camped for the night."

Cindy interrupted, "Anyway, in addition to living under bridges, trolls are said to be able to foretell the future, possess great strength, and have an eye on their tail for defense and–I suppose–to compensate for the one eye missing on their faces."

"What about the worms?" asked Dan.

"That was gross," replied Cindy.

"No," prodded Dan, "any mention in your mythology class about worms?"

Cindy only repeated herself, "That was gross."

Looking at Sam and sensing disappointment, Dan admitted, "Sam, I'm sorry. I really meant to tell you earlier. It's just that ... well ... we were all tired and I thought it could wait until dinner."

"Next time," ordered Sam, "tell me immediately."

"I promise," replied Dan.

Lowering himself to his heels, Sam removed the burned venison from the fire saying, "I hope you like your meat well done."

While Dan assembled the mess kits, Cindy offered to check on Jimmy; Sam accompanied her to the patient.

Removing the homemade bandages from Jimmy's shoulders and upper chest, Sam was still astonished with the severity of the wounds. The only consolation was that Jimmy's shoulder blades prevented a deeper penetration of the Oswagi's talons. Cindy treated the injuries; Jimmy remained motionless. Once the bandages were reapplied, Sam pulled the sleeping bag over Jimmy's shoulders. He and Cindy returned to the campfire, where Dan had the three plates of venison and chips ready. After Dan said grace, the three did their best to cut and chew their charred meal.

Since it was a late meal, after cleaning the area, Cindy volunteered for the first patrol watch. After a lengthy debate with Dan about whether or not he should patrol, due to his recent hand injury, the teenager eventually won, reasoning that his hands would not adversely affect his patrol.

Reluctantly, Sam accepted Dan's questionable logic.

Before leaving the safety of the fire, however, it was agreed that before each watch, the person starting their patrol would tend to Jimmy.

The following morning over breakfast, the three watchers were grateful to report that nothing out of the ordinary transpired during the previous night or early morning. Unfortunately, Jimmy had not stirred, even when the treatments were administered.

While watching Cindy drop a pill into Dan's bandaged hands, Sam asked, "How are your hands this morning?"

"Better, thanks," replied Dan.

"Nonetheless," said Sam, "I want you to endure the therapy for at least another day."

"But, Sam," replied Dan, "they feel fine."

While lifting a piece of dried cereal from his bowl, Sam clarified, "Dan, what's the point in coming all this way and then unable to use your hands once we reach the castle?"

"Alright," agreed Dan, "I'll take the bottle one more day."

Cindy entered the conversation saying, "What should we do today?"

"I guess," suggested Sam, "there's the usual. We could mend some clothing, treat Jimmy's wounds, and if there's time, maybe a little hunting and water gathering."

"Can I go hunting with you?" asked Dan.

"Let's see how much time we have after the chores," replied Sam.

Dan was determined to keep himself as busy as possible that day, since he suspected it would keep his mind off the castle and William. It seemed so unfair to the teenager that after all the group had sustained–and now with the castle only hours away–they couldn't proceed, not until Jimmy had the strength.

Rising to their feet, the travelers began their assigned chores.

At midday, as the three gathered for lunch, Cindy reported that she had finished the mending, while Dan informed the group that all the supplies were reasonably clean–since no water was used–and repacked.

Desperately wanting to go hunting with Sam, Dan updated, "Sam, last night was the last of the venison."

"Well then," said Sam, "I guess I'll go hunting this afternoon."

"Can I come along?" asked Dan.

"I think it would be better if you stayed here with Cindy and Jimmy," answered Sam, "just in case something wanders into the campsite."

As much as he had set his heart on hunting, Dan knew that Cindy and Jimmy could probably use his protection more than Sam. With mild disappointment, Dan replied, "Okay, I'll hang around the camp."

As Sam grabbed his bow and arrow and headed off the path for the deeper recesses of the forest, Dan and Cindy neared Jimmy's sleeping area. With the utmost care, Dan removed Jimmy's bandages, while Cindy applied the liquid antiseptic. To their amazement, Jimmy jerked.

"That's a good sign, right?" asked Dan.

"Yeah," answered Cindy, "it means he's slowly pulling through."

While Dan's concerns for Jimmy's recovery were somewhat eased, he was also relieved for himself since Jimmy's modest movement signaled that the group would resume their hike to the castle sooner rather than later.

"Jimmy," said Cindy, "can you hear me?"

No movement or verbal response was heard from the patient.

In a louder voice, Dan said, "Jimmy!"

Again, there was no reaction.

Not having received a verbal response as they had hoped, the two disappointed travelers reapplied the bandages and proceeded to the fire which was quickly fading.

"I better gather some more timber," offered Dan.

"That might not be a bad idea," remarked Cindy, as she offered an over-the-shoulder glance to Jimmy.

As Dan disappeared into the nearby woods, Cindy rearranged the few charred timbers in the fire to make room for the new supply. Within minutes, Dan returned with an armful of wood which he intentionally dropped to the forest floor near the campfire, hoping the noise would induce Jimmy to stir again. With the loud thump, two six-inch beetles scurried across the footpath, as if in a competition for the trees beyond.

"I'm surprised they didn't have teeth," remarked Cindy, as she stepped from the path of the rushing insects. "It seems like everything in this world has teeth."

"I suspect," replied Dan, "that a lot of creatures in these woods have teeth or poison for self-defense."

Cindy offered another glance at Jimmy, who was in his sleeping bag about ten feet behind, as Dan sat on the log directly opposite Cindy to keep Jimmy in full view. Cindy returned her gaze to Dan and said, "I wonder how Sam's doing."

"I'm sure he's fine," replied Dan, in an attempt to reassure Cindy.

"You should have gone with him," said Cindy. "I would have been fine here by myself."

Thinking back to her warrior days at the lakeshore, Dan replied, "Yeah, I'm sure you would be, but Sam thought it was best that I stay here."

Changing the subject, Cindy asked, "So, how long do you think it'll take us to reach the castle?"

"I can't imagine it taking more than a few hours," answered Dan, "assuming Jimmy's well enough to travel at our normal pace."

"Any ideas where we should look in the castle for your brother?" asked Cindy.

Without even a moment's hesitation, Dan answered, "I had a dream once where I saw him resting upon a cot on the sixth floor." Detecting a look of doubt on Cindy's face while mentioning his vision, Dan quickly added, "But, I'm sure there'll be clues in the castle which will lead us to him."

"Then what?" asked Cindy.

"Then," replied Dan, "we hightail out of the place, head for the majestic oak, and then home."

The word home took Dan back to the night some two weeks ago when he was saying goodbye to his folks. He vividly recalled how excited he was to leave town, if only for a month, and enter the forest. Now, he wanted nothing more than to leave the forest and return home with his brother at his side.

Cindy, likewise, reminisced about her mother and the day that she bid her only parent farewell and walked to the chartered buses. She wondered how her mother was holding up since her disappearance.

Both teenagers were drawn from their thoughts by a branch

snapping in the nearby forest. Grabbing their lances, the two travelers jumped from their logs to witness Sam returning with four rabbits.

Holding up his game, Sam asked, "Was I lucky or what?"

"Oh my gosh," said Cindy, "they look great!"

"Did you come across anything weird in the forest?" asked Dan.

"No," replied Sam, "unless you call squirrels rummaging through the forest undergrowth weird. Actually, everything went more smoothly than I thought it would." After wiping rabbit blood from his hands to his pants, Sam joked, "Maybe you teenagers are bad luck on my hunts."

As Sam set the rabbits on the ground and grabbed Dan's machete, he asked if there was any change in Jimmy.

"Yes," replied Cindy.

Sam dropped the knife, looked up at Cindy, and then glanced behind her at Jimmy, who was still resting motionless in his sleeping bag. There was no denying the fact that Sam had developed a deep friendship with the teenagers, including the impulsive Jimmy.

"When Dan and I were treating him," explained Cindy, "Jimmy jerked a bit, though he didn't say anything or open his eyes. We even talked to him, but there was no response."

"That's alright," said Sam, "as long as he moved, that's a pretty good sign that he's on the road to recovery." Elated with the latest prognosis, Sam grabbed the machete from the soil and began butchering the rabbits for the meal that night, as well as the next couple days. Within an hour, the first rabbit was ready for the fire.

Looking at Cindy, Sam said, "If you don't mind, I'll leave you to the cooking while I hike to a small pond which I discovered during my hunt–only about a half-mile away–to gather some water."

"Sure, Sam," replied Cindy.

After grabbing two lances and the rope, Sam sat upon a log, where he reconstructed his water collection bucket.

"Sam," asked Dan, "can I come along?"

As much as he thought it would be better for Dan to remain with Cindy and Jimmy, he had to admit that the teenager would come in handy for lugging as much water back as possible. Looking at Cindy, Sam asked, "Will you be alright by yourself?"

"Jimmy and I will be fine," replied Cindy. "You two get the water."

Before Cindy even finished her statement of assurance, Dan was reaching for the two empty plastic containers.

"We'll be back as soon as we can," promised Sam.

"Take your time," said Cindy, "we'll be fine."

As the two men marched off, Cindy reached for a pan in the backpack, placed a rabbit inside, and set it atop the fire. While the meal was cooking, Cindy decided to take another look at Jimmy. Slowly removing his bandages, she was pleased to see that the bleeding had finally stopped. A slight grunt was heard from Jimmy, who slowly opened his eyes.

"Jimmy," exclaimed Cindy, "you're awake!"

Closing his eyes again and then licking his lips, he feebly asked, "Where's.... ." He took a deep breath, swallowed with difficulty, and resumed, "Where's the bird?"

"Don't worry," assured Cindy, "it's long gone. You're safe at the campsite."

Jimmy opened his eyes again.

Attempting to keep him conscious, Cindy continued, "You gave us quite a scare, Jimmy; you've been out for nearly twenty-four hours." While resting her hand on his forehead to check for a fever, Jimmy closed his eyes again. "No fever," Cindy said to herself.

With his eyes still closed, Jimmy struggled to ask, "What happened?"

"Once the bird dropped you into its nest atop the boulder," explained Cindy, "Dan and I scaled the rock to lower you with a rope to Sam below."

Opening his eyes, Jimmy muttered, "Thanks."

Noticing that Jimmy was watching her, and in an attempt to keep her friend awake, Cindy added, "Sam speared four rabbits today; so once the meal's ready, I'll bring you a plate. You need to eat to regain your strength."

Cindy wanted so much to tell Jimmy about Dan's discovery a few miles up the trail, but decided against it, thinking that Jimmy would play the hero and act like he was fully recovered before he was ready for the hike.

Hearing the men return from the pond, Cindy yelled, "Sam, Dan, come quick."

After carelessly dropping their liquid cargo to the ground, the two men dashed to Cindy's side fearful that Jimmy had taken a turn for the worst. As the men approached, they immediately noticed Jimmy's opened eyes.

"Hey," exclaimed Dan, "welcome back."

"Yeah," added Sam, "glad to see you're awake."

Again, with great difficulty, Jimmy said, "Thanks ... thanks for saving me."

"Now we're even," joked Dan.

"No, not quite," replied Jimmy.

Dan smiled, for he knew that with the return of Jimmy's sense of humor, he'd soon be back to his old self.

That night, Jimmy feasted on a small portion of the rabbit, but quickly fell asleep shortly thereafter. At Cindy's suggestion and Sam's approval, the cure-all was suspended that night. As a result, Jimmy enjoyed many hours of uninterrupted sleep.

CHAPTER TWENTY-TWO

Torturous Thoughts

THROUGH THE OAK TREE AND INTO THE TRAVELERS' WORLD OF birth, Nancy Clay was true to her word. She and her husband met with the Parkers and Ms. Somer periodically in their home. After a few visits, the Clays convinced the families to join them every morning at church after the morning Mass. Even Sara Somer, who wasn't Catholic, felt an indescribable peace as she prayed for the safety of her daughter beneath the statue of Saint Michael the Archangel. When praying under the protective gaze of the artwork, Nancy Clay felt reassured that Dan was alive. Every morning, without exception, Father James led the families in prayer for the three teenagers' and Sam White's safety.

One morning, Father James pulled Jeff and Nancy aside and asked if they had received any more notes from Dan.

"No, Father," replied Nancy. "But Jeff and I remain hopeful that he'll return on the thirtieth as he promised."

Beyond a doubt, Father James now knew that Dan had indeed entered another world and was unable, at the present time, to communicate with his family.

After the prayers were recited, the families departed and agreed to meet the same time the following morning. Jeff kissed his wife goodbye before driving to work. The Parkers, as they had done every morning since meeting the group to pray, offered Nancy a ride home. And as the Parkers suspected, Nancy politely declined their kindness stating that she enjoyed saying additional prayers during the walk home.

As Nancy turned the corner several blocks from the church, she realized that the discomfort in her hands, which she initially experienced nearly two days ago, was finally subsiding. At the onset of the pain, she decided against telling Jeff, since the last time she mentioned a soreness in her ankle and neck, Jeff insisted that she visit their family doctor, who—on seeing no abrasions or cuts on her ankle or neck—was completely baffled with her condition. As painful as it was, Nancy couldn't understand why there were no visible wounds. She remained oblivious that what she was experiencing was the direct result of a close bond she shared with her son. Rather, she thought, *I'll take Father James' advice and offer up the suffering for the safety of Dan and the other missing persons.* The only time she enjoyed a brief respite from the pain was in prayer below her new favorite statue, Saint Michael the Archangel.

Back in the parallel world, Sam, Dan, and Cindy awoke at 7:00, while Jimmy, thankfully, remained sleeping well into the afternoon hours. Throughout the morning, the three travelers busied themselves with minor chores, aware that silence was to be maintained.

Near the fire and away from the sleeping patient, Dan asked, "Sam, when do you think Jimmy will be well enough to travel?"

"I don't know," replied Sam, "we'll just have to check on him every day to see how he's healing."

As much as Dan genuinely hoped for Jimmy's complete recovery, the idea of William in the castle and the thought of losing precious travel time kept nagging him.

"Sam," asked a hesitant Dan, "do you think I could venture to the castle myself?"

Sam dropped the utensils he was cleaning, spun around to face Dan, and exclaimed, "Are you nuts? Of course you can't go there alone! My gosh, do you know what you're asking? Do you have a death wish or something?"

Quite uncomfortable with Sam's disturbing questions, Dan nervously slipped his hands in his pockets and replied, "No; I just thought it might be easier on everyone if I went alone, while you and Cindy stayed here with Jimmy."

Suspecting that Dan might attempt to undertake the unthinkable in the dead of night, Sam remarked, "Dan, I know you're an honest man, so I must ask you to promise me that you will not, under any circumstances, travel to the castle alone." With no immediate response from the teenager, Sam sternly added, "Dan, I mean it!"

The teenager removed one hand from his pocket and, while running his fingers through his hair, unwillingly promised.

Cindy, who had just finished tidying up her sleeping area, neared the fire when she overheard Sam's harsh tone. "What's going on?" she asked.

"Nothing," snapped Dan.

"Nothing?" questioned Sam. "I'd hardly call attempting to hike to the castle alone as nothing."

"Dan," exclaimed Cindy, "are you insane? No one could ever make it alone. Besides, you can't hide it from me; I know your hands are still hurting."

"Look," replied Dan, "I promised Sam I wouldn't, so end of story."

"Well then," said Sam, "now that that's settled, let's start some lunch."

As Sam grabbed the food bag, Dan walked away in Jimmy's direction; Cindy followed.

"Hey, Dan," said Cindy, once the two were out of Sam's earshot, "I know you promised Sam, but now I need you to promise me something."

"What's that?" asked an annoyed Dan.

"Promise me," demanded Cindy, "that if you break your promise to Sam, you'll tell me and together we'll reach the castle and find your brother. Personally, I dread visiting the castle, but I also don't want you attempting the rescue mission alone."

Dan remained silent.

"Dan," urged Cindy, "promise me!"

"Alright... alright," replied Dan. "But I made a promise to Sam already and I never go back on my word."

Just then, the two heard Sam calling them over to help with lunch–in a rather soft voice–so as not to wake Jimmy.

Sensing that Dan might break both promises, Cindy tried to gain his trust by confiding in him, "I'll see what I can do to convince Sam to head to the castle sooner rather than later."

"Thanks," said Dan.

As Sam was warming one of the precooked rabbits, Dan aligned the mess kits, while Cindy reached for the cookie fragments.

During the meal preparations, Cindy posed, "Sam, when do you think we'll move on?"

"Like I told Dan," replied Sam, "we'll check on Jimmy regularly to see how he's healing."

"I don't suspect it'll be too much longer," continued Cindy, "since he's already begun to heal."

Suspecting that she was trying to coerce the group into leaving prematurely, Sam remarked, "Okay, you two, I know what you're up to and I partially agree with you. Sure, I'd also like to leave today if we could, because the sooner we leave, the sooner we'll get back." After brushing a spider which had settled upon his knee, Sam asked, "But don't you think we'd all feel guilty if we left too early, before Jimmy had time to heal, and he ended up in a worse predicament because of his poor strength?"

Cindy and Dan had no response; they knew Sam was right.

Sensing growing frustration with the situation, Sam proposed, "I'll treat Jimmy's wounds later today and again tomorrow morning. When he stirs again, I'll tell him of the castle's discovery and let him make the decision. But I'll only mention the castle to him if I think he's recovered enough. Is this agreeable to you two?"

"Yes," replied the teenagers.

"Good," said Sam, "then we'll not mention this conversation until tomorrow." Returning his attention to the fire, Sam continued, "It looks like the rabbit's done; pass me your plates."

Cindy handed her plate to Sam for rabbit, and then to Dan for a few cookie crumbs. The meal was enjoyed in relative silence, while each took turns glancing in Jimmy's direction.

TORTUROUS THOUGHTS

To the amazement of everyone, Jimmy awoke at 3:00 in the afternoon; by 5:00 he was walking around the campsite and by 6:00 his appetite had returned. For the first time in awhile, the four travelers enjoyed a meal together, though nothing was mentioned about when the hike would resume. On patrol that night was Cindy, followed by Dan and then Sam.

The next morning during breakfast, while enjoying one handful of dry cereal, half of a roasted marshmallow, and Doctor O'Brien's medication, none of the three watchers had anything unusual to report from their patrols.

Once again, Sam was pleased to see that Jimmy was still sleeping. *After all,* Sam thought, *he needs a great deal of rest for the healing process to take hold.*

After cleaning the campsite, the three had a few hours to themselves. Sam occupied his time cleaning his revolver and sharpening his lances; Cindy busied herself reorganizing her personal belongings, while periodically checking on Jimmy; and Dan spent the morning hours reading Scripture. Dan was just turning the page in the Bible when, from the corner of his eye, he witnessed Jimmy sit up in his sleeping bag.

"How are you feeling?" asked Dan.

"Much better," replied Jimmy, after a prolonged yawn.

On overhearing the men talking, Cindy and Sam approached Jimmy's sleeping area.

"So, trooper," said Sam, "are you up for a snack?"

"Yeah, Sam," replied Jimmy, "that sounds great."

As Sam headed to the campfire to grab a few handfuls of cereal and a cup of water, Cindy reached for the liquid cure-all resting beside Jimmy and poured a small dose on his shoulders, once Dan had removed the patient's shirt and bandages. To Dan and Cindy's surprise, Jimmy hardly twitched.

Returning to Jimmy's side, Sam set the pieces of cereal on the sleeping bag and carefully inspected Jimmy's injuries. "Well," said Sam, "your wounds are healing nicely." Detecting the smell of alcohol and seeing Cindy holding the opened bottle, Sam asked, "Did it sting just now?"

"Not much," replied Jimmy.

Sam handed Jimmy the cup of water.

"Jimmy," said Sam, "there's something I need to ask you."

With a mouthful of dry cereal, Jimmy only nodded.

"The other day when Dan was atop the Oswagi's nest," explained Sam, "he spotted the castle directly west, less than a day's walk from here."

Jimmy's eyes widened, as he looked at Dan seeking confirmation of the story.

"Yeah, Jimmy," verified Dan, "I saw it."

Sam rested his hand on Jimmy's forearm to draw his attention back to him. "Anyway," added Sam, "I don't want to press forward until you're ready. We don't want anything else to befall you in your weakened condition."

"Thanks, Sam," replied Jimmy, "but I think I'm good to go this afternoon."

"It might be better if we wait until tomorrow," recommended Sam, "once you've had another full night's rest."

"No, Sam," replied Jimmy, "I'd rather move out today."

"Tell you what," proposed Sam, "we'll leave later this afternoon, but at the first sign of weakness, we stop for the day, agreed?"

"Okay," replied Jimmy.

"And, Jimmy," warned Sam, "I'll be watching you like a hawk."

After the group enjoyed lunch–including Jimmy, who only minutes earlier had eaten a few handfuls of cereal–all pitched in to clean the area. Like every day since their entry into the world, the group meticulously cleaned the area and removed all evidence of their stay to prevent any creature from picking up their scent and tracking them. At 2:30 in the afternoon, Sam took the lead for the castle with Jimmy at his side for close supervision; Cindy and Dan followed immediately behind, each bearing a lance.

Two hours into their hike, Sam asked, "Jimmy, how are you holding up?"

"Fine," replied the teenager.

In an effort to appease his doubts, Sam added, "Do you want to keep moving?"

"Sure," answered Jimmy. "My shoulders are a little sore, but the nicks on my legs from the nestlings hardly hurt at all."

"Be that as it may," advised Sam, "we'll take it slow."

Meanwhile, Dan swung his duffle bag off his back and held it in front as he walked, feeling inside to confirm he had the essentials he'd be taking inside the castle. First he felt William's stuffed animal, then the asthma medication, the holy water bottle, and finally, the blessed votive candle.

"Sam," asked Dan, "do you have your lighter on you?"

After checking his pockets, Sam responded, "Yeah."

"Is there plenty of lighter fluid in it," questioned Dan, "or is it running low after all the campfires?"

Removing the lighter from his pocket, Sam shook it and answered, "Yeah, there's plenty of fluid left, why?"

"No reason," replied Dan.

At 6:30, the group stopped for dinner, knowing that if they started a campfire any closer to the castle it would be detected. Sitting down for another rabbit meal, the topic quickly turned to the Reclaimers.

Sam did his best to recount the stories he had heard from Doctor O'Brien twenty years ago concerning the evil men. "The main thing to always–and I mean always–remember is never to make direct eye contact with a Reclaimer. Doctor O'Brien told me once that their will power is infinitely stronger than any human's and that the serpent men can effortlessly persuade anyone to take up permanent residence in their castle, regardless of the visitor's determination never to step foot inside the fortress."

"Are the Reclaimers fearful of light?" asked Cindy.

"I doubt it," replied Sam, "since Spiritus Malus occasionally travels to the oak tree during full moons, and Reclaimers have been known to wander the forest which, as you know, isn't brilliantly lit, but there's some light."

"Do the Reclaimers have supernatural powers?" asked Jimmy.

"That's a good question," replied Sam. "I'm not really sure; but I don't think so."

Detecting a sense of uneasiness, Sam reiterated, "Look, the main thing is not to look into their eyes. If we can avoid eye contact, then we'll be fine."

Throughout the conversation, Dan remained silent, sitting against a tree several feet from the group, and staring westward. One can only imagine the thoughts which preoccupied his mind.

"Dan," said Sam.

The teenager remained in a daze.

"Dan," said Sam again, but in a louder voice.

There was still no reaction from the teenager.

Finally, Sam threw a spoon at Dan, who quickly jolted from his trance. "Sorry... what?" asked Dan.

"Have you been listening to any of this?" asked Sam.

"Kind of... sorry," replied the teenager.

"Dan," restated Sam, "it's very important that if you encounter a Reclaimer you don't look into his eyes. Do you understand?"

"Yeah," answered Dan.

To drive the point home, Sam stressed, "Dan, I'm serious. This could make the difference between being held captive in the castle and returning home."

"Yeah, Sam," said Dan, "I know, don't look into their eyes."

Glancing around the campsite area, Sam noticed that everyone displayed a traceable look of fear in his or her eyes. Rising to his feet, Sam recommended, "I think it would be a good idea that when we resume our hike tomorrow, we avoid the footpath and cross deeper into the woods to avoid detection."

The young travelers agreed.

"And finally," concluded Sam, "it probably goes without saying, but we must be exceedingly vigilant on our patrols tonight."

Again, all members agreed.

The conversation about the Reclaimers and the ghastly castle resumed well into the night, at which time Sam remarked, "I suggest that we get a good night's sleep. Cindy, why don't you take the first shift? Then I'll patrol, followed by Dan and then Jimmy."

Once in his sleeping bag, Dan reached for his lantern and Bible to read Saint Luke's account of our Lord's Passion for courage and strength. He knew he'd need those virtues the next day.

The following morning, even though the travelers were too excited–or nervous–to eat, Sam insisted. Over their meal, no one had anything unusual to report from their patrols, except Cindy, who mentioned that toward the end of her shift she heard a disturbing creaky noise, then a loud bang, and then silence.

At once, the explorers scanned the footpath and the forest fringes for a probable cause of last night's clamor. Unfortunately, the thick forest cover obscured their views. Returning their sights to the immediate area, the group resumed their meager breakfast which was consumed in record time. However, before rising from the campsite to clean the area, Cindy pulled four pills from her pocket and then reached for the whiskey to administer a final cleansing on Jimmy's shoulders. With the application, none of the travelers were more astounded than Jimmy when he didn't twitch.

I guess we're as ready as we'll ever be, thought Sam.

Within thirty minutes, the camp area was cleaned and the four rescuers were trudging to the castle. After an hour's hike through the rough terrain and its steady uphill climb, the four stopped only feet within the outer edge of the forest to survey the clearing and castle ahead. The fortress was composed of massive, irregular, black stones which soared six stories high with only a handful of openings in the wall facing them, which Sam suspected were used to detect approaching guests. However, the most prominent feature which the group noticed was the lack of trees a thousand feet or so outward from the castle wall and extending around the structure's perimeter, from what they could see. Except for a few scattered cumulus clouds, the sun shone brightly that morning. Yet, the castle itself remained somewhat darkened. It was as if an invisible barrier prevented the sun's rays from penetrating the castle, or perhaps the rays chose not to enter. Whatever the reason, a dark threatening castle sat atop a large hill with the sunlight abruptly ending just above the four watchtowers on each corner of the structure and within feet of the castle walls.

After several moments analyzing the castle, suddenly, and without warning, the travelers began to shake spastically. It wasn't fear that overcame them, but rather a flood of evil and doubtful thoughts which dominated their minds. Every shameful word and deed that each member of the group had spoken or committed during their lifetime plagued their thoughts instantaneously. They were grief stricken.

Dan fell to his knees. While in a position of mercy, he felt the torturous thoughts slightly diminish. *I wonder...* he thought, as he prostrated himself on the ground. Once flat on the soil, his mind was totally at ease. Rolling onto his back, he witnessed his friends still physically trembling. Dan jumped to his feet and threw each friend to the forest floor and ordered them to remain on the ground. Within moments, a great calm engulfed the travelers as they exhaled a sigh of relief.

"What the heck was that?" asked Jimmy, while flat on the ground.

"I'd guess it's something in the air," answered Dan, "since we can't feel its effects on the ground."

To confirm Dan's speculation, Sam rose to his feet, but faced away from the castle to determine whether the effects were caused by the sight of the castle or a smell in the air. Within thirty seconds, he began to shake again; Jimmy leveled him.

After catching his breath again, Sam yielded, "I think you're right, Dan; it's probably something in the air. So, I suggest we near the castle on our stomachs or at least on our knees."

All travelers wholeheartedly agreed.

"But why," asked Cindy, "didn't we experience these vile feelings last night or earlier this morning when we were approaching the castle?"

"Maybe," replied Sam, "we were too far away to be vulnerable to whatever's in the air. And I'm sure that the dense woods acted somewhat like a filter."

Once the four travelers were breathing normally, Sam recommended that everyone remain flat on the ground while he rose to his knees to resume his initial survey for their point of entry into the castle. After taking a deep breath, Sam rose to his knees. The mental torture increased the longer Sam remained above the ground. Within a minute, he began shaking. On witnessing his deteriorating condition, Dan and Jimmy lunged at Sam, knocking him to the ground.

"Sam!" yelled Dan.

Sam remained flat on his back unable to speak and still shaking.

"Sam!" yelled Dan again.

"Come on, Sam," yelled Cindy, "pull through!"

Eventually, Sam's shakes subsided. "I'm okay," he whispered.

After giving Sam a few more minutes to recover, Jimmy asked, "What'd you find out?"

Sam cleared his throat and explained, "From what I can tell at this distance and from this angle, there's a moat surrounding the castle." Sam paused to take another deep breath and then reported, "It looks like the bank of the moat on the side nearer the castle is at an incline; obviously, I couldn't make out the bank on the side closer to us. The only point of entry I saw was the drawbridge and it's closed, which is fine. If we want to enter undetected, the drawbridge is not the answer."

"Closed?" questioned Cindy. "Why would the drawbridge be closed if the Reclaimers want guests?"

Sam shrugged his shoulders before remarking, "Who knows? But I think it's best for us that it's closed."

"Hey," blurted Jimmy, "maybe the loud bang Cindy heard during her patrol last night was the drawbridge closing. And maybe it's closed to prevent ..."

"But, Sam," interrupted Cindy, "if we can't use the drawbridge, then how will we get in?"

"I'd suggest," said Sam, "that we crawl on our bellies across the clearing, swim across the moat, and then climb the inner embankment later tonight. The darkness of night will conceal our crossing the clearing. It'll be a rough crossing, but I think we can do it."

"But how," asked Cindy again, "do we enter the castle if the drawbridge is the only access and we can't use it?"

"If the castle is as old as legends say," explained Sam, "then there's bound to be a loose or missing rock in its massive structure, and we'll find it."

The remainder of the day was spent in that particular location, resting flat on the ground. Occasionally, however, a traveler would rise to his or her knees and conduct a quick scan of the clearing to see if anyone or anything was approaching. Cindy spent part of the day stitching an experimental two-layered bandanna from tattered clothing, hoping it would deter whatever foul chemical which infested the air from penetrating the travelers' nasal passages. Volunteering to test the latest survival gear, Dan rose to his feet and remained standing for nearly three minutes without enduring any evil thoughts or shakes.

"Hey," exclaimed Dan through the bandanna, "it works!"

With plenty of time on her hands, Cindy made several more double-layered bandannas in the event one or two proved defective.

At 5:00 in the evening, with a campfire out of the question, the four gathered for cold rabbit.

Halfway through the meal, Sam suggested that everyone remove all nonessential items from their backpacks to lighten the load. "Whatever you take with you," reminded Sam, "is what you'll have to drag through the clearing, across the moat, and throughout the castle until we return to this site."

Within an hour, the travelers had inventoried their backpacks and removed most of their spare clothing, knowing that they wouldn't be changing clothes anytime soon. Then all the essential items–the sparse food supply, water, weapons, whiskey, rope, flashlight, first-aid kit, and lantern–were equally distributed between the four backpacks.

After concealing his holy water, votive candle, asthma medication, and stuffed animal under a patch of fallen leaves beside him, Dan made a mental note to return his personal essential items to his duffle bag immediately before the group resumed their journey later that evening. Still not completely convinced that light didn't torment the Reclaimers, Dan asked, "Sam, do you still have your lighter?"

Again, Sam reached into his pocket and replied, "Yes; Dan, why are you so concerned about my lighter?"

Without skipping a beat, Dan responded, "If, by chance, the Reclaimers are fearful of light, then it would come in handy."

"Like I explained before," remarked Sam, "I doubt the Reclaimers are afraid of light. After all, even though the sun's rays never fully penetrate the castle's barrier, I'm sure there's some natural light in the castle."

Dan remained silent, but hopeful.

CHAPTER TWENTY-THREE
Dark Waters

THAT EVENING, THE SUN DROPPED BELOW THE HORIZON AT 7:15. By 7:30, the rescuers, protected with bandannas, were crawling on their stomachs, hoping to deter the dangerous effects of the odorless gas in the clearing, while also attempting to avoid detection from someone or something that may be posted in the watchtowers. Lugging their essentials—and Dan, his personal possessions—they quietly inched their way to the moat's edge. At 8:00, they reached their destination.

"Oh great," whispered Sam as he noticed the embankment's vertical drop on the near side of the moat. "I guess we'll have to jump," added an uneasy Sam. "There's no doubt it'll make some noise, but I don't see any other way."

Discreetly, Sam rose to his feet and took several steps back, preparing himself for the thirty-foot fall.

Cindy remained staring into the moat, while Dan and Jimmy slightly rotated from their stomachs to their sides, supported themselves on one elbow, and gazed back at Sam. The senior traveler had only begun to lunge forward, when Cindy sprang to her feet and intercepted Sam, knocking both to the ground.

"What are you doing?" whispered Sam in a harsh voice.

"I saw something move in the water," answered a troubled Cindy.

"What do you mean something moved in the water?" questioned Sam.

Dan and Jimmy, who were still resting on their sides facing Cindy and Sam, rotated again and directed their sights to the murky waters below.

"I don't see anything," said Jimmy. "Do you, Dan?"

"No," answered Dan. Amid his downward stare, Dan speculated, "Maybe it was a fish or something."

Still seated on the ground from his collision with Cindy, Sam grabbed a rock which was within arm's reach, crawled to the edge of the moat, and remarked, "We'll just see," as he released the stone over the moat.

Cindy scurried to the edge on all fours.

The moment the rock hit the surface, the dark waters agitated violently. The travelers stared in complete disbelief. Once the water's fury subsided, Sam turned to Cindy and admitted, "Sorry I doubted you. Thanks."

As the four peered into the dark, veiled waters trying to decipher the movement's origin, Jimmy whispered, "What do we do now?"

"I'm thinking," replied Sam.

"Maybe we could…" started Dan.

"I've got it," interrupted Sam. "It'll be an allnighter, but I'm sure it'll work."

"What's that?" questioned Dan.

"I'd guess," said Sam, "that the distance across is fifteen feet."

"Yeah," confirmed Dan, "about fifteen feet."

"I suggest," detailed Sam, "that we gather several sturdy fallen limbs greater than fifteen feet in length from the forest, bind them with the rope, and then roll them uphill to the moat."

"Uphill?" questioned Cindy. "Isn't there an easier way?"

"I'm afraid not," answered Sam. "It'll take us a few hours, but the sun's only recently set."

Dan, knowing that he must enter the castle for his brother, was the first to whisper, "Let's do it."

Dan's approval was seconded by Jimmy and–after a lengthy deliberation–Cindy ultimately agreed.

Shortly before 8:30, the four travelers retraced their crawl back to the cover of the forest. Once under its protection, the travelers rose from the ground and searched for long fallen limbs which were durable and not decayed. For their own protection, Sam demanded that the four look together, no more than ten feet away from one another.

Dan was the first to find a long sturdy limb. It was only four inches thick, but knowing that it would be bound with several other limbs of similar size, Sam affirmed through his bandanna, "That should be the perfect size."

Even though Jimmy was still experiencing slight pain in his shoulders, he helped Dan carry the timber to the border of the forest. The second suitable limb was also discovered by Dan.

"Great job," replied Sam, as he and Dan lugged it and set it alongside the first branch.

Eventually, Cindy located a qualifying limb; then Jimmy, then Dan again, and then Sam. Within three hours, twelve appropriate-sized limbs were located, all within a hundred yards of the forest's edge. Once the branches were aligned, Sam unpacked his rope and bundled the timbers together. Fully aware that the limbs would be literally a life line for his friends and himself, Sam took extra care to wrap the rope around the timbers three times and at four separate points. Each cord was secured with several knots. The entire process took nearly an hour.

"There," said Sam, "that ought to hold."

"Ought to hold?" questioned Cindy.

"I mean," corrected Sam, "will hold."

The four explorers dropped to their stomachs–with their backpacks attached and their bandannas secured–and slowly, but forcefully, pushed the timber uphill. Considering the weight of the wood and the steady uphill push, the team required several breaks along the way. Even Jimmy, who was now enduring growing discomfort in his shoulders, proved valuable in pushing the massive timber.

At approximately 4:00 a.m., the manmade bridge rested several feet from the moat's edge. Knowing that the four travelers must make the crossing before sunrise, the group wasted no time in attempting to raise the cumbersome limb. Since Jimmy had not fully regained his upper body strength, Sam suggested that Jimmy and Cindy anchor their feet at the base of the log to prevent it from sliding forward, while he and Dan use their combined strengths to raise the timber vertically.

After several failed attempts, success was finally attained, as the bulky branch towered overhead and then fell in the direction of the castle over the moat. Longer than required, the log grazed the castle wall. The resounding thump produced by the limb hitting the ground on the opposite side of the moat forced the travelers to the ground, hoping to escape detection from any would-be onlookers. The group remained completely motionless for a few minutes. Then, with added caution, Sam raised his head and scanned the area. Detecting no one or no creature nearby, he whispered to his companions that it was safe to cross the moat.

In the unlikely event that the timber isn't strong enough, thought Sam, *and since I'm the second heaviest person in the group, next to Jimmy, I'll test the apparatus first.*

After tightening the bandanna around his face, Sam straddled the log and then pulled himself two feet forward. Several cycles later, Sam arrived safely on the opposite side of the moat. Throughout his harrowing journey, he was elated that the timber exhibited no signs of strain.

From across the moat, Sam gestured Cindy to tighten her bandanna, which was slipping down her face. Then he motioned her to approach the roped limbs.

With visible trepidation, Cindy slowly and methodically crossed the timber, never once glancing down. Within minutes, she was in Sam's waiting arms. Jimmy's trek across the bundled wood set a new record in speed.

Dan retightened the straps on his duffle bag, secured his bandanna, dropped to the timber, and was soon making great headway across the log. Barely five feet across, Dan felt the wooden bridge shake and then creak. *Oh, no,* he thought, *it's giving way!* Across the moat, his three co-travelers also heard the ill-fated squeak. Dan turned his head and glanced behind, hoping not to detect any indications that the branches were separating. As he turned to face the castle wall, a troll quickly spun itself from under the log only a few feet from Dan; the suspended teenager gasped. Fortunately, with its four-clawed hands gripping the tied timbers for balance, the troll's talons were virtually useless against its prey. At the same time, Dan's firm grasp on the wood prevented him from knocking the creature from the log.

DARK WATERS

Sensing a forthcoming lunge from the troll—similar to the troll that leaped upon him in the forest—Dan immediately dropped his face and chest to the timber.

With one quick spring, the troll landed on Dan's back, only lightly tearing into his flesh. Six of the troll's claws secured themselves onto Dan's duffle bag; two claws tore into Dan's back. While holding on for dear life with his hands and squeezing the log with his thighs, Dan rocked violently, attempting to release the troll from his back. With each spastic roll, the troll instinctively sank its claws deeper into Dan's back and further into his duffle bag. Amid one last powerful rocking motion, the troll lost its grip, and fell from Dan's back.

Grasping at anything within reach to save itself from plummeting, the troll seized Dan's left leg and while sliding down to his boot, shredded the traveler's jeans and tore a gash in Dan's leg from his calf to his ankle. Dan withstood the pain, refusing to scream for fear of alerting the Reclaimers to the group's presence.

Sam had his revolver drawn, but knowing that a shot would summon the Reclaimers and put the remaining teenagers' lives at risk–not to mention the fact that the early morning darkness prevented him from a clear aim at the troll–Sam's weapon was useless.

The troll remained suspended in midair over the moat hanging from Dan's boot. As Dan turned his head slightly from the timber and saw the troll dangling, he also noticed the waters churning slowly. A drop of blood left Dan's bleeding calf and hit the water; a giant eel–easily forty feet long with an elongated head, bulging eyes, and an open mouth displaying numerous protruding teeth–whipped its powerful posterior muscles to propel itself twenty-five feet into the air and sank its fangs into the hanging troll, releasing it from Dan's boot and pulling it to its watery grave. Dan immediately shut his eyes and pressed his face and chest even more firmly against the log, while raising his legs and placing them behind him atop the timber–far from the predator's sight and reach.

In a state of shock, Dan remained in the same spot, unable to speak or move, while his co-travelers–watching from across the moat–tried to snap him out of it.

"Dan," said Sam in a low voice, so as not to be overheard by the castle residents, "you can do it; come on."

With no reaction from Dan, Jimmy knew he had to act quickly to save his friend. Disregarding the potentially fatal consequences for himself, Jimmy straddled the log and crawled to Dan. When he was only a couple feet from his friend, Jimmy urged, "Come on, buddy. We can do it ... the two of us together."

Dan remained silent.

"Dan," reminded Jimmy, "we've got to save William."

That was all Dan needed to hear. The injured teenager slowly lowered his legs alongside the timber and gripped it with his thighs. Then he raised his face and chest from the bundled branches, grasped the log several inches in front, and pulled himself forward, while Jimmy performed the same routine in reverse. Within five painstaking minutes, the two teenagers arrived safely on the opposite side of the moat with the rest of the group.

Resting his hand on Jimmy's shoulder, Sam whispered, "That was a brave thing you did."

"Yeah," whispered Cindy, "thanks."

Dan–with his head lowered–whispered, "Sorry I freaked out."

Touching his clenched fist against Dan's chin and then raising it, Sam replied, "There's nothing for you to apologize for. Any one of us, including myself, would have reacted the same way."

Dan's leg gave way; luckily Sam caught the teenager before he collapsed.

Jimmy rushed to support Dan's other side. Very carefully, the two men lowered Dan to the ground and placed him on his stomach.

Once Dan's damaged duffle bag was removed, Sam, Cindy, and Jimmy noticed a fair amount of blood on the teenager's shirt.

"I'm fine," lied Dan, "it doesn't really hurt."

"Nonsense," whispered Sam, "of course it hurts."

Glancing up at Cindy and then down at Dan, Sam regrettably remarked, "I hate to do this to you now, Dan," as he accepted the whiskey bottle from Cindy, "but it's for your own good."

Realizing that a loud noise from Dan would easily attract attention, Sam ordered Cindy to rip a piece of timber from the nearby log. After visually confirming the absence of castle residents, Sam and Jimmy gently removed Dan's shirt and lifted his pant leg.

At Sam's nodding, Jimmy raised Dan's head slightly, while Cindy placed the strip of wood firmly between his upper and lower jaws. Dan squeezed Jimmy's and Cindy's hands as Sam disinfected the young man's back and leg. Though only a weak moan was heard, Dan was suffering unbearable pain; however, he didn't pass out. Once again, the teenager silently endured the anguish for the safety of the group.

As Cindy bandaged Dan's injured leg and back with the limited clothing in the backpacks, Sam adventured to the moat's edge, determined to salvage the rope. Unfortunately, since the cord was wrapped around the timber at four separate points and secured with several knots, it was impossible to retrieve without climbing over the moat and risking an encounter with the eel. With Jimmy's help, Sam pushed the log into the water below to discard all evidence of their unannounced arrival. Glancing into the moat, neither Sam nor Jimmy saw any movement of the creature and both were grateful that the bundled branches sank below the dark waters. After only a few minutes of respite at Dan's side, Sam raised the teenager to his feet and assisted his young friend to the castle wall. The sun would rise soon and the group needed to find cover quickly.

As the four trespassers began their hike around the fortress, looking for a loose stone or a hole in the foundation, Cindy was the first to mention the unnatural terrain between the castle wall and the moat, saying, "It looks like someone or something has recently turned the soil."

Looking ahead, the group noticed that the entire area bore the curious soil markings, as far as they could see in the relative darkness.

"Alright," whispered Sam, "enough with the ground; we need to be on the lookout for a missing stone, a hole in the foundation, or an opening. And since our rope's at the bottom of the moat, the opening has to be within arm's reach."

All scanned the immense fortress for a break or fracture in its base or an opening, but nothing was discovered. Turning the corner of one of the castle walls, the group walked another five minutes before Jimmy spotted an opening without iron bars and only a few feet above the ground.

As the travelers neared the opening, Sam whispered, "Shush," as he heard the remote sound of voices.

Once the group was alongside the opening, each clearly heard two men talking. While resecuring his grip around Dan's waist, Sam failed to notice Jimmy and Cindy crawling on all fours–to avoid detection–to the opposite side of the opening. The four explorers pressed their backs firmly against the castle wall; Cindy and Jimmy on one side of the opening and Sam and Dan on the other. The group patiently waited for the voices to cease.

After nearly ten minutes and with no indication that the conversation would be ending soon, Sam stole a quick peek through the opening. In less than two seconds, he yanked his head from the opening and thrust himself against the outside castle wall.

Cindy pushed herself from the wall, leaned in Sam's direction, and in the softest of whispers, asked, "What's wrong?"

After a noisy gulp, Sam whispered, "There are two men preparing meals by candlelight."

"So," whispered Jimmy.

"Except," explained Sam in a soft voice, "they aren't really men."

"What are they?" asked Dan.

"I don't know," answered Sam. Though curious to steal another glimpse, Sam resisted the growing temptation and admitted, "I've never seen anything like them ... even in this world. They're men with huge pincers, like a crustacean."

"Men with claws?" asked a doubtful Dan.

"Shush," warned Sam.

Within the kitchen stood two creatures bearing the most gruesome features. Part crayfish, part human, and part fish, each beast walked upon eight legs, while displaying two oversize anterior claws and a pair of probing antennae. Between its pincers and first set of legs, each primeval crustacean brazenly unfurled a pair of three-foot retractable fins which closely resembled the swimming appendages affixed between its third and fourth series of legs. An unheard-of elongated whip-like tail, complete with a deadly stinger, remained suspended beyond the rear of the creature.

Although the upper frame of the beasts appeared partially human with a man's head, shoulders, two arms, and chest, their upper bodies were inhumanly disgraced with lengthy gills which extended on either side of their cold-blooded bodies–directly below the armpit to the waist–and two miniature dorsal fins attached to their shoulder blades.

Sam's immediate, yet alarming, belief was correct. Unlike the travelers' home world, the prehistoric claw-men–like the Oswagi Bird–had escaped extinction in the parallel world. Eons ago, the ancestors of these crustacean creatures populated the rugged terrain and murky lake waters of the forest, thus justifying their gills and fins.

Curiosity got the better of Jimmy, who pushed himself off the wall and peered through the opening. He exhaled a loud gasp and then recoiled to the wall's safety.

Suddenly, the voices within the structure stopped and were replaced with the sound of clacking crustacean feet upon the hard floor growing louder and louder; a claw-man was approaching the opening. Before the creature reached the hole in the wall, Sam gestured Cindy and Jimmy to slip further away; he and Dan did likewise. The crayfish poked its head slightly into the opening, but the inner casing prevented it from glimpsing around the corner. Within seconds of pulling its head back inside the castle, the creature shot its tail–complete with stinger–through the opening and physically inspected the nearby walls. The stinger came within two feet of Jimmy, as he and Cindy slid even further away. Suddenly, the ugliest bird the travelers had ever seen–dark green with gray spots and its eyes so far down its head that they rested alongside its beak–landed in the opening.

"Oh," said the claw-man at the opening, "it's only Ekim," as he petted the disfigured bird.

All travelers breathed a very faint sigh of relief.

For as brief as Sam's glance was earlier through the opening, he noticed fruits and vegetables sitting on a dilapidated wooden table; he was determined to retrieve some of the produce, since the group's food supply was frightfully low.

Eventually, from inside was heard, "That ought to do. Let's deliver the meals to the guests."

After a few moments of silence from within, Sam whispered, "Jimmy, come over here and support Dan."

Once Dan's arm was across Jimmy's shoulder, Sam directed, "You three stay here and out of sight, while I gather a little food; it looks like this is the castle's kitchen."

"Can I come along?" pleaded Jimmy.

"Absolutely not," snapped Sam. "You're to stay here and watch Dan."

Suddenly, more voices were heard, but from around the corner of the castle, no more than twenty-five feet from where the travelers stood.

"Quick," whispered Sam, "everybody through the opening."

"But I thought you just said... ." remarked Jimmy.

"Shut up, Jimmy," blurted Sam, as he helped Jimmy lift Dan to the opening.

Cindy, who volunteered to climb through the opening first, assisted Dan to the floor inside the castle. Once the group was in the kitchen, they remained in a squat position—which proved exceedingly painful for Dan—against the wall directly below the opening in the likely event the men or creatures outside towered above the opening. Taking a glance to his right and upward slightly, Sam eyed two stingers hovering outside the opening and then watched them depart.

While Sam monitored the movement outside the opening, Jimmy scanned the table ten feet ahead which was overflowing with produce. Though fruits and vegetables weren't his favorite food groups, he hadn't had a juicy apple or ripe tomato in such a long time that even they looked appetizing to him.

Once Sam signaled that the coast was clear, Cindy assisted Dan to the table. Jimmy was already there with his bandanna lowered and enjoying an apple. Dan snatched an apple and continued walking across the kitchen floor—doing his best to conceal his aching leg, but was poorly convincing.

While nearing the table of produce Sam lowered his bandanna and warned, "Don't make our pilfering obvious."

Glancing at the table and then at Sam, Jimmy remarked, "Look at all this." Then pointing to another table which was also loaded with produce in the corner of the kitchen, the teenager added, "And there's more over there. I don't think they're going to miss a few apples and tomatoes."

Once he saw the second table, Sam yielded, "Alright, but like I said, don't make it obvious," as he grabbed an apple and took a healthy bite.

Touring the kitchen, Sam noticed that its appearance was as if time itself feared the castle and passed it by. Everything appeared suitable to the Middle Ages, including the wooden ladles, plates, and bowls. In the kitchen's fireplace, hung a large metal pot, which upon closer inspection, Sam speculated was used regularly or at least recently for cooking vegetable stews.

Turning around, Sam eyed Cindy and Jimmy loading their backpacks with produce. "Hey you guys," whispered Sam, "I'm sure they'll notice all of that missing."

In their rush to load the enticing fruits and vegetables, Jimmy splattered a tomato to the kitchen floor. Knowing that all evidence of their covert entry must be removed, Jimmy reached for a rag resting on the table's edge. Noticing something peculiar on the fabric, Cindy ripped it from Jimmy's hands.

"Oh my God," exclaimed Cindy, as she unraveled the rag.

In her hands, she held a child-sized jersey with the number '7' still attached and the name 'CLAY' clearly visible, though the 'L' lettering was missing from the shirt. The heavy jersey, though severely faded, appeared to have been hardly used.

Dan, who was standing only several feet from Cindy, darted–as fast as his aching leg would allow–to the clothing and yanked it from her hand.

"It's William's," exclaimed Dan. "He's here!"

"Shush," warned Sam, as he neared the group at the table.

"But, Sam," interjected Dan, "this is William's soccer jersey." Detecting an obvious look of doubt on Sam's face, the teenager continued, "Look, Sam," as he pointed to the lettering on the shirt, "it even has 'CLAY' on it. I knew he was here."

In an effort not to needlessly raise the young man's hopes prematurely, with the distinct possibility that his hopes could be shattered in the very near future, Sam reasoned, "Dan, maybe someone from the Clay family in this world visited this castle years ago."

"Come on, Sam," said Dan in a sarcastic tone. "What are the chances?" Dan took another look at the jersey and repeated, "I knew he was here."

Sam took a step in Dan's direction and accepted the shirt for a closer inspection. "Alright," conceded Sam, "for argument's sake, let's say this is your brother's jersey. Then that means he was here thirteen years ago." Sam returned the shirt to Dan. The sixty-year-old traveler struggled for a few moments, but ultimately voiced the unthinkable, "Look, Dan, given the harsh environment of this world and the legends of the Reclaimers–not to mention William's medical condition–there's a real possibility that your brother . . ." Sam abruptly ended his suspicion.

"That my brother, what?" demanded Dan. "That he died in this castle or in the forest in the past?"

"I'm sorry, Dan," said Sam in a comforting tone, "but we have to face the grim reality that it's entirely possible."

As a disheartened Dan walked from the group, Sam vowed, "Dan, if your brother is alive and in this place, I promise we'll find him. But in the meantime, we can't leave any evidence of our arrival."

Dan turned and displayed a puzzled look.

"The jersey," explained Sam. "We have to put it back where we found it. Regardless of how insignificant it may seem, it could very well disclose our presence." Suspecting a forthcoming refusal from Dan to surrender the soccer jersey, Sam reminded, "Your friends have suffered a great deal to ensure our arrival at this fortress. Don't further endanger their lives by removing something from the castle which could conceivably draw attention to them."

As much as Dan hated Sam's logic and abhorred the idea of relinquishing William's shirt, he knew that Sam was right. With great reluctance, Dan tossed the jersey to Sam, who returned it to the table. Dan resumed limping to the kitchen's entryway where the claw-men had only recently exited.

Sam dashed in Dan's direction as the young man stuck his head through the doorless entryway and peered around the corner.

Seeing that the coast was clear, Dan placed his injured leg into the hallway.

Only now arriving at the teenager's side, Sam grabbed Dan's shoulder and foiled his complete entry into the corridor.

"Dan," exclaimed Sam, "what are you doing? There will be plenty of time."

Dan made a second attempt, but Sam repelled his advance with greater force. "First," suggested Sam, "we need a game plan."

Dan turned to face Sam and asked, "A game plan? What do you mean?"

Helping his young friend retrace his steps to the center of the kitchen, Sam explained, "Well for starters, this is a big castle and we haven't the foggiest idea where your brother is ... if he's even here."

"I know he's here," insisted Dan. "He's on the sixth floor; you've got to believe me."

Realizing that Dan had suffered much over the past couple weeks, and since Sam didn't want to dampen the young man's spirits, especially now that they were in the heart of the castle–a place where every member of the group had to be alert and attentive–Sam restated, "If William's here, we'll find him ... even if it means taking the second full moon home."

Not knowing when the claw-men would return, Sam placed a firmer grip around Dan's waist and advised, "Come on, let's get out of sight."

As Sam and Dan neared their co-travelers, the hushed conversation, which Cindy and Jimmy had only recently begun, abruptly stopped. All heard the dreaded voices of the claw-men from the hallway growing louder and louder.

The four travelers raced to the opening which they had entered only minutes earlier. As Sam and Jimmy were lifting Dan to the opening, they clearly heard a second conversation–but this one was originating from outside the opening. Sam and Jimmy lowered Dan and then skittishly scanned the kitchen for another escape route.

"Hey," whispered Cindy, "what about this?" as she opened a dumbwaiter.

With no other options available, and with the conversation in the hallway so close now that the travelers could almost decipher what was being said, Sam whispered, "It'll have to do," as he raised Dan to the dumbwaiter. "They sure don't make them this big anymore," commented Sam in a low voice, while helping Cindy into the antique compartment and handing her two backpacks, the lantern, and two lances.

Though the dumbwaiter was larger than anyone had ever seen, regrettably, it could accommodate only two members of the group at a time.

"Where does it lead?" questioned Dan.

"I don't know," whispered Sam, "but wherever it ends up, I'm sure it'll be safer than the kitchen."

Immediately upon closing the door of the dumbwaiter, Sam reopened it and reminded, "Don't forget to send it back right away for Jimmy and me."

With that, the two teenagers were gone ... somewhere.

As Sam and Jimmy waited in the kitchen for the return flight of the dumbwaiter, Sam suddenly let out a slight gasp when he spotted three stingers suspended outside the opening, while the claw-men in the hallway were now so close that the two stranded travelers could actually hear what was being discussed.

"I'll grab the produce and meet you in the Grand Foyer," came from the hallway.

"Alright," was then heard from the corridor, "but hurry."

"Come on, Cindy," whispered a nervous Jimmy.

With the absence of a door at the kitchen's entrance, Sam's heart sank to his stomach when he spotted a claw-man's left pincer only inches inside the entryway. With a vulnerable teenager trembling behind, and not knowing where he sent Cindy and Dan–but aware that the group was in the core of the demonic castle–Sam broke a promise he made to himself years ago. While clutching the handle of the dumbwaiter, Sam prayed, "God, help."

ENDNOTES

1 "Prayer to Saint Michael the Archangel," composed by Pope Leo XIII, 1810–1903.
2 "The Memorare," prayer historically attributed to Saint Bernard of Clairvaux, 1090–1153, though some accredit its composition to Father Claude Bernard, 1588–1641.